WHAT FEARS]

An Anthology from The

Edited by Jeani Rector

WHAT FEARS BECOME

http://www.thehorrorzine.com

FIRST EDITION

Imajin Books - http://www.imajinbooks.com

September 2011

ISBN: 978-1-926997-20-9

Cover designed by Sapphire Designs - http://www.designs.sapphiredreams.org

Praise for WHAT FEARS BECOME

"You won't be able to put WHAT FEARS BECOME down, not even for a second…Darkly humorous…Each spine-tingling chiller takes the reader into the depths of eerie imaginations…Thanks to Rector, get used to names such as Philip Roberts, Larry Green, and Cheryl Kaye Tardif because you're going to be hearing from them in the future!" —Jorge Solis, *Fangoria*

"There's nothing like a good scary story, except a lot of them, collected in an anthology from some of our top horror/suspense writers. So read one and be scared, or read a few and be good and scared, or read the whole book and lock all the doors and stay up all night listening to the house creak…They're terrific." —William Martin, New York Times bestselling author of *Back Bay*

"*What Fears Become* is a bold, brilliant collection of some of the most innovative and eloquent voices in modern horror. A must read for any avid horror fan." —Gabrielle Faust, author of *Eternal Vigilance*

"What an inspired mix of energetic and captivating horror. Here is work from acclaimed writers and a host of talented newcomers. This anthology is like a fearful breath from an ancient crypt; enter if you dare!" —Trevor Denyer, *Midnight Street Magazine*

"Dip in and you're hooked. WHAT FEARS BECOME is a high-bar mix of new and established talent." —Stephen Gallagher, author of *Kingdom of Bones*

"From the producers of *The Horror Zine*, this anthology of frightful fiction pulls in an impressive cast including some of the old masters of the genre, several bright luminaries and a handful of newcomers, promising that the top quality of the fiction, poetry and art is the only thing that matters." —Djibril al-Ayad, editor of *The Future Fire*

"This anthology showcases unusual and deeply disturbing horror fiction by numerous distinguished authors. Ramsey Campbell's story, in particular, will surely strike terror into the hearts of all aspiring writers." —Margaret L. Carter, author of *Different Blood: The Vampire as Alien*

"The stories in "What Fears Become" epitomize what Stephen King has called "the bad death." Whether they're jealous mirrors, irradiated vampires, clueless ghosts, or carnivorous homes, this anthology's shadows render the world a deadly place that gets most of its stories' protagonists in the end. Unless the protagonist is a monster—or already dead. That happens, too." —Paula R. Stiles, editor of *Innsmouth Free Press*

"The well crafted stories, and list of writers new and well known make WHAT FEARS BECOME a must read for horror lovers." —Selina Rosen, author of *The Host* trilogy

For the loyal readers of *The Horror Zine*

Acknowledgments

As editor of *The Horror Zine*, I would like to take this opportunity to thank all the talented writers, poets, and artists that make us what we are. There would be no *The Horror Zine* without all of you. I want to especially thank the best-selling professional writers who so generously and graciously lent us their works for this book.

I also want to thank all the hardworking and underpaid (think working for free!) editors of print and online magazines who strive diligently to give the writers, poets, and artists a venue in which to display their talents.

I particularly want to thank Trevor Denyer of *Midnight Street Magazine* for introducing me to Ramsey Campbell a couple of years ago, which basically started this whole adventure. I want to extend my thanks to Geoff Nelder for introducing me to Conrad Williams. I would like to thank Matt from the online forum Shocklines and also Ed from Cafe Doom for their unselfish devotion to giving people like me a venue to share my news and also to promote my endeavors.

I want to thank Trudy Hunter, Julia Cross, Sue Quiberg, Cheryl Babcock, and Kathleen Matranga for their continuing support. I would like to thank Heather Rector and Eric Rector for their refreshing uniqueness that never fails to inspire me.

And finally, I would also like to thank Cheryl Tardif, Lisa Hazard, Jennifer Johnson, Dean H. Wild and Toni Lopopolo for making this book possible.

TABLE OF CONTENTS

POETRY

THE ARTISTS

THE EDITOR'S CORNER

Foreword by Simon Clark:
A SMALL MATTER OF LIFE AND DEATH

I want to talk to you about a mystery. An interesting and important mystery. One that is, well, a matter of life and death.

And what has this extraordinary volume, *What Fears Become,* got to do with that *extraordinary* mystery?

Because the book you hold in your hands is part of a unique gift that we enjoy as a species. That gift is 'story.' As far as we know, we are the only creatures to tell, invent, and enjoy stories. And stories are important. We owe our existence to them. They sustain. Interpret. Educate. Encourage. Give hope. They allow us to see through the eyes of our fellow humans. They nourish empathy. Stories develop the strength and breadth of our amazing imaginations. They give us the power, from time to time, to cheat death. They are vitally important to the human race. Stories mean life.

Many anthropologists will cite singing and dancing as being the glue that cemented early tribal society together. I believe our 'species survival and growth package' includes other vitally important elements, such as a talent for the visual arts, a compulsion for physical and mental games, and stories—our universal passion for the made-up tale. Fiction pumps through our veins.

Where's the origin of this apparent inborn need to tell and to hear stories? The mystery lies in the origins of this *need*. We can't say precisely where the first fable was spun. Or when. Perhaps a gene mutated in one of our ancestors two hundred thousand years ago. For some mysterious reason our great (many times great!) grandmother or grandfather found themselves saying words that broadly mean "Once upon a time." And then relating events that never actually happened, yet which contain iridescent truths that illuminate human life.

Soon I'm going to talk about *What Fears Become*. First, I should say something about my dramatic statement that stories are so important we owe our existence to them. After all, I can't glibly toss out the opinion "that stories are a matter of life and death" in your general direction, then saunter away, can I? So, Ladies and Gentlemen of the jury, I present my case. The facts are, at the time of this writing, scientifically accurate. Of course, I'm a writer of fiction (every cell of my body positively throbs with that 'story' gene: yours, too!), so I paint my facts onto the canvas of imagination.

Here we go. We're traveling back twenty thousand years. Back to a world of woolly mammoth and saber-toothed cats. Silently, we follow a lone figure limping through the forest. This is the last of the Neanderthals. The anatomy of the figure is typical of the Neanderthal species. A very stocky build. Sturdy legs. The jaw juts out fiercely. Large eyes peer from beneath prominent brow ridges. The arms are muscular, biceps are bulging. She is so powerful that she can easily snap the neck of a wild pig.

Her body language radiates confidence and strength. Her formidable torso is protected by a long cloak made from reindeer hides. She carries a spear tipped with a flint that's as sharp as a surgeon's scalpel. For months she has been searching for more of her kind. A quest doomed to failure. She can't possibly know that she is the last of her species. Nor would she understand that something happened in the last few generations that caused the Neanderthal to begin a headlong rush to extinction.

The last Neanderthal is living on borrowed time.

In the forest she hears voices. Though the language is unfamiliar, she is suddenly excited. Her species have communicated with each other in a remarkably sophisticated way for thousands of years, using spoken words and tongue clicks. Her heart pounds. This female is certain she has found another family grouping of Neanderthals. The chances of joining the group are slim—typically Neanderthal tribes are insular, they seldom interact—just the thought, however, of setting eyes on her own kind is so thrilling that she begins to run.

At the edge of the clearing the female pauses. Something is wrong. Yes, the men, women and children she sees walk on two legs, they call to one another, a couple are arguing, juveniles are laughing as they throw sticks into a tree. The figures wear animal skins, carry spears that are remarkably similar to the weapon she carries. Yet they are not the same as her species. Their bodies are so slender they seem almost fragile. Their faces are peculiar, too. They have small chins; the foreheads rise straight up instead of sloping back like those of her race.

The last Neanderthal is disappointed. These aren't of her blood. Yet she finds their behavior interesting. Although it is decidedly bizarre. Not much of it makes sense to her. Lack of food has made her drowsy. So why not settle down here in the bushes? Rest. Observe these delicate creatures for a while.

From her vantage point, concealed in the vegetation, she watches. The peculiar-looking creatures start a fire. They butcher a roe deer with flint knives. Soon they are enjoying a meal. Even though they have been hunting during the day they don't doze after the feast like Neanderthal hunters would do.

These eccentric individuals chase one another about the camp. The young men make a competitive game of jumping over a rock. Meanwhile, a group of children scratch lines in the dirt with twigs. She realizes that the lines resemble horses. This is very perplexing because her own species never did anything like this. Nor did they carve figures as a man appears to be doing right now to a section of mammoth tusk. Just as darkness pulls in, when all sensible Neanderthals would be bedding down for the night, these people start to move about the fire. They clap their hands in a rhythmic way. Sounds come from their delicate, little mouths. They seem to be saying the same words at the same time, then they begin to sway to the rhythm.

Song never featured in the Neanderthal way of life. Dance is alien to her.

After the dancing a silver-haired woman begins to speak. All the tribe gather round to listen. They are captivated by what she is saying. The last Neanderthal notices the expressions on the faces in the audience. She's incapable of figuring out that the *Homo sapiens* are listening to invented situations that befall a fictional character. And because other tribes of *Homo sapiens* are eager for new stories, different tribes meet and share their fables. Therefore, they don't experience the tribal isolation that has brought the socially shy Neanderthal to the brink of extinction.

The family group she watches from her hiding are vibrant, outgoing, and passionately interested in life. Their restless curiosity always means that they expand their contact amongst neighboring tribes, so the gene pool is ever-growing. These highly imaginative humans are equipped to survive, even flourish.

The female stares at the creatures listening to the story. The faces of the children shine with delight. They are learning without even realizing a lesson is being taught. Or that the muscles of imagination are being strengthened to the point imagination becomes a tool of incredible power in its own right.

The last Neanderthal continues to stare as the stars come out one by one. She no longer blinks. Not even when a spider begins to methodically spin a pure white shroud for her face.

II

Story. So very important. So vital to the survival of our species. And fiction is important to us individually. You probably remember the first story you heard that fascinated you, and invoked the power of your imagination. Certain films and TV dramas undoubtedly still linger in your mind, even though you saw them as a very young child.

I grew up loving movies that featured monsters, aliens, and robots. When I was three-years-old I watched a film on television that, for the first time, seemed to light up the atoms of my very being. For the life of me, I can't name the film, or the actors. But, *wow!* I can still remember the hulking, great robot that stomped down a metal ramp with so much force that sparks flew from its iron feet.

Bouncing up and down on the sofa, I shouted, "That's great! I'm going to watch it again next week!" The adults carefully explained to the diminutive Simon, with his wide, shining eyes, that it was a film, not a TV series. That it wouldn't be back next week. That didn't matter. Not at all! Because my imagination had been brought to life. Whenever I wanted, I could recall in vivid, dazzling, awesome detail that huge robot clumping along, sparks blazing from its feet.

So, like my fellow human beings everywhere on Earth, I found my love of story. Books, comics, television, film, radio. Stories pulsated everywhere. My family told tall tales. My uncles had a never-ending supply of haunted house yarns. "Simon. Do you see that house by the canal? There are ghosts in there…" An uncle would point to the creepy old building and I'd believe every word.

Fiction nourished me as much as potatoes, gravy and the sweet puddings we were served at school. What I devoured most in the way of books were anthologies. Fortunately, the school library had a fine stock of ghost stories for children. I gobbled them up one after another. And birthdays brought me the *Armada Ghost Book* series.

And it was only later that I appreciated that many of the pieces I enjoyed were first printed in magazines, such as the nineteenth century monthly *The Strand Magazine,* and *Weird Tales*, hailing from the 1920s. These publications used the latest print technology to deliver their content in what was then a fresh and inventive way. *The Strand Magazine* not only published great text by the likes of Sir Arthur Conan Doyle, there were also dramatic illustrations of soldiers brandishing swords, or explosions, or thrilling cliff-top fights. *Weird Tales* boasted vivid covers, which were broadly based on the *Beauty and the Beast* theme. Gorgeous females being menaced by alien creatures were a resounding favorite. Back in the gloomy depression between the World Wars they would have screamed excitement from the newsstands. *Buy Me! I can take you away from your worries!* Readers would be carried away on strange adventures from the pens of H.P Lovecraft, Robert E. Howard and the top pulp writers of the day. Imaginations would blaze; the reader would step into the hero's shoes. They'd be empowered. Even when the reader was back in the real world again after closing the magazine, they could face the day-to-day struggles with renewed energy and hope.

That's what stories, do. They help our species to survive.

With every new generation there's always an inventive, new way to feed our appetite for fiction.

So, imagine my delight when I heard about *The Horror Zine*.

Let me tell you about the e-zine.

Launched by Jeani Rector in 2009, this is a glorious online treasury of fiction, artwork, photographs, articles and poetry. With that first click of the mouse I saw that there was something special about *The Horror Zine*. Lavish color, photos, and illustrations blazed from the screen. Its very look proclaimed a fresh approach to online publishing.

The Horror Zine is divided into different departments. Each one features short stories, poetry, art, or non-fiction. Jeani Rector is a lady with vision. Shrewdly, she understands what horror fans enjoy. Jeani Rector ably ushers in artists, authors and poets for us to enjoy.

There is provocative artwork. Some subtly erotic, some disturbing, some eerie, and some just plain beautiful. All of it very, very good. And instead of simply displaying the artwork of talented individuals, *The Horror Zine* becomes a vehicle that can take us to the artist's website, or invites us to contact them. In this way, Jeani Rector's e-magazine acts as both an art gallery and a marketplace, where publishers and individuals might seek to commission original artwork that is stimulating and visually exciting.

The same applies to the fiction department. We step into the pages of new and gifted writers who create such remarkably unique and imaginative fiction that it stays with us long after we are finished reading. We can read the story; we learn something about the writer, then once more the door swings open for us to visit the authors' websites.

Besides the new writers, *The Horror Zine* also has a remarkable list of established authors: Graham Masterton, Melanie Tem, Ramsey Campbell, Piers Anthony, Scott Nicholson, Conrad Williams, Ronald Malfi, Cheryl Kaye Tardif, Elizabeth Massie and others, who have entrusted their work to the editor's decidedly capable hands.

A click of the mouse and we're conveyed to the poets: Joe R. Lansdale is among them. *The Horror Zine* poets create fluid and artistic lines well worthy of the time spent to savor them.

Elsewhere in the e-zine we find The Banners Page, a portal to other sites in keeping with *The Horror Zine's* morbid theme. "The Oddities in the News Page" features factual items culled from the newspapers: a medieval 'vampire' burial, plans to clone extinct animals, a 75-year-old mystery in Los Angeles that may or may not be related to Peter Pan, and the like. Anyone who has ever stepped into Ripley's Odditorium will love this. I know I do!

"The List of Zines Page" is devoted to an extensive directory of both print zines and e-zines that that are potential markets for the work of writers, poets, and artists. Best of all, "The List of Zines Page" is kept current and all of the links work.

"The Morbidly Fascinating Page" invites us to peek into some dark corners. Here we find pictures and articles - famous criminals of the past, haunted houses, ancient bodies preserved in bogs, shrunken heads, Victorian post-mortem photography, and an assembly of macabre curios and bizarre exhibits. There is a different subject every month to, well, morbidly fascinate us.

And *The Horror Zine* holds its contributors in heartwarmingly high esteem. My work features there. I contributed a short piece of fiction entitled *The Pass*. Working with Jeani is a happy experience. She took a great deal of care in ensuring *The Pass* was displayed attractively, smartly illustrated, and I was extremely gratified that the reader has the opportunity to find out about my latest novels. Believe me, this gladdens an author's heart. I'm sure other contributors to *The Horror Zine* have been and will be looked after superbly.

Just when this seems the point where I invite everyone to hurry over to *The Horror Zine* to immerse themselves in this groundbreaking creation, I holler "Wait!" Because Jeani isn't content to deliver a great online magazine. Jeani has also embarked on editing a very beautiful book.

I'm honored to be able to introduce to you the Jeani Rector-edited anthology here in your hands: *What Fears Become: An Anthology from The Horror Zine.*

Maybe this book is in the form of paper and ink, or you might be reading it in an electronic format. Rest assured, however, that you are about to step into worlds of wonder where dreams and nightmares are waiting to steal into your heart.

Here you'll find the kind of artwork in book format that elevates *The Horror Zine* into something so special. Your editor has selected a fabulous array of stories, poetry, and artwork for this book.

Let me give you a little background about some of the contributors. Ramsey Campbell was encouraged in his writing by HP Lovecraft's friend, August Derleth, and has rightly gained a legendary status in the genre. Graham Masterton's skill as a writer shines from the page. Pick one of his stories and read the masterful dialogue aloud. You'll see what I mean.

Piers Anthony's novels have appeared many, many times in the *New York Times* bestseller lists. I've been fortunate to take part in a convention event with Melanie Tem, and found myself wishing I could make notes about her insights into the craft of the tale. Elizabeth Massie is a well-established writer of novels, short stories and radio plays, and has legions of fans.

A favorite movie of mine is *Bubba Ho-Tep,* which was inspired by a novella from the prolific and gifted Joe R. Lansdale. Here he turns his skillful hand to verse. Conrad Williams is carving a big name for himself in the horror world. His fans would agree; as does Peter Straub, who describes Conrad's work as "beautiful and blazing."

Scott Nicholson is the celebrated author of *The Red Church.* The latest in a long line of fine books by Scott is *Drummer Boy.* Cheryl Kaye Tardif is a versatile writer, and a rising talent of the Canadian book world. A talent destined for worldwide appreciation.

And then there's Ronald Malfi. Always a joy to read, Ronald Malfi's writing-style shines with a diamond-bright brilliance that always leaves me wanting more, *much* more.

Bentley Little is ferociously loyal to the horror genre. He has been rightly described by Stephen King as "a master of the macabre." In the last twenty years he has built up a dedicated following for his terrific supernatural fiction. Bentley Little's *The Mailman* is a personal favorite of mine and is wickedly entertaining fare.

Those are the established writing stars. Which make this book an essential must-buy in its own right. However, Jeani Rector hasn't forgotten the new authors. These new authors prove that *The Horror Zine* has a healthy appetite for writers who have a taste for the adventurous and the innovative.

Online, *The Horror Zine* attracts the best talent. The well-known, the soon-to-be-well-known. Jeani Rector deserves our applause for producing such a visually stimulating, enchanting and downright exciting website. Now those elements are enshrined here in *What Fears Become.* This wonderful anthology continues the important traditions of the first story-teller. That ancestor of ours that first spoke the words: "Once upon a time…"

Here is proof that humanity is still confidently exploring the world of imagination. And as we continue our voyage into the future we will always tell one another stories. After all, it truly is a matter of life and death.

Simon Clark
England
August 17, 2010
http://www.bbr-online.co.uk/nailed/

Abstract Green Houses
Ricardo Di Ceglia

Save the Depot
April A. Taylor

FICTION

BAST
by Christian A. Larsen

The fluorescent light flickered like the minds of the residents. Sometimes it lit up the entire breadth and depth of the hallway, and sometimes—most times—it only interrupted the peace of the darkness.

"I hate this place," muttered Marty, counting off the room numbers. The patients, end-stage dementia sufferers and terminal cancer victims shambling past in flapping terrycloth robes, gave him the absolute willies. They looked like something out of a George Romero movie. He hated the smell worse, though—a mix of piss, disinfectant and ointment that made the nursing home stink like a giant litter box.

The woman at the nurse's station smiled when he walked past, but never looked up from her Sudoku game. In fact, the smile never reached her eyes. "Can I help you, sir?" she asked automatically, scrawling numbers in a grid without pausing for an answer. A fat black cat lifted its head from a porcelain bowl where it had fallen asleep. It followed Marty with its good eye. The other was sewn shut and made it look like it was winking at him.

Marty mumbled a perfunctory *no thanks* to the nurse and shuffled into his grandmother's room. The sun was a sinking tangerine and the lights were off, but he could hear her breathing raggedly—a faint snore repeating through her diminished frame.

"Grandma?" he asked and wondered why. He hadn't had a real conversation with her in weeks. Not since a couple of months after she checked into the home, since the beginning of her great inexplicable— but not totally unexpected—geriatric decline.

"Hubert? Is that you? It's too bright. I can't see."

"Grandma, it's me. Marty," he answered, drawing a chair closer to her bed. With the faint purple coming in through the windows, he could see the outline of her face like a silhouette portrait cut from black construction paper.

"They were having a party outside, Hubert."

"Who was?"

"The people in the white coats."

"The doctors? Where? Out in the hall?"

"No, the people in the *white coats* were having a party, Hubert. Don't you *listen*?"

Marty didn't know why he was bothering with the conversation, given that she thought he was his years-dead grandfather Hubert, but at least they were connecting, at least a little, and it might be for the last time too. At least he hoped it might be. "Where was the party?"

"Across the river," she sounded angry.

"Didn't they invite you?"

"No, they wouldn't *stop* inviting me!"

For a long time, he couldn't draw anything else intelligible out of her. She moaned and groaned about the cat trying to kill her, how she was afraid to swim, that she wasn't ready, and why did she have to go in the first place? Marty patted her hand. Her skin felt thin and loose, like it was ready to slide off of her bones in a pile, and it made him shiver. Willpower. Old-fashioned German bull-headed willpower. That was the only thing holding her together.

The doctors had said she had six months left in her, tops. That was thirteen months ago, and it beat Marty up every time he came back to see her, a little less there than the last time. But enough of her was left to fight that inevitable slide. How he wished *that* part of her was the first to go. He didn't mind seeing her bruised from the IV lines, or feeding her a cafeteria version of Thanksgiving dinner. What he minded was seeing her living through these nightmares like they were real, and waking up meant dying. Maybe she would be better off really dying.

Marty slumped back in the chair and watched the sunlight drain from the twilight. His grandmother was sleeping, or some variant of it, but he told her about his day, anyway. The mundanities, the trivialities about his job, how his wife was handling grad school courses—whatever came to his mind. It was reflexive. He didn't actually intend any of it. It merely came out as the room fell into nighttime, with only the flickering fluorescent trapezoid cut by the doorway casting any light.

Something brushed up against Marty's leg and he reached down in that momentary panic—where the small unknown seems life-threatening—and barely missed the fluff of the cat's tail. It sprang onto his grandmother's bed, settled between her feet, and looked at Marty with its single, slitted, radioactive eye.

"Shoo, puss. Go on, go," said Marty, waving his hands at the animal. It looked back at him with something akin to bemusement. "I said go!" he repeated, reaching for the cat. It hissed at him and bared its teeth. When it reared back, the light from the door caught a white splotch on its chest shaped like a swinging noose.

Marty settled back into his seat. It wasn't doing him any harm. Yet. But then it started to crawl up toward his grandmother's face, the blades of its shoulders pistoning higher than its sleek black head. Marty looked over his shoulder toward the nurse's station.

"Can someone come in here and get this cat?"

When he turned back, the cat had settled on his grandmother's chest, where it proceeded to lick its paws. There was a faint wheezing noise coming from the bed, like a broken motor or an air-hose leaking from a pinhole. The sound drew Marty forward, and for a couple of seconds, he thought it might be the cat purring, but it wasn't. The sound was coming from higher up, and then it shaped itself into words in his grandmother's voice.

"I c-c-can't breathe, Hube-b-b-bert-uhh."

"Grandma!" shouted Marty, reaching for the cat with both hands. It stood its ground and glowered at him with its one chartreuse eye. Marty tried to pick it up, but it seemed to weigh more than a thousand pounds. It let out a long purr that sounded like a burp.

Then the room went quiet.

"Grandma? Grandma?" whispered Marty, suddenly and surprisingly very afraid that she might be dead when just a few minutes before he had hoped as much. He took her hand in his and he patted it. It felt cold. He fumbled around her wrist and couldn't feel a pulse. "Nurse!"

"What's the problem, sir?" asked the nurse sleepily as she entered the room.

"My grandma's not breathing and I can't get this cat off her chest!"

As he was saying that, the cat jumped off the bed and padded past Marty with its tail sticking straight up, flashing its anus at him. In the oddly cast shadows, the animal looked bigger than a small dog. The nurse called the staff physician and he declared Marty's grandmother dead a few minutes later. "I'm sorry, Mr. Gustafson," the doctor offered.

"Doctor, there was a cat in here…"

"That's Bast, a shelter cat. She's a favorite around here. Named after the Egyptian cat goddess."

Marty didn't know why any of that was important when they should have been talking about his grandmother. "Why does that cat have the run of the place? That cat sat on my grandmother's chest."

"Bast snuggles up to people when she's feeling affectionate, and the residents seem to like her. She brings their spirits up."

"You didn't hear me. That cat, doctor, sat on my grandmother's chest and squeezed the air out of her."

"Now, Mr. Gustafson, I'll admit she's overfed, but old Bastie doesn't weigh more than twenty-five pounds, give or take. She doesn't weigh enough to do what you described. Besides, if you were so concerned, why didn't you just pick her up?"

"I tried. I couldn't move it."

"I understand," said the doctor. "Some people don't like cats. I'll talk to the director of the home about keeping the cat out of places she's not welcome. And again, I'm very sorry for your loss. We'll make the arrangements for you."

Marty felt like arguing, but let it go because of the offer of arrangements. Still, he felt like pointing out that he didn't have feelings about cats one way or the other—at least cats in general. But this Bast he didn't like at all, from its one-eyed glare to the noose on its chest, to the way it squashed the tidal breath out of his grandmother's dying body. Still, he was too numb to take it any further, so instead he worked with the home about the arrangements for his grandmother's body, and afterward, he walked back down the flickering hallway. Most of the residents were asleep this time, but Marty still had the willies for some reason.

"Well, Grandma, I guess you won't have to be afraid of being alone in the dark anymore," Marty said out loud, feeling like he was whistling past a cemetery. He signed out at the visitor's check-in, spun himself through the revolving door and out of that litter box smell.

But the outside didn't smell any better. Marty supposed it was either on his clothes or up both nostrils, and he'd have to shower when he got home. Hell, he needed a shower anyway, but it would have to wait until after he walked Freya. She was wagging her tail in the backseat. He waved at her with his free hand as he felt the door handle catch with the other.

It was in that last split second that she growled and bared her teeth, too late to be an effective warning. He thought—as quickly as only such thoughts can be—how odd she looked, and then something hit him like the sweet spot of a baseball bat, right between the shoulder blades and knocked him down to the pavement.

The dog was going nuts inside the car, a million miles away. There was a terrible weight on his back and another noise, breathing just above his ear, the hissing of a cat. He felt it curl its claws between his shoulder blades and start to press the air out of his lungs, just like he'd watched it do to his grandmother, and he couldn't even gather the breath to shout for help. His eyesight was graying out, and the last thing he would ever see was his bald tires. *I guess I didn't need that alignment after all,* Marty thought.

Freya, though, tested the door with her weight and it gave. Marty heard her scramble out, her claws and jaws snapping and scrambling onto the pavement. Marty felt her weight on his legs and hips, but even for a dog her size, it was reassuring. The cat hissed and dug its claws deeper into Marty's back—this time a move not of predation, but of desperation. One cat paw moved off of Marty's back and Freya whimpered, drawing back. Marty's hopes went up in smoke. *The cat got Freya. There goes my last chance.*

But he was wrong again. Freya leaped back, snapped at Bast, got a hold of something, and pushed her weight against Marty's side, peeling the cat off of his back. Bast mewled pitifully, raked its claws across Marty's back, and then was gone. He managed to look up. Freya's teeth were red with cat blood, her lips curled in a feral snarl.

Marty dragged himself off the pavement and sat against the side of the car. "Good girl, Freya. Good dog." Freya dropped Bast's wrung and punctured corpse in front of Marty and sat down, panting like her master. Marty reached up and scratched the deep pile under the dog's throat. His arms trembled, a nervous reaction to his near-death experience with a house cat, but he'd be okay to drive home if he just gave himself a minute.

Bast was a mess, the cat's tail and hind leg braided together at disturbing angles, its throat mangled, and its innards draped over its wounds like the pulsing bodies of coiled nightcrawlers. Marty watched the heat from the cat's body seep into the spring night air. It smelled like his own rejuvenation and rebirth. Finally he felt strong enough to stand, brush the asphalt off his jeans, call the dog into the car, and put this night behind him. "Come on, Freya."

But the dog was investigating something under the car next to him—the car he had been sitting against. The cat was nowhere to be seen, but there was a track of gore leading from where Bast had been to the underside of that other car, and he could hear an obscene yowling coming from there.

"Freya, get into our car...now!" said Marty, shooing her inside. Jumping into the driver's seat, it wasn't until he pulled onto the highway that he took another breath. "That cat—that damned cat—it still has a couple lives to work through. I don't want to be there when it does."

The lights from the highway rolled over the glass of the windshield and Marty flicked on the radio. Ted Nugent was singing "Cat Scratch Fever" and Marty laughed a laugh out of relief more than amusement. "Hey, Freya, how's that for serendipity?"

When he looked into the rear view mirror, he could see that Freya's ears were flat and her tail was down. Anxiety rimmed the dog's wide eyes.

Marty felt his smile fade under the weight of that stare, dreading the sinister yowl coming from the car's undercarriage—the dead giveaway of a feline stowaway. He checked his gas gauge and calculated in his head how long he could keep the car moving. Not long enough.

About Christian A. Larsen

Christian A. Larsen grew up in Park Ridge, Illinois and graduated from the University of Illinois at Urbana-Champaign. He has worked as a high school English teacher, a radio personality, a newspaper reporter, and a printer's devil. His work has appeared in magazines such as *Golden Visions, Lightning Flash, An Electric Tragedy, Eschatology, Indigo Rising*, and *Aphelion*. He lives with his wife and two sons in Kenosha, Wisconsin. http://www.exlibrislarsen.com

DOGLEG
by Bentley Little

I never liked Darla. No reason, really. At least no logical one. It's just that some of your kids' friends you like, and some you don't. As an adult, you can see in the children the seeds of the grownups they are going to be.

And I could see that Darla was going to grow up to be someone I couldn't stand.

But she was Stacy's friend and her mom was June's friend, and I didn't say anything to either of them. She wasn't a Bad Seed or a female Damien or anything, she was just...annoying.

So on those rare occasions when June was out and Darla came over and I was left alone to babysit the two girls, I usually let them do whatever they wanted in Stacy's room or the backyard, while I watched TV and tried to ignore them.

This time was no different. It was a Saturday afternoon and USC was playing—a game I really wanted to see—so when Darla knocked on the screen and asked if Stacy was home, I told her to come on in. Stacy was in her bedroom, and the two of them did something in there for a while before going in the kitchen and snacking on some Goldfish crackers. The game got really exciting, and I lost track of them after that. It wasn't until halftime that I started wondering where they were and what they were doing.

Just at that moment, the back door slammed, and Darla came running into the house. She stopped breathlessly in front of my chair and grabbed my hand. "Mr. Harrison! Come outside! I have to show you something!"

"Why don't you just tell me?"

"No," she whined. "You have to *see* it! Hurry *up*! Stacy's *waiting*!"

Knowing that I should be checking on them anyway, I feigned an interest I did not feel and allowed myself to be dragged out of the house, through the back yard, to the chaotic jumble of boards that Stacy called her "clubhouse." Darla pushed aside the swinging piece of plywood that covered the entrance and went inside. I ducked and followed, entering the makeshift structure's only room.

Blood was everywhere, and at first I did not even understand what I was looking at. I blinked dumbly. There was a dead dog in the left corner, a mutilated Labrador corpse that I recognized as Scout, our next door neighbor's pet. To the right of that, on top of the low coffee table we had scrounged from another neighbor's garbage, was a wiggling form covered by a raggedy, red-soaked cloth. A bloody ax leaned against the wall behind it. My heart started jack-hammering in my chest. Underneath the table, I could see a length of crimson-spattered flesh that looked like a leg.

Darla walked up to the table and pulled aside the cloth. "See what I did, Mr. Harrison? See?"

I did see. Darla had chopped off Stacy's leg above the knee and had somehow grafted the dog's leg in its place. I swooned for a second, felt like fainting, felt like vomiting. The strangest thing—the most horrifying thing, perhaps—was that Stacy seemed to be feeling no pain. She was laughing and excited, and she sat up, then stood, showing off. She was wearing nothing but her underwear, and where the hairy leg of the dog met her own thigh, the transition was smooth, unnoticeable.

Darla was looking up at me, and I wanted to hit her, wanted to smack the neediness and self-satisfaction off her smarmy little face. "Don't you think I did a good job? Huh, Mr. Harrison? Doesn't it look good?"

Stacy took a step forward. The leg screeched when she moved it, a horrible shriek that sounded like bad brakes on an old car. She said something to me, but I couldn't hear it. She could not walk and talk at the same time. The sound of her leg was so loud, she had to stop all movement in order for me to hear her speak.

She did stop, and she looked up at me and smiled. "Isn't it great, Daddy? Darla said she could do it, and she did!" Stacy looked sad for a second. "I didn't think Scout would die, though." Immediately she brightened. "But I love my new leg! It's a lot better than my old one!"

Stacy gestured toward the discarded appendage under the bloody table, and I threw up. I managed to lurch to the left first, and heaved in the corner away from the girls. I wasn't disgusted, exactly, it was just...all of it. The sight, the smell, the sound, Darla, Stacy, the dead dog, the amputated leg, the bloody room, everything was swirling inside me, and my body expressed its emotions by vomiting.

I wiped my mouth on my sleeve. Outside the clubhouse, I heard June's voice, bright and cheerful and entirely clueless, thanking Kristie,

Darla's mom, for going shopping with her. Darla immediately ran out of the clubhouse, the plywood door swinging shut behind her. Stacy was shouting excitedly—"*Mommy*," I think—but she was hurrying after her friend at the same time, and her voice was drowned out by the horrible screech of her leg.

I sucked in a deep breath, then pushed the plywood aside, holding the door open for Stacy, who hobbled through the opening. Her new leg, I noticed, was shorter than her old one, and she listed to the right.

Darla was babbling to her mother, bragging about what she had done. June seemed confused, but she glanced over as Stacy emerged from the clubhouse.

She took one look at her daughter.

And fainted.

June adjusted to it.

I don't know what I expected to happen once my wife came to her senses. A rush to the Emergency Room? A call to the police? But I didn't expect what actually happened: a calm discussion with Darla and her mother that resulted in an *understanding*. I was the only one screaming and yelling, the only one calling names and making threats, and I would never forgive June for that. Never. But recriminations would have to come later. Right now, I just needed to figure out a way to get my daughter whole again.

Before Kristie and Darla left, June actually *thanked* them.

I wanted to hit her.

From down the hall, I could hear Stacy walking around her bedroom, the dogleg screeching.

I walked back there, standing in the hallway and watching her through the open doorway while everyone else said their goodbyes. I remembered what it had been like when my dad had given me a bad haircut. I'd been the laughingstock of the school for an entire week, the object of attention everywhere I went. I could only imagine what it would be like for Stacy, having a dogleg.

She limped from her bed to her closet, from the closet to her dresser, looking down at her hairy leg and grinning all the while. I felt June's hand on my shoulder and nearly jumped. "She'll be fine," June said. "Look how happy she is."

"That's what's so wrong," I explained, but she didn't understand.

It had happened on a Saturday.

Against my better judgment, I called neither the cops nor the paramedics. As June so rationally pointed out, how would I explain what had happened? At the very least, Child Protective Services would take her away from us for observation, until what had happened could be sorted out and dissected. I didn't want that to happen.

That afternoon, I buried Scout in the backyard. I also tried to salvage and clean up Stacy's real leg, but it was dead, shriveled down to the thickness of bone, the skin brown and dry and leathery.

I buried it, too.

All day Sunday, I kept crying, bursting into tears at odd and inappropriate moments. I loved my daughter, had loved her since the moment she'd been born, and it was the little things that set off my emotional fireworks. Remembrance of the past, thoughts of the future. Recalling the times she had run to me when I got home from work, jumping into my arms and hugging me tightly. Wondering what she would do when there were school dances.

And always there was the screeching of the joint where the dogleg was fused right above her knee, a shriek-like squeal that was almost metallic. I heard it every time she moved, a constant reminder of what had happened. Like the telltale heart, it nagged at me, gnawed at me, made me realize that if I had supervised my daughter more closely, if I had watched her play with her friend instead of watching the football game, this never would have happened. She would be a normal little girl, we would be a normal family, and I wouldn't be dealing with this horror.

Finally, I decided to do something about it.

Night had fallen, and both June and Stacy had gone to bed. I was still up, watching TV in the living room, and I walked back to our bedroom, checking to make sure June was asleep. She was. Stacy was asleep, too, in her own room, in her own bed, although she had kicked off part of the covers, and I could see the dogleg sticking out.

I moved forward, bending down to examine it more closely. From even a foot away, the hairy animal appendage appeared to blend into Stacy's smooth white skin, transitioning seamlessly. But from this intimate vantage point, I saw that there was a definite line of demarcation. Reaching out, I touched the dogleg, feeling a strong sense of revulsion as my fingers stroked rough fur.

The dogleg could be amputated. Even if they couldn't reattach her own leg, doctors could affix a prosthetic limb, I told myself. Anything would be better than this...*abomination*.

Stacy moaned, stirring in her sleep, and the leg joint creaked, its metallic squeak loud enough to be heard on the other side of the house. I felt like throwing up again, but I didn't.

I knew what had to be done.

The previous day, I had cleaned off the ax and returned it to the garage, where Stacy and Darla had originally gotten it. Now I went into the garage and brought the ax back with me to Stacy's room. For a moment, I wasn't sure I'd be able to go through with it, and I put the blade of the ax down on the floor and leaned on the handle like a cane, watching my daughter as she slept. The dogleg was still exposed, and I thought of the girls, so proud of what they'd done, so utterly uncomprehending of the tragic consequences.

Picking up the ax, I chopped off the dogleg with one mighty swing, gratified to hear an ear-splitting screech that came not from my daughter's mouth, but from the joints of the leg itself. There was blood all of a sudden, much more than I would have expected, and I dropped the ax and moved forward to stem the flow, vaguely aware that there was the sound of screaming coming from somewhere behind me. And then—

I was out.

I felt nothing, no pain, at least not until I woke up, and by then Stacy was gone. June had taken her. I ran through the house, my head throbbing where I'd been hit, but their clothes were gone and so were some of Stacy's stuffed animals and a lot of things I couldn't quite recall. I'd apparently been out for some time, because it was light outside, and the clock on the DVD player said it was one forty-five.

Opening the front door of the house, I saw that the car was gone. They'd taken it. But where? To the police station? To June's parents' house? I didn't know, but I started calling. I phoned everyone I knew, dialed every number in our address book, which for some reason June hadn't taken. No one had heard from them, and no one knew where they were.

I decided to wait, hoping they would come back, hoping June would cool off and bring my daughter back to me. But a day passed, a week, and there was still no sign of them.

The only thing left was the dogleg.

It was not part of Stacy, but somehow it was.

It had been left on her bed, right where I'd chopped it off, and that gave me hope. Wherever they were, whatever they were doing, Stacy was free. All of her body parts were her own. That seemed important, somehow.

I prayed that she was still alive, that June had gotten her medical attention, though none of the local hospitals I called would admit to treating anyone matching my daughter's description.

I took the dogleg and put it on ice, in the extra freezer we maintained in the garage. I found myself going out there constantly to check on it, an obsession that only grew worse as the days passed. I would touch the leg sometimes, holding back tears. I even kissed the leg once. It had been a part of Stacy, if only for a little while, and I felt closer to her as I stroked the frozen fur, thinking of how happy she'd been when she'd first jumped off the table and run over with her new leg to give me a hug.

Perhaps I had been wrong to deprive her of it.

"Stacy," I said, sobbing. "Stacy..."

It was the second Sunday after June and Stacy had left, and I was sitting numbly in front of the television, staring at a football game, but not watching it. The doorbell rang, and when I went to answer it, I saw Darla standing on the stoop, looking up at me with bright eyes. "Is Stacy feeling better? Can she come out to play?"

Stacy's not here, I wanted to say, *Stacy's gone.* But I couldn't get my mouth to say the words.

Darla just stood there, looking at me in a way that made me think she'd known that all along. I started to close the door, but stopped when she said, "I have an idea, Mr. Harrison. Do you want to hear my idea?"

As much as I disliked the girl, hearing her talk was like having a link to my daughter, and I found myself nodding.

Fifteen minutes later, I was in the clubhouse with the dogleg. Darla had gone home to get what she needed and had just returned. She looked at me I nodded, and I laid down on the table. Darla smeared cat food on my leg, spit on the cat food, then pressed a leaf against it. I felt nothing until she started singing. The words were nonsensical, something about dancing birds and bears in the trees, and they were set to the same tune that underlay a lot of children's songs, the one for "Twinkle, Twinkle Little Star" and the ABC's. The second she started singing, there was a tingling in my leg, a weird sensation that was not just skin deep, but went down to the bone.

Was this what Stacy had felt?

Darla smiled at me, and lifted the ax.

"Ready?" she asked.

About Bentley Little

Bentley Little was born in Arizona a month after his mother attended the world premiere of Psycho. He is the author of numerous novels, short stories, articles and essays. He originally came up through small presses.

Bentley Little is notorious for not participating in anything on the Internet, so he does not have an official website. The Horror Zine communicates with Bentley Little though mail delivered by the U.S. Post Office.

A BAD STRETCH OF ROAD
by Dean H. Wild

Max Drummond was in the depths of a heavy driver's daze, the toll of endless miles since sunup and too much to think about, he conceded, but for some reason the sight of the interchange rising out of the distance brought him around. He gave his surroundings a waking-dreamer's blink. He was somewhere in the back-forty of the Midwest surrounded by dust devils and afternoon heat shimmers. Other than that, he was uncertain of his location. Someplace where they didn't bother to post highway signs, he could say that much. Not a single directional sign graced the roadside for as far as he could see. Now that he was looking, he noticed not a single billboard advertisement either. Not even a friendly reminder of the local speed limit, only cars racing off the ever-closer interchange ramps at a steady pace, flooding the highway with metal and glass and chrome. On the one hand, he reminded himself how much he hated busy highways, and on the other hand told himself it didn't matter. All that mattered was he make Milwaukee by sundown, reach Linda by nightfall, and cling to the thinly wrapped hope she would open the door when he came knocking unannounced.

Just ahead, an ancient structure—a kind of bridge or trestle—stretched over the highway. He hadn't noticed it at first, but there it was, acting as a gateway to the weave-work of feeder ramps beyond. It held its ground with entitlement like a tribal elder. In fact, its rigid profile struck him as possessing a sort of—well—wisdom. The old bridge would be his starting line, he decided. True, his journey began hours ago in St. Louis, but this would be the point where the agonizing fell away, like stages of a rocket, leaving him light and unburdened. He considered it with a sudden pang of hopefulness. Welcomed it, even.

"And we're off," he sighed and punched the Volvo's accelerator as he swept under the trestle.

The sensation was surprising and exquisite. His view of the road gained a harsh, bright-glass clarity that caused him to squint into the two northbound lanes alive with bumper to bumper trucks and cars. What momentarily drew his attention, however, (and brought a hint of unease) were the interchange ramps. There were more than he'd first realized, and they snaked away one after the other into the distance at ridiculous, drastic angles. They joined with mysterious elevated and unmarked roads, or sometimes fed into other ramps.

The only thing worse than a busy stretch of highway, he decided as he twisted anxiously at the wheel, was a busy stretch whose designer graduated the Dr. Seuss School of Highway Planning.

His cell phone was on the seat next to him. He fingered it and thought about the sound of Linda's voice, how it always had the ability to calm him when things got tense. The old Linda's voice, that was, the one full of sweetness and trust. Certainly not the Linda's voice from this morning which seemed to traverse the distance from Fond du Lac, Wisconsin to St. Louis like a hail of arrows. "How could you?" she had asked him three, maybe four times, demanding an answer, insisting he talk about it. He couldn't. It was all he could do to make the call. To go into any great depths was beyond him.

"It's over with me and her," he had told Linda, and it seemed to be the only defense he could conjure, followed by, "I want to forget it ever happened."

Finally, Linda hung up.

And it really *was* over with the other woman. Over because he'd chosen to end it. *That had to count for something*, he thought as he snatched up the phone and dialed Linda's number with a new conviction. There was no backing down on this side of the starting line, after all. No blocking the forward momentum. He was going to tell her that he was coming home so things could go back to the way they were, that was it. No surprises. No need for discussion.

"Yeah," he let out a shaking breath as he depressed the final key on the phone pad, "this ought to go well."

The phone let out a short, piercing squeal and fell silent. He recoiled from it and gave it an irritated wince. The screen was backlit but featureless, only a blank and dim rectangle and he studied it with more than a little puzzlement. Feedback? But from what? As if in response, the landscape outside his window changed to beige blankness as steep concrete embankments flanked the road. They towered over the roofs of the traffic, blocking his view of the complementing southerly lanes and all but the nearest on- and off-ramps. *Phone's out and I just went down the gullet of the Hooberbloob Highway. Could I hate this any more?*

He dropped the phone into the passenger seat with an uneasy laugh. Uneasy because when he tried to recall this odd stretch of highway from his trip down to Missouri, (and he was certain he was following the same route back) he couldn't. And the Hooberbloob with its arterial passages and Kali arms was something not easily forgotten. Perhaps he had taken a wrong turn while in the grips of his driver's daze. If only he could find one signpost, one bit of direction. If only he were in the right-hand lane so he could exit—

A small white hatchback cut in behind him with a screech of tires. The car directly to his right pulled ahead of him and blatantly rammed the bumper of the sedan riding in front of it. He tensed and evaluated this new situation: tailgater behind, unreasonable driver at two o'clock and there was nowhere for him to go. He was sandwiched in, part of a solid mass of speeding cars, and all he could do for the moment was keep pace with them. He flexed his hands on the steering wheel and found them greasy with sweat.

A grinding crunch shook the Volvo.

"What?" he barked and glanced around.

The white hatchback had rammed him, for Christ's sake. He watched it swerve out and move up on his right, gobbling up any available space. The driver was a young woman with long hair tied back in a ponytail. She seemed totally unaware that she had hit him, did not even turn her head, but cruised along until she was the better part of a car-length ahead of him. Her rear license plate read SAMI. He snatched up his phone, his teeth gritted, sweat popping out on his forehead. Well, SAMI, you might not think there's a problem, but let's see what the local cops have to say about your driving habits. He coaxed the Volvo to the left, toward the narrow shoulder that buffered the concrete wall from the edge of the highway. He wanted to pull off and inspect the damage to his bumper prior to making his call. A horn blared, high and shrill like a flat chord from a church organ. A rusty blue four-door squeezed by him on the left, kicking up gravel and road debris like buckshot. He could feel the vibration of its humming machinery through the Volvo's window. Its door panel picked off his side mirror with a crunch. Reflective fragments flew.

"Goddamn it," he roared and veered back into his own lane.

A glance in his rearview mirror confirmed that the left shoulder corridor had become an impromptu lane of its own, stacked full of racing vehicles. They whooshed past him in rapid succession.

He tossed the phone aside to clamp both hands back on the wheel. Ahead of him, in the right-hand lane, a yellow Volkswagen raced up to SAMI's back bumper and unceremoniously rammed it. Bits of tail light lenses scattered like flung rubies.

"What is wrong with you people? We're not on the bumper cars at the goddamn county fair," Max called out and then blinked uncertainly at the hatchback. "What the hell?"

SAMI had a rider. He hadn't noticed one earlier, but now a small, hairless silhouette was visible in the passenger seat. A child, standing and bracing itself against the dashboard. *This road's a hell of a place for a kid,* he thought, and wondered why the blow from behind a minute ago hadn't knocked the little rug rat off the seat and right out of its Pampers.

Another feeder ramp allowed more vehicles to crowd onto the main highway ahead. He watched them merge, transfixed by their dumb voracity. He'd seen brewery bottles bustle onto a conveyor belt like that once. It was during a beer-making tour he insisted they go to in downtown Milwaukee. Linda followed along politely that day, absorbing facts and details with her usual quiet interest, and after the tour she suggested they go to the art museum. Out of fairness, he respected her wishes only to realize later he'd enjoyed both portions of the day equally. He never admitted this, but he was pretty sure she knew. Smart girl, his Linda. And intuitive. That's why he loved her, he guessed.

The flow of traffic changed again, just enough to allow him to pull up alongside SAMI. At that moment he saw her passenger reach out to embrace her with long arms. Overlong gray arms. Max blinked, all his attention suddenly drawn to the interior of SAMI's car. The rider tipped its oddly large head toward him as if it sensed his stare. A mask, he thought, the child in the seat wore a disguise that turned its forehead into something high and creased with perpetual rage. The nose was an insignificant hump vented by two slits and the mouth was a lipless gash, all of it the color of ashes. Added to that was a pair of novelty shop goggles. The type where huge painted eyeballs (a solid deep orange in this case) might pop out on springs and waggle partway down the cheeks of the wearer. He regarded it with a tenuous brand of amusement, knowing he should watch the road, but unable to look away. The face of SAMI's rider caught the sun in that second and he felt his breath leave him. The rider's mouth moved liquidly to show sharp nubs of teeth. It was almost a smile, but not quite. Its large eyes, not goggles at all and not equipped with springs of any kind, glimmered and pulsed at him with embryonic heat like steam engine coals. And they blinked, wet and alive.

He shook his head, still unable to look away. SAMI's passenger clamped its hands around her throat. The hatchback swerved and Max jerked his wheel to the left to avoid a collision, but he was allowed little play. A tan sedan piloted by a portly man in a short-sleeved shirt and necktie now cruised the shoulder to his left. The sedan held its ground and Max compensated again. He had enough time to notice another small hairless figure, similar to SAMI's rider, in the portly man's back seat. It tapped its gray fingers on the headrest, impatient, its mouth rolling up into a mocking smile.

"This can't be," he said and glanced back to SAMI.

SAMI's passenger climbed onto her while she drove. No, climbed wasn't right. It mounted her, facing her. Its arms slipped around her neck and it pressed itself against her. The hatchback remained on a steady course, steering itself perhaps, even as the young woman's hands began to claw wildly at the air.

"Get it off of you," he cried out to her.

She tried to twist her head, her saw her make the attempt, but her face became buried in the flat underbelly.

The gray flesh of the rider began to ripple and reform, becoming loose and dangling strands. In unison those strands, ropy and wet, stretched through the air and slipped over SAMI's face, her neck, her thrashing arms. Max realized he was watching a drowning woman, one who pulled not dark and swampy water into her lungs, but invading cables of gray matter. He felt the air in his own lungs grow thin and hot as he fought to keep the Volvo on track. SAMI's rider lost all shape, becoming a woven membrane which sealed itself in a shroud-like pod around the blonde behind the wheel. Her throes were momentarily visible as twitches and overlong bulges, then the gray sac clenched and a small spray of crimson bloomed on the underside of the skin. All movement stopped inside. After an eternal pause, the pod began to shrink, rapidly reclaiming shape as Max stared on—a head, a narrow body, long arms. Seconds later it was the gray rider once again, now facing front, its horn-like claws clittering on the wheel. The only thing reminiscent of the previous driver was a short nub of matter, somewhat like her ponytail, which waggled from the back of its head. Max turned away, a new kind of daze calling him away from the act of driving—this one charged not with fatigue but with disbelief. The hatchback broke away, squeezed between two vehicles which traveled the right-hand breakdown lane, and zipped up one of the twisted exit ramps. He barely noticed.

"Figure this out," he coached himself between deep breaths, "Think it through."

The driver of the tan sedan on the left shoulder punched his brakes hard enough to make the tires squawk. Max glanced his mirror in time to see a dusky form hop out of the back seat and flop onto the man's chest. A second later a stripe of blood painted the middle of the sedan windshield. A chorus of horns rose up. A heavy crash followed.

"Where are those things coming from?" Max asked through a violent shudder.

Several car lengths ahead of him a man leapt from the seat of his moving convertible as if performing a standing long-jump, arms outstretched, dark shirt and Roman collar stark against the clear sky. His legs pumped enthusiastically as if the God who had called him into service and gave him his daily bread might now pluck him from the air and set him down tenderly at the roadside so that he may run away from this bad stretch of road. He crashed into the windshield of the yellow Volkswagen, tumbled over its roof and landed in the right-hand lane. A dark colored Cadillac riding behind the Volkswagen bounced over him importantly. The man's abandoned car veered sharply and cut between vehicles in the right lane to crash into the concrete wall. An opening formed between the Caddy and the yellow Volkswagen and Max cut his wheel hard to the right. The Volvo slipped into the space neatly and Max rapped the steering wheel, calling out with excited accomplishment. "Almost there. The next exit ramp is mine, baby!"

Don't celebrate yet, he thought, *not as long as you're on this road—*

A musky reek flooded the car. It reminded him of old leather and wet weeds, the scent of things flung off into the ditch to rot. He checked his rearview mirror just as the shape in his back seat slipped forward. Its round lantern eyes twitched, calculating, sizing him up. A web-work of black veins pulsed beneath its skin.

"What do you want?" he called out.

The thing made a small, wet grunt and tilted its head the way an old woman might ponder produce in the grocery store, thoughtful and perhaps a little skeptical. Its claws came up and gave his shoulder a tentative, exploring poke.

"No, you don't," he told it and wrenched the steering wheel hard to the right.

His rider toppled to the backseat floor with a surprised squawk. Momentum swept the Volvo to the edge of the breakdown lane and directly into the path of a massive recreational vehicle. Its horn sounded and its grille flashed in his rear window like the snarl of a gigantic beast. Max switched back to the travel lane instinctively and his trunk nearly sheared off the nose of the ensuing Cadillac, which had already begun to claim the open space. The RV rumbled up along his side. Its driver glowered down at him, hunched and gray-skinned, contempt in its eyes. He switched his gaze back to the creature in his backseat. It rose up and clicked its claws anxiously as if readying fine instruments for delicate but necessary work. Its eyes lingered on him with want and determination.

"I said no!" Max jerked the wheel and slammed sidelong into the RV.

The RV's side panels buckled and grated against the Volvo, raising shrill, prolonged screeches. His rider raised its hands in an attitude of fussy distress, and then clamped them over its head. To his amazement, it flopped backward and began thrashing on his back seat, kicking its legs as if throwing a tantrum.

"Don't like that racket, eh?" he asked it, even as the two vehicles parted and the screeching stopped. "Then don't even think about coming over the top of that seat." He gave the steering wheel a slight tug, lurching the car to punctuate his point. "I'll do it again, longer next time if you try. I swear to God."

The RV drifted to the right and sailed up an exit ramp like a wounded cur in retreat. Damn it, he hadn't even seen the exit coming up. But there was another, not too far. A mile maybe.

The Cadillac rammed his back bumper anxiously.

"Oh yeah?" he asked as he glanced his rear view mirror, "Oh yeah?"

Something thumped beneath him. Dumbly, he checked the instrument panel with a twisting fear that the car might not be weathering the unexpected abuse. The last thing he needed was to break down in the middle of this hellish, swarming mess. But it was not a thump brought on by failed suspension or a wobbling tire, it was something closer. More intimate. It was...inside. He checked the floor just as a gray arm shot out from under the car seat. Spiny fingers clawed at his ankles. He took another sharp hit in the rear from the Caddy. A second arm unfurled and claws scrabbled at the floor between his feet. With deliberate slowness a gray head began to emerge from under the seat, mashed into an impossible contour as it moved through the narrow space. Eyes, alight with flat determination, peered up between Max's knees. The caved-in condition of its head made the eyes looked crossed. The obscenity of it made him want to laugh, something harsh and humorless, but he was afraid if he started he would not be able to stop.

It's not coming over the seat, he thought with that same dark, lunatic humor, *I'll give it that much.*

The rider twisted around and rammed the heels of its hands down on his accelerator foot like a medic doing field compressions. The Volvo shot forward and rammed the rear end of the Volkswagen before he could pull back. Horns blared around him and he gave a helpless sweeping glance to the tight raft of traffic, and the tighter confines of the Volvo cabin. There was no room to put up a fight. His cell phone rested on the seat, however, its blank face still casting drab light onto the upholstery. He snatched it up.

"Please," he said with hoarse hopefulness as he pushed the redial button. "Don't connect. I don't want you to connect."

The screech that pealed out of the phone's earpiece seemed to fill the interior of the car. The creature glared at him with alarm. He thought it might attack him, latch onto his throat and just start tearing, but instead it slipped away from him, scrambled into the foot well on the passenger side and crouched there like a terrified child, its features limned with distress.

"I'd say the reception sucks around here," he said through a lunatic near-grin as he redialed again. "What do you think?"

The second squeal seemed louder. Max thrust the phone forward in a menacing manner and the creature shrank away. Now if he could only pop the passenger door open somehow and toss the little creep out on his bony gray ass...

The feedback ended and the phone fell startlingly silent.

The creature vaulted from its place, its face pulled down into an expression of hatred, and it two-handedly sunk its claws into his extended arm and opened him up from elbow to wrist. Pain rocked him like a sickening blow. The phone popped out of his fingers, rapped sharply against the windshield and then tumbled to the floor. Its housing came off in two jagged pieces revealing gleaming components, and a small fragment of internal parts bounced a few inches away on the floor mat. The phone display screen went dark.

The creature leapt onto the passenger seat. Max balled his free hand into a fist and drew back. Blood squelched in his palm. The creature's eyes widened with a sudden urgency and for a moment he wondered if it had read his intentions so clearly that it nearly felt the imminent blow. Its eyes, however, were no longer fixed on him. They goggled toward the road ahead.

"What? What's up there?" he asked it.

The rider did a frustrated double-take and lunged at him, suddenly wild and thrashing. Desperate. Claws gouged his cheeks, raked his forehead and he did his best to fend off the attacks. One talon pulled a long furrow down the side of his neck. He lost his grip on the wheel, regained it. His front fender nicked somebody and the Volvo's front bumper rang like an ill-tuned chime. The creature's feet tramped on his thighs and then it stood before him, blocking his view, its face hardened by something like triumph, an athlete about to make an eleventh-hour score.

Max brought his fist around and delivered a hard smack to the side of the thing's head. The creature rocked back and for a moment he could once again see the road ahead, the strands of cars that stretched out before him and slipped, row by row, past the last remaining exit of the entangled interchange. But there was one other structure before the ramps were gone and the cement walls gave way to low, flat landscape once more. An ancient trestle, as diligent, monumental and wise as the first.

Dim realization bloomed in his thoughts. The rider pressed itself against him. Its naked chest scrubbed against his cheeks, filling his lungs with the scent of rotted leaves and stagnant runoff. Its pelvis humped up against his throat. Tissue began to slide over him, rubbery cords working furiously to knit up around him, draw him in. He tried to veer off the road, perhaps collide with another vehicle—any type of distraction would do—but the Volvo's wheel was locked and unmovable. So much for forward momentum, he thought.

He slammed on his brakes.

The Cadillac rear-ended him with a grinding force. The jolt snapped his head backward. The creature was flung into the back seat in a tangle of gray limbs and a spiteful flash of orange eyes. Max hit the gas and nosed the Volvo blindly into the breakdown lane. A speeding van clipped his right fender, sending another shockwave through the car. The creature made an incensed bleating sound. Max steadied the Volvo and set his sights on the trestle ahead, on the broad shadow traced like an ashen thumbprint across the highway. Finish line, he thought with grim assurance. He glimpsed the mirror one final time. The creature lunged at him from the back seat, its hands locked in a vicious claws-out rigor.

Max closed his eyes and braced for the blow. The Volvo passed beneath the trestle. Shadows clenched at him, but their hold was ardent one moment, insubstantial the next. No claws slashed him, but there was a slight pass of air at the back of his neck and then nothing but the rumble of his tires on the craggy breakdown lane.

He opened his eyes to the realization he was once again alone in the car, and that he needed to steer if he wished to stay on the road. He clamped the wheel tightly. Pain sizzled inside each cut on his arms, his face, his scalp, burning deep down like cruel betrayals and things unsaid.

He took the next off ramp (a green sign properly designated it as an "Exit" and informed him that Dubuque, the next city of notoriety, was 42 miles away) and the road ahead expanded to three lanes. He chose the center lane because it seemed the least congested.

The first gas station he came to had a phone booth just inside the plate glass entrance and he pulled in. Blood ran from his cheeks and onto his chin like oily tears as he dialed Linda's number, the well-worn handset pressed to his ear. When she answered, his first utterance was a broken sigh of relief. But she knew it was him. She asked, with real concern, what was wrong. Where was he? Was he coming home? So smart, his Linda. So intuitive.

Outside, traffic glittered and passed benignly in the afternoon sunshine.

About Dean H. Wild

Dean H. Wild has been writing for over twenty years, and most of his work is in the horror and dark fantasy genre. Some of Dean's work in print include: "The Laughing Place," published in Brian Hopkins' *Extremes 5: Fantasy and Horror from the Ends of the Earth*, and "The Kid," included in William Simmons' *Vivisections*. He is the Assistant Editor of The Horror Zine. http://www.deanwild.com

THE HOUSE AT THE END OF SMITH STREET
by Stephen M. Dare

The two men stared at the small, partially burned house at the end of Smith Street. It was bordered on one side by the high trees of the Park Woods, and on the other by a vacant lot full of tall grass, weed-trees, and the junked hulls of appliances and cars. They stared, amazed that so much of the house was still standing; so much was still intact, somehow surviving the fire. The worst of the fire looked to have scorched the house's right side where some blackened bricks of the foundation had been kicked over, probably by kids in the neighborhood—kids in rags and bruises on their unwashed bodies, most without shoes, but all with rings in their ears and noses.

Kids, the men thought, not much younger and not much different than their sister Rachel's boy, Eddie. Head-shaven Eddie, with the new stainless steel gauge in his earlobe, a bit less expensive than the diamond Rachel had studded into him when he was six months old. Eddie was eleven now, bearing their father's eyebrows and cheekbones and their mother's pouty mouth.

Eddie hadn't been to school in three days. The school had finally called his Uncle Shane, one of the men who was now staring at the house. Shane had called his own brother Al, the other man. Al worked the second shift, so he was home now; two brothers staring at their sister's home across the street, and wondering where Rachel was right now. The last they knew, she had wound up in some friend's trailer, after the fire had broken out, though now in a meth-haze.

A few days ago, the brothers had gone to the trailer to try to reason with her. Rachel wailed that she "didn't know nothing" about Eddie until Al shoved her head against the wall. That was when she finally cried out, "The house has him! The house has my Eddie, and it won't let him go!"

Disgusted with her drug-induced psychosis, the two brothers had left in Shane's Mustang to find out for themselves if Eddie was trying to live inside the burned house. Once there, they talked in front of the house, watching its burned silence behind a single strand of yellow police tape over the front door. Shane lit a cigarette, and Al kept nodding at what he was saying until Shane pointed with his cigarette across the lot at another house just like Rachel's. This one was surrounded by a ragged wire fence, yard stomped to dust by dogs and kids. One of the kids—a child certainly no older than three, diaper sagging yellow around its middle—stood at the fence staring at them. The child stared and stared and stared so long that both Al and Shane soon believed the child could not blink.

Across the street and in the tall grass of the other lot waited an older child dressed only in cut-off jeans so baggy that the boxer shorts underneath were in full display. The boy was smoking a gray joint. He watched them as if waiting for something before finally sitting on the crumbling curb. A dog barked with menace down the pitted road somewhere.

Shane pulled his palm across his forehead. The heat had stilted the air to a smother. Maybe there would be rain later, but this early, the sky was white with August fatigue.

Al said, "No crickets here."

"No crickets anywhere," Shane said back. Then he finished his cigarette and tossed it into a pothole in the street, and they went together to the path scrawled through the weeds up to the house.

Rachel's satellite dish had been moved since they were last here. Rachel and her goddamn daytime TV and her Xbox, and all the while Eddie ran wild over God knew the hell where. The brothers had long known that Rachel lived only for Rachel. Plasma TV Rachel, iPhone Rachel, Wi-Fi computer Rachel; probably all stolen. And the latest was that BioFab one of her old boyfriends had installed; that penthouse-designer carpet you never had to vacuum. That was their sister. Gotta have every new and trendy thing because she was tweaking all the time and always needed a distraction, and go screw the rest of you.

Approaching the front stoop, the brothers saw that a rotting board was set on cinderblocks as a step before the battered screen door. Al broke the single strand of yellow tape, pulled the screen door open, and tried the knob on the weather-warped storm-door behind it. Shane would have gone instead to one of the windows along the side of the house, but each window had been barred, probably so that Rachel's stolen items wouldn't get re-stolen when she had lived there. With all those bars, it was amazing that anyone had gotten out that night when the house had caught fire.

Al pushed the big front door open and they both stepped in. Though it was mid-morning, it was dark inside, the air smelling of old fire. It was close and stale, but with something in it that made them both pause. Al didn't like it and said so. Shane grunted. It was like wetness, he said. Wetness from the firemen's hoses, hauled in like heavy snakes through the front door. Wetness and rot. Like a pile of vegetable scraps and meat left to rot in the sun. But Al thought of something more: it made him think of rank digestion.

They shut the door against the outside and waited in the dark for their eyes to adjust. They couldn't turn on any lights since Rachel hadn't paid her bill before she left. No electricity for almost a week before the fire. Maybe she couldn't stand the lack of TV and Xbox and that was why she left. It sure wasn't the smell of the burned roof; Rachel had lived like this for years. She might have continued living here, even with the fire damage and its rank smell. Except neither of the brothers could remember when the smell had been this bad.

Al called for Eddie several times, his voice filling the empty house. Nothing. You could tell when someone was hiding out in a house. An empty house felt empty, vacant and hollow. The feel of it here said that Eddie was sure as shit gone. Probably living with someone, some girl maybe.

In the dimness, as they waited and talked in near-whispers, Al thought he heard something move across the designer carpet to their right. A mouse, maybe. They were all over these places, rats too. But it didn't sound like a mouse. It sounded like something pushing its way over the floor, jabbing in one long, darting movement through the paper and trash. Not scurrying like a mouse, but something more like a snake.

"Snakes're all over out here," Shane said when Al spoke about it, "'specially under these houses. Foundations're crawling with the fuckin' things. Fire could have drove them out though."

"We need a flashlight," Al said.

"We need to get this place searched and done with."

"You lead, then. You deal with the snakes."

Shane stepped through a heap of wet, soiled clothes. He kicked sopping pizza delivery boxes, Cheetos and Lay's potato chip bags, and mildewed newspapers out of the way. The big room—really, no larger than Shane's garage—doubled as a TV room and kitchen, the kitchen set to one side of the room. Dishes crusted with macaroni and dried spaghetti and pot pie tins were piled in the rust-spattered sink. A Breyer's vanilla ice cream box left on the peeling counter had dribbled a tacky white stream down a scarred cabinet door to a pool on the linoleum.

Against the wall by the fridge were towering stacks of Budweiser, Mountain Dew, and Coca-Cola cans. Some of the stacks had fallen over, the remaining contents in the cans having trickled to a sticky pale sheen on the floor. A Monster energy drink can lay by the trim-strip where the linoleum met the BioFab carpet. Some of the carpet had frayed there and bits of its curly strands lay across the linoleum. Their ends were pasted into the tacky pool of puke-colored energy drink.

The men moved through the kitchen onto the carpet and bent down to examine it. The BioFab carpet looked like a graham-colored Berber, but unblemished by stains. Somehow it had survived the fire completely intact. Al moved another box away to find a half-eaten piece of pale pizza crust stuck to the carpet. He nudged it with his boot, but the crust didn't budge, the BioFab pinning it down tight like glue. Soon the BioFab would have made the crust disappear altogether.

"That designer carpet shit actually works," he said, amazed.

"The lazy housekeeper's dream," Shane said. "Look at this place. It'll be condemned, I'll betcha."

They went through the trash to the window on the far side of the room and moved the fire-eaten curtain away. Through the filthy window, they could see two new shirtless boys standing on the edge of the weed-lot across the street where the older boy had been. They were watching the house, their tanned skin like tough bronze. They were barefoot and in cut-off shorts. One had a mohawk, the other a mullet, they were both smoking cigarettes or joints. Eddie's long lost friends, Al thought.

"Let's see what they know," Al said.

"After we look in the bedroom," Shane said.

They went back across the carpet and around the kitchen wall into the bedroom. Most of the fire damage was here, where Rachel and Eddie had shared a bed. It had probably been someone's cigarette that started the fire. The walls and ceiling were ravaged by fire as it had consumed up and into the roof before the firemen could put it out. Had Eddie come back to hide out?

They searched the closet, glanced under the ragged bed. No Eddie. So Eddie was gone, all right. Maybe he had hooked up with that gang everyone was so scared of over on Adams Street.

"What now?" Al asked.

"Let's go outside and talk to those kids out front," Shane said. "Those kids look like they know something, the way they were watching the house. Like they're waiting for something to happen."

Al peered out the window to the backyard. Through the bars, he saw the edge of the woods running away and the sea of yellow weeds reaching up past the window. There were power lines further out, leading to brick apartments on a distant grassy hill. Too far off, Al thought, to tell if anyone is standing on a balcony of one of the apartments, grilling something good with an icy Busch beer at their side. Al swallowed, wanting to taste it. He waved a couple of fingers at the invisible griller. *Be there soon. Save a cold one for me.*

Back in the combined living room and kitchen, the light had brightened as the sunlight shifted. It looked as though somehow there was more trash on the floor, and more light on the far side of the room. They remembered that there was a plant on a stand in the corner, some viney tropical thing living on neglect. A perfect plant for their sister.

But the old wooden stand had toppled, and the pot fallen away from it onto the carpet. The plant still lived, its vines and leaves rolling over a greasy Domino's pizza box. Frayed grayish strands of BioFab carpet had curled into the spilt black soil. In here the light had moved enough for them to see that several fuzzy strands had climbed the walls in long twists. The brothers looked closer and closer until they each had their faces hovering several inches from the BioFab's strands, which were hooked into the wallpaper, curled like stiff worms underneath it—not pulling the wallpaper out, but having pushed through it, some of it forced into the drywall itself and into the wall.

One strand had ventured high enough to grasp the low corner of the smoke-greased HD television and hung there.

Al tugged on a strand, pulled it away from the wall, but plaster powdered down with it, and he cursed, letting it go fast and cursing again and again and holding his finger away from him in the sunlight. It dripped with bright blood, spotting his jeans leg and shoe.

"Sumbitch bit me," he said, "bit me hard."

"What bit you hard?"

"What d'you think bit me, fuckin' carpet got me."

"Bullshit."

"Bullshit, lookit." He held his bleeding finger out at Shane. "Bit me like with a tooth or razor."

Shane bent to look at the strand Al had pulled off. Held it between his fingers like a string. He quietly ran it between his fingers. Then he winced. He held the strand up to the light. A very tiny fragment was hinged on the strand so that it was able to flip up and down. It was no longer than a quarter-inch. A black tooth. Sharp. Snake-fang sharp.

"Jesus Mary Christ, brother," Shane said. He ran his fingers a ways down the strand. There seemed to be a tiny burr at its end. It gleamed like steel in the light, as long as a carpenter's trim nail, with an edge like a razor.

Al saw the lump in the new light first, the small risen area in the corner where the BioFab had swollen like something pregnant. And then he knew what had tipped the plant-stand. The lump had moved toward the dark corner, tipping the plant stand into the room long after Gotta-

Have-It-Rachel had fled in her piece-of-shit Ford Escort. The lump had moved to a dark spot to get tucked away and hidden, like an engorged python digesting a goat in sleepy seclusion.

Shane took his Buck knife and plunged it into the lump, slicing through the BioFab. A tiny hissing sound like a broken steam-hose came from somewhere under their knees or behind them as they stripped the rug back with their knives, the lump feeling soft at first, but then hard under them. A warm, wet vomit-acid reek came around them, filling their skulls, springing hot tears to their eyes.

Al fell away, stumbling backward. Coming out of him was a combination of screaming and choking noises. Shane held a flap of rug away with the blade of his knife, the strands twisting, dangling like silkworms in August country air, and peered at the squashed thing inside the hole.

It was a bony, flattened torso, the pink arm and leg bones; pale, moist flesh pitted like Swiss cheese, and stringy meat was glistening underneath. The slick and pitted pink skull gaped up at him. A stainless-steel gauged earring lay beside it in the warm, red-black, rotting muck. The entire thing was compressed, all folded tightly into itself, as if stuffed into a suitcase.

Shane was holding the earring up to the light with his knife as Al ran to the front door, both hands gripping the handle and twisting together. He pulled hard, but the door wouldn't move, wouldn't even budge. He fell to his knees, spitting and cursing. He looked up at the door, blinking, not comprehending the slight bow in the wood before him, bulging out at him in the middle, and falling away into its frame at the sides.

Then Shane was there beside his brother, studying the BioFab by the floor-trim, his eyes traveling upwards along the doorjamb. The trim covering the jamb had flexed away from the wall. Shane cursed, squeezing the tips of his fingers behind the trim, prying it outward only to see that the BioFab had curled under it, stuffing itself into the quarter-inch space between the wall and jamb. Stuffing itself like insulation but only tighter, so tight that even as Shane dug his fingers into it, he could barely make purchase. The twisted strands had snaked high, burrowing into the space, squeezing the jamb so tight it flexed the door inward, compressing it to not open, freezing it tight.

"Christ, brother, what's it done?" Al cried with frustration and fear.

"What's it look like?" Shane said as he forced his nails into the strands, managing to pull several frays out until finally he had enough to seize. He began stripping them outward, away from the jamb, the trim leaning by the few nails holding it to the wall. His hands worked, stripping the frays like long gray licorice. His eyes were wide with what he and his brother now realized had happened, this seeming entrapment. The strands came away only a few at a time, but revealed a newly twisted mass hardened into the jamb, the loose ones twisting against the frame and door like silkworms.

The blood began to trickle a little at first. It ran down Shane's wrists and then his forearms, over his faded snake tattoo, beading on hairs and blooming against his shirt and pants like bright red paint.

Al said his brother's name several times before finally rushing to lurch him away from the door. Blood ran down Shane's pants and into his shoes and down the sides of them onto the carpet where the rich stains disappeared in moments, as if they were never there. When he got to the deeper strands, the hinged fangs slipped into him like surgeon's needles, biting through his flesh and muscle. He didn't stop, as if he couldn't, his will hijacked by some outside and foreign determination. Blood dashed over the door, streamed down to the threshold, pooling on the carpet where Al thought he heard something like a sucking sound, like someone using a straw in a deep, emptying cup.

Then Al was on his knees too, and then over his brother and what was left of his brother's arms and hands. Flesh hanging like torn, wet paper, tendons like wet black cables, muscle and white fat stripped apart; a few of the strands had caught in the torn fat and muscle and hung there, but other strands were twisting in the air and over his ruined body. They were squirming like they were alive, tiny furry things with their ends moving back and forth like the heads of worms. Some wiggled into the lacerations on Shane's arms, disappearing into them.

It was Shane who spoke what Al knew by then. It was Shane who put it together, but too late.

Not just the carpet stranding to the pizza crust in the TV room, not the strange kids watching the house from the lot, not just the kids keeping away, far away from the house, knowing something. There had been more, and it had come when they had seen Rachel in her doped rant about the house. About something bad with the house. The house has him! The house has my Eddie, and it won't let him go!

"It got Eddie, it got me too, brother," Shane said, his eyes already death-sheen glassy. "It let us in because it was hungry, it wanted more. Now that it's got us, it ain't going to let us out. I couldn't help tearing at it. Something about it got in me to make me keep cutting myself, making myself bleed. Feeding it with myself." He spat blood over his chin. "Call 911 on your cell."

Al screamed, "I didn't bring it! Christ, I didn't think to bring it!"

But Shane went on, not listening, his voice fading. He said, "It grew out of itself, brother. Eddie always had those bloody noses. Fuckin' rug got a taste of blood. No rats left here. No cockroaches, no crickets. No Eddie, and now nothing left to eat but us."

After Al shut his brother's eyes, he had moved off the carpet to stand on the tiny linoleum area by the door. Against the far wall of the TV room, something hissed, and when he looked, he saw that the sliced-open section around what had once been his nephew in the floor had gotten smaller. Gray fibers had run across the hole like threads trying to stitch together a gaping wound. The hissing came again right next to him, and when he turned he saw that several strands had run themselves over Shane like tiny ropes pinning down a giant.

He remembered the window in the bedroom, knew he could break the glass out, and beg the staring kids for help. *Please help me! Please, please get someone...*

And what would that help be? To summon someone—the police? Never, not down here, not in this neighborhood. Some kid's dad with a blowtorch to cut the goddamn bars away? No one would venture toward this house; he knew it in his bones. By the look of the kids across the street, they'd seen or heard things down here that would make even grown men like Al go pale. And things from this house too. It wasn't the fire that had kept them away. Maybe they had heard what happened to Eddie. Maybe they heard Eddied screaming as the carpet strands wrestled him to the floor; furry, sharp tendrils snaking into his bleeding nose and mouth, into his ears, up his asshole. Or maybe, Al thought, maybe it had gotten Eddie as he slept. Maybe Eddie had never woken up.

He needed to get out of the living room. There was only one place that had no carpet: the kitchen.

It was watching him as he was trapped in the kitchen, sitting on the counter. The sun faded low, the house succumbing into dimness. The sun's light changed orange and purple in the window across the room. He could hear the hissing sound come more and more and from every side so that eventually no moment was silent. It came from the attic and from inside the walls.

And now the kitchen was no longer a safe haven. Out of the corner of his eye, Al saw the linoleum floor below him move. So it was spreading. It wasn't just the carpet anymore.

Al pushed himself into the corner on the counter and held himself, his muscles cramping. He no longer smelled stale fire; now he sensed new decay, sweet and bitter as the hissing went on into the black night, his eyes finally adjusting to see shapes moving from the floor. The hissing pierced him like talons so that soon—sweat beading down his face and back—it became just white noise, familiar, like a fan. It lulled him to sleep, letting him nod off, only to snap him awake, his heart drubbing in his throat.

Nodding off, then waking, over and over; clinging to the countertop, thinking of Eddie. Dreaming of Eddie. Eddie on his first day of school. Eddie's first birthday. Fatherless Eddie. Drug-addict mom. We should have been there for you more, Eddie. We should've knocked your mom's teeth out a long time ago, taken you with us. Raised you ourselves. Raised you right and good and with a chance in this hell of a world. Gave you what you needed. Sorry, Eddie, sorry.

He felt his cheeks wet. Tears, hot and thick. Wiping them away, but with the sting of salt like a stab in his eyes, and then his hand snagging into the fabric of his shirt collar and then another stab and another in his hand and up his nose and inside both eyeballs, exploding him awake so that he fell and his face met the floor with a painful, furious slam.

The police came shortly after the house was condemned, but the search for the two men and the boy ended quickly and quietly. What was strange, the police decided, was that it was the only house on Smith Street that wasn't a haven for rats and snakes. Even cockroaches were absent, which was okay. Just a bit peculiar. Just like the things left behind—the Xbox, an iPhone, and the charred remains of several marijuana plants. The woman who owned the place was supposed to be strung up and crazy, but not so crazy she couldn't vanish sometime in the night from the friend's trailer she'd been staying at. Vanished, someone thought, to head out West. California maybe, or Mexico even.

They razed the two-room house in the grassy lot with a bulldozer and backhoe and dump trucks that came and went only twice in a span of two hours.

The demolition crew had pushed soil vaguely over the house's crumbling foundation. Bits of wood lath and plaster and remnants of carpet had mixed into the earth and brick. Eventually, under the sun and rain and wind, new weeds sprouted wild, accompanied by tiny bits of grayish strands of carpet that twirled over timothy and ragweed. In some places, whole mats of carpet had stretched over patches of barren soil, clinging in bland colors like the soil itself. It was moving across the lot toward the other crumbling houses; moving away for the distant hilltop apartments, toward young wives with toddlers, toward men grilling on their balconies in late summer-wear and sunglasses, who were sipping their final cold beer.

About Stephen M. Dare

Stephen M. Dare lives with his wife and three children in Delavan, Illinois, which is a small town founded by H.P. Lovecraft's uncle. He has a master's degree in English and teaches at a private school.

Stephen has been writing horror since the eighth grade, but he has been reading it and watching movies in that genre for much longer. He appreciates good, deep horror fiction and has a passion for Algernon Blackwood's novella *The Willows*, which achieves a profound level of horror rarely seen in contemporary fiction, and that is unfortunate.

Besides horror, Stephen's other passion is gardening, and he is attracted to carnivorous plants. He has actually created a carnivorous plant bog in his front yard.

GNAW
by Lala Drona

3:20 AM

The movement in the second-floor apartment rocked and swayed the rest of the decaying building like gelatin. The oven alarm blared from the adjacent room, burning their ears. The TV added to the noise; an old western shooting-scene seemed to shake the cheap apartment, forcing the two lovers to compete with the televised battle. Broken dishes laid in pieces on the living room floor next to a lamp lying on its side; the bulb flickered in the static-charged air.

He didn't deserve this love. She slapped him in the face.

Pounding from broomsticks, smacking from hands, and thuds from fists on the other sides of the walls shook the apartment as neighbors futilely protested the noise. He held his jaw, looking up and down the black trails of makeup on her cheeks. He said, "I love you."

The room quit spinning when she squeezed his face between each of her palms and whispered, "Now you can taste the ache I feel every day." She released him and turned away. The televised battle transitioned into a clamoring word from the program's sponsors, and the flickering bulb finally went out. He caught her wrist and secured her back in. The light flickered back on, but just for a moment, then off for the final time.

His chest was to her back while he turned her face and delicately kissed her until her body went soft. He didn't know her. Their relationship was like a one-night-stand that never ended, and he felt as if he had only just met her, even though he had been staying with her for a while. His iron-flavored kiss went deep, and before it had ended, he pulled away. "Now you can taste mine too," he breathed.

7:05 AM

Dieter didn't have to open his eyes to know it was morning. The light shone hard on his eyelids, causing him to see a pink hue. His skin burned and ached from the night before. His jaw swelled from Renee's blow. The sheets and mattress were unmoving beside him, so either she had left the night before, or she was still next to him, sleeping. Dieter found it was the latter as he rolled over to the other side of the bed and bulldozed over a tiny body.

"Eh!" Renee protested, struggling from under him. "What's the big idea? Can't a girl sleep past seven o'clock these days?" Dieter reverse-rolled over, taking the blanket back with him. She frowned through crusty black make-up, her eyes puffy and sleepy. The black trails still ran down her face.

"I swear, you're a machine. A robot. Robots don't need sleep, y'know." Her fingers wrapped around the yellowed sheet and she pulled it over her shoulder while rolling onto her side. She looked back at him, frowning, but then a smile broke loose, so she hid her face in the lumpy orange pillow. Dieter pulled the blanket off her shoulders and watched the skin move across her back while she breathed. His fingers walked up her back, skipping, using freckles like stepping-stones.

Dieter pulled himself close by her ear. "Hey, Bird…" Her back began to jump up and down as if she were attempting to fly away. Then, Dieter heard the giggles follow. Her back stopped moving and she yelled into the orange pillow, but the sound was not muffled. One of the neighbors thudded against the wall in response.

"Okay, okay!" Renee called to the unseen neighbor, then flipped over and put her hands behind her head as Dieter laid his head on her chest.

The ceiling fan stopped, the television went black, and a car alarm blared outdoors. "This building," Dieter complained. "It should be condemned."

Dieter felt Renee's hand tap his cheek, hard enough to create yet another welt on him. "Hey now…" she said, wrinkling the white skin on her forehead.

Before Dieter could say a word to apologize about his building remark, a loud crash hit the room. Dieter and Renee didn't move, didn't open their eyes, as the sizzling noise of dust from the shifting building entered their ears. They waited.

Finally, Dieter opened his eyes and saw Renee's eyes flashing back at him. His head jerked up at the sound of the wall behind them cracking, splitting further up to the ceiling. Dieter saw the lines form and fold on Renee's forehead while she pinched her eyes closed. The bed began to shake and the building stirred, echoing the sound of bowling balls rolling on wooden floors. Renee slapped her other hand across Dieter's head and squeezed his scalp skin between her fingers. The shaking ceased and the noise dwindled; the room became still.

The pressure on Dieter's scalp decreased. Renee's shoulders lifted and fell quickly with every breath, but slowed with the passing seconds. Her eyes started flashing again, blinking between her black mascara, but ending in small slits.

"Earthquake?" Dieter asked, reaching up to feel her hand on his scalp. He brought his hand down, peeking at his fingers, expecting to see blood. Dieter struggled to sit up, begging Renee to loosen her painful grip on his hair. He looked around the room and lightly stepped off the bed, taking two steps toward the window before he looked back to Renee.

"Earthquakes in Germany?" Renee scoffed. She untangled the sheets from around her legs and stepped onto the floor behind him. Dieter felt her light body wrap around his arm, and they walked toward the window together.

Outside, car alarms blared and dust filled the air between the buildings. Neighbors stumbled out from their apartment buildings dazed. The sounds of their voices quickly went from a low hum to a jarring rattle. More bodies spilled onto the street. The dust began to clear, revealing buildings that stood shorter, closer to the ground than before. Renee's fingers tightened around Dieter's hand and elbow. They looked out into the street from their second floor room, now almost level with the swarming bodies in bathrobes and nightclothes.

Renee loosened her hold on Dieter, but then grabbed him again and pulled him in the direction of the front door. The yellowed walls were cracked and the dust was beginning to settle. Dieter put his hand on her freckled shoulder. "Wait," he said. He walked up to the door and noticed the floor had pushed up from under it. His eyes traced the wood and above he saw the top jammed into the ceiling. Dieter gripped the side of the door and tried to force it open, the wood whined, but did not budge an inch. Dieter wiped his hands on his thighs and looked to Renee standing with her arms crossed in front of her, rubbing the skin up and down. He shook his head and shrugged.

Renee looked around again and sighed. "Well, it's a good thing I like you, because it looks like we're in it for the long haul." She laughed and tapped him on the elbow playfully. Dieter smiled and rushed her, taking her over his shoulder and throwing her on the bed. He considered following her, but stopped first to take a light bulb from the closet and replace the damaged one. Then he jumped back into bed.

10:47AM

They were standing now. Tears slipped past her eyelids and trailed down the salty black paths etched in her cheeks. Lying chest to chest, she punched her lips to his again. Her arms reached back, behind his neck to pull his kiss deeper; the iron taste now washed with tears. He pulled her closer in order to feel her chest rise and fall against his, and then squeezed the skin on her back. His hands outlined the sides of her body and he rested his palms on the back of her neck and shoulders, pulling his mouth off hers, holding a knuckleful of short, feathery hair. She raked her fingernails across his bare back, digging deep.

The new light bulb behaved like the old one; flickering off and on. She kissed his body until she felt her back hit up against the wall next to the bed. He pressed himself up against her and started to slow his motions as she continued to consume him frantically. His hips pressed against her again, making her skin squeak against the wall that vibrated from a new frenzy of thudding brooms, knocking fists and slapping palms. The light was still flickering, and the oven alarm began buzzing once again while the television began another shoot-'em-up Western.

Suddenly the room broke into a quiver and the floor began to crack. Sounds similar to trains and bowling balls invaded their ears. "Not again," Renee said, reaching for him. Dieter pushed Renee onto the bed, feeling the floor drop from under him as soon as his toes pushed his body off the wooden surface. Dieter and Renee held each other while each drop of the floor brought more debris down onto them. Large pieces of plaster and cement, wood and metal shards, fell from the collapsing building. They held the copper bedposts and coughed from the air thickening with dust. They attempted to shield their heads with their arms. Dieter could barely focus enough in the chaos to see the window being covered by dirt and cement. He saw the light on Renee's face dim; the shadows were winning over her closed eyes and wrinkling forehead. The building had dropped into the ground possibly an entire foot.

The vibrations began to die down, and it all stood still again.

The room was dark, foggy, and coated in the smell of soil and rotting wood. Renee's body started jerking slightly, and she let out a guttural scream. The scream bounced off every flat surface perpendicular to what should have been the floor. The sounds pounded into Dieter's skull. Dieter felt as if the screaming exhale went on forever, but then recognized pauses in between. His head ached and his vision was blurred; the whites and blacks blended into inconsistent grays. The light peeked in from the top of the window, but the dust in the air made it impossible to see. The smell of metal and cold dirt came and went with the pounding of his head.

Dieter shook himself into lucidity and then blindly began to feel around Renee's body. "Are you okay?" he asked her.

She didn't reply. Her breaths accelerated into high-pitched heaving, in then out in one-second intervals.

His fingers patted the skin on her face lightly, but as soon as he touched her, the room shook for another moment and Dieter recoiled from her. Immediately the room was still again. A sob built up in his chest and escaped through his teeth, causing saliva to blow onto his chin. The room stood still, but Dieter heard a sound similar to the low buzz of a weed whacker in the room. When the buzzing started, Renee's breaths stopped.

The buzzing ceased and Renee's sharp breaths continued. The breaths reverberated off the surfaces perpendicular to the bed, and entered Dieter's ears like splintered wood. He put his hands over his ears and tried to see Renee's face through the dust and darkness. He rubbed his eyes again and leaned closer to her body. The heaving continued. He held himself above her and listened to the violent breaths, raspy and high pitched, but her body did not move. It wasn't Renee who made the sounds.

Dieter lightly patted down Renee's motionless body, searching for injuries. His fingers traveled down her shoulders until they crashed into a large, rocky obstacle that crushed the tiny body beneath it. Dieter clenched his jaw and pushed the cement fragment off Renee's chest. It tumbled to the floor, and Dieter jumped as he heard the buzzing begin and the heaving stop again. The buzzing noise came closer, became louder than before, but he ignored it.

His fingers grazed over Renee's chest. A sob built up, but Dieter held it in. His fingers touched her left side. The bars of her ribcage remained strong, but on the right, his fingertips dipped into where he could feel the semi-solid remnants of the ribcage caved in. Her tight nightclothes covered the broken and softened parts below.

Realizing she was dead, Dieter recoiled from her and covered his face. The iron taste in his mouth made him gag. He swallowed it down, and then patted his way over to her wounds again. The wet bed sheets slimed over solid fragments and slipped through his grip. He couldn't tell which pieces were hers and which were the bed and rubble. Dieter traced the outside of Renee's nightclothes. The material was the only thing that held her together, and Dieter could feel her seeping out of it.

The buzzing stopped and the heavy breathing sounds replaced it. Dieter threw his arms around Renee's body and exhaled his relief. Maybe he had been wrong, maybe she wasn't dead.

"Bird, stay with me," he told her, but he felt her body, and it was as cool as the blood surrounding it. Her body did not react to him, and he did not feel her sharp breaths on his skin, yet he heard breathing close by.

Dieter froze, and his heart raced, causing his blood to feel as if it boiled. Straightening up, he closed his eyes and tried to feel the room, to reevaluate it. He directed his listening to all parts of the room, and he released his grip from Renee's lifeless body. The heaving sounds continued from somewhere else in the room.

Renee was gone, and something else was in that room with him.

His breaths became shorter and faster, taking in more dust from the wreckage. He touched around the bed, wishing he could hold his lover, but instead his fingers found the cold copper bedpost and he held onto it, trying not to cough.

He knew he had to leave. He knew he would die just like Renee if he stayed in that building much longer. Dieter's toes tested the slippery floor beneath him. The rocks and gravel at his feet cracked and scratched the floor while he turned to face the bed, both hands around the copper knob on the top corner of the bedpost. The bed shook abruptly, and Dieter jumped back. He could hear Renee's body drop from the bed onto the floor.

The coils whined from the weight of another replacing her. Dieter could feel the other in the room, but Dieter couldn't see.

The foundation of the building began to creak and Dieter felt the floor sway side to side until it broke into a violent shake. He tried to pull his body close to the copper bedpost, but slipped on the wet floor, his knee crashing with rock, and his hip cracking from the impact with the floor. Dieter screamed in pain while being thrashed against the debris from the wreckage. He saw the light in the room dimming as the soil crawled further up the window. He screamed until his breath ran out, but could not hear it in the jarring noises of the sinking building. The shaking decreased and the building settled a little deeper into the ground.

He heard a scream, not realizing it was his own. He struggled to his knees, putting most of his weight on the uninjured one. Dieter began to feel the floor in front of him and started to find his way through the chaos. Dust coated the air in a thick cloud, making visibility impossible. Dieter coughed and squinted, trying the see in the room blackened by dust.

His fingers patted the large cement fragments and he crawled around them. In the blackness, he approached a fleshy obstacle. He patted what felt like skin leading to a large arm. The skin was cold, but it wasn't Renee's. A sob built up in Dieter's chest and escaped through his teeth, "Please?"

The fragmented cement and rocks shifted under the other body while it sat up, Dieter's hands still on its skin. "Please? Whoever you are, please help? I need out." Dieter could feel the warm saliva drip down his chin as he laid his head on the other's thigh.

He felt a cold, rough hand on the back of his head, and then it moved down his neck and onto his back. He heard the breathing start again, each breath like a hiccup. A shrill between pauses. The rhythm accelerated, louder, like a machine starting up, but all thoughts of saving Renee's body left his mind; now he only wanted to save himself.

Dieter looked up into the darkness, sniffling and slurping up the liquids spilling from his face. His pulse quickened. The other's hand on his back became heavier, curled into a fist, and gripped his shirt.

Dieter held his breath and closed his eyes. The heavy hand lifted him to his feet. Dieter hopped on his uninjured leg, which caused the cracked bones on his other side to swing in the flesh bag that held them together. Dieter bit his lips and groaned as his leg collapsed from under him, but the hand held him up. The pain was overwhelming. His fingers found the other's shoulder, and he tried to get a hold of it in order to support himself. He heard a sharp crack, then a pop, and felt the other's neck jerking as it thrashed from side to side. He found himself losing his grip on the other's cold body.

Dieter placed both of his hands around the other's neck. *Crack.* The cold body began pulling itself closer, and he felt a long, cold, slimy tongue lap at his cheek and ear. *Crack.* The head jolted back, whipping the wet tongue on Dieter's skin. *Crack.* The head snapped again, and what felt like another tongue followed the same path. He broke from the hold and pushed the other away.

Dieter swung his arms around in the dark, spinning and slipping on one foot. The sounds of the breathing were all around him, bouncing off every surface and tearing at his eardrums. The hand grabbed at the back of his head and a leg snaked around the thigh and shin that supported him. All within the matter of moments, the other pulled back and thrust its mouth into Dieter's shoulder. *Crack.*

The other's head jerked, breaking the bone that lay beneath its grip. An iron flavored kiss, one similar to Renee's. For a second, he welcomed it, because it made her seem alive to him again.

But then he realized this wasn't Renee, and this wasn't going to end with the kinky sex which had always been his reward for enduring her physical abuse. The other gnawed around his clavicle and left the insides of his flesh exposed.

The two bodies fell to the ground, and Dieter screamed from the pain, but he could not hear the noises that left him because the razor-sharp buzzing smothered all other sounds. His body lay over sharp metal and manmade rock, and he could feel the sticky warmth of his own blood on his shoulder. His hands searched for a weapon. He gripped a piece of plywood, but did not have the strength to lift it. His fingers fell upon a piece of cement, small enough to curl his fingers around. Dieter tightened his hand around the rock and threw his arm up, bringing the rock down on the other's head. The gnawing stopped long enough to let Dieter roll to his side. He kicked at the floor, pushing his body across it, but hitting debris with his bleeding shoulder.

The dust in the room was beginning to settle, and Dieter could see the other in front of him, the sun peeking through the top of the window at its back. He lay on his back and squinted through the gray cloud. The body towered over him, blocking the light with its shadowy mass. He could hear the sounds of wet fleshy pieces rubbing and smacking.

Dieter watched the other's head jerk to the side and heard it snap. Its black profile formed what seemed like large pinchers coming from its face. Dieter couldn't breathe. The other grabbed hold of his ankle. *Crack,* it snapped the bone beneath, and began to pull him back. The head jerked again. *Crack,* and the body was on top of him once more, gnawing his wounded shoulder, tearing flesh away from bone.

Frantically Dieter struggled to get away from the other's grasp as he searched the area for another piece of masonry, but his hand met with a metal shard. He lifted the shard and then brought it down into the other's upper back.

The shrill buzzing relaxed into quick heaving again. He was enveloped in a searing pain from his shoulder and he needed to get out. Dieter kicked at the floor, now sliding more easily across it due to the other's maroon, slick blood. The room began to freckle in white, and all that he could taste or smell was iron. The pain pulsed strong through his body, pulsed stronger, and then dulled. It dulled until the pain ended, and all he could hear was the other's rapid breathing behind him, but now there were pauses in between, and in those silences, were the lapping sounds before the gnawing.

About Lala Drona

Lala Drona is a freelance writer, poet, artist and jane-of-all-trades. She is the perpetual foreigner in a world of seek and hide.
http://www.laladrona.com

REFLECTION OF EVIL
by Graham Masterton

It was raining so hard that Mark stayed in the Range Rover, drinking cold espresso straight from the flask and listening to a play on the radio about a widow who compulsively knitted cardigans for her recently-dead husband.

"It took me ages to find this shade of gray. Shale, they call it. It matches his eyes."

"He's dead, Maureen. He's never going to wear it."

"Don't be silly. Nobody dies, so long as you remember what they looked like."

He was thinking about calling it a day when he saw Katie trudging across the field toward him in her bright red raincoat with the pointy hood. As she approached he let down the window, tipping out the last of his coffee. The rain spattered icy-cold against his cheek.

"You look drowned!" he called out. "Why don't you pack it in?"

"We've found something really exciting, that's why."

She came up to the Range Rover and pulled back her hood. Her curly blonde hair was stuck to her forehead and there was a drip on the end of her nose. She had always put him in mind of a poor bedraggled fairy, even when she was dry, and today she looked as if she had fallen out of her traveler's joy bush and into a puddle.

"Where's Nigel?" he asked her.

"He's still there, digging."

"I told him to survey the ditches. What the hell's he digging for?"

"Mark, we think we might have found Shalott."

"What? What are you talking about?"

Katie wiped the rain from her face with the back of her hand. "Those ditches aren't ditches; they used to be a stream, and there's an island in the middle. And those lumps we thought were Iron Age sheep-pens, they're stones, all cut and dressed, like the stones for building a wall."

"Oh, I see," said Mark. "And you and Nigel, being you and Nigel, you immediately thought, 'Shalott!'"

"Why not? It's in the right location, isn't it, upstream from Cadbury?"

Mark shook his head. "Come on, Katie, I know that you and Nigel think that Camelot was all true. If you dug up an old tomato-ketchup bottle you'd probably persuade yourselves that it came from the Round Table."

"It's not just the stones, Mark. We've found some kind of metal frame. It's mostly buried, but Nigel's trying to get it out."

"A frame?"

Katie stretched her arms as wide as she could. "It's big, and it's very tarnished. Nigel thinks it could be a mirror."

"I get it…island, Camelot, mirror. Must be Shalott!"

"Come and have a look anyway. I mean, it might just be scrap, but you never know."

Mark checked his watch. "Let's leave it till tomorrow. We can't do anything sensible in this weather."

"I don't think we can just leave it there. Supposing somebody else comes along and decides to finish digging it up? It could be valuable. If we have found Shalott, and if it *is* a mirror—"

"Katie, read my lips: Shalott is a myth. Whatever it is you've dug up, can't you just cover it up again and leave it till tomorrow? It's going to be pitch dark in half an hour."

Katie put on one of those faces that meant she was going to go on nagging about this until she got her own way. They weren't having any kind of relationship, but ever since Katie had joined the company, six weeks ago, they had been mildly flirting with each other, and Mark wouldn't have minded if it went a little further. He let his head drop down in surrender, and said, "Okay…if I must."

The widow in the radio-play was still fretting about her latest sweater. "He's not so very keen on raglan sleeves…he thinks they make him look round-shouldered."

"He's dead, Maureen. He probably doesn't have any shoulders."

Katie turned around and started back up the hill. Mark climbed down from the Range Rover, slammed the door, and trudged through the long grass behind her. The skies were hung with filthy gray curtains, and the wind was blowing directly from the north-east, so that his wet raincoat collar kept petulantly slapping his face. He wouldn't have come out here at all, not today, but the weather had put him eleven days behind schedule, and the county council were starting to grow impatient.

"We're going to be bloody popular!" Nigel shouted. "If this is bloody Shalott!"

Katie spun around as she walked, her hands thrust deep in her duffel-coat pockets. "But it could be! A castle, on an island, right in the heart of King Arthur country!"

Mark caught up with her. "Forget it, Katie. It's all stories— especially the Lady of Shalott. Burne Jones, Tennyson; the Victorians loved that kind of thing. A cursèd woman in a castle, dying of unrequited love. Sounds like my ex, come to think of it."

They topped the ridge. Through the misty swathes of rain, they could just about make out the thickly-wooded hills that half-encircled the valley on the eastern side. Below them lay a wide, boggy meadow. A straggling line of knobbly-topped willows crossed the meadow diagonally from south-east to north-west, like a procession of medieval monks, marking the course of an ancient ditch. They could see Nigel about a quarter of a mile away, in his fluorescent yellow jacket and his white plastic helmet, digging.

Mark clasped his hands together and raised his eyes toward the overbearing clouds. "Dear Lord, if You're up there, please let Nigel be digging up a bit of old bedstead."

"But if this *is* Shalott—" Katie persisted.

"It isn't Shalott, Katie. There is no Shalott, and there never was. Even if it is—which it isn't—it's situated slap bang in the middle of the proposed route for the Woolston relief road, which is already three-and-a-half years late and six-point-nine million pounds over budget. Which means that the county council will have to rethink their entire highways-building plan, and we won't get paid until the whole mess has gone through a full-scale public enquiry, which probably means in fifteen years' time."

"But think of it!" said Katie. "There—where Nigel's digging—that could be the island where the castle used to stand, where the Lady of Shalott weaved her tapestries. And these were the fields where the reapers heard her singing! And that ditch was the river, where she floated down to Camelot in her boat, singing her last lament before she died!"

"If any of that is true, sweetheart, then this is the hill where you and I and the Historic Site Assessment Place would go instantly bankrupt."

"But we'd be famous, wouldn't we?"

"No, we wouldn't. You don't think for one moment that we'd be allowed to dig it up, do you? Every medieval archeologist from every university in the western hemisphere would be crawling all over this site like bluebottles over a dead hedgehog."

"We're perfectly well qualified."

"No, darling, we're not, and I think you're forgetting what we do. We don't get paid to find sites of outstanding archeological significance or interest, we get paid *not* to find them. Bronze Age buckle? Shove it in your pocket and rediscover it five miles away, well away from the proposed new supermarket site. An Iron Age sheep pen, fine. We can call in a JCB and have it shifted to the Ancient Britain display at Frome. But not Shalott, Katie. Shalott would bloody sink us."

They struggled down the hill and across the meadow. The rain began to ease off, but the wind was still blustery. As they clambered down the ditch, and up the other side, Nigel stood up and took off his helmet. He was very tall, Nigel, with tight curly hair, a large complicated nose, and a hesitant, disconnected way of walking and talking. But Mark hadn't employed him for his looks or his physical co-ordination or his people skills. He had employed him because of his MA in History and his diploma in Archeology and Landscape, which were prominently displayed on the top of the company notepaper.

"Nigel! How's it going? Katie tells me you've found Shalott."

"Well—no—Mark! I don't like to jump to—you know—hah!— hasty conclusions! Not when we could be dealing with—pff! I don't know!—the most exciting archeological find ever! But these stones, look!"

Mark turned to Katie and rolled up his eyes in exaggerated weariness. But Katie said, "Go on, Mark. Look."

Nigel was circling around the rough grassy tussocks, flapping his hands. "I've cut back some of the turf, d'you see—and—underneath— well, see?" He had already exposed six or seven rectangular stones that were the color of well-matured Cheddar cheese. Every stone bore a dense pattern of chisel-marks, as if it had been gnawed by a giant stone-eating rat.

"Bath stone," said Nigel. "Quarried from Hazlebury most likely, and look at that jadding…late thirteenth century, in my humble opinion. Certainly not cut by the old method."

Mark peered at the stones and couldn't really see anything but stones. "The old method?"

Nigel let out a honk of laughter. "Silly, isn't it? The old method is what quarrymen used to call the new method—cutting the stone with saws, instead of breaking it away with bars."

"What wags they were. What makes you think this could be Shalott?"

Nigel shielded his eyes with his hand and looked around the meadow, blinking. "The location suggests it, more than anything else. You can see by the way these foundation-stones are arranged that there was certainly a tower here. You don't use stones five feet thick to build a single-story pigsty, do you? But then you have to ask yourself why would you build a tower here?"

"Do you? Oh yes, I suppose you do."

"You wouldn't have picked the middle of a valley to build a fort," said Nigel. "You would only build a tower here as a folly, or to keep somebody imprisoned, perhaps."

"Like the Lady of Shalott?"

"Well, exactly."

"So, if there was a tower here, where's the rest of it?"

"Oh, pilfered, most likely. As soon its owners left it empty, most of the stones would have been carried off by local smallholders for building walls and stables and farmhouses. I'll bet you could still find them if you went looking for them."

"Well, I'll bet *you* could," said Mark, blowing his nose. "Pity they didn't take the lot."

Nigel blinked at him through rain-speckled glasses. "If they'd done that—hah!—we never would have known that this was Shalott, would we?"

"Precisely."

Nigel said, "I don't think the tower was standing here for very long. At a very rough estimate it was built just before 1275, and most likely abandoned during the Black Death, around 1348 or 1349."

"Oh, yes?" Mark was already trying to work out what equipment they were going to need to shift these stones and where they could dump them. Back at Hazelbury quarry, maybe, where they originally came from. Nobody would ever find them there. Or maybe they could sell them as garden benches. He had a friend in Chelsea who ran a profitable sideline in ancient stones and 18th century garden ornaments for wealthy customers who weren't too fussy where they came from.

Nigel took hold of Mark's sleeve and pointed to a stone that was still half-buried in grass. There were some deep marks chiseled into it. "Look—you can just make out a cross, and part of a skull, and the letters DSPM. That's an acronym for medieval Latin, meaning 'God save us from the pestilence within these walls.'"

"So whoever lived in this tower was infected with the Black Death?"

"That's the most obvious assumption, yes."

Mark nodded. "Okay, then..." he said, and kept on nodding.

"This is very, very exciting," said Nigel. "I mean, it's—well!—it could be stupefying, when you come to think of it!"

"Yes," said Mark. He looked around the site, still nodding. "Katie told me you'd found some metal thing."

"Well!—hah!—that's the clincher, so far as I'm concerned! At least it will be, if it turns out to be what I think it is!"

He strode back to the place where he had been digging, and Mark reluctantly followed him. Barely visible in the mud was a length of blackened metal, about a meter-and-a-half long and curved at both ends.

"It's a fireguard, isn't it?" said Mark. Nigel had cleaned a part of it, and he could see that there were flowers embossed on it, and bunches of grapes, and vine-tendrils. In the center of it was a lump that looked like a human face, although it was so encrusted with mud that it was impossible to tell if it was a man or a woman.

Mark peered at it closely. "An old Victorian fireguard, that's all."

"I don't think so," said Nigel. "I think it's the top edge of a mirror. And a thirteenth century mirror, at that."

"Nigel…a mirror, as big as that, in 1275? They didn't have glass mirrors in those days, remember. This would have to be solid silver, or silver-plated, at least."

"Exactly!" said Nigel. "A solid silver mirror—five feet across."

"That's practically unheard of."

"Not if The Lady of Shalott was true. She had a mirror, didn't she, not for looking at herself, but for looking at the world outside, so that she could weave a tapestry of life in Camelot, without having to look at it directly!"

And he began to sing:

"'There she weaves by night and day
A magic web with colors gay.
She has heard a whisper say
A curse is on her if she stay
To look down to Camelot.
But moving through a mirror clear
That hangs before her all the year,
Shadows of the world appear…'"

Katie joined in:

"And in her web she still delights
To weave the mirror's magic sights
For often thro' the silent nights
A funeral, with plumes and lights
And music, went to Camelot."

"Top of the class," said Mark. "Now, how long do you think it's going to take to dig this out?"

"Oh…several weeks," said Nigel. "Months, even."

"I hope that's one of your University of Essex jokes."

"No—well!—it has to be excavated properly. We don't want to damage it, do we? And there could well be other valuable artifacts hidden in the soil all around it. Combs, buttons, necklaces, who knows? We need to fence this area off, don't we, and inform the police, and the British Museum?"

Mark said, "No, Nigel, we don't."

Nigel slowly stood up, blinking with perplexity. "Mark—we have to! This tower, this mirror—well!—they could change the entire concept of Arthurian legend! They're archeological proof that the Lady of Shalott wasn't just a story, and that Camelot was really here!"

"Nigel, that's a wonderful notion, but it's not going to pay off our overdraft, is it?"

Katie said, "I don't understand. If this is the Lady of Shalott's mirror, and it's genuine, it could be worth millions!"

"It could, yes. But not to us. Treasure trove belongs to HM Government. Not only that, this isn't our land, and we're working under contract for the county council. So our chances of getting a share of it are just about zero."

"So what are you suggesting?" said Nigel. "You want us to bury it again, and forget we ever found it? We can't do that!"

"Oh, no," Mark told him, "I'm not suggesting that for a moment." He pointed to the perforated vines in the top of the frame. "We could run a couple of chains through here, though, couldn't we, and use the Range Rover to pull it out?"

"What? That could cause irreparable damage!"

"Nigel—everything that happens in this world causes irreparable damage. That's the whole definition of history."

The rain had stopped completely now and Katie pushed back her hood. "I hate to say it, Mark, but I think you're right. We found this tower, we found this mirror. If we report it, we'll get nothing at all. No money, no credit. Not even a mention in the papers."

Nigel stood over the metal frame for a long time, his hand thoughtfully covering the lower part of his face.

"Well?" Mark asked him, at last. It was already growing dark, and a chilly mist was rising between the knobbly-topped willow-trees.

"All right, then, bugger it," said Nigel. "Let's pull the bugger out."

Mark drove the Range Rover down the hill and jostled along the banks of the ditch until he reached the island of Shalott. He switched on all the floodlights, front and rear, and then he and Nigel fastened towing-chains to the metal frame, wrapping them in torn T-shirts to protect the moldings as much as they could. Mark slowly revved the Range Rover forward, its tires spinning in the fibrous brown mud. Nigel screamed, "Steady! Steady!" like a panicky hockey-mistress.

At first the metal frame wouldn't move, but Mark tried pulling it, and then easing off the throttle, and then pulling it again. Gradually, it began to emerge from the peaty soil which covered it, and even before it was halfway out, he could see that Nigel was right, and that it *was* a mirror—or a large sheet of metal, anyway. He pulled it completely free, and Nigel screamed, "Stop!"

They hunkered down beside it and shone their flashlights on it. The decorative vine-tendrils had been badly bent by the towing-chains, but there was no other obvious damage. The surface of the mirror was black and mottled, like a serious bruise, but otherwise it seemed to have survived its seven hundred years with very little corrosion. It was over an inch thick and it was so heavy that they could barely lift it.

"What do we do now?" asked Katie.

"We take it back to the house, we clean it up, and we try to check out its provenance—where it was made, who made it, and what its history was. We have it assayed. Then we talk to one or two dealers who are interested in this kind of thing, and see how much we can get for it."

"And what about Shalott?" asked Nigel. In the upward beam of his flashlight, his face had become a theatrical mask.

"You can finish off your survey, Nigel. I think you ought to. But give me two versions. One for the county council, and one for posterity. As soon as you're done, I'll arrange for somebody to take all the stones away, and store them. Don't worry. You'll be able to publish your story in five or ten years' time, and you'll probably make a fortune out of it."

"But the island—it's all going to be lost."

"That's the story of Britain, Nigel. Nothing you can do can change it."

They heaved the mirror into the back of the Range Rover and drove back into Wincanton. Mark had rented a small end-of-terrace house on the outskirts, because it was much cheaper than staying in a hotel for seven weeks. The house was plain, flat-fronted, with a scrubby front garden and a dilapidated wooden garage. In the back garden stood a single naked cherry-tree. Inside, the ground-level rooms had been knocked together to make a living room with a dining area at one end. The carpet was yellow with green Paisley swirls on it, and the furniture was reproduction, all chintz and dark varnish.

Between them, grunting, they maneuvered the mirror into the living room and propped it against the wall. Katie folded up two bath towels and they wedged them underneath the frame to stop it from marking the carpet.

"I feel like a criminal," said Nigel.

Mark lit the gas fire and briskly chafed his hands. "You shouldn't. You should feel like an Englishman, protecting his heritage."

Katie said, "I still don't know if we've done the right thing. I mean, there's still time to declare it as a treasure trove."

"Well, go ahead, if you want the Historical Site Assessment to go out of business and you don't want a third share of whatever we can sell it for."

Katie went up to the mirror, licked the tip of her finger and cleaned some of the mud off it. As she did so, she suddenly recoiled, as if she had been stung. "Ow," she said, and stared at her fingertip. "It gave me a shock."

"A shock? What kind of a shock?"

"Like static, you know, when you get out of a car."

Mark approached the mirror and touched it with all five fingers of his left hand. "I can't feel anything." He licked his fingers and tried again, and this time he lifted his hand away and said, "Ouch! You're right! It's like it's charged."

"Silver's very conductive," said Nigel, as if that explained everything. "Sir John Raseburne wore a silver helmet at Agincourt, and he was struck by lightning. He was thrown so far into the air that the French thought he could fly."

He touched the mirror himself. After a while, he said, "No, nothing. You must have earthed it, you two."

Mark looked at the black, diseased surface of the mirror and said nothing.

That evening, Mark ordered a takeaway curry from the Wincanton Tandoori in the High Street, and they ate chicken Madras and mushroom bhaji while they took it in turns to clean away seven centuries of tarnish.

Neil played *The Best of Matt Monroe* on his CD player. "I'm sorry...I didn't bring any of my madrigals."

"Don't apologize. This is almost medieval."

First, they washed down the mirror with warm soapy water and cellulose car-sponges, until all of the peaty soil was sluiced off it. Katie stood on a kitchen chair and cleaned all of the decorative detail at the top of the frame with a toothbrush and Q-tips. As she worried the mud out of the human head in the center of the mirror, it gradually emerged as a woman, with high cheekbones and slanted eyes and her hair looped up in elaborate braids. Underneath her chin there was a scroll with the single word *Lamia*.

"Lamia?" said Mark. "Is that Latin, or what?"

"No, no, Greek," said Nigel. "It's the Greek name for Lilith, who was Adam's first companion, before Eve. She insisted on having the same rights as Adam and so God threw her out of Eden. She married a demon and became the queen of demons."

He stepped closer to the mirror and touched the woman's faintly-smiling lips. "Lamia was supposed to be the most incredibly beautiful woman you could imagine. She had white skin and black eyes and breasts that no man could resist fondling. Just one night with Lamia and—pfff!—you would never look at a human woman again."

"What was the catch?"

"She sucked all of the blood out of you—hah!—that's all."

"You're talking about my ex again."

Katie said, "I seem to remember that John Keats wrote a poem called Lamia, didn't he?"

"That's right," said Nigel. "A chap called Lycius met Lamia and fell madly in love with her. The trouble is, he didn't realize that she was a blood-sucker and that she was cursed by God."

"Cursed?" said Katie.

"Yes, God had condemned her for her disobedience forever. 'Some penanced lady-elf…some demon's mistress, or the demon's self.'"

"Like the Lady of Shalott."

"Well, I suppose so, yes."

"Perhaps they were one and the same person…Lamia, and the Lady of Shalott."

They all looked at the woman's face on top of the mirror. There was no question that she was beautiful; and even though the casting had a simplified, medieval style, the sculptor had managed to convey a sense of slyness, and of secrecy.

"She was a bit of a mystery, really," said Nigel. "She was supposed to be a virgin, d'you see, 'yet in the lore of love deep learnèd to the red heart's core.' She was a blood-sucking enchantress, but at the same time she was capable of deep and genuine love. Men couldn't resist her. Lycius said she gave him 'a hundred thirsts.'"

"Just like this bloody Madras chicken," said Mark. "Is there any more beer in the fridge?"

Katie carried on cleaning the mirror long after Mark and Nigel had grown tired of it. They sat in two reproduction armchairs drinking Stella Artois and eating cheese-and-onion crisps and heckling *Question Time*, while Katie applied 3M's Tarni-Shield with a soft blue cloth and gradually exposed a circle of shining silver, large enough to see her own face.

"There," she said. "I reckon we can have it all cleaned up by tomorrow."

"I'll give my friend a call," said Mark. "Maybe he can send somebody down to look at it."

"It's amazing, isn't it, to think that the last person to look into this mirror could have been the Lady of Shalott?"

"You blithering idiot," said Nigel.

"I beg your pardon?"

Nigel waved his can of lager at the television screen. "Not you. Him. He thinks that single mothers should get two votes."

They didn't go to bed until well past 1 AM. Mark had the main bedroom because he was the boss, even though it wasn't exactly luxurious. The double bed was lumpy and the white Regency-style wardrobe was crowded with wire hangers. Katie had the smaller bedroom at the back, with teddy-bear wallpaper, while Nigel had to sleep on the sofa in the living room.

Mark slept badly that night. He dreamed that he was walking at the rear of a long funeral procession, with a horse-drawn hearse, and black-dyed ostrich plumes nodding in the wind. A woman's voice was calling him from very far away, and he stopped, while the funeral procession carried on. For some reason he felt infinitely sad and lonely, the same way that he had felt when he was five, when his mother died.

"Mark!" she kept calling. "Mark!"

He woke up with a harsh intake of breath. It was still dark, although his travel clock said 07:26.

"Mark!" she repeated, and it wasn't his mother but Katie, and she was calling him from downstairs.

He climbed out of bed, still stunned from sleeping. He dragged his toweling bathrobe from the hook on the back of the door and stumbled down the narrow staircase. In the living room the curtains were drawn back, although the gray November day was still dismal and dark, and it was raining. Katie was standing in the middle of the room in a pink cotton night shirt, her hair all messed up, her forearms raised like the figure in *The Scream*.

"Katie! What the hell's going on?"

"It's Nigel. Look at him, Mark, he's dead."

"What?" Mark switched the ceiling-light on. Nigel was lying on his back on the chintz-upholstered couch, wearing nothing but green woolen socks and a brown plaid shirt, which was pulled right up to his chin. His bony white chest had a crucifix of dark hair across it. His penis looked like a dead fledgling.

But it was the expression on his face that horrified Mark the most. He was staring up at the ceiling, wide-eyed, his mouth stretched wide open, as if he were shouting at somebody. There was no doubt that he was dead. His throat had been torn open, in a stringy red mess of tendons and cartilage, and the cushion beneath his head was soaked black with blood.

"Jesus," said Mark. He took three or four very deep breaths. "Jesus."

Katie was almost as white as Nigel. "What could have done that? It looks like he was bitten by a dog."

Mark went through to the kitchen and rattled the back door handle. "Locked," he said, coming back into the living room. "There's no dog anywhere."

"Then what—?" Katie promptly sat down, and lowered her head. "Oh God, I think I'm going to faint."

"I'll have to call the police," said Mark. He couldn't stop staring at Nigel's face. Nigel didn't look terrified. In fact, he looked almost exultant, as if having his throat ripped out had been the most thrilling experience of his whole life.

"But what did it?" asked Katie. "We didn't do it, and Nigel couldn't have done it himself."

Mark frowned down at the yellow swirly carpet. He could make out a blotchy trail of footprints leading from the side of the couch to the center of the room. He thought at first that they must be Nigel's, but on closer examination they seemed to be far too small, and there was no blood on Nigel's socks. Close to the coffee-table the footprints formed a pattern like a huge, petal-shedding rose, and then, much fainter, they made their way toward the mirror. Where they stopped.

"Look," he said. "What do you make of that?"

Katie approached the mirror and peered into the shiny circle that she had cleaned yesterday evening. "It's almost as if...no."

"It's almost as if what?"

"It's almost as if somebody killed Nigel and then walked straight into the mirror."

"That's insane. People can't walk into mirrors."

"But these footprints...they don't go anywhere else."

"It's impossible. Whoever it was, they must have done it to trick us."

They both looked up at the face of Lamia. She looked back at them, secret and serene. Her smile seemed to say, *wouldn't you like to know?*

"They built a tower, didn't they?" said Katie. She was trembling with shock. "They built a tower for the express purpose of keeping the

Lady of Shalott locked up. If she was Lamia, then they locked her up because she seduced men and drank their blood."

"Katie, for Christ's sake. That was seven hundred years ago. That's if it really happened at all."

Katie pointed to Nigel's body on the couch. "Nigel's dead, Mark! That really happened! But nobody could have entered this room last night, could they? Not without breaking the door down and waking us up. Nobody could have entered this room unless they stepped right out of this mirror!"

"So what do you suggest? When we call the police?"

"We have to tell them!"

"Oh, yes? And is this what we tell them? 'Well, officer, it was like this. We took a thirteenth-century mirror that didn't belong to us and The Lady of Shalott came out of it in the middle of the night and tore Nigel's throat out?' They'll send us to Broadmoor, Katie! They'll put us in the funny farm for life!"

"Mark, listen, this is real."

"It's only a story, Katie. It's only a legend."

"But think of the poem, The Lady of Shalott. Think of what it says. 'Moving thro' a mirror clear, that hangs before her all the year, shadows of the world appear.' Don't you get it? Tennyson specifically wrote *through* a mirror, not *in* it. The Lady of Shalott wasn't looking at her mirror, she was inside it, looking out!"

"This gets better."

"But it all fits together. She was Lamia. A blood-sucker, a vampire! Like all vampires, she could only come out at night. But she didn't hide inside a coffin all day...she hid inside a mirror! Daylight can't penetrate a mirror, any more than it can penetrate a closed coffin!"

"I don't know much about vampires, Katie, but I do know that you can't see them in mirrors."

"Of course not. And this is the reason why! Lamia and her reflection are one and the same. When she steps out of the mirror, she's no longer inside it, so she doesn't appear to have a reflection. And the curse on her must be that she can only come out of the mirror at night, like all vampires."

"Katie, for Christ's sake...you're getting completely carried away."

"But it's the only answer that makes any sense! Why did they lock up The Lady of Shalott on an island, in a stream? Because vampires can't cross running water. Why did they carve a crucifix and a skull on the stones outside? The words said, *God save us from the pestilence within these walls*. They didn't mean the Black Death...they meant *her!* The Lady of Shalott, Lamia, she was the pestilence!"

Mark sat down. He looked at Nigel and then he looked away again. He had never seen a dead body before, but the dead were so totally dead that you could quickly lose interest in them after a while. They didn't talk. They didn't even breathe. He could understand why morticians were so blasé.

"So?" he asked Katie, at last. "What do you think we ought to do?"

"Let's draw the curtains," she said. "Let's shut out all the daylight. If you sit here, perhaps she'll be tempted to come out again. After all, she's been seven hundred years without fresh blood, hasn't she? She must be thirsty. "

Mark stared at her. "You're having a laugh, aren't you? You want me to sit here in the dark, hoping that some mythical woman is going to step out of a dirty old mirror and try to suck all the blood out of me?"

He was trying to show Katie that he wasn't afraid, and that her vampire idea was nonsense, but all the time Nigel was lying on the couch, silently shouting at the ceiling. And there was so much blood, and so many footprints. What else could have happened in this room last night?

Katie said, "It's up to you. If you think I'm being ridiculous, let's forget it. Let's call the police and tell them exactly what happened. I'm sure that forensics will prove that we didn't kill him."

"I wouldn't count on it, myself."

Mark stood up again and went over to the mirror. He peered into the polished circle, but all he could see was his own face, dimly haloed.

"All right, then," he said. "Let's give it a try, just to put your mind at rest. Then we call the police."

Katie drew the brown velvet curtains and tucked them in at the bottom to keep out the tiniest chink of daylight. It was well past eight o'clock now, but it was still pouring with rain outside and the morning was so gloomy that she need hardly have bothered. Mark pulled one of the armchairs up in front of the mirror and sat facing it.

"I feel like one of those goats they tie up, to catch tigers."

"Well, I wouldn't worry. I'm probably wrong."

Mark took out a crumpled Kleenex and blew his nose, and then sniffed. "Phwoaff!" he protested. "Nigel's smelling already. Rotten chicken, or what?"

"That's the blood," said Katie. Adding, after a moment, "My uncle used to be a butcher. He always said that bad blood is the worst smell in the world."

They sat in silence for a while. The smell of blood seemed to be growing thicker, and riper, and it was all Mark could do not to gag. His throat was dry, too, and he wished he had drunk some orange juice before starting this vigil.

"You couldn't fetch me a drink, could you?" he asked Katie.

"Ssh," said Katie. "I think I can see something."

"What? Where?"

"Look at the mirror, in the middle. Like a very faint light."

Mark stared toward the mirror in the darkness. At first he couldn't see anything but overwhelming blackness. But then he saw a flicker, like somebody waving a white scarf, and then another.

Very gradually, a face began to appear in the polished circle. Mark felt a slow crawling sensation down his back, and his lower jaw began to judder so much that he had to clench his teeth to stop it. The face was pale and bland but strangely beautiful, and it was staring straight at him, unblinking, and smiling. It looked more like the face of a marble statue than a human being. Mark tried to look away, but he couldn't. Every time he turned his head toward Katie he was compelled to turn back again.

The darkened living room seemed to grow even more airless and suffocating, and when he said, "Katie...can you see what I see?" his voice sounded muffled, as if he had a pillow over his face.

Soundlessly, the pale woman took one step out of the surface of the mirror. She was naked, and her skin was the color of the moon. The black tarnish clung to her for a moment, like oily cobwebs, but as she took another step forward they slid away from her, leaving her luminous and pristine.

Mark could do nothing but stare at her. She came closer and closer, until he could have reached up and touched her. She had a high forehead, and her hair was braided in strange, elaborate loops. She had no eyebrows, which made her face expressionless. But her eyes were extraordinary. Her eyes were like looking at death.

She raised her right hand and lightly kissed her fingertips. He could feel her aura, both electrical and freezing cold, as if somebody had left a fridge door wide open. She whispered something, but it sounded more French than English—very soft and elided—and he could only understand a few words of it.

"My sweet love," she said. "Come to me, give me your very life."

There were dried runnels of blood on her breasts and down her slightly-bulging stomach, and down her thighs. Her feet were spattered in blood, too. Mark looked up at her, and he couldn't think what to say or what to do. He felt as if all of the energy had drained out of him, and he couldn't even speak.

We all have to die one day, he thought. But to die now, today, in this naked woman's arms...what an adventure that would be.

"Mark!" shouted Katie. "Grab her, Mark! Hold on to her!"

The woman twisted around and hissed at Katie, as furiously as a snake. Mark heaved himself out of his chair and tried to seize the woman's arm, but she was cold and slippery, like half-melted ice, and her wrist slithered out of his grasp.

"Now, Katie!" he yelled at her.

Katie threw herself at the curtains, and dragged them down, the curtain-hooks popping like firecrackers. The woman went for her, and she had almost reached the window when the last curtain-hook popped and the living room was drowned with gray, drained daylight. The woman whipped around again and stared at Mark, and the expression on her face almost stopped his heart.

"Of all men," she whispered. "You have been the most faithless, and you will be punished."

Katie was on her knees, struggling to free herself from the curtains. The woman seized Katie's curls, lifted her up, and bit into her neck with an audible crunch. Katie didn't even scream. She stared at Mark in mute desperation and fell sideways onto the carpet, with blood jetting out of her neck and spraying across the furniture.

The woman came slowly toward him, and Mark took one step back, and then another, shifting the armchair so that it stood between them. But she stopped. Her skin was already shining, as if it were melting, and she closed her eyes. Mark waited, holding his breath. At the same time, Katie was convulsing on the floor, one foot jerking against the leg of the coffee-table, so that the empty beer-cans rattled together.

The woman opened her eyes, and gave Mark one last unreadable look. Then she turned back toward the mirror. She took three paces, and it swallowed her, like an oil-streaked pool of water.

Mark waited and waited, not moving. Outside the window, the rain began to clear, and he heard the whine of a milk-float going past.

After a while, he sat down. He thought of calling the police, but what could he tell them? Then he thought of tying the bodies to the mirror, and dropping them into a rhyne, where they would never be found. But the police would come anyway, wouldn't they, asking questions?

The day slowly went by. Just after two o'clock the clouds cleared for a moment, and the naked cherry tree in the back garden sparkled with sunlight. At half-past three a loud clatter in the hallway made him jump, but it was only an old woman with a shopping-trolley pushing a copy of the Wincanton Advertiser through the letterbox.

And so the darkness gradually gathered, and Mark sat in his armchair in front of the mirror, waiting.
"'I am half-sick of shadows,' said The Lady of Shalott."

About Graham Masterton

Graham Masterton has published over one hundred novels, including thrillers, horror novels, disaster epics, and sweeping historical romances.

He was editor of the British edition of *Penthouse* magazine before writing his debut horror novel *The Manitou* in 1975, which was subsequently filmed with Tony Curtis, Susan Strasberg, Burgess Meredith and Stella Stevens.

One of his best sellers, *Blind Panic*, was published by Leisure Books in January 2010, and tells of a final devastating conflict between the characters that first appeared in *The Manitou*—Harry Erskine the phony mystic and Misquamacus, the Native American wonder-worker.

After the initial success of *The Manitou*, Graham continued to write horror novels and supernatural thrillers, for which he has won international acclaim, especially in Poland, France, Germany, Greece and Australia.

His historical romances *Rich* (Simon & Schuster) and *Maiden Voyage* (St. Martins) both featured in *The New York Times* Bestseller List. He has twice been awarded a Special Edgar by Mystery Writers of America (for *Charnel House*, and more recently *Trauma,* which was also named by *Publishers Weekly* as one of the hundred best novels of the year.)

He has won numerous other awards, including two Silver Medals from the West Coast Review of Books, a tombstone award from the Horror Writers Network, another gravestone from the International Horror Writers Guild, and was the first non-French winner of the prestigious Prix Julia Verlanger for bestselling horror novel. *The Chosen Child* (set in Poland) was nominated best horror novel of the year by the British Fantasy Society.

Several of Graham's short stories have been adapted for TV, including three for Tony Scott's *Hunger* series. Jason Scott Lee starred in the Stoker-nominated *Secret Shih-Tan.*

Apart from continuing with some of most popular horror series, Graham is now writing novels that have some suggestion of a supernatural element in them, but are intended to reach a wider market than genre horror.

Trauma (Penguin) told the story of a crime-scene cleaner whose stressful experiences made her gradually believe that a homicidal Mexican demon possessed the murder victims whose homes she had to sanitize. (This novel was optioned for a year by Jonathan Mostow.)

Unspeakable (Pocket Books) was about a children's welfare officer, a deaf lip-reader, who became convinced that she had been cursed by the Native American father of one of the children she had rescued. (This novel was optioned for two years by La Chauve Souris in Paris.)

And then, of course, is Graham's seventh Jim Rook novel *Demon's Door*, recently published in December 2010.
http://www.grahammasterton.co.uk

Deviant Queen of Clubs
Felicia Olin

Of What Was Everything
Elizabeth Prasse

WANDERING DANIEL
by Jagjiwan Sohal

Daniel feebly dragged the narrow box through the heavy black sand. It was another dusty night, the moon long concealed by a thick cloud of ash and the stars peeking out here and there. Daniel had no need for light, though. His heightened senses told him where he was and how long it would take to get to his destination. Not that he had anything or anyone waiting for him.

The box was pulled by rusty chains wrapped around Daniel's once-meaty forearms. Lacquered and ornamental, it once housed a famous philanthropist, but was now Daniel's constant companion, his only refuge from the scorched world around him. He thought of naming it, but that would be silly. Why would anyone name a coffin?

Daniel stopped, the sweat cascading down the back of his torn shirt. He hated feeling so soiled, but the heat caused perpetual sweating. He took off his cloak and placed it in the box, wondering why he put the thick wool article on in the first place. He shrugged. Maybe he was just pining for the good ol' days.

He sat on the box, ruminating on this thought. He looked around the desert, remembering how easy it used to be to travel it. Not too long ago, he could fly it in an hour or so, soaring on the wind, back when there was a wind to soar on. Or even blast through on the hot pavement road in his old vintage convertible, his golden locks blowing as the speedometer begged for mercy. What was the make of that car, Daniel wondered. Was it a Ford? Maybe a Japanese model? He honestly couldn't remember.

He stretched, his muscles exhausted. He never used to feel so weak, so foul, so empty. It had been months since he last fed and he remembered how painful the hunger was that time, a stabbing in his guts that only subsided when his belly was full. Nowadays, the hunger was barely noticeable, the agonizing pangs almost forgotten. *How much longer can I go without feeding?* Daniel wondered. Probably best not to think about it.

He grasped the chains again, aware that the city was not too far off. He looked to the sky and saw that the ash was subsiding and the sun was beginning to peek through. With the ozone layer completely decimated, the sun's ultraviolet beams were more dangerous than ever. Already Daniel could see the desert coming alive with flame and soon, he would be close to disintegration. Nevertheless, he smiled at the danger and even dared to hold out his arm against the sun's rays. It made his skin sizzle and he was almost grateful, as this little risk broke up the monotony of a dull night.

He quickly shed his clothes, opened the box and hopped in. He would be safe in here, the coffin fireproof, although the heat still caused him to sweat. It would cool down soon, though, and then he could sleep.

These few hours before the sun changed were often the most boring. A few months ago, Daniel would spend the time planning for the future, but now every day was the same, wandering the land and dragging the box behind him. Instead, he would try to remember how things used to be. It was heady work as nostalgia was a great enemy for survivors.

Daniel remembered that last evening. It had been a cool night, a welcome change from a relentless summer. He had been trying to sleep in his quaint suburban home, his old coffin far more spacious than this new box, and it had been lined with exquisite cottons imported from the Punjab. Of course, living in the suburbs had meant noise as the incessant hum of air conditioners and growls of lawnmowers often resulted in a fitful slumber. However, the suburbs had also provided a wonderful hunting ground, and that outweighed everything else.

On The Last Night, Daniel had decided to take a stroll in the park, knowing that supple young teenagers often congregated there to partake in a vice or two. He dressed well for the occasion (as he was prone to do) and he had liked the way designer labels like Gucci and Armani often adorned his slender frame. He knew he had looked damned good on The Last Night, despite not being able to see his reflection to verify this. Of course, he was a bit out of place in suburbia, where rubber flip flops, torn jeans and cheap polo shirts were considered high fashion, but Daniel didn't care. No one really noticed him anyway since he only came out at night.

That evening, a fifteen-year-old named Jenny had caught his eye. A sweet young thing in jean shorts and a tank top, Daniel especially liked her long plume of black hair. He had watched as Jenny and her friends sat by the statue of the founder of the park, some degenerate fool who murdered aboriginals to help establish this settlement. He could tell this little morsel had some wickedness in her as she and her friends took turns drinking from a wine bottle, obviously lifted from a parent. Her freckled face blushed after a few sips and Daniel smiled, smitten by her antics.

And so had he waited by a great oak tree, away from the light of the lampposts that dotted the park. Almost invisible, he stayed like this for forty-five minutes until the teens finally had enough and stumbled off together. He was hoping Jenny would be walking home by herself, instead of being accompanied by her unappetizing friends. It would have been difficult to make a move, as summertime meant there still could be neighbors out, sitting on their porches, downing their cheap swill and smoking their poison. He had known he could only take Jenny if she was alone and at first it hadn't appeared feasible that night as her group looked to be leaving together.

Daniel had cursed his luck and sadly observed the delicious Jenny, demoralized that the night's hunt had been a waste. As he watched the drunken girls clumsily follow the stone path leading out of the park, a hunger pang had jolted his body. *Damn,* he had thought. *I really wanted her.*

Despite his frustration, Daniel had continued to spy on Jenny, his powerful nose catching a hint of peach schnapps on her breath. It tingled his body and he unconsciously touched his fangs with his tongue, feeling them grow long and sharp. He had pondered making a move for if he was brazen and took her fast, it wasn't like anyone would have been able to catch him. Those few crackpots that believed they could hunt his kind were merely a bunch of old drunks who got lucky once or twice. He could never be slain by one of those stupid oafs.

He had tensed as Jenny and her friends stopped at the park gate. They hugged each other and waved good night and to Daniel's delight, Jenny had turned away from her friends, going home on her own. Without hesitation, he had leapt into the air, quickly soaring toward the young girl. *I have to have her,* he thought. *Damn the consequences.*

She had gasped as he landed smartly in front of her and before she knew it, she was writhing helplessly against him. He loathed having to take her in the open street like this, but there was no other option. She tried to scream, but he had already clamped his mouth down on her throat, her shriek extinguished and replaced by a painful moan. Her salty-sweet blood had filled his salivating mouth and he drank and drank and drank, finally pausing for a breath as he cradled her inert body.

What had happened next was anyone's guess. Daniel could have sworn he heard an explosion of some kind, almost like a sonic boom. He remembered dropping Jenny to the sidewalk and scanning the sky with his heightened sight. Were they missiles? It all happened so damn fast...

Then the entire world ignited. He had felt the wave of searing heat, becoming terrified as he watched the skin and flesh rip from his body. He remembered seeing the neighborhood burning to cinders and looking down at Jenny's body, his beautiful young prey being reduced to a skeleton and then, at last, to ash. And he remembered the pain as he fell to the ground. So much pain.

And then, of course, the regeneration. He could feel the single cell of blood on his ribcage multiply over and over until he was whole again, his muscles and organs rebuilt, his survival possible because he had fed just before the bombs went off. Fresh blood had given him the ability to come back.

He remembered being naked, his designer clothes gone and everything around him aflame. It hurt to stand and the question he had asked as he watched the world burn on that Last Night wasn't: *What happened?* It was: *What do I do now?*

Daniel hated coming to the city. The suburbs were where he went to chase easy prey, but the city was where he really *lived*. He loved the smoggy night air in the summer and the large gleaming skyscrapers that pierced the sky. He even loved the constant automobile traffic and frequent siren whoops. And nothing compared to a hunt in the city on a Saturday night.

And so it was quite painful for Daniel to be here now. Those once-mighty buildings were now charred, rusted and barely standing. And the parked cars were melted into the roads, a tar-like residue encasing them. Daniel didn't pay much attention to these sights and after ditching his box at a bone-dry water fountain at some now-useless corporate office tower, he went on a tour of the city, the acrid smell of burnt rubber all around him.

I wonder if Vincent survived, he thought, as he made his way to a familiar condo building. He smiled at it, relieved that damage from the attack was evident but not catastrophic, although the lofty structure was still a threat to collapse. He squatted down and readied his aching muscles. It was time to test his seldom-used abilities.

The tendons in Daniel's blood-starved body crackled as he launched himself up the building. The fact that he could still fly even though he hadn't fed for months pleased him and he landed rather easily at penthouse-level, although he had to wait a few moments to rest his taxed body. *What a rush,* he chuckled as he straightened up.

Once up on the top level, he realized to his dismay that the penthouse was completely ravaged by fire. Even so, Daniel searched the wreckage for a sign of anything familiar: an antique chair, an expensive painting, a photograph of anyone he knew. Or more importantly, any sign of life. After a while he stopped. *If Vincent was alive, I would've run into him by now,* he muttered to himself.

He missed Vincent terribly. Not the most handsome or debonair of his kind, but perhaps the most accomplished, Vincent was cursed with remaining in his current physical shape upon his turning. Still, being saddled with an unattractive and portly shell never seemed to bother the man. In fact, nothing ever really did. And what a teacher! Never hesitant to share the tricks of the trade to an inexperienced whelp like Daniel and always conducting himself as a true gentleman, Vincent was definitely one of the best.

Daniel peered into the empty swimming pool and was surprised to see the skeletons of what must have been two young females, probably in their early twenties. *Poor Vincent had most likely been entertaining when the bombs hit,* Daniel thought with a shake of his head. *If Vincent had fed on these humans right before detonation, he'd still be around. And then it would just be us, two degenerate blood-suckers ruling the world.*

Daniel mused on this as he strolled to the penthouse ledge. He sighed at the city, his beloved metropolis reduced to a disgusting ashtray. He looked around and finally settled upon on an old subway station, covered with debris from adjacent buildings.

A wave of happy memories overtook him as his eyes followed the station to the old clubbing district, where there had once been a collection of discos and singles bars. He remembered gallivanting there with Vincent and especially loved his companion's various little quirks while on the hunt, particularly his fondness of a heavy metal rock club that only catered to white skinheads. According to Vincent, feeding on these wretches was sending an important message: *Hey Skinheads, no matter how supreme you may deem yourself to be, you are still merely cattle to us.*

Then suddenly, Daniel felt miserable. For all these months, he had been alone, but until now he'd never felt lonely. He took one last look at the penthouse and leapt off the building, but this time he didn't try to fly. He just sank through the heavy air, closing his eyes as he waited to hit the ground.

He was surprised at how much it hurt. He used to be able to do these things and emerge unscathed. He lay there, feeling his body as it went about the lengthy process to heal itself after his "fall." Paralyzed with pain, Daniel clenched his jaw and sprawled on the cracked pavement, feeling his broken bones set themselves and the scraped skin regenerate. It was because he hadn't fed in so long that his body was slow to react to trauma.

Finally, the torture ended and when he was able, Daniel stood. He retrieved his box and continued on. He walked through every borough of the city, dragging his coffin behind. He found himself picking out a stray memory here and there as he passed a men's clothing store, a university campus, and even a deplorable strip joint on the east side, an establishment earmarked for when he and Vincent wanted to go slumming.

Eventually, Daniel found himself on the outskirts of the city and wandered into a gated community distinguished by so-called posh homes and large plots of land. He stopped at one mansion, a charming Victorian-style building in which the owner, most likely a pompous architect, must have wanted to re-fashion into something he deemed eclectic. Daniel felt drawn to this residence because it was startlingly intact considering the demolition of the rest of the city, and he wanted to explore it.

So after dropping his box off by the front door, Daniel quietly entered, a thrill of excitement coursing through him. He first made his way to the ruined kitchen and began to rummage through the few cupboards that remained upright, finding nothing but expired cans, most likely fruit cocktail or dog food. For a wild moment, he considered opening one and blindly consuming its contents, but thought better of it. *It'd probably make me deathly ill,* he reminded himself. *I can't eat human food.*

He continued to search the house, poking through every drawer and closet he could find. He did this often when he came across an interesting dwelling, although he detested feeling like a lowly scavenger. He reconciled this by noting it was just curiosity as he rarely kept anything he found.

After awhile, Daniel found himself in the master bedroom, a high-ceilinged chamber laden with wooden beams, perhaps to showcase a rustic look. He tested the bed and coughed as a puff of dust whorled into the air. He then pulled off the covers, surprised to see the mattress was still relatively clean. How had this place survived a nuclear attack? Without hesitation, he laid his tired body down and peered over to the only window of the room, concluding that if he did fall asleep, the sun would narrowly avoid him. *I'll just lay here for a second and catch my breath,* he sighed wearily. *It's been a long night.*

Then Daniel heard something. It was a kind of frantic rustling downstairs, which caused him to quickly sit up and focus his senses. Someone was making their way up to the second floor and Daniel, who had only heard his own noises in the last year, was suddenly very frightened.

To compensate, he slowed his breathing to calm his nerves and quickly leapt to the ceiling, hiding next to one of the beams. He concentrated so that he could relax. What was there to fear? He had done this sort of thing so many times.

Letting his senses do the work, he surmised that the person was a child, based on weight and movement. As he sniffed the air, a mental image of a small person began forming in his mind. *Definitely female,* he smiled to himself as the hibernating thirst slowly reawakened in him.

He closed his eyes and listened as the girl climbed the stairs. Anticipation almost overcame him as she entered the room. How lucky he was that out of all the rooms in this house, she had chosen the one in which he waited for her.

Her movements were quick and almost hyperactive, but Daniel didn't make much of it, as she was probably half-crazy from a world gone awry, just as he was. He figured she was unaware of his presence, and he wanted to bide his time and do this just right.

She finally stopped, resting almost directly beneath him and he felt his dormant fangs go long and sharp. It had been a long time since they had last come to life and he was relieved that they still could.

I can't wait any longer, he thought, as he felt the sweat on his hands. The hunger wracked his body, but he welcomed the pain.

Without hesitation, he dropped from the ceiling, his eyes tightly closed, and savagely fed. He clamped down with all his teeth, the blood filling his mouth, the kill better than any he could remember. He even became feral for the first time in his life, eagerly ripping at the flesh with his fingernails as his prey collapsed and died noiselessly. He continued to suck hungrily and kept his eyes closed as to further savor this meal that he had waited so long to find.

Eventually, Daniel stopped, exhausted by the effort. He sprawled on the floor, feeling giddy as he felt the blood travel to his stomach. This had always been the best part—the anticipation of the supernatural strength that a new feeding would give him.

Then suddenly he recoiled, as if he had swallowed a vial of acid. He painfully retched and vomited until his meal was completely expelled from his body. He continued to vomit long after his stomach was empty and the dry heaves wracked his body and wrenched his guts.

Finally his spasms subsided. Weakly, he opened his eyes, expecting to see a prone human girl, and what he saw instead shocked him. Once he saw *it*, he wished he hadn't.

The cockroach was immense, mutated by radiation. It lay dead in a puddle of black blood and yellow ooze, although a spindly leg still kicked out furiously. Looking at this slaughter horrified Daniel and he felt like vomiting again, but his body had nothing left to expel.

Instead, he wiped his mouth and groaned, frantically brushing his face to remove all of the insect's remains. Then he rose, swayed a bit, and desperately stumbled out of the house and into the nuclear aftermath that was the night.

About Jagjiwan Sohal

Born and raised near Toronto, Canada, Jagjiwan Sohal holds a BA and MA in Political Science, but upon graduation, he (to his parents' chagrin) entered the world of film and television. Now an up-and-coming screenwriter, he spends his time bombarding his agent with new material and is currently developing all kinds of projects, including cartoons, sitcoms and films. "Wandering Daniel" is Jagjiwan's first stab at horror fiction. http://www.facebook.com/jagjiwansohal

NEXT TIME YOU'LL KNOW ME
by Ramsey Campbell

Not this time, oh no. You don't think I'd be taken in like that now, do you? This time I don't care whose name you use, not now I can tell what it is. I only wish I'd listened to my mother sooner. "Always stay one step ahead of the rest," she used to say. "Don't let them get the better of you."

Now you'll pretend you don't know anything about my mother, but you and me know better, don't we? Shall I tell everyone about her so you can say it's the first time you've heard? I *will* tell about her, so everyone knows. She deserves that at least. She was the one who helped me be a writer.

Oh, but I'm not a writer, am I? I can't be, I haven't had any of my stories published, that's what you'd like everyone to think. You and me know whose names were on my stories, and maybe my mother did finally. I don't believe she could have been taken in by the likes of you. She was the finest person I ever knew, and she had the best mind.

That's why my father left us, because she made him feel inferior. I never knew him, but she told me so. She taught me how to live my life. "Always live as if the most important thing that ever happened to you is just about to happen," she'd advise, and she would always be cleaning our flat at the top of the house with all her bracelets on when I came home from the printer's. She'd have laid the table so the mats covered the holes she'd mended in the tablecloth, and she'd put on her tiara before she ladled out the rice with her wooden spoon she'd carved herself. We always had rice because she said we ought to remember the starving peoples and not eat meat that had taken the food out of their mouths. And then we'd just sit quietly and not need to talk because she always knew what I was going to tell her. She always knew what my father was going to say too, but that was what he couldn't stand. "My dear, he never had an original thought in his head," she used to affirm.

She was one step ahead of everyone, except for just one exception—she never knew what my stories were about until I told her.

Next you'll pretend you don't see how that matters, or maybe you really haven't the intelligence, so I'll tell you again: my mother who was always a step ahead of everyone because they didn't know how to think for themselves didn't know what my ideas for stories were until I told her, she said so. "That's your best idea yet," she would always applaud, ever since she used to make me tell her a story at bedtime before she would tell me one. Sometimes I'd lie watching my night light floating away and be thinking of ways to make the story better until I fell asleep. I never remembered the ways in the morning and I never wondered where they went, but you and me know, don't we? I just wish I'd been able to follow them sooner and believe me, you'll wish that too.

When I left school I went to work for Mr Twist, the only printer in town. I thought I'd enjoy it because I thought it had to do with books. I didn't mind at first when he didn't hardly speak to me because I got to be as good as my mother at knowing what he was going to say, then I realised it was because he thought I wasn't as good as he was the day he told me off for correcting the grammar and spelling on the poster for tours of the old mines. "You're the apprentice here and don't you forget it," he proclaimed with a red face. "Don't you go trying to be cleverer than the customer. He gets what he asks for, not what you think he wants. Who do you think you are?" he queried.

He was asking so I told him. "I'm a writer," I stated.

"And I'm the Oxford University Press."

I laughed because I thought he meant me to. "No, you aren't," I contradicted.

"That's right," he stressed, and stuck his red face up against mine. "I'm a second-rate printer in a third-rate town and you're no better than me. Don't play at being a writer with me. I'm old enough to know a writer when I see one."

All I wanted to do was to tell my mother when I got home, but of course she already knew. "You're a writer, Oscar, and don't let anyone tell you different," she warned. "Just try a bit harder to finish your stories. You ought to have been top of your class in English. I expect the teacher was just jealous."

So I finished some stories to read to her. She was losing her sight by then, and I read her library books every night, but she used to say she'd rather have my stories than any of them. "You ought to get them published," she counselled. "Show people what real stories are like."

So I tried to find out how. I joined a writers' circle because I thought they could and would help. Only most of them weren't published and tried to put me off trying by telling me that publishing was full of cliques and all about knowing the right people. And when that didn't work they tried to make me stop believing in myself, by having a competition for the three best stories and none of mine got anywhere. The judges had all been published and they said my ideas weren't new and the way I told them wasn't the way you were supposed to tell stories. "Take no notice of them," my mother countermanded. "They're the clique, because they want to keep you out. You're too original for them. I'll give you the money to send your work to publishers and just you wait and see, they'll buy it and we can move somewhere you'll be appreciated," and I was just going to when you and Mrs. Mander destroyed her faith in me.

Of course you don't know Mrs. Mander either, do you? I don't suppose you do. She lived downstairs and I never liked her and I don't believe my mother did, only she was sorry for her because she lived on her own. She used to wear old slippers that left bits on the carpet after my mother had spent half the day cleaning up even though she couldn't see hardly, and she kept picking up ornaments to look at and putting them down somewhere else. I always thought she'd meant to steal them when she'd got my mother confused about where they were. She came up when I wasn't there to read books to my mother, and now you can guess what she did.

Oh, I'll tell you, don't worry, I want everyone to know. It was the day they told Mr Twist not to print any more posters about the old mines because the tours hadn't gone well and they'd stopped them, and I was looking forward to telling my mother that the grammar and spelling had put people off, but Mrs. Mander was there with a pile of paperbacks you could see other people's fingermarks on that she'd bought in the market. As soon as I came in she got up. "You'll be wanting to talk to the boy," she deduced, and went out with some of her books.

She always called me the boy, which was another reason why I didn't like her. I was going to say about Mr Twist and then I saw how sad my mother looked. "I'm disappointed in you, Oscar," she rebuked.

She'd never said that before, never. I felt as if I were someone else. "Why?" I inquired.

"Because you led me to believe your ideas were original and every one of them are in these books."

She showed me where Mrs. Mander had marked pages for her with bits of newspaper. By the time I'd finished reading, I had a headache from all the small print and fingermarks. I was almost as blind as she was. All the books were the number one best seller and soon to be major films, but I'd never read a word of them before, and yet they were all *my* stories, you know they were. And my mother ought to have, but for the first time ever, she didn't believe me. That's the first thing you're going to pay for.

I had to take some aspirins and go to bed and lie there until it was dark and I couldn't see the small print dancing any more. Then my headache went away and I knew what must have happened. It was being one step ahead, I knew what stories were going to be about before people wrote them, except they were my stories and I had to be quick enough to write them first and get them published. So I went to tell my mother, who was still awake because I'd heard her crying, though she tried to make me think it was just her eyes hurting. I told her what I knew and she looked sadder. "It's a good idea for a story," she dismissed as if she didn't even want me to write any more.

So I had to prove the true facts to her. I went back to the writers' circle and asked what to do about stolen ideas. They didn't seem to believe me, and all they said was I should go and ask the writers to pay me some of their royalties. So I looked the writers of the books up in the Authors and Writers Who's Who, and most of them lived in England because Mrs. Mander liked English books. None of the writers' circle were listed, so that shows it's all a clique.

I couldn't wait until the weekend and I could tell the writers they were my ideas they'd used, but then I realized I'd have to leave my mother for the first time I ever had and keep the money from my Friday pay packet to pay for the train. She hadn't hardly been speaking to me since Mrs. Mander and her books, she'd just kept looking as if she was waiting for me to say I was sorry, and when I told her where I was going she looked twice as sad. "That's going too far, Oscar," she asserted, but she didn't mean to London, she meant I was trying to trick her again when I hadn't really even once. Then on Friday evening when I was going, she entreated, "Please don't go, Oscar. I believe you." But I knew she was only pretending that to stop me. I felt as if I was growing out of her and the further I went, the more it hurt, but I had to go.

I had to stand all the way on the train because of the football, and I'd have been sick with all the being thrown back and forth except I couldn't hardly breathe. Then I had to go in the tube to Hampstead. The sun had gone down at last, but it was just as hot down there. But being hot meant I could wait outside the writer's house all night when I found it and I could see he'd gone to bed.

I lay down on what they call the heath for a while and I must have fallen asleep, because when I woke up in the morning I felt like toothache all over and there was another car outside the big white writer's house. When I could walk I went and rang the bell, and when I couldn't hear it I banged on the door with my fists to show I didn't care it was so tall.

A man who looked furious opened the door, but he was too young to be the writer and anyway I wouldn't have cared if he had been when he'd made my mother lose her faith in me. "What do you want?" he interrogated.

"I'm a writer and I want to talk to him about his book," I announced.

He was going to shut the door in my face, but just then the writer clamoured, "Who is it?" and his son vociferated back, "He says he's a writer."

"Let him in then, for God's sake. If I can let you in I might as well let in the rest of the world. You and I have said all we have to say to each other."

His son tried to shut the door, but I wriggled past him and down the big hall to the room where the writer was. I could see he was a famous writer because he could drink whisky at breakfast time and smoke a pipe before getting dressed. He gave me a look that made his face lopsided and I could see he really meant it for his son. "You're not here for a handout as well, are you?" he denied.

"If that means wanting some of your money, I am," I sued.

He wiped his hand over his face and shook his head with a grin. "Well, that's honest, I can't deny that. See if you can make a better case for yourself than he's been doing."

His son kept trying to interrupt me and then started punching his thighs as if he wanted to punch me while I told the writer how I'd had his idea first and the story I'd made it into. Then the writer was quiet until he acclaimed, "It took me a quarter of a million words and you did it in five minutes."

His son jumped up and stood in the middle. "You're just depressed, Dad. You know you often get like this. All he did was tell you an anecdote built around your book. He probably hasn't even the discipline to write it down."

I caught the writer's eye and I could see he thought his son was worried about whatever money he'd asked for, so I winked at him. "Get out of the way," he directed, and shoved his son with his foot. "Who the devil are you to tell us about discipline? Keep a job for a year and maybe I'll listen to you. And you've the gall to tell us about writing," he enunciated and looked at me. "You and I know better, whatever your name is. Ideas are in the air for whoever grabs them first and gets lucky with them. Nobody owns an idea."

He went over to his desk as if the house was a ship. "I was about to write a cheque when you appeared, and I'm glad I can do so with some justice," he relished. "Who do I make it out to?"

"Dad," his son bleated, "Dad, listen to me," but both of us writers ignored him, and I told his father to make the cheque out to my mother. He started pleading with his father as I put it in my pocket and ran after me to say his father had only been trying to teach him a lesson and he'd give him it back for me. But he didn't touch me because he must have seen I'd have burst his eyes if he'd tried to steal my mother's cheque.

I didn't want her to apologise for doubting me, I just wanted her to be pleased, but she wasn't that when I gave her the cheque. First she thought I'd bought it in a joke shop and then she started thinking the joke was on me because the writer would stop the cheque. She had me believing it had been too easy and meaning to go back to make him write another, but when I got round her to pay it into her account where she kept her little savings the bank said it had been honored. Then she was frightened because she'd never seen five hundred pounds before. "He must have taken pity on you," she fathomed. "Don't try any more, Oscar. I believe you now."

I knew she didn't and I had to carry on until she did, and now there was money involved I knew who to go to, the solicitor who'd got her the divorce. He didn't believe me until I told him about the cheque and then he was interested. He told me to write down all my ideas I didn't think anyone had used yet for him to keep in a safe at the bank, though Mr. Twist tried to put me off writing in my lunch hour, and then he said we'd have to wait and see if the ideas got written after I'd already written them. That wasn't soon enough for me and I went off again at the weekends.

You'd been putting your heads together about me though, hadn't you? The writer in the Isle of Man would only talk to me through a gatepost and wouldn't let me in. The one in Norfolk lived on a barge where I could hear men sobbing and wouldn't even talk to me. And the one in Scotland pretended she had no money and I should go to America where the money was. I wasn't sure if I believed her, but I couldn't hurt a woman, not then. Maybe that's why you chose her to trick me. She'll be even sorrier than the rest of you.

So I went to America instead of the seaside with my mother. I told her I was going to sell publishers my stories, but she tried to stop me, she didn't think I could be published anymore. "If you go away now you may never see me again," she predicted, but I thought that was like saying the other time she believed me and I kept on at her until she gave me the money. Mrs. Mander promised to look after her, seeing as she wouldn't go away without me. I only wanted the money for her and to make her believe me.

I got off at New York and went to Long Island. That's where the number one best seller who stole my best idea lives. Maybe he didn't know he was stealing it, but if I didn't know I'd stolen a million pounds I'd still be sent to prison and he stole more than that from me, all of you did. He had a big long house and a private beach with an electric fence all around, and it was so hot all the way there when I tried to talk to the phone at the gate all I could do was cough. The sand was getting in my eyes and making my cough worse when two men came up behind me and carried me through the fence.

They didn't stop until they were in the house and threw me in a chair where I had to rub my eyes to see, so the writer must have thought I was crying when he came in naked from the beach. "Relax, maybe we won't have to hurt you," he prognosticated as if he was my friend. "You're another reporter, right? Just take a minute to get yourself together and say your piece."

So I told him about my idea he'd used and tried to ignore the men standing behind me until he nodded at them and they each took hold of one of my ears just lightly as if I'd be able to stand up if I wanted to. "Nothing my friends here like better than a tug-of-war," the writer heralded, then he leaned at me. "But you know what we don't like? Bums who try to earn money with cheap tricks."

I was going to lean at him, but I couldn't move my head after all. My ears felt as if they'd been set on fire. Suddenly I knew I could show him it wasn't a trick, because all at once it was like what my mother did, not just knowing what someone was going to say, but knowing which idea of mine he was going to steal next, one I hadn't even written down. "I can tell you what the book you're going to write is about," I prefaced, and I did.

He stared at me, then he nodded. The men mustn't have understood at first, because I thought they were tearing my head in half before they let me go. "I don't know who you are or what you want," the writer said to me, "but you'd better pray I never hear of you again. Because if you manage to get into print ahead of me I'll sue you down to your last suit of clothes, and believe me I can do it. And then my friends here," he nuncupated, "will come visit you and perform a little surgery on your hands absolutely free and with my compliments."

They marched me out and on a lonely stretch of path where I couldn't see the house or the bus stop. They dragged me over the gravel for a while, then they dusted me off and waited with me until the bus came. There was a curve where you could see the house and when I looked back off the bus I saw the writer talking to them and they jumped into a car. They followed me all the way to New York and either the writer had sent them to find out how I'd known what he was thinking or to get rid of me straight away.

But they couldn't keep up with the bus in the traffic. I got off into a crowd and wished I could go back to England, only they must have known that's where I'd go and be watching the airport if they'd read any books. So I hid in New York until my holiday was over because if I'd gone to any more writers they might have given me away. I didn't hardly go out except to write to my mother every day.

When I got to the airport I hid at the bookstall and pretended to be choosing books until the plane was ready, and that's how I found out what you'd done to me. I leafed through the best sellers and found all my ideas that were locked in the safe, and the date on all the books was the year before I'd locked my ideas up. You nearly tricked me like you tricked everyone until I realised the whole clique of you'd put your heads together, publishers and writers, and changed the date on the books.

I bought them all and couldn't wait to show them to the solicitor. I was sure he'd help me prove that they'd been written after I'd written them first. I thought about all the things I could buy my mother all the way home on the plane and the train and the bus. But when I got home, my mother wasn't there and there was dust on the furniture and my letters to her on the doormat, and when I went to Mrs. Mander she told me my mother was dead.

You killed her. You made me go to America and leave her alone, and she fell downstairs when Mrs. Mander was at the market and broke her neck. They couldn't even get in touch with me to tell me to go to the hospital because you were making me hide in New York. I'd forgive you for stealing my millions before I'd forgive you for taking way my mother. I was so upset I said all this to the newspaper and they published some of it before I realised that now the Long Island men would know who I was and where to find me.

So I've been hiding ever since and I'm glad, because it gave me time to learn what I can do, more than my mother could. Maybe her soul's in me helping, she couldn't just have gone away. Now I can tell who's going to steal one of my ideas and which one and when. Otherwise, how do you think I knew this story was being written? I've had time to think it all out down here and I know what to do to make sure I'm published when I think it's safe. Kill the thieves before they steal from me, that's what, and don't think I won't enjoy it too.

That's my warning to you thieves in case it makes you think twice about stealing, but I don't believe it will. You think you can get away with it but you'll see, the way Mrs. Mander didn't get away with not looking after my mother. Because the morning of the day I hid down here I went to say goodbye to Mrs. Mander. I told her what I thought of her and when she tried to push me out of her room I shut the door on her mouth then on her head and then on her neck, and leaned on it. Goodbye, Mrs. Mander.

And as for the rest of you who're reading this, don't go thinking you're cleverer than me either. Maybe you think you've guessed where I'm hiding, but if you do I'll know. And I'll come and see you first, before you tell anyone. I mean it. If you think you know, start praying. Pray you're wrong.

About Ramsey Campbell

Living in England, Ramsey Campbell is perhaps the world's most decorated author of horror, terror, suspense, dark fantasy, and supernatural fiction. He has won four World Fantasy Awards, ten British Fantasy Awards, three Bram Stoker Awards, the Horror Writers' Association's Lifetime Achievement Award, and has been named a Grand Master of Horror.

Ramsey Campbell's work is notable for both its focus and its breadth. His novels, short fiction, and even nonfiction always seem to address emotions. Characteristic themes weave throughout Campbell's works: the uncertain nature of reality, the dangers of repressed fears and desires, and the reactions of ordinary people in extraordinary circumstances.

Douglas E. Winter praises Campbell's "stylish sophistication and intensely suggestive vision" and The Horror Zine's Poet Gary William Crawford writes in *Ramsey Campbell* (1988) that Campbell's prose "is like no other in supernatural horror fiction."

S.T. Joshi, in which his book *Ramsey Campbell and Modern Horror Fiction* (2001) studies the writer, says: "Ramsey Campbell is worthy of study both because of the intrinsic merit of his work and because of the place he occupies in the historical progression of this literary mode." Joshi went on to say: "Future generations will regard him as the leading horror writer of our generation, every bit the equal of Lovecraft or Blackwood."

Campbell is always refining his craft. "As far as I'm concerned," Campbell stated in a 1990 interview by Stanley Wiater, "the whole business of writing is a process of trying to do things you didn't do last time."

Ramsey Campbell is the prolific author of thirty novels, twenty books of short stories, two chapbooks, and two non-fiction books. He has edited fifteen anthologies, and has had one or more of his stories appear in 132 multiple-author collections. You can visit Ramsey Campbell at: http://www.ramseycampbell.com

3 AM
by James Marlow

At 3AM, the mind likes to travel on dark and strange roads. Your thoughts seem more real while your actions have a dream-like quality. It's a time when reality is fluid and drips slowly. It's also a time to tell yourself lies.

Much soul searching happens at 3AM. It's the beginning of *The Tomorrow*, as in: "I'm going to quit smoking tomorrow." Or, "Tomorrow I turn things around," and the ever popular, "My diet begins tomorrow!"

These thoughts are easy to swallow at 3AM. If we want to be honest, at 3AM they are the truth. The Gospel. They are words carved in stone by the finger of God. It's only after sleeping that we come to see the truth has turned to lies.

I may be biased toward 3AM. My father died at 3AM. My ex-wife caught me with another woman at 3AM, and I was thrown in jail for the first and only time at 3AM. Also (this may mean nothing or it may explain everything and I'm just not smart enough to figure it out), I was born at 3AM.

I'm a security guard at a warehouse today because I drank and partied too hard in college yesterday. I work the midnight shift because I have the least amount of seniority. The job's a breeze. I sit in a little shack and watch video monitors. Every two hours I walk the warehouse and the grounds looking for anything out of place.

Nothing is ever out of place.

Except at the 3AM walk-through.

And I've noticed that the 3AM walk is getting worse.

At first, it was subtle. Just little oddities I could chalk up to being tired or tricks of shadows. I would catch movement from the corners of my eyes, always just outside my flashlight beam. I'd swing the light to the movement and nothing would be there. Sometimes I would hear faint voices echoing through the building.

And, of course, there was the first time I saw a ghost.

That night, I thought we had a prowler, so I opened the door to the main warehouse and saw a person walking down the aisle. I yelled at him to stop, but he never turned around. Then he ran, and I pursued, with him screaming the whole time. Instead of going out to the docks, he turned left and I knew I had him. There was nothing down that way but a dead end. I rounded the corner, flashlight held over my shoulder, still lighting my way, but also ready to knock the prowler out, and skidded to a stop when I saw I was alone.

My knees shook and I had to put my hand on the wall to keep from falling. I stood there and took a few deep breaths, replaying the chase in my mind. I hated myself for not expecting something like this. The Corps had taught me to be prepared for anything and I should have known 3AM would send the supernatural after me. Then I thought of the thing screaming and I smiled. I had scared 3AM.

3 AM was becoming a *thing*.

The next night I decided to confront 3AM. After the little adventure the night before, I felt I had the advantage. I was wrong.

I had thrown open the door to the warehouse, feeling bold, and yelled at 3AM to talk to me. No more tricks, man to man, or as close as we could get. The warehouse greeted me with silence which I had mistaken as a good sign.

My confidence increased as I strutted down the central aisle. I felt nothing, saw nothing and the only sound was my shoes slapping the concrete and my occasional profanity-filled taunt. I was, if I do say, one major league Hip Cat.

Until I made it to the loading dock.

There, a semi burned with a strange black-red flame. I knew it wasn't real; it couldn't be. It was only another trick of 3AM, but I could feel the heat and smell the acrid smoke. I had stood, mesmerized by the strange ghost-fire, and then I was falling.

I screamed until my throat bled, a raw animal yell I didn't think could come from a human's mouth. I landed with enough force to shatter bone. Somehow I was able to stand up again and I was amazed that I was still alive.

But my screams had drawn attention, and dark forms moved toward me. I heard laughter tinted with screams and fell to my knees. As soon as I was down, the dark forms swarmed me.

When I was a kid my dad had taken me fishing every weekend. One misty morning we were in his jon boat, anchored under some trees and my rod tore through one of those spider nests you see all over the place. Thousands on tiny spiders rained down on us. I tried to brush them off, but they were everywhere. If my dad hadn't grabbed me and thrown me in the river, I would have gone crazy.

That is what the dark forms felt like, only there was no river in that warehouse, so I had no escape.

I prayed my mind would break, but sanity remained. I don't know how long the dark forms were on me. It could have been only seconds, or it could have been days. There was no perception of time. All I knew was that when the feeling stopped, I opened my eyes and I was suddenly back in my office.

When I pulled myself together, I looked at the clock on the wall and saw it was 3AM. I broke a little then; laughter and cries mixed together. But then the sound reminded me of the dark place with its creeping things and I shut my mouth.

3 AM passed and I recovered until the next night. That next night, I was more cautious. I could still hear the echo of footsteps, but the warehouse seemed more normal, more real than it had for as long as I could remember. I started to relax, thinking maybe 3AM had used all of its power with the previous display.

I was wrong again.

The entire loading dock was suddenly covered with those black-red ghost flames. I could see shapes running in the flames. They looked human, but it was hard to tell. One shape ran at me and I let out a little cry when I saw it was Bill Lucas, the midnight shift dock foreman. I wanted to run, but my legs were frozen.

"You son of a bitch!" Bill yelled at me, and when he opened his mouth I saw the black-red fire dance on his tongue.

I backed away from Bill, shaking my head. "Not my fault," I said.

Bill had tried to grab the front of my shirt, but his hands were melting. He looked at them, confused, then gave me an accusing stare. And then, of course, 3 AM passed.

But now, it's 3AM more often than not.

I've almost gotten used to the ghost flames and all the screaming people. These nights, I try yelling back at Bill, and telling him that he is getting what he deserves. They're *all* getting what they deserve. I often hope that my anger will drive the demons off, but it only seems to draw their attention to me. Now *all* of them run at me. I don't know why I thought I could yell at 3AM and get my way, but it never works.

I am on my third 3AM walk through (I average five a night now), and things seem different. The warehouse is bigger for one. I don't explore all of it; in fact, I am unable to make myself stray from my normal route, but it *feels* bigger. I pause at the loading door, preparing myself for the ghost flames as best as I can. It is pitch-black inside; the flames never burst into life until I enter.

I step through the opening and fall a good four feet to the ground because the docks are gone. I sit on the ground, more amazed that I am unhurt than anything, and stare at where the docks should be.

I can make out the concrete dividing walls that mark the lanes to the big over-head doors, but they are cracked and overgrown with weeds. I can see that the perimeter fence is about a hundred yards closer than it should be. I chuckle despite my fear. 3AM has outdone itself this time. I give a tip of my hat in the direction of the now-closer fence.

I get up and find my way back to the office, but it too looks old and worn out. The video monitors are off and have thick layers of dust on them. All the windows are broken and my chair is torn and rotten with mold. I am on the verge of panic when I look at the filth-covered clock and see it is 3AM.

Of course, I think, and a warm sense of the familiar washes over me. I am about to go back out for my 3AM walk-through when I hear a voice.

"You don't have to do this any more."

I spin around. "Who said that?"

"I did," the voice says and a woman appears before me. She looks to be in her forties and is strangely dressed.

"Who are you?" I ask, even though I already know.

"My name is Madame Claire and I've been asked to talk to you."

"Oh yeah?" I say. "By who?"

"The owners of this property asked me to speak with you. They'd like you to leave."

That makes me angry. "I work here. If old man Benny wants to fire me, he can be a man and tell me to my face."

She shakes her head and looks sad. "You're mistaken, my friend. You haven't worked here for thirty years."

I laugh. "That's a good one since I'm only twenty-eight."

"I wasn't making a joke," Madame Claire says. "Do you remember the explosion?"

"What explosion?" I ask. A memory tries to surface. I reach for it, but grab only pain and creeping darkness.

"On June twelfth, 1981, you drove a semi-truck full of explosives into the loading dock, killing everyone working here that night."

"No," I say. "That's not true. I wouldn't do something like that. You ask anyone here. I'm a good guy."

"You had a breakdown and killed sixty people back then, including yourself. Now you're scaring people. They can't sell this property. They can't even keep a night watchman. No one wants to walk in the warehouse at 3AM."

I almost believe her. Somewhere a blurry memory of hate floats and I can almost see the surprised look on Bill's face when I slam the semi into the docks.

But two things stop me from listening to her sweet, commanding voice. One is I remember that it is 3AM and that whatever appears to be the truth at 3AM is most certainly a lie. And two, I notice that I can see her heart beating.

I smile as I advance. "I know what you are," I say and reach into her chest.

She screams as I grab her heart. I squeeze and she falls, dead before she hits the floor.

"My name is Henry Dobbins," I say, standing over the ghost corpse. "I know it's 1981. And I know it's *always* 3AM."

About James Marlow

James Marlow fell in love with horror after sneaking over to a friend's house to watch *American Werewolf in London*. He has been writing fiction in one form or another all his life. He lives with his wife and children in Indiana and is currently working on his first novel. He can be found on Facebook by searching James J Marlow.
https://www.facebook.com/pages/James-J-Marlow/253209748028257

LOSING JUDY
by Andy Mee

He could hear his Labrador barking, and the sound seemed to be traveling farther away. The man in the pale red Macintosh shouted the dog's name. "Judy! Where are you, girl? Judy!"

Inquisitive at first, it was the sort of bark Judy made when questioning the sanity of her owner for throwing the evening's leftovers into the bin; then the barking became louder, urgent, almost hysterical. The growing howls of canine angst were coming from inside the yellow-brown autumnal wood. That was the point at which the man in the Mac realized something was wrong. Judy sounded uncharacteristically agitated.

The man in the Mac had been careless, losing Judy ten minutes previously. The dog had been sniffing its way along the line of leaning brown-red oaks by the side of the half-frosted lake, searching for the last of summer's old stale bread that the ducks had missed when people fed them. The night-lights from the old mansion house on the opposite bank shimmered on the glassy lake. Morning stars faded as the dawn's light came on. The man looked down and was certain he saw ice forming at the lake's edge. Cold enough, he thought, bitter cold.

Judy had wandered off, deep into the old oak and weeping willow woodland. The man in the Mac had been sitting on the bench smoking his rolled Swan Vesta and enjoying the beauty of the early morning. It was the only time he could smoke without his ears bleeding from the verbal abuse of his wife.

He sat, dormant in the cold morning rain, savoring each berate-less inhale, admiring the young mallards as they floated their way toward the old bridge on the southern side of the lake, and watching the swans as they bathed in the grey, autumn morning drizzle.

And then the ferocious barking suddenly ceased with a high squeal, concluding into an eerie silence; even the ducks became quiet.

He got up from the bench, and half cursing, threw his cigarette on the ground and began calling for his dog. He scanned the peripheries of the semi-leaved ashen-brown woods. No sign of her. "Damn dog," he whispered hoarsely to no one.

She was a placid dog, and always had been, so all this barking had been uncomfortably unusual. The man in the Mac made his way over the frozen grass into the woods and felt sleety rain-specks fall on his grey-black hair, still calling for his dog as he half-strode, half-ran.

There was no answering bark, no howl, no whine. He changed to a semi-sprint and felt his heart thumping at his rib cage. He entered the brown wooded area, breathing heavily as he ran.

"Judy!" he shout-panted.

The sleet gave way to rain, and then a downpour ensued. The noise of the raindrops hitting the broken woodland canopy made a low echoing rumble, making the man in the Mac think of tribal drums and, although he refused to acknowledge it, terror began to tug at his chest. Something was wrong.

Inside the woods, the grayness of mid-autumn had gotten much dimmer as he ran through the heavy browns of mid-winter. The further into the forest the man ventured, the darker it got, but still the damn dog refused to acknowledge his calls.

The oaks and alders made way for the deep green pines, closing around him so that three to four at a time were within touching distance. Rain ran down the man's face in blinding rivulets, his grey hair now soaked, eyes stinging. He shivered. The frosted, glassy leaves crunched and cracked under his racing feet. His calling had become a hard-forced wheezing, his lungs emptied by each cry. "Judy!" sounded more like a dead-beat, rasping 'Hoodee.' Still nothing.

Then came the buzzing.

It was a low humming at first. The man questioned whether he was just imagining it. Was it the head-buzz of exhaustion he sometimes got on that darn treadmill? The man in the Mac slowed to a half-walk, heading in the general direction of the strange, low humming.

The rain was starting to raid the forest, robbing it of its musky autumn aroma. Warnings were probing the back of his mind, telling him to go back to his bench by the lake, but he felt a strange compulsion to head toward the humming, an inquisitive yearning; and besides, he needed to find Judy. He loved that damn dog. This was the direction where he'd last heard her. He knew it. But where was she?

"Judy?" he whispered, not realizing he even spoke.

As the man got nearer to it, the buzzing drowned out the noise of the falling rain. His eyes were half-blurred. Wiping his face with soaked coat sleeves had been effective before, but now it was futile as he squinted into the dark alcove of thick pines. The forest had a choking, deep musky taste, which was beginning to linger in the back of his throat as he gasped for another lungful of cold morning air, and he struggled to catch his breath.

The hypnotic, almost orchestral buzzing, slowly drawing him, appeared to be coming from behind a mass of evergreen bushes just ahead. There seemed to be life in them; they had a luminous greenness amidst the grays and dead browns. And, God, the buzzing! It was now almost deafening.

The man's head began to throb. The loud noise, combined with the blanketed anxiety now smothering him, became ingredients for the dull pain witch-dancing within his temples.

Still, like a magnet pulling a cold steel tack, the man in the Mac was drawn to the green shimmer ahead. The pine trees closed around him and he felt sure they were gathering inwards. The woods grew even darker; a thick, purple-grey.

And then the man noticed the smell.

Decay. Rotting meat. The forest not only looked dead, it smelled dead. The only sense of life in the woods were the glowing evergreen bushes ahead. The bushes looked incandescent, too bright, like a beacon.

"Jooodeee?" he called, still feeling the fingers of fear on his spine.

The man saw small white stones on the ground, lying on top of wet leaves. Chalk or limestone, he thought. The stones seemed to have been arranged into the shape of some type of Celtic cross. *Kids,* the man thought, but still found himself looking over his shoulder to stare back at the stone cross many yards after he had passed it.

"Jooo..."

The man noticed a small cloud of flies (too small for bluebottles?) escaping from somewhere inside the bushes. It was strange to see flies so late in the season. And certainly such small insects couldn't be the cause of all that noise.

"...deee?"

The noise was now deafening, painful. He clasped his soaking sleeves to his ears. He had no idea what it could be. It sounded as if it might be something radioactive, and he kept telling himself that he should probably turn back. But he couldn't; he had to find his dog. His wife would kill him if he didn't come back with Judy.

The man in the Mac kept moving toward the light-colored bushes, unable to resist the draw of the buzzing.

The man reached the bushes.

He reached out to move a branch, touching it; inspecting it. It was then that he saw the larvae. Thousands of squirming white insect larvae were completely covering the leaves. The man had never seen such an infestation in all his life. The bushes looked alive, white with crawling vermin.

Repulsed, the man moved quickly past the bushes into the crow-black clearing beyond. And there on the ground was a multitude of milling insects; a swarm so grotesquely huge that it made the air seem coal-black. There were millions of them! The man's mouth dropped open. He turned and looked to his left as the mouth of the swarm drew open around him.

And then he saw what remained of Judy.

A Labrador carcass, almost devoured, was being impossibly held in mid-air by countless swarms of demonic flies.

The man in the Mac was frozen to the spot, eyes unbelieving. Then the swarm began to close its mouth around him, and his vision grayed like a television losing transmission.

From the depths of a slowly fading sanity, a voice in his mind screamed *"Run!"* His immobile legs suddenly obeyed.

Stumbling backward, he coughed out disbelieving monosyllables, unable to muster enough breath to scream, as his black boots drove his weaving body through the dense bracken. The rainwater in his stinging eyes made the world around him a kaleidoscope of browns, greens, and heavy grey blurs.

He scurried blindly into the thick bottle-green foliage of ferns and nettles, stumbling over vine tripwires, while the thunderous buzzing grew in intensity above him. Instinctively swatting, flailing like a drowning man, he hurled his rain-glossed red arms upwards, repeatedly throwing fists into the buzzing black blur as he wove through the stinging thorns of bramble and nettle. He ran blindly through the trees, branches slapping his soaked face.

Suddenly, burning pain flared as his ankle twisted, and he fell on the potholed forest floor. Thudding heavily upon the soft, mud-soaked earth, the last of the man's breath was driven from his lungs, coming out in a groan.

He could feel insects moving on his back; a heavy crawling overcoat that weighed him down. He crept onwards, silently mouthing *Help me* in a last, desperate plea for salvation. He gritted his teeth and summoned one last ounce of strength, and tried to stand.

Rising, he threw his arms into the black cloud as it swallowed what was left of the dull gun-metal light. Mind-shattering pain seared his hands. The gloves he wore began disintegrating. The carnivorous flies were devouring him like piranhas.

The man could feel the buzzing insects enter his open, screaming mouth, as the agonizing pain began to spread through his entire body, burning in his throat and then his lungs. He never saw the flesh of his arms turning black; huge blisters growing and bursting like flowering plants exploding into deep crimson geysers. Bone, yellow-white, showed through his flesh as it became a bubbling swarm of living-black.

Finally, with his last breath, the man screamed.

The screaming echoed across the lake, and a few of the swans bolted, rising out of the water and flying away from the woodlands to land on the other side of the lake.

And then all was silent. The ducks continued their trip to the bridge and the swans went back to searching for food. And Judy was never coming home.

About Andy Mee

Andy Mee is a teacher of English Literature working and living in the Welsh valleys with his wife and young daughter. Occasionally, when finding time away from analyzing other authors' writing in the classroom, he likes to dabble with language and spin a yarn of his own. Andy has written short stories and poetry for a number of small press publications. http://www.facebook/andymee

FISH NIGHT
by Joe R. Lansdale

It was a bleached-bone afternoon with a cloudless sky and a monstrous sun. The air trembled like a mass of gelatinous ectoplasm. No wind blew.

Through the swelter came a worn, black Plymouth, coughing and belching white smoke from beneath its hood. It wheezed twice, backfired loudly, died by the side of the road.

The driver got out and went around to the hood. He was a man in the hard winter years of life, with dead, brown hair and a heavy belly riding his hips. His shirt was open to the navel, the sleeves rolled up past his elbows. The hair on his chest and arms was gray.

A younger man climbed out on the passenger side, went around front too.

Yellow sweat-explosions stained the pits of his white shirt. An unfastened, striped tie was draped over his neck like a pet snake that had died in its sleep.

"Well?" the younger man asked.

The old man said nothing. He opened the hood. A calliope note of steam blew out from the radiator in a white puff, rose to the sky, turned clear.

"Damn," the old man said, and he kicked the bumper of the Plymouth as if he were kicking a foe in the teeth. He got little satisfaction out of the action, just a nasty scuff on his brown wingtip and a jar to his ankle that hurt like hell.

"Well?" the young man repeated.

"Well what? What do you think? Dead as the can-opener trade this week. Deader. The radiator's chickenpocked with holes."

"Maybe someone will come by and give us a hand."

"Sure."

"A ride anyway."

"Keep thinking that, college boy."

"Someone is bound to come along," the young man said.

"Maybe. Maybe not. Who else takes these cutoffs? The main highway, that's where everyone is. Not this little no-account shortcut." He finished by glaring at the young man.

"I didn't make you take it," the young man snapped. "It was on the map. I told you about it, that's all. You chose it. You're the one that decided to take it. It's not my fault. Besides, who'd have expected the car to die?"

"I did tell you to check the water in the radiator, didn't I? Wasn't that back as far as El Paso?"

"I checked. It had water then. I tell you, it's not my fault. You're the one that's done all the Arizona driving."

"Yeah, yeah," the old man said, as if this were something he didn't want to hear. He turned to look up the highway.

No cars. No trucks. Just heat waves and miles of empty concrete in sight.

They seated themselves on the hot ground with their backs to the car. That way it provided some shade—but not much. They sipped on a jug of lukewarm water from the Plymouth and spoke little until the sun fell down. By then they had both mellowed a bit. The heat had vacated the sands and the desert chill had settled in. Where the warmth had made the pair snappy, the cold drew them together.

The old man buttoned his shirt and rolled down his sleeves while the young man rummaged a sweater out of the back seat. He put the sweater on, sat back down. "I'm sorry about this," he said suddenly.

"Wasn't your fault. Wasn't anyone's fault. I just get to yelling sometime, taking out the can-opener trade on everything but the can openers and myself. The days of the door-to-door salesman are gone, son."

"And I thought I was going to have an easy summer job," the young man said.

The old man laughed. "Bet you did. They talk a good line, don't they?"

"I'll say!"

"Make it sound like found money, but there ain't no found money, boy. Ain't nothing simple in this world. The company is the only one ever makes any money. We just get tireder and older with more holes in our shoes. If I had any sense I'd have quit years ago. All you got to make is this summer —"

"Maybe not that long."

"Well, this is all I know. Just town after town, motel after motel, house after house, looking at people through screen wire while they shake their heads No. Even the cockroaches at the sleazy motels begin to look like little fellows you've seen before, like maybe they're door-to-door peddlers that have to rent rooms too."

The young man chuckled. "You might have something there."

They sat quietly for a moment, welded in silence. Night had full grip on the desert now. A mammoth gold moon and billions of stars cast a whitish glow from eons away.

The wind picked up. The sand shifted, found new places to lie down. The undulations of it, slow and easy, were reminiscent of the midnight sea. The young man, who had crossed the Atlantic by ship once, said as much.

"The sea?" the old man replied. "Yes, yes, exactly like that. I was thinking the same. That's part of the reason it bothers me. Part of why I was stirred up this afternoon. Wasn't just the heat doing it. There are memories of mine out here," he nodded at the desert, "and they're visiting me again."

The young man made a face. "I don't understand."

"You wouldn't. You shouldn't. You'd think I'm crazy."

"I already think you're crazy. So tell me."

The old man smiled. "All right, but don't you laugh."

"I won't."

A moment of silence moved in between them. Finally the old man said, "It's fish night, boy. Tonight's the full moon and this is the right part of the desert, if memory serves me, and the feel is right — I mean, doesn't the night feel like it's made up of some soft fabric, that it's different from other nights, that it's like being inside a big, dark bag, the sides sprinkled with glitter, a spotlight at the top, at the open mouth, to serve as a moon?"

"You lost me."

The old man sighed. "But it feels different. Right? You can feel it too, can't you?"

"I suppose. Sort of thought it was just the desert air. I've never camped out in the desert before, and I guess it is different."

"Different, all right. You see, this is the road I got stranded on twenty years back. I didn't know it at first, least not consciously. But down deep in my gut I must have known all along I was taking this road, tempting fate, offering it, as the football people say, an instant replay."

"I still don't understand about fish night. What do you mean, you were here before?"

"Not this exact spot, somewhere along in here. This was even less of a road back then than it is now. The Navajos were about the only ones who traveled it. My car conked out, like this one today, and I started walking instead of waiting. As I walked the fish came out. Swimming along in the starlight pretty as you please. Lots of them. All the colors of the rainbow. Small ones, big ones, thick ones, thin ones. Swam right up to me...*right through me!* Fish just as far as you could see. High up and low down to the ground.

"Hold on, boy. Don't start looking at me like that. Listen: You're a college boy, you know something about these things. I mean, about what was here before we were, before we crawled out of the sea and changed enough to call ourselves men. Weren't we once just slimy things, brothers to the things that swim?"

"I guess, but —"

"Millions and millions of years ago this desert was a sea bottom. Maybe even the birthplace of man. Who knows? I read that in some science books. And I got to thinking this: If the ghosts of people who have lived can haunt houses, why can't the ghosts of creatures long dead haunt where they once lived, float about in a ghostly sea?"

"Fish with a soul?"

"Don't go small-mind on me, boy. Look here: Some of the Indians I've talked to up north tell me about a thing they call the manitou. That's a spirit. They believe everything has one. Rocks, trees, you name it. Even if the rock wears to dust or the tree gets cut to lumber, the manitou of it is still around."

"Then why can't you see these fish all the time?"

"Why can't we see ghosts all the time? Why do some of us never see them? Time's not right, that's why. It's a precious situation, and I figure it's like some fancy time lock — like the banks use. The lock clicks open at the bank, and there's the money. Here it ticks open and we get the fish of a world long gone."

"Well, it's something to think about," the young man managed.

The old man grinned at him. "I don't blame you for thinking what you're thinking. But this happened to me twenty years ago and I've never forgotten it. I saw those fish for a good hour before they disappeared. A Navajo came along in an old pickup right after and I bummed a ride into town with him. I told him what I'd seen. He just looked at me and grunted. But I could tell he knew what I was talking about. He'd seen it too, and probably not for the first time.

"I've heard that Navajos don't eat fish for some reason or another, and I bet it's the fish in the desert that keep them from it. Maybe they hold them sacred. And why not? It was like being in the presence of the Creator; like crawling back inside your mother and being unborn again, just kicking around in the liquids with no cares in the world."

"I don't know. That sounds sort of..."

"Fishy?" The old man laughed. "It does, it does. So this Navajo drove me to town. Next day I got my car fixed and went on. I've never taken that cutoff again — until today, and I think that was more than accident. My subconscious was driving me. That night scared me, boy, and I don't mind admitting it. But it was wonderful too, and I've never been able to get it out of my mind."

The young man didn't know what to say.

The old man looked at him and smiled. "I don't blame you," he said. "Not even a little bit. Maybe I am crazy."

They sat awhile longer with the desert night, and the old man took his false teeth out and poured some of the warm water on them to clean them of coffee and cigarette residue.

"I hope we don't need that water," the young man said.

"You're right. Stupid of me! We'll sleep awhile, start walking before daylight. It's not too far to the next town. Ten miles at best." He put his teeth back in.

"We'll be just fine."

The young man nodded.

No fish came. They did not discuss it. They crawled inside the car, the young man in the front seat, the old man in the back. They used their spare clothes to bundle under, to pad out the cold fingers of the night.

Near midnight the old man came awake suddenly and lay with his hands behind his head and looked up and out the window opposite him, studied the crisp desert sky.

And a fish swam by.

Long and lean and speckled with all the colors of the world, flicking its tail as if in goodbye. Then it was gone.

The old man sat up. Outside, all about, were the fish — all sizes, colors, and shapes.

"Hey, boy, wake up!"

The younger man moaned.

"Wake up!"

The young man, who had been resting face down on his arms, rolled over. "What's the matter? Time to go?"

"The fish."

"Not again."

"Look!"

The young man sat up. His mouth fell open. His eyes bloated. Around and around the car, faster and faster in whirls of dark color, swam all manner of fish.

"Well, I'll be...*How?*"

"I told you, I told you."

The old man reached for the door handle, but before he could pull it a fish swam lazily through the back window glass, swirled about the car, once, twice, passed through the old man's chest, whipped up and went out through the roof.

The old man cackled, jerked open the door. He bounced around beside the road. Leaped up to swat his hands through the spectral fish. "Like soap bubbles," he said. "No. Like smoke!"

The young man, his mouth still agape, opened his door and got out. Even high up he could see the fish. Strange fish, like nothing he'd ever seen pictures of or imagined. They flitted and skirted about like flashes of light.

As he looked up, he saw, nearing the moon, a big dark cloud. The only cloud in the sky. That cloud tied him to reality suddenly, and he thanked the heavens for it. Normal things still happened. The whole world had not gone insane.

After a moment the old man quit hopping among the fish and came out to lean on the car and hold his hand to his fluttering chest.

"Feel it, boy? Feel the presence of the sea? Doesn't it feel like the beating of your own mother's heart while you float inside the womb?"

And the younger man had to admit that he felt it, that inner rolling rhythm that is the tide of life and the pulsating heart of the sea.

"How?" the young man said. "Why?"

"The time lock, boy. The locks clicked open and the fish are free. Fish from a time before man was man. Before civilization started weighing us down. I know it's true. The truth's been in me all the time. It's in us all."

"It's like time travel," the young man said. "From the past to the future, they've come all that way."

"Yes, yes, that's it…Why, if they can come to our world, why can't we go to theirs? Release that spirit inside of us, tune into their time?"

"Now, wait a minute…"

"My God, that's it! They're pure, boy, pure. Clean and free of civilization's trappings. That must be it! They're pure and we're not. We're weighted down with technology. These clothes. That car."

The old man started removing his clothes.

"Hey!" the young man said. "You'll freeze."

"If you're pure, if you're completely pure," the old man mumbled, "that's it…yeah, that's the key."

"You've gone crazy."

"I won't look at the car," the old man yelled, running across the sand, trailing the last of his clothes behind him. He bounced about the desert like a jackrabbit.

"God, God, nothing is happening, nothing," he moaned. "This isn't my world. I'm of that world. I want to float free in the belly of the sea, away from can openers and cars and —"

The young man called the old man's name. The old man did not seem to hear.

"I want to leave here!" the old man yelled. Suddenly he was springing about again. "The teeth!" he yelled. "It's the teeth. Dentist, science, foo!" He punched a hand into his mouth, plucked the teeth free, tossed them over his shoulder.

Even as the teeth fell, the old man rose. He began to stroke. To swim up and up and up, moving like a pale, pink seal among the fish.

In the light of the moon the young man could see the pooched jaws of the old man, holding the last of the future's air. Up went the old man, up, up, up, swimming strong in the long-lost waters of a time gone by.

The young man began to strip off his own clothes. Maybe he could nab him, pull him down, put the clothes on him. Something…God, something…But, what if *he* couldn't come back? And there were the fillings in his teeth, the metal rod in his back from a motorcycle accident. No, unlike the old man, this was his world and he was tied to it. There was nothing he could do.

A great shadow weaved in front of the moon, made a wriggling slat of darkness that caused the young man to let go of his shirt buttons and look up.

A black rocket of a shape moved through the invisible sea: a shark, the granddaddy of all sharks, the seed for all of man's fears of the deeps.

And it caught the old man in its mouth, began swimming upward toward the golden light of the moon. The old man dangled from the creature's mouth like a ragged rat from a house cat's jaws. Blood blossomed out of him, coiled darkly in the invisible sea.

The young man trembled. "Oh God," he said once.

Then along came that thick dark cloud, rolling across the face of the moon. Momentary darkness.

And when the cloud passed there was light once again, and an empty sky.

No fish.

No shark.

And no old man.

Just the night, the moon, and the stars.

About Joe R. Lansdale

Joe R. Lansdale is the multi-award-winning author of thirty novels and over two hundred short stories, articles and essays. He has written screenplays, teleplays, comic book scripts, and occasionally teaches creative writing and screenplay writing at Stephen F. Austin State

University. He has received The Edgar Award, The Grinzani Prize for Literature, seven Bram Stoker Awards, and many others.

His stories Bubba Ho-Tep and Incident On and Off a Mountain Road were both filmed. He is the founder of the martial arts system Shen Chuan, and has been in the International Martial Arts Hall of Fame four times. He lives in East Texas with his wife, Karen.
http://www.joerlansdale.com

METHODS OF DIVORCE
by Philip Roberts

Before the darkness nearly tore away the front of their car and sent both Steven and Candice Lane tumbling into the high weeds along the side of the road, the two had been arguing.

Steve had been in the middle of shouting something when the shriek of metal cut his words off just a split second before the windshield splintered and nearly tore inward. Steve realized that his hands were gone from the wheel as he brought them up to protect his face.

When the car came to a halt, Steve could hear Candice beside him, hyperventilating, her fingers held tightly over her eyes. She looked old and tired to him, all the years they'd trudged through together suddenly accumulated in her face, in her skin, and in her very being. Steve wondered why he was thinking such thoughts now, when he had just been in a car accident.

But then reality returned. The true Candice, who he suddenly realized was the false Candice, took her hands off of her eyes.

"My God, what did you do?" Candice shrieked.

I'm fine, thank you, Steve thought, even though he didn't bother to ask Candice if she was all right or to answer her question.

He couldn't get the seatbelt unlocked, so he opened the console and retrieved a knife, cutting cleanly through the tight material. He handed the knife to Candice in the darkness rather than bother to cut hers as well, and did his best to push open the bent driver's side door.

The moon provided the light he needed to see the damage. He could hear Candice as she struggled to get her door open, but Steve's attention was focused on the amount of destruction to the front of his car.

There was no blood visible within the tangle of metal, and no sign of the animal he must have hit. Even on the road, he could see no carcass, or any streaks of blood to mark where the animal might have been flung.

"There's a house over there," Candice called out to him, and Steve's gaze shifted toward the faint lights in the distance, further in the field, where a lone house stood.

Immediately a slight chill ran through him. "We get smashed by something almost directly in front of what looks to be the only house around for miles," Steve said.

"Well, in case you forgot," Candice hissed at him, her face flushing red, visible even in the dim moonlight, "you were the one who said we shouldn't take our cell phones along. You wouldn't even let me take my Blackberry or my laptop! *A quiet night with just the two of us to patch things up, get over all our problems.* That's what you said, Mr. Big Ideas. So now what's your next big idea, huh? What are we supposed to do? Stand here all night and hope another car comes by?"

"I'm just saying..." He trailed off because it didn't matter what he was saying. From behind him, from the other side of the road, he heard the sound of something moving.

Steve saw the faint rustling in the grass, saw the light wash over a very large form, hunched but still appearing to walk on two legs. And ever so briefly its head turned toward him, light reflecting in two massive eyes embedded into a grotesque face, mouth starting to split open to reveal an abyss that somehow became even darker than the night surrounding it.

Oh my god, Steve thought. *Was that what I hit? Did I mangle it? It must be hurt; I have to help it.*

And then he went into action. Steve ran past the vehicle and through the field, chasing the creature that was running away. Candice, who hadn't managed to get sight of the monstrosity, lingered for just a second before following after him. Steven only knew she was following because of her cry of surprise and by the soft crackling of her feet stamping down on the grass.

He hadn't run this fast or this hard in twenty years, and already his side was burning, his lungs rubbing like sandpaper. He could feel sweat soaking into his shirt.

And then he lost sight of the creature, and a helpless sense of panic and anger overcame him. There was nowhere else to go but to the house. It was the only house around for miles.

"What...did you...see?" Candice cried out through gasps for air as she caught up to him.

Steve didn't answer. They soon realized that it wasn't a house, but a barn that loomed ahead of them, nearly in front of them, and they came to a stop.

They stared at the large barn. The house was a little farther past, and much smaller than the larger structure before them. Inside the barn, a lone light shined through a window on the second floor.

"Anyone there?" Steve called.

Candice interrupted him. Tears sent streaks of make-up down her face. "Please tell me what you saw."

But he ignored her because both of them heard the movement, and both of them saw the hulking shape come from out of the tree-line. This thing, just like the other one Steve had seen, stood on two feet, but it was so hunched over that its massive upper body hung down to its knees, making it appear as though it walked on all fours.

And that was when Steve realized it wasn't the impact of his car that made the creature look this way.

Two large eyes watched them, and then the thing's mouth pulled open to reveal a void darker than anything Steve had ever seen. One massive claw-like hand slapped the ground and sent dirt spraying up into the air as the creature lumbered toward them.

"Oh my god!" Candice screamed, and Steve rushed to the barn, not even taking the time to make sure his wife was following. As soon as he was through the door, he glanced over his shoulder to see the creature reaching the barn as well.

Its arm stretched through the door a second before Steven could slam it shut, but the wood was thick, and a faint, oddly subdued howl wailed into the night before the creature's arm pulled back and the door closed completely.

The moment Steve turned, a slap caught him across the face.

He stared into Candice's wet, bloodshot eyes. "You didn't even look back to see if I was behind you before you slammed that door shut!" she screamed.

There was no surprise at her accusation, and Steve's attention was already turning to the surroundings. He saw that they were in an old, wooden room.

Very little light managed to make it into the small room, though to their right they could see a hallway that led into the rest of the barn. Outside, something scratched the wood, and then hammered a muscular hand against it.

"It's going to get in and kill us," Candice whispered.

"I'm not going to die that way," Steve said as he moved down the hall.

The hallway curved to the right, and opened into a much larger room that had at one point been filled with hay, he figured, but times had changed and given it a new purpose. Now the centerpiece of this room appeared to be the platform ten feet up from the ground, acting as a loft. And above that platform a single light bulb burned with life. So this was the light they had seen from the outside.

And then the pounding at the door grew louder. A deep, low wail made Steve shiver. How many of those things were out there now?

And then, through the attempts by the creatures to get in, Steve heard another sound. It was the sound of a person breathing heavily. He ran toward the ladder that connected the first floor to the loft, Candice still trailing behind him.

His arms felt weak and distant, with barely enough strength to pull himself up the ladder, but finally his head peeked over the edge and he could see a man laying on the floor of the loft, his chest covered in blood, and a gun gripped firmly in his hand. His eyes were closed, but his chest kept rising and falling, the movements ragged.

Steve pulled himself completely onto the platform and saw there was no hay up here anymore either, but a bare, wooden floor. Black, circular shapes were painted on the floor, and contained several lines drawn out from the epicenter.

When his attention turned back to the stranger, Steve saw the man watching him, and the gun was now pointed at him. With a surprising instinct for survival, Steve lunged at the stranger and attempted to pull the gun out of his hand, but not before it discharged. Steve heard both the shot and Candice's scream at the same time. Pain stabbed through his arm. He fell on top of the wounded man and managed to deflect another shot before it could get him, this second bullet digging harmlessly into the ceiling.

And then he used what little strength he had left to yank the gun out of the stranger's hand. Steve rose, clutching the gun, his chest heaving with exhaustion.

In the glow of the light bulb, he could see that the man who had nearly killed him was older than himself by a good ten years, the man's hair already graying, and a bundle of wrinkles playing around the edges of his eyes. More wrinkles lined the middle of the man's forehead, and his teeth were dark and rotting. Judging from his clothes, the stranger looked more like a farmer than anything else.

"Why'd you try to kill me?" Steve demanded.

"I thought you were, you know..." the man trailed off, then refocused his gaze and asked, "Who are you?" His right hand clutched tightly at a cloth that he held against his wounded chest.

"We had an accident on the road," Steve explained, and noticed Candice step up beside him. For the first time he realized the bullet that had clipped him might've hit her, but he saw no wound. He repeated, "Why did you try to kill me?"

The stranger's eyes shifted to the floor, and his left hand was shaking as it rose to point at the markings. "Need blood to seal it," the man said. "Couldn't be my blood to seal it, because my blood opened it."

"Seal what? And what are those things outside?"

"They are what you think they are. They'll keep coming out of the rift if no one seals it back up. I shouldn't have done it. Shouldn't have opened the rift. Now it's too late. They're here, and more will always keep coming."

Steve moved past the man and toward the window in the side of the barn to see the outpouring of shapes running from the dark house beyond. But he could also see humans strewn near the door of the house, most of them torn to nothing, wet redness splashed along the porch.

"Whose blood, then?" he asked, finding his normally practical logic momentarily thrown away in the face of the impossible.

"Life's blood," the man whispered. His breathing was becoming shallow. Candice knelt beside him, and extended a shaking hand toward his wound.

"That gash is deep," she said, speaking to Steve. "He's going to bleed to death unless we can get an ambulance." Then she added, "There won't be any ambulance, will there? No help is going to come."

Steve fell to his knees in front of the man whose eyes began to grow distant. "Are you telling me that one of us has to bleed in order to stop this?"

"Not just bleed," the man rasped, "but one of you has to die. And it has to happen here in this barn."

"You can't be serious!" Candice blurted.

The man managed a weak nod before his eyes closed. His chest kept moving, but Steve had a feeling the man wasn't about to wake up again. Outside, the cracking sounds grew louder, the claws digging into the wood.

"Do you believe it?" Steve asked his wife.

"You're asking *me*?" Candice said, her own eyes fixed on the still-moving chest of the stranger. "I guess a life and death situation is finally enough to get my opinion requested."

"If you believe it's true, then one of us has to die, and I figured you might want to have a say in *that* one."

She stood up and stared at him, but her face contained no hostility, no malice, and from what Steve could tell, no fear of any kind. Candice had always been able to grab onto a form of faith Steve himself couldn't help but deny, and he had to admit a certain envious feeling at seeing her so composed.

"It seems we only have two real options here," she said. "If we believe him, then one of us dies. If we choose not to believe him, then we wait for those things to get in and kill us anyway. I don't think either one of us really has a say in the matter, Steve."

Perhaps her choice of words was meant as a jab at him, or perhaps he was too nervous and paranoid to think of anything else, but her final statement just briefly made him snap his head toward the ground in an effort to drive away the fury at his inability to control the situation.

"So, what are we going to do?" Candice asked, still composed, still accepting whatever fate had in store while Steve himself tried not to vomit.

A much louder crack shook through the barn. Steve stared down below at the creature's claws moving through a hole in the barn's wall below.

And then the answer came to him. They had to try to seal it, and he could decide who died.

"We seal this with *my* life," he said, and saw the surprise on Candice's face.

"We could...we could leave it up to chance," Candice said, reaching out to him.

His features were firmly set when he moved toward her. "There's no reason for you to end your life. Try to live on and make something better than what the two of us had. Remember that...I...I love you," he said, and felt the smallest pang of guilt as he saw the look spreading across Candice's face. How long had it been since he'd said that? He couldn't remember, but he could remember the moment, nearly seven years ago, when he'd first realized that he didn't love her anymore, and no horrifying situation such as this could make that change.

Still, he liked the idea of leaving her with a moment of sentiment, and it made him feel as though within the relationship, he was still able to maintain control to the very end.

He stepped wordlessly into the middle of the circle and brought the gun up to his temple. He was about to close his eyes when Candice shoved him back, catching him by surprise, and making him drop the gun.

As Steve fell onto the floor of the loft, his ears filled with the howling cries of the creatures and the sharp snapping of wood giving way. He saw Candice on her knees in the middle of the pentagram with the gun below her chin and her eyes filled with tears.

A huge BOOM thundered, and in a split second, it took Candice's life and drowned out the sound of the monsters pouring in through the hole they had made in the barn's wall. Steve had to look away from the grotesque thing that Candice had become as she tumbled back, sprawled in the middle of the pentagram.

Behind him, the ladder shook as something tried to pull itself up, and Steve managed to regain sense enough to kick the ladder back from the edge of the loft. It left him stranded, yet protected, on the second floor.

He stood up in a daze. He walked past Candice's headless body. He walked past the now-dead body of the man who had started this. He stared through the window toward the dark house, and saw no more monstrosities pass through its door. Whatever rift had been opened appeared now to be shut, so there would be no more new creatures pouring out of the gateway from hell. But the things that had managed to make their way out of it before the rift was sealed still remained.

He realized that for the last twenty years, he had been making decisions for his wife, and none for himself. He wasn't sure he knew how to live for himself anymore. These thoughts amazed him because he had always been so certain that Candice was the problem, not himself.

Steve suddenly wanted to die with his wife. He didn't want her to leave this world without him because he didn't know what to do with himself if she did. Could it be that he still had feelings for her and hadn't realized it until now? If so, he had wasted so much time in both of their lives by all the needless resentments he had harbored.

He knelt down and pulled the gun from his wife's fingers without looking at the remains of her head. He pressed the still-warm barrel against the side of his own head and pulled the trigger again and again, but only hollow clicks sounded in his ear.

So there would be no easy way out for him. He threw the gun over the edge of the barn loft toward the scrambling mass of creatures trying to get to him. He reached into his pocket for his knife. There was nothing there. In his mind he could see himself toss it to Candice rather than cut her seatbelt for her.

Standing on the edge of the platform, Steve stared down at the mass of squirming, black shapes below; they looked like cockroaches scurrying over each other, their massive, clawed hands pointed upward, groping toward him. He leaned out, trying to decide his next move, as the turbulence below became more urgent with anticipation.

Forty-three years of good grades, hard work, fast promotions, and always wanting to be right had led me to this, he thought, but the idea only reignited his anger. He turned from the creatures, his eyes so wide with anger they hurt, his foot swinging out to connect with the man who had started it all. He couldn't make himself stop kicking at this stranger, his foot swinging repeatedly until the man's jaw had shattered and four of his teeth skidded across the wooden floor.

"I'm not dying that easily!" Steve cried, his face hot with pumping blood, his fingernails digging sharply into his palms. He even found himself smiling through clenched teeth as he told the creatures, "You're going to have to work for this kill."

He stared at the window in the loft and at the house beyond it. If he could gather his courage, he figured he might be able to jump out the window. But first he needed to distract the monsters below.

He knelt in front of the dead man and started rolling the corpse toward the edge of the platform. He didn't know if the creatures merely wanted food, or something else, but he hoped even a corpse would divert them for a little while. When he had the body by the edge, he turned toward Candice's remains, knelt to begin pushing her as well, but found himself pausing instead.

He might not have loved her the way he had when he first walked down the aisle with her twenty years before, but as he knelt before her now, aware of the years they'd spent with each other, Steve figured those years counted for something. He couldn't bring himself to let those monsters rip her apart.

He slipped off her wedding ring and put it in his shirt pocket before he returned to the dead man. A swift kick sent the body tumbling toward the ground floor, landing amongst the demons below. A warbling cry erupted from the group, and all of them began ripping at the body, no longer looking up at Steve.

Anger gave him a large burst of strength as he charged across the platform and threw open the window in the loft wall that led to the world outside. Arms outstretched, fingers groping for the edge of the aged wood, he knew his last act would be a leap for freedom. Splinters tore through his hands and nearly dropped him, but he managed to stop himself so he could peer out into the night. He glanced down at the twenty-foot drop to the ground. "This is my decision and I am controlling my fate," he whispered, and leapt over the edge.

He went limp before impact, his right arm taking the brunt of the fall, a deep breath of dirt kicked up from the impact making him choke, and he felt the tears streaming down his cheeks from the jolt of pain.

He couldn't believe he had survived the fall; never would he have anticipated that he would live. And the idea that he hadn't died from the fall gave him hope.

The creatures were still in the barn and from what he could tell, none of them had seen him pull himself up and start jogging as best he could away from the barn. He didn't bother with the house; he was too afraid it would trap him inside. He just wanted to make it back to the car. Maybe the car was still drivable.

He didn't know how far he'd gone when the sounds of snapping wood first reached him. He didn't bother looking back, instead focusing ahead at the waving grass in the faint moonlight. He didn't need to look back to know they were coming after him. Maybe the creatures hadn't seen him at first, but by now they had figured out that he had escaped. He could hear their feet and hands hammering the dirt, crunching down the grass, their mouths opened into that never-ending abyss.

But he didn't dwell on the thunder rushing toward him, the pain spiking through his side with each additional step, or his knees and legs that were so numb he could barely feel them. Steve kept moving into the night, running the best he could in a lop-sided gait.

When the first shape barreled into him and knocked him down onto the tall grass, Steve felt himself being ripped apart; eaten alive. Even as the weight bore down on him and the pain tore into his back, he thought, *I shouldn't have suggested the ride in the car to try to work things out. I should have agreed to the divorce because Candice deserved better.*

About Philip Roberts

Philip Michael Roberts lives in Nashua, New Hampshire and holds a degree in Creative Writing with a minor in Film from the University of Kansas. Although a beginner in the publishing world, Philip is a member of the Horror Writer's Association, and has had numerous short stories published in a variety of publications, such as the *Beneath the Surface* anthology, *Midnight Echo,* and *The Absent Willow Review.*
http://www.philipmroberts.com

AND BABY, YOU CAN SLEEP WHILE I DRIVE
by Elizabeth Massie

Andy stole a car to drive Alicia across country to her mother's funeral. Andy's own '93 Dodge had broken down a couple weeks earlier, he didn't have enough money to get it fixed because, as the mechanic laughed and said, "This one's gonna need a major overhaul. Transmission, brakes, steering. Why didn't you take care of this earlier?"

Andy didn't answer. There was no answer except that he was poor and getting poorer and that was that.

The Chevy Nova Andy stole was a two-door blue thing with one white door and mismatched tires, though "stole" was too severe a term for what he'd actually done. Andy knew Mick, who owned the car. Mick was a colleague, sort of, an eternally angry piss-ant of a man who was employed as a custodian at the American Safety Razor plant where Andy worked as a security guard, and Andy *did* leave Mick a note in his little cubby, reading, "I'll have someone drive this back to you in two weeks, man, and I'll pay you something for your trouble," so it was more of a borrow than a steal. When Alicia had called him in the middle of the night from home crying, "Mama's dead!" he knew right away that he'd have to plan for transportation to Seattle. They couldn't afford a train or a plane, and Alicia was scared of buses. But Andy loved his wife and he would get her to the funeral in one way or other.

Alicia's mother had lived the last three years in the Oak Hill Nursing Home just a mile from Andy and Alicia's apartment in Nashville. She'd been pretty healthy for a woman who'd smoked two packs a day for fifty-some years. Yet over the past year, she'd begun to go soft in the head, and everyone knew it wouldn't be long before she died. Alicia's bitchy older sister Barb told everyone, "Mama will be buried here in Washington state where she was born. We've already got her a plot close to Daddy's. When the time comes, we're shipping her here."

The time came three nights ago, when Mama got up out of bed and slipped on a puddle of her own urine. Her head came down—*SMACK*—against the stainless steel sink, bounced off, then struck the steel footboard of her bed—*CRACK*—and then she dropped to the floor.

Barb was furious, seemingly more so about the fact that Mama had died in a foreign state than the fact she had died. Barb never liked it that Mama was in "Nastyville" in the first place. But Alicia had always been Mama's favorite girl, and when Mama's health was declining she wanted to be close to her baby. Oak Hill was an acceptable place, if you didn't look too closely. The daytime attendants were spiffy and alert. The nighttime attendants were much like nighttime attendants anywhere that the public didn't go during off hours—bored, cynical, careless.

Andy opened the Nova's passenger door for Alicia, tossed her suitcase and his duffle bag onto the back seat, and helped her in. She was hardly an invalid; Alicia was small, but she was a strong, funny woman most of the time. But today, she was listless and quiet. Her mother's death had hit her hard. She knew her mother was declining—hell, she'd been on the downward spiral for months—but that didn't ease the pain.

"Thanks," Alicia whispered as Andy helped her with her seatbelt. He kissed her head, went around to his side (Mick's side, actually) and climbed in behind the wheel. He handed Alicia a paper bag he'd filled with her favorite candies, hard butterscotch pieces and Hershey kisses. She took the bag, but held it, unopened, in her lap. She hunkered down against the seat and stared out the window.

Andy had been glad to find the Nova came with almost a full tank of gas, but by the time they reached St. Louis they needed to stop for a refill and Alicia had to pee. Andy had brought what was left of his weekly paycheck in his wallet, three hundred-thirteen dollars. If he could make it across country with this clunker on the money he had, if he and Alicia made it to the funeral and then more importantly, to the reading of the old woman's will, all would be good again in life-land. Mama had Alicia's name at the top of the list. Mama had shown a copy of the will to Alicia back in the spring. Barb had been a bane of Mama's existence, telling her what to do, where to live, when to eat, when to shit, but Alicia had always let Mama do her own thing. That is why Mama came to Nashville when she needed assisted living. That is why Mama planned on leaving her Seattle house (in which Barb had been living since Mama upped it across country), her savings, and her jewelry (a diamond ring and earrings and her gold wedding band, though that was about as far as the bling went) to her younger daughter. This inheritance would be enough to pull Alicia and Andy's heads way above water. Andy could almost taste the new car, the paid bills, and the computer he'd been wanting for a couple years now.

Andy stuffed the gas nozzle back into its cradle, went inside to pay the cashier, looked longingly at the cigarettes, then returned to the car. Alicia was still in the can. She was moving slowly these days, but that was okay. She was just tired and sad. Andy opened the passenger's side door and got himself a Hershey's kiss to stave off the craving for a smoke. He had to do this trip carefully, because what would happen if they ran out of money? Barb wouldn't care enough to wire them any, and since his bankruptcy in March, Andy didn't have any credit cards.

"C'mon, babe," Andy hissed toward the convenience store. "We got miles to make before we crash tonight. We got to make it at least to Denver."

He slid in on the seat and punched the glove box button. It was locked. He found a small key on the key ring he'd taken from Mick's employee cubby back at the plant, and poked it in the glove box keyhole. The box popped open.

"Hallelujah!" said Andy. There was a pack of cigarettes, well, Virginia Slims, but beggars couldn't be choosers. Andy tugged his lighter from his jacket pocket, lit up, and leaned back. He took a long, deep drag and held it in as long as he could. He closed his eyes and felt the soft, familiar sting. Then he let the smoke out.

"Ahhh," he said.

He took another drag, held it, let it out. Behind his eyelids, pink and orange patterns played against the black. The dark colors shifted endlessly, like leaves off an autumn tree. Then they began to cluster, to come together into something odd...

What's that?

...something unsettlingly familiar. A round shape, with dark punctuations near the top, a slash near the bottom.

A face? A woman's face?

The punctuations blinked and widened as the colors around it continued to collect themselves into human form. The slash opened up into a twisted sneer, and it and hissed long and loud.

Andy's eyes flew open and he leapt from the car, nearly dropping his smoke to the oily pavement.

"What the fuck...?" he shouted.

"What's the fuck?" This was Alicia, behind him. He looked around at her worried face.

"Nothin', just dropped ashes on my lap's all."

"Okay."

"Get back in the car," he said, holding the door wide open. Alicia slid in. "We'll be in Denver quicker than you can imagine. You just sleep all you want."

They hit the road again, Andy digging in the duffle bag in the back for the sticks of beef jerky he'd brought from home, Alicia snoring softly beside him. He finished his cigarette, tossed out the butt, and chewed on the beef. Interstate driving was beyond tedious. He read each road sign aloud so he wouldn't drift off.

A tractor-trailer pulled up on his ass and rode him a good couple miles, then finally went around. *Asshole.* More trucks and more trucks passed by him, a good ten over the limit.

Andy felt snot trickle down his nose. Was he coming down with a cold? Yep, that was just what he needed. He tugged the rearview mirror around to have a look at the snot, to wipe it away before Alicia woke up and got grossed out.

But it wasn't his face in the mirror. It was a hideous countenance, eyes as wide and white as bleached river rocks, the lips peeled back revealing red-streaked teeth, three long and bloody gashes across her nose, forehead, chin. A piece of chewed-through tongue lashed out like a mangled snake and licked the glass from the inside, leaving shiny pink spittle.

"Holy shit!"

Andy steered the car to the shoulder, slammed on the brakes, and shoved the mirror up so it faced the ceiling.

"Jesus, did we wreck?" screeched Alicia, coming immediately out of her sleep and clutching the door handle with both hands.

"No," said Andy, swallowing hard. "We're okay."

"We are? You sure? What happened?"

I saw a bloody dead woman in the rearview!

"Tractor-trailer. Passed too closely. Scared the bejeezus out of me," wheezed Andy.

"Well, okay."

"Okay."

They sat on the side of the road many long minutes, and then Andy steered back into the traffic.

It's just stress, he told himself. *Like those dudes who came home from Vietnam and the Gulf. Just stress playing with me, is all.*

Andy gripped the wheel tightly. The hairs on his knuckles stood at attention.

It sure couldn't be what it looked like. It sure couldn't be...her.

Andy wiped his lips, his nose.

I don't believe in that kind of shit. The old woman's dead!

Alicia closed her eyes and leaned against Andy's shoulder.

There are no such things as ghosts.

Five miles down the road, he smelled it. It came from the back, rolling up over the seat like a stinking wave, wrapping itself around his head. It was a putrid stink, a smell of hot steel and festering puss. He wrinkled his nose and rolled down the window. It didn't help. He gagged into his hand.

What the fuck is that?

It smelled like a corpse, a three-day dead body. A bloody, putrid human slab…coming back for revenge.

But dead can't come back to haunt the living! Dead people are dead!

Dead, like Mama. Dead like when Andy was through with her the other night. He'd tiptoed from his hiding place in the nursing home bathroom, pulled out her catheter, let the pee drain to the floor, then knocked her head against the sink. She fell to the floor on her own.

He had to do it. During their visit last Saturday, the old woman had mumbled to Andy that she was changing her will. Barb had called and said God would punish her if she didn't, Barb being the firstborn and all. Mama was just whacked and drugged enough believe what she was told. "I can't go against God, now, can I, Paul?" That was her dead husband's name.

And Alicia and I will go on whirling down the drainhole! Andy had thought as he and Alicia walked home from Oak Hill.

Alicia nuzzled Andy's shoulder and continued to snore.

The smell in the car grew even stronger. Andy swerved back and forth in his lane, trying to lose it through the open window. Alicia muttered against him.

A passing truck honked; Andy glanced in the side view mirror and saw not the truck or the road, but the mangled, bleeding face of the woman, shouting silently at him, blaming him. Her fingers scrabbled up at the surface of the mirror. Then they came out of the mirror and clutched at his collar.

"Noooooo!"

Andy jerked the steering wheel and the car rumbled off the road, the shoulder, and went airborne. It flipped in mid-air. Alicia screamed. Andy's sunglasses flew out the window. The suitcase and duffle bag jumped from the back seat to the front. The car landed on its top.

Alicia, dangling upside down in her seatbelt, shook Andy violently. Andy's seatbelt was holding up tightly at the throat. "Andy! Are you okay?"

I didn't want to kill her, I had to! We need the money!

"She's here to get me!" he managed.

"Who?"

"The car is haunted! You're mother's after me!"

"What? Stop it, that's crazy talk!"

Alicia unbuckled her belt and fell in a heap on the car ceiling. She jabbed the release button on Andy's, and he dropped down with her then rolled over, righting himself. The windshield was shattered, the hood crumpled like a piece of old school paper. Neither door would open.

I want out of this car!

"I saw her, coming after me…" he began.

Alicia took Andy's face in her hands. "You've got a bump to the noggin," she said anxiously. "Shh! Shhh! Everything's gonna be okay."

Red and blue swirling lights pulled up beside them and behind them. Men in uniforms swarmed the car, talking in soothing, encouraging tones.

The rearview mirror was banged back down and was covered with a spider web of cracks. Andy glanced in the glass. The bloody, butchered woman leered at him and winked her dead white eyes.

"Get me out!" Andy screamed, slapping at the mirror.

The Jaws of Life tore open the Nova door. Alicia and Andy were pulled into the sunlight. Police swarmed the area, keeping the huddled curious back up on the shoulder.

Someone strapped Andy onto a stretcher. A policeman came up to him before he went into the ambulance.

"Well, buddy," he said from behind his dark glasses. "I can see why you were running away from Nashville. Pretty nasty business you got mixed up in back there, huh? But we got you now."

Andy started to weep. "I was crazy," he said. "Okay? It was extreme duress! She was going to change the will, leave us out, leave Alicia out! Alicia needs the money! I don't care about me, just her! And I didn't really kill her mother, exactly, I just pushed her and she fell and hit her head!"

The policeman's nose twitched. "Hmm," he said. "I'll make note of that murder, too. But right now I'm talking about the young lady in your trunk."

"The who?"

"Mick Conners called us this morning. Reported his Nova stolen, his wife missing. You flip this car, we run the plates, and viola. How about that? Mrs. Conners, beat, cut, and dead in the trunk. You killed her with a machete's what it looks like."

"Mick's wife?"

"You're one sick fuck," said the policeman.

No, wait, wait, Mick was always bitching about his wife...!!

"Mick's wife is dead in the trunk? That wasn't me, it had to be Mick. I borrowed his car, it was bad timing...!"

"Shit yeah, bad timing." The police looked around to be sure no one was watching, and punched Andy soundly in the face. Andy felt his jaw, already loosened in the wreck, give way like a bag of marbles. His head flopped over, and amid flashes behind his eyes and the agony in his chin, he could see the woman they'd removed from the trunk. He caught a glimpse of her face before they zipped the body bag closed.

It was the woman he'd seen in the mirror, not Mama. He recognized the three deep cuts, the near-white eyes. Her mouth hung partially open and he could see where she'd bit her tongue nearly off at the time of her murder.

"You haunted the wrong person, you bitch!" Andy screamed as he was shoved into the ambulance next to Alicia. "You fucking, stupid bitch!"

Alicia began to cry. The ambulance door slammed shut.

The policeman rubbed his sore fist and went back about his business.

About Elizabeth Massie

Elizabeth Massie is a two-time Bram Stoker Award-winning author of horror novels, historical novels, media tie-in novels, radio plays, short fiction, and chapters and units for American history textbooks. Her works include *Sineater, Welcome Back to the Night, Homeplace, The Fear Report, Shadow Dreams, The Tudors: King Takes Queen, The Tudors: Thy Will Be Done,* and many more. A former public school teacher, Beth presents creative writing workshops to students in elementary schools, middle schools, high schools, and colleges.

Beth is also the creator of the Skeeryvilletown menagerie of bizarre cartoon characters, which are featured on clothing and other items at www.cafepress.com/Skeeryvilletown.

Her newest works are the psychological horror/humor novel *DD Murphry, Secret Policeman* (co-authored with Alan M. Clark) and the comic book in which Julie Walker is *The Phantom in the Race Against Death.* Several of Beth's novels are now available as e-books through Crossroad Press, including a new mainstream novel, *Homegrown.*

Elizabeth lives in the Shenandoah Valley of Virginia with illustrator Cortney Skinner. http://www.elizabethmassie.com

CHUPACABRA
by Ronald Malfi

I am a nervous wreck coming into Salinas Cove, my sweaty hands slipping on the steering wheel. I have come from Durango, down through Mesa Verde and across the Rio Grande toward Las Cruces, and the air is warmer. Even at twilight.

I peer through the windshield at the oncoming darkness.

It is a rundown motel outside the city. An illuminated sign promises its employees speak English. I pull into the parking lot and turn off the engine. It ticks down in the silence. There is less light out here, outside the city. Mine is the only car in the parking lot.

The girl who signs me in is dark-skinned, pretty. She definitely does not speak English. I scribble my signature on a clipboard and fork over my driver's license. Behind the counter, a wall-mounted television set flickers with the black-and-white, static-marred image of Cary Grant.

And for a moment, I zone out. I hear the man with the ironworks teeth saying, *You do not look like him.* He says, *Your brother—you do not look like him.* Yet he extends his hand anyway.

The room is bleak, tasteless, the color of sawdust. The shower stall is filthy and ancient, and there is the distinct impression of a foot stamped in grime on the shower-mat. Sketches of hunting dogs and wind-blown cattails cling to the walls in spotty frames. The bed looks miniscule, like something from a child's fairytale about a family of bears, and it is packaged in an uncomfortable-looking bedspread adorned with fleur-de-lis. The ghosts of cigarettes haunt the room. Yet none of this troubles me at the moment. I stand in the center of the room and look at the miniscule bed and am nearly knocked over by the sudden strength of my exhaustion.

Immediately, I strip. I go straight for the bed and do not turn down the comforter and do not turn out the lights, for fear cockroaches will trampoline on my body in the dark. So I remain in bed, my hands behind my head, listing to my own heartbeat compete with the chug of someone's shower through the wall. And despite my utter exhaustion, I cannot find sleep.

I am thinking of the man with the ironworks teeth, and how he extended to me a set of pitted brass keys. *Kees,* he pronounced it. *Keees, chico.* And then I think of my brother, of Martin, and the way he looked after returning from the Cove, like some vital fluid had been siphoned from him. When he first saw me at the trailer park, he tried to smile, but his smile was all busted up, his lips split, his teeth jagged. His eyes were bulbous, swollen, amphibian in their protrusion. *They did me real good, bro.* Sure they did. Sure.

Somehow, I become hostage to a series of dreams. They all have the sepia-toned quality of old movies. Shapeless, hair-covered creatures shuffle along the periphery of a nightmare highway; each time I try to look at them, they break apart into glittering confetti.

At one point, I awake. I think I hear Martin talking somewhere in the distance. He speaks with the marble-mouth distort of a stroke victim. Because I cannot sleep, I rise and do calisthenics just beyond the foot of the bed in the half-gloom. I am too wired to sleep.

Before I know it, morning breaks through the half-shaded window across the room. I shower with the dedication of a death row inmate. Brushing my teeth with my finger, I try to think of old songs on the radio to hum, but I cannot think of anything.

With some detachment, I dress. And it is still early morning by the time I'm back in the car. I drive for some time without seeing anything, then finally pull over at a gas station to refill the tank. I purchase a cup of black coffee and a chocolate chip cookie nearly the size of a hubcap. The gas station is practically a ghost town; only a mange-ridden mutt eyes me from across the macadam. Back in the car, I drive for an hour and breeze by the twisted carcasses of chupacabra along the side of the highway.

I glance out the window to my left and watch the mesas watch me. I'm surprised I haven't seen any border patrol vehicles yet. This relaxes me a bit. I cross into Mexico with little difficulty, sticking to the route previously outlined for me by the man with the ironworks teeth.

I pull into a deserted parking lot outside a diner somewhere west of Ciudad Juárez. An ice cream truck sits slumped and tired-looking in the sun, mirage-like in a halo of dust. The sun seems to be at every horizon. I park alongside the ice cream truck and step quickly from the car to survey the vehicle. It could be an elephant. Or maybe a bank safe. Its color suggests it was once a pale blue, the color of a robin's egg. But both the desert sun and the passage of time have caused it to regress to a monochromatic gray, interrupted by large magnolia blossoms of rust and speckled with muddy chickenpox. Cryptic phraseology has been spray-painted along one flank. Reads, "Sho'nuf." Reads, "Denis Does Daily."

Its windshield is grimy, but in one piece and the tires, all four of them, look new.

Inside, I sip a glass of tasteless soda while picking apart a *sopapilla* stuffed fat with beans that look like beetles. I wait. Soon, a young, scarecrow-faced man with a too-wide mouth and baggy dungarees materializes beside my table. He introduces himself as Diego. He seems friendly enough. He sits across from me and orders a 7-Up. To quell my nerves, he tells me about a helicopter ride into the Grand Canyon and how there is this entire Indian tribe living down there, just tucked away like a secret behind some waterfall, and I listen with mild interest. Then around noon, just when I think nothing is going to happen, I catch a glint of chrome on the horizon morph into a prehistoric Impala as it draws closer to the diner.

"That's him," Diego says.

His name is Caranegra and his face is indeed almost black as tar. He does not smile—not like the man with the ironworks teeth, the man who gave me the *keees, chico*—and he tries hard to be stoic when we first meet. He wears a tattered Iron Maiden concert tee which I find somewhat comical and his knuckles are alternately covered with tattoos and intricate silver rings.

"I'm Gerald," I say and am not sure if I should shake this man's hand or not. I opt for a slight nod and leave it at that.

Caranegra acknowledges both Diego and me with a grunt. "You are Martin's brother?"

"Yes."

"You do not look like him."

"Yeah, that's what the other guy said."

"Pinto? Who gave you the keys?"

"Yes. Pinto." I hadn't known his name.

"You look nervous to me, boy," Caranegra says. And before I can answer, he says, "Your brother, he was not careful. That is why his face looks like it does. He has been doing this for a long time, *muchacho*, and he got careless. If you get careless, then the bad things can happen. If you do not get careless, *muchacho*, you will not have a face that looks like his."

"I won't be doing this for very long," I say quickly. For whatever reason, I feel I need to make this clear. "I'm just working off what Martin owes."

"Why?"

"Because he's my brother."

Caranegra leans back in his chair. I can smell marijuana about him like body odor. His face is heavy with lines and creases, like a map that has been folded too many times, and I cannot tell if I am looking at a genius or an imbecile. "Martin, your brother, was not a stupid man," he says. "He was a smart man. He just got careless. Did he ever tell you about his last crossing?"

"Some of it."

"Not all?"

"He told me enough. He just left some parts out."

"I would bet," says Caranegra, "those are the parts that make him look careless." And he smiles sourly.

"I have to piss," Diego says and rises automatically from the table. "Can we hurry this along? I've got things."

Caranegra watches Diego cross the diner and, when he is out of earshot, says, "He is my sister's boy. He is the good kid." Then he leans toward me over the table. Suddenly we are ancient friends and longtime conspirators. "How old are you?"

"Twenty."

"You look younger."

"I can show you my driver's license."

Caranegra waves uninterested fingers at me. "This is the delicate work, *muchacho*. Do you understand?"

"You don't have to worry about me."

"You have the map?"

I remove a roadmap from my rear pocket and splay it out across the table. With a fat red thumb, Caranegra presses down on a section just southwest of Guerrero. "Debajo Canyon. Up here, then up here, then—do you follow? Then up here." His eyes never leave mine. "But this is the delicate work, *muchacho*."

"You don't have to worry."

Caranegra thumps his thick bronze fingers on the tabletop. Says, "Come with me."

Outside, he pats the side of the ice cream truck. "Pinto give you the route, no? The directions?"

"Yes."

"That is the best route. Pinto knows all the best routes. You stay on that route and you will have no worries."

"What's in the truck?"

"Your brother was careless," Caranegra says. "Also, he started to ask many questions."

Diego saunters out into the broad sunshine, hitching up his too-big dungarees. He smiles when he sees us as if happy to see old friends.

"Diego will take you to Debajo Canyon to get the I.D.," Caranegra says. "From there, you will travel alone."

Awkwardly, I move to shake his hand.

Carangera just laughs. Says, "You do not look like him." Says, "Get lost now."

No more than a minute later, Diego and I are kicking up dust in the ice cream truck, leaving the ruddy-faced Caranegra standing in the parking lot of the diner, his ridiculous Iron Maiden tee-shirt flapping in the breeze. The truck drives horribly, and I can feel every bump and groove in the roadway. It gives off the distinct aroma of burning steering fluid and someone has spilled M&M's into the radiator ducts; they rattle like ball bearings from one side of the dash to the other with each sharp turn.

Debajo Canyon is due south, near Guerrero, and we are closer to it now than I thought we were. Diego stares at the map and talks to himself and hums hair metal songs under his breath while drumming his fingers on his knees. Having driven all this way by myself, his presence is practically suffocating, despite the fact that we hardly speak to one another. Then, finally, Diego mentions Martin.

"Did he ever tell you about this?" he asks. "About the job?"

"A little."

"He ever say what he carried in the trucks?"

"I don't know."

"Didn't you ask?"

"Sure."

"Frankenface didn't tell you?" And he seems pleased with himself for coming up with the name.

"I just assumed drugs," I said. "Or guns. Something like that."

"Do you know who did that to his face?"

"No. He never said."

"It was Pinto," Diego says. "Used his big fists."

For whatever reason, this upsets me.

"They sure banged him up pretty good," Diego continues. "Had a B.A.G."

"What's that?"

"Busted-Ass Grille."

"Let's drop it."

Something flickers just to the left of my line of sight. My breath catches. Immediately my mind returns to the dreams, and to the shapeless beasts that scale the highways. Chupacabra. Goat-suckers.

"What?" Diego asks, sensing my sudden unease.

"Chupacabra," I say. "Martin used to scare me with stories of the chupacabra when I was little."

"He raise you?"

"Our parents died when we were young, yeah."

"So now you feel you need to pay him back? To finish what he started?"

I roll my shoulders. "I don't know."

"This is not the business for that, bro."

"It's just this one time."

"Christ." Diego sinks down into the passenger seat. "Chupacabra's a myth. They're coyotes. Your brother saw coyotes."

"I saw something large and hairy dead on the side of the road coming down here. Looked too big to be a coyote."

"You're ridiculous," Diego says.

Am I? Because I am thinking of the horror stories Martin used to tell me when I was younger and he'd return from weeks and sometimes months on the road. He would tell me of the chupacabra and of the way they drained the fluids from livestock and how, sometimes, they drained the fluids from people, too. Of course, I know now that there are no such creatures, but seeing the dead coyote along the side of the road and thinking, too, of Martin instill within me a certain disquiet. Suddenly, I feel like turning around and driving the hell home.

It is late by the time we pull into Debajo Canyon. It is nothing more than a sandstone bluff overlooking a scrub grass valley, milky in the oncoming darkness, interrupted at intervals by ramshackle hovels and peeling, sad-looking campers. I have no idea what to expect from Diego's associates, but I can sense an urgency in Diego the moment we cross onto the rutted gravel roadway leading toward the semicircle of campers. In the distance, a small bonfire winks at us. The sky is dizzy with stars.

Diego has unraveled a worn slip of paper and looks at it now the way an explorer might scrutinize a treasure map. Says, "Pull off to the left here, Gerald."

I pull off to the left. Say, "Which one is it?"

Diego points past the windshield. "Straight ahead. One with the lights on." It is a beat-up trailer with automobile tires nailed to the roof. It is one of the few with lights in the windows.

Diego pops the passenger door and climbs down from the ice cream truck. For the first time, I catch a glimpse of a pistol butt jutting from the waistband of his dungarees, hidden beneath his shirt. "Let's shake a tail feather, bro. I got things."

I pop my own door and hop down, kicking up dust with my sneakers, and follow Diego to the trailer. Diego mounts the two abbreviated steps to the door then knocks and waits. Knocks again. My discomfort increases and I take a step back. Across the sandstone courtyard, very few lights are on in any other homes, and even the distant bonfire has disappeared. I scan the horizon for a sign of civilization beyond the trailer park, but I am kidding myself. We are alone.

The trailer door opens and we're suddenly scrutinized by a barrel-chested Mexican in a wife-beater, his thick, hairless arms as red as the sunset. His matted, corkscrew hair informs me we've just woken him from a nap.

Briefly, Diego and the man exchange pleasantries in Spanish. I understand very little of what is said. It isn't until I recognize my brother's name that I feel I am included in all this, and the big man in the wife-beater grins bad teeth at me.

Inside the trailer is like being in a coffin. The air is stale and palpable. It is a home for papers and paperwork, of overflowing manila folders and spools of adhesive tapes, an ancient reel-to-reel recorder that blindly stares, and the like. Unwashed plates are stacked like ancient tablets in the sink. The whole place smells not of a structure of human residency and occupancy, but rather of mildewed library cellars and wet paperback novels and discarded and forgotten towers of time-yellowed newspapers.

"*Aquí,*" the barrel-chested man says, and quickly directs me to stand against one wall. Suddenly, I am looking across the cramped trailer at the lens of a digital camera. The man rattles off a succession of photos then, moments later, perches himself in front of a computer monitor.

Startled by movement in a darkened corner of the trailer, I squint to find a set of dark eyes staring back at me. An ancient Mexican woman, nearly skin and bones, watches me from a Barcalounger across the trailer. She has a knitted afghan pulled over her legs, and her hands, like the talons of a prehistoric bird, sink into the divot of her lap. Like a ghost, she watches. I suddenly taste my own heartbeat.

Then she starts cackling.

"Here," says the barrel-chested Mexican, stabbing a freshly-minted driver's license in my direction. He has something else in his other hand—something that quickly steals Diego's attention. It's marijuana, a few ounces of the stuff, in a Ziploc bag.

"Hey, Frodo," Diego says. "Go wait in the truck."

Cold, uncomfortable, I climb back into the truck and punch off the headlights. I sit in the simmering quiet of a desert night. I wait for decades. Soon, Martin is seated somewhere behind me in the truck, whispering my name. He makes me promise to be careful and to not ask too many questions. I call him an idiot and tell him I'll be home soon. He asks if I've seen the chupacabra and I snort…but deep down inside I am that lost, little boy again, fearful of the goat-suckers, of the desert vampires. *You know they don't exist, Gerald, right?* he soothes me now.

Yet I frown and tell him it's too late, damn it, that he has already poisoned me with his stories, years of poisoning, years of waiting in my own sad little trailer for him to come home and raise me and act like a responsible adult. Is it fair that I should have to act like the responsible adult for both of us now? Is it?

It was an accident, he whispers. *I drove a truck into a river.* Then: *They did me real good, for driving the truck into the river. They did me real good, bro.*

Sure they did.

Sure.

Across the bluff, Diego spills through the trailer door. He staggers to the ice cream truck and motions for me to take down the window, which I do.

"Hey," he says, "you know where you're going, right?"

"I have the map."

"Yeah. Uh, I'm gonna crash here, all right?"

"I don't need to drive you somewhere?"

"Take it easy, Gerald."

I spin the wheel and pull back on to the main road, this time heading north. I drive for nearly forty-five minutes, the only living creature among miles and miles of desert. And when I think I see something shapeless and black moving alongside the highway, I can't help but slam on the brakes and straddle the highway's center line like a tightrope walker. And I think, Chupacabra! I am breathing heavy and sweat stings my eyes. Behind me, somewhere in the darkness, I hear Martin assure me that the chupacabra are not real. Vampire devils. Goat-suckers. His face, he says—what they did to his face is real, but the goat-suckers are not.

It is always brighter the moment you step out of a vehicle in the desert, no matter how dark it is. Now, it is cold, too. When people think of perishing in the desert, they usually don't imagine themselves freezing to death, but that is the truth of it.

I step around the side of the ice cream truck, my ears keying in on every desert sound. The chatter of insects is deafening. I cannot seem to get my heartbeat under control. With one hand tracing along the body of the truck, I move to the rear of the vehicle and peer through the darkness. I am not shocked when I see the reflective glow of two beady eyes staring back at me from the cusp of the highway; rather, a dull sense of fatigue overwhelms me.

It is a coyote. I see it clear enough as it turns and scampers further down the shoulder of the roadway. And while I am relieved, I am quickly accosted by a delayed sense of fear that causes my armpits to dampen beneath my sweatshirt and my mouth to go dry. I turn and begin to head back to the cab when I hear a sound—some sound, some thump—echo from the rear of the truck. From within.

My footfalls are soundless on the blacktop of the midnight highway. There is no lock on the rear doors—just a simple bolt slid into a ring. Unhinging the bolt, I peel the doors open and stare into the black maw of the truck. The sick-sweet stink of decay breathes out. I climb into the rear of the truck. There are coolers affixed to the floor and metal boxes on shelves. There are a number of cardboard ice cream boxes lining the shelves here too, but they are empty and so ancient that a slick, brown mildew coats every box. Looking down, I expect the coolers to be locked with padlocks, but they are not, and I am surprised.

Chupacabra? I wonder, and open one of the coolers. The hinges squeal and I fumble around my jacket pocket for a pen light. Shine the light into the back of the truck.

At first, it does not even register with me. And even after it does, I do not fully understand what I am looking at.

There are a number of them, bronze-skinned and wide-eyed, staring up at me, pressed so closely together that they are indistinguishable from one another. They reek of fear and sweat, their expressions just as uncomprehending as my own. Their clothes are filthy, their faces greasy with perspiration. So many of them, it is a wonder they can even fit. Finally, before I ease the cooler lid down, one of them says, "*Muchacho.*"

"I'm sorry," I say…although I am unsure if I am actually speaking or am just hearing the words funnel through my head. And I hear Martin saying, *They did me real good, for driving the truck into the river.*

It is a long, quiet ride back across the border.

About Ronald Malfi

Ronald Malfi was born in Brooklyn, New York in 1977. Along with his family, he eventually relocated to Maryland where he spent most of his childhood growing up along the Chesapeake Bay. He professed an interest in the arts at an early age and is also known to be a competent artist and musician. In 1999, he graduated with a degree in English from Towson University. For a number of years, he fronted the Maryland-based alternative rock band Nellie Blide.

Ronald Malfi is the author of the well-received novel *Snow* and most recently, *The Ascent*. Recognized for his haunting, literary style and memorable characters, Malfi's horror novels and thrillers have transcended genres to gain wider acceptance among readers of quality literature. He currently lives along the Chesapeake Bay. You can visit Ronald Malfi at: http://www.ronmalfi.com

THE ORPHANS OF LETHE
by Rachel Coles

The "blessed" day finally arrived with cussing that would have boiled holy water into steam. We checked into the hospital. I don't think we were in the labor suite for twenty minutes before my husband Bill ogled at the Romanesque design of the bathroom. I imagined choking him and ripping his nuts off. That helped, but not as much as the epidural.

Before my eyes slid shut, I zoned out and stared at a shadow in the corner behind the heart monitor, and realized that it wasn't the shadow of the monitor.

A day later, Bill wandered into my room with the rich aroma of pastrami and buttery rye following him like an elderly Brooklyn deli phantom, poaching my fries on the way.

"I got your Reuben, as requested."

"Are you eating my fries?"

He paused, an errant fry poking out of his mouth. "No…just quality assurance…"

I snatched the bag and stuck my entire face inside, inhaling the greasy goodness. "Stay out of my food, or I'll eat you."

He snorted and leaned back in the chair and stretched his legs. "I heard something interesting today. They're closing down one of the last units for psychiatric folks in the city at University Hospital. The only one left will be Denver Health. If Denver's full, they'll have to go to Fort Logan, or get shuffled through the Emergency Department and then back out onto the street."

"University is closing their psychiatric unit?" I said through mouthfuls of meat. "I thought they just got that new huge building. It was supposed to be the whole point of moving out to the east end of nowhere, so they could have more room. What are they doing with it after the psych unit closes?"

"Luxury rooms for the wealthy. They want to attract more money to the hospital. So they are turning the space that used to be the psych ward into single-patient rooms for body-scans." Bill shook his head. "I'll be doing the rest of my residency in the park across from the Denver Rescue Mission, because that's where my low-income, mentally ill patients will end up."

I stopped chewing and looked around at my own semi-lavish surroundings in the labor room.

He seemed to read my thoughts and smiled. "Don't feel so guilty. They wouldn't have turned this back into a mental health wing anyway. The suites in the previous labor and delivery wing were like prison cells. They needed an overhaul."

I poked at a blob of sauerkraut, and glanced out the window. A blanket of snow was swirling around lumps of roadside dirt and iced grime until everything was shifting, glittering white. The wind blew a cruel blast against the double-pane. My attention was caught by my own reflection in the mirror. My image and I swiped at a beige smear of Thousand Island dressing on the wrong cheek. Bill laughed as I pawed both my hands over my face and licked the dressing off my hand.

Then the eyes in the mirror changed. They weren't smiling or laughing anymore. The face was an expressionless mask. As soon as I focused on it, the face became my face again. I glanced at Bill, but he was busy eying the other half of my sandwich.

It was good to be home, minus dozens of hours of sleep. A chilly draft blasted across the room when Bill came in from work, bundled in a hat and scarf and smelling like frost and ozone. No paternity leave for the wicked.

"Shut the door!" I squealed and dove beneath a mound of flowered fleece. Baby Tom snuggled against my chest in a swath of fabric, yawned, and looked unimpressed by the waft of frigid air.

"It's windy. Jeez. You've been here for five years. Aren't you ever going to get used to cold? Oh yeah, I forgot, your people have been lost in the desert for forty years. Would you feel more comfortable if I shipped in some sand dunes?" He ducked as a couch pillow sailed past his head and whumped against the front door.

"Sure! Ask your people to build us a teepee," I shot back.

He grinned, "Wrong tribe, dork! We lived in longhouses. And...hell no."

"Whatever. You all look alike."

He shook his fist and kissed me on the top of the head, kissed Tom on his button nose and crossed his eyes at the baby. Tom stared at him in fascination. His head wobbled off my chest and he grabbed Bill's finger, pulling it toward his mouth. "Oh, guess what! He's hungry again, what a surprise! 'Feed me, Seymour.'"

I sighed. "I'm tapped out. We'll need to use formula."

"I can take this shift if you want to sleep early."

"Are you sure? You just got off call."

"Maybe so, but I'm going to have a hard time sleeping right now anyway. One of my patients didn't come back for her follow up. The schizophrenic girl from Russia. Police found a body matching her description in the alley behind the King Soopers on Thirteenth Street. It looks like she died of exposure." He slumped into the worn chair across from me. "We should have kept her, but there weren't any spots left on the unit. It was an insane night, and now that folks from the VA are being shipped over too..."

I felt badly for him. I knew he was wondering if he could have somehow prevented the woman's fate. "It wasn't your decision to release her. It was the attending doc."

"I know. But I just can't stop thinking about how somehow, this is my fault."

"It isn't your fault." I handed Tom over because I knew it would help, and it did. Bill's face relaxed and lit up as Tom gurgled and drooled onto his scrubs.

A few weeks in a tiny house with no sleep and my 'helpful,' anxious mother drove me out into the cold, looking for commodities we needed at the store. Or anything. Once I was done in the supermarket, I rattled the cart briskly toward my car in the parking lot. Tom was just a fuzzy mountain of blankets in the cart with two dark eyes peeping out.

Suddenly a voice startled me, causing my heart to try to leap out of my chest. "Just feel free to run me over! Christ, I'm homeless, not invisible!"

I gasped and jumped a foot in the air when the grungy figure near the sidewalk moved toward me. "I'm so sorry!" I cried before I could think. Then, as I tried to calm my rapidly beating heart, I told him, "I know you're not invisible, but I really didn't see you."

His hard eyes softened. "It's all right. I didn't mean to scare you. You got a little one there. Boy or girl?" He peered at Tom.

"Boy."

"He's a teeny one! How old?"

"A few weeks."

"Jesus Christ! What're you doin' out in this weather?"

"I've been in the house for three weeks. My mother's been here for two."

He laughed. "I see. You needed a little fresh air and a little get-away."

I dug for my wallet.

"You don't have to do that, miss. I don't want your money. I'm doin' all right." He held up his cup of ratty bills. "I got the shelter at night, my coat, my wits."

His wrinkled, leathery face grew distant for a second. "That's more 'n some out here..." He drifted off, and then his eyes sharpened, and he said, "It's really cold, and here comes the rent-a-cop. You'd better get that little bundle of yours inside."

As a square-shouldered security guard stalked toward us, the homeless man warned, "You be careful. Some folks out here aren't okay."

"What do you mean?"

"The weather makes it worse for some of us," the homeless man explained. "People get lonely, and scared of dyin' out here. Nobody sees them, like you didn't see me with your cart."

"I said I was sorry."

"I know you are. But before that cop gets here to chase me off, let me finish. Some of us homeless folk start out just like you. Nice home, nice job. And then they get sick, and they never get better. You know, 'cause they're sick in the head. Some from addictions, others, from no reason other than just because. And then their families don't want 'em, or can't keep track of 'em, and after a while, the sick people are on their own."

He hesitated, then turned to me and lowered his voice, like he was going to let me in on a secret. "Their names get lost. Their real names, not what we call them. Hell, I hang out with the likes of Dirty Pete, Hobo Jim, Nuke Girl, and Old Crystal. They have their stories. But after a while, sometimes they lose those, too." He nodded at me and bobbed his chin toward the security guard who now stood in front of us.

"You can't stay here, sir," the security guard said.

"Have a nice night, Miss." My acquaintance loped off across the street.

I hurried to my car and shivered while Tom pulled the strings out of the puff-ball on my hat that was sitting on top of the Cocoa Puffs.

Sleep deprivation did odd things to my perception. One night I awoke during the wee hours to Tom's hungry cries from the other room, and turned on the light by my bed.

When I sat up, my shadow didn't move.

I paused, at first thinking I was still asleep, locked within a dream. I rubbed the sand out of my eyes, and looked again. My shadow seemed to move back and forth, right at the peripheral edges of my sight. When I looked directly, it was a normal silhouette cast by the lamp light.

And then I noticed that the reflection in the mirror on top of my dresser also moved out of synch in my peripheral vision. It was still when I looked at it. My memory tugged at me; I had seen something like this before and was overwhelmed with a strong feeling of déjà vu.

And then I remembered the heart monitor in the labor room when I had delivered Tom. I slid off the bed and threw my sheet over the mirror. I swept through the hallway to the baby's room, grabbed Tom, and threw on the lights and the TV. Then I sat, feeding Tom and trembling until I fell asleep with him wrapped in my arms.

The alley was dirty, like a dozen alleys, like every alley. A lump of dingy clothes were piled in the corner nook next to a dumpster, almost buried under a blizzard drift. The lump had a smudged, pale face surrounded by an unraveling hat and shawl. Her delicate, frost-rimed eyelashes looked like dragonfly lace. Her eyes were closed, and her lips were parted and cracked. Her rough hands rested upon her chest. An empty cigarette package was barely discernible under the snow that was heaped upon parts of her body, and an empty lighter dangled from her fingers that were the colors of the Arctic sea.

I jerked awake. I had never seen Bill's Russian girl, but it was dream logic. *Let's just stick Darth Vader and Yoda in there and call it a day,* I thought. A groan escaped me as I stood up and trudged with Tom into his room as the watery light outside paled. He was still asleep and I was ready to fall over.

Maybe the dream affected me. Or maybe it was the homeless man I had met outside the grocery store who'd been dismissed by the security guard.

But I started volunteering at the Denver Rescue Mission in June. I sat at donations intake and sifted through an ocean of boxes, sorting piles of pants, shirts and other clothing articles. It was amazing the things people got rid of because they didn't have the time to barter on Ebay or hold a good old-fashioned garage sale. All hail the alley recycling system. I found a Chinese gong once, a set of skis, and a baby iguana in a full-sized tank, complete with the topping from a Big Mac that some kid probably figured it would eat. If I found it, it ended up here at the shelter. Jana, the operations manager, peered at the stuff and then at the door, on the other side of which was a legion waiting to receive my alley-finds when the doors opened.

"Seems like there's more every day," Jana said, nodding at the crowd.

"Economy," I said. That was a great explanation for everything these days.

She snorted. "Then how come even when the economy is booming, we still have hoards of homeless? You know that most of these folks have mental problems no matter what Wall Street is doing." She knew everybody there. She could tell you anything about anyone, and often did.

There was Hobo Jim. He was an old-fashioned boxcar hobo. He hopped trains. He had started out as the manager of a company, and then his wife died, the love of his life. Whatever had happened to her had destroyed him. From that point on, the material world had no interest for him. He lived day to day, enjoying the open sky and stars and the people he met. He was a gentle soul who wished every person he saw on the street a great day and really meant it. It was a good day for him if he saw you smile.

There was Old Crystal. No one knew how old he was. He loved the magic mushrooms, or had before meth had come along. Then he'd loved the meth for years that had seemed like hours to him. His teeth and skin were rotted from consuming the food of Faery. One night, after he had run out of his stash, the demon music faded and the dancers vanished. The powers the Queen had given him were gone and he lay alone, hacking with pneumonia in an abandoned house that he saw as a feasting hall. A cop had found him because of a complaint report and, instead of taking him to the station, had taken him to a hospital. He had been clean for a year, but still couldn't keep a job or a home. The fairies still followed him around corners, compelling him every second he was awake, offering him things he couldn't touch. And then, they laughed and cavorted in his dreams.

There was Patrick Reilly, the homeless man I had nearly run over with my cart outside the supermarket. Patrick Reilly, from Boston. That was his real name, and he insisted that others use it. He never talked about his past or his life. "What's done is done. Life goes on," he would say, gazing at you with eyes that could have been those of a twenty-year-old, or a sixty-year-old, or centuries older. But he always held onto his name.

And then there was Nuke Girl, or had been until last winter. Nuke Girl was the Russian woman Bill had told me about, and she had talked to animals and thought they talked back. She had gotten her moniker because she smoked like Chernobyl, and always offered a light. Jana suspected she had been smuggled here and then forced into the sex trade to pay her passage. Until she died, this had been the longest Nuke Girl had ever stayed in a place.

As I left the crowd to go pick up Tom, someone said that Old Crystal was in the hospital again. Patrick Reilly shook his head and spat near the scraggly base of a tree. "He likes them hospitals. Course, I would, too, if I was in his shape. He's falling to pieces."

"Do you think he'll be okay?" I asked.

"Hard to say. Every time he goes in we think he ain't coming out this time and he always does. Spent his life cheatin' death, that one."

I nodded and started to walk back to my car, but he grabbed my arm. "Give 'em their names back," Patrick Reilly said. "When they come to you. Those things."

His pale eyes pinned me, and I knew he wasn't talking about his companions. My blood went cold.

"How?"

He smiled. "Talk to them. Them things you see were people once." He disappeared into the food line.

In front of me is a young boy, dark-eyed, in a green tunic and pants. I know he is my son. But his eyes are distant and cold like the landscape around him. We're separated by mist and rain and everything is barren and muddy. He reaches into his bag for a drink of water, but when he holds it to his mouth, the dirty, yellow rain gets in and he pours it out. He keeps trying.

I call to him; he looks at me and doesn't answer. He makes sounds, but cannot speak, not even to tell me he's okay. He isn't. Around him, shifting through the air, are disturbing creatures cruel and alien, denizens of no genetic tree I ever saw on Earth.

I gasped as I woke. Great. The first of many nightmares I was sure I'd be having about my kid, not the least of which would be when he learned to drive. Then I'd never sleep again.

But now, still a baby, Tom had stopped feeding and looked at me. His eyes held none of the roaming lack of focus characteristic of infants. Old Crystal's story mixed with the nightmare of my son crawled through my mind. True Thomas cursed by the Faery Queen, who disappeared from the world of Men, to return when everyone he knew was gone. I cuddled my son as he made a reassuring burbling sound, and blew a bubble with his spit.

When Bill came home, I asked him if he had found any records of Old Crystal at the clinic or hospital.

He shook his head, eyes darting around the room. "I know you asked me to check. He wasn't my patient, but I know the doctor who treated him. And he told me that there are no records for anyone with his identity."

"What about medical charts?"

"Nothing."

"Could the computer have lost it?"

"At that place? It's possible. Their system is archaic."

"So it's like, what, three years old?"

He flashed a computer-geek grin. "Bite me, Neo-Luddite."

"Well, what else did he say about Old Crystal?"

Bill shrugged, apologetic. "Not much; his recollection of him was a bit hazy. Docs can get burned out at that hospital. Remember, they take everyone. Which means it's crowded and busy all the time."

A chill went up my spine in the arid heat. "Or maybe more than his file disappeared." And then I sighed as I sat down into a chair. "You look like shit."

His smile faded. "These guys at the clinic are really tragic. I saw a guy a couple weeks ago, complained of pain in his foot. Well, when we pulled his boot off, it came off with a sucking sound because his foot was rotten. And I don't mean he just had stinky toes. I mean he had gangrene that was never even seen, let alone treated. He lost his leg up to his knee. And he doesn't have the money for a prosthetic. We can get him a chair, but not much else."

He stared into space for a second.

"There's something I want to tell you..." I said slowly. "I've been seeing weird things."

He glanced at me warily. "Weird like what?"

"Like shadows, doing things they oughtn't." I told him what I had seen. Or thought I had seen.

"Listen," Bill said, "I'm a doctor, or at least an intern, and the laws of physics say that your shadow is just a silhouette in a light stream. And a mirror is just a coating of silver covered by glass. But things have gone wonky around here. I've seen those things too."

"Do you believe in ghosts?"

"Many Native Americans do. We know there are spirits."

"What about you?"

"Maybe," he said, "but I never believed that I would see one." He let out a nervous breath. "Well, what do you want to do about this?"

"Let's call your mom. You know, don't you have that Enemy Ghost Way?"

He burst into a laugh, and rolled his eyes. "That's Navajo. Wrong tribe."

"Does that matter for ghosts?"

"It does because Mom doesn't know how to do it. That's like asking an electrician to fix a water main. Do you know any Navajos?"

"No."

"Me neither."

I ran for the phone. There had been lovely calm for a few weeks, barring the routine feeding of Tom The Black Hole. The phone rang, and at first I thought it was a crank call. Panting was all I could hear for a couple seconds.

"Schmuck!" I yelled. "Move out of your Mommy's basement!" I almost hung up.

"Wait, you there?" Bill caught his breath.

"Bill? What's up?"

"Remember when you asked about Old Crystal's records?"

"Yeah."

"Well, there are others that I recalled. Their records have all vanished too, and they all have something in common. They all had trouble either remembering who they were, or some psychosis where they lost a chunk of time."

I shivered and said nothing.

"The Russian girl, you know, Nuke Girl, believed she was displaced in our century, and that she was pursued by an ancient weather figure. Old Crystal believed the fairies stole years of his life. Christ, I think there's probably more." His voice echoed on the connection. "But I can't report this, because there's no way to prove it. No one seems to remember the files, much less the people. I can't prove they existed. I don't know what to do."

The room was cold and my brain raced. How many of these people drifted through time, bumping into other people only occasionally in a brief moment of contact? They were dark figures flashing by on a corner holding signs for passersby. How long had some of them been there? Some of them had been there for years. Decades? And where did they go, and why didn't anyone besides Bill and I remember them?

But I said none of my thoughts out loud. "Please come home." I hung up.

It's started again. And now it has involved both of us. The shadows shift and move even when we stare straight at them. They reach for us and brush dark fingers toward our bodies, but never quite touch us. Sometimes they separate into multiples of shadows.

There are no mirrors in the house. Bill smashed them earlier and threw them away after his image in the cabinet mirror put its hands on the surface when he was brushing his teeth, as though it would come right through.

They never rest. Not for a second. The edges of the silhouettes are like bacteria in Brownian motion, cilia rippling. Bill calls in sick, and hasn't slept for days on top of the sleep deprivation he was already suffering. But we must stay alert.

I can't stay awake much longer, but I won't let them get to Tom. He's crying most of the time, unable to sleep because I always shift and jerk, and we won't set him down in his crib alone. I remember what happened to him in my dream, when he is older.

Finally, Bill gets that science-guy look on his face and runs to the garage. He drags every single lamp he can find into the large walk-in closet. Then he tosses everything in the closet out onto the main room floor. His hands are shaking with fatigue.

"If we use a smaller space with no obstacles, it will be easier to illuminate the place bright enough so that there won't be shadows. Dammit, that won't work! It would have to be directly overhead, and then it would only work if we never moved."

"What about total darkness?" As soon as the words leave my mouth we both shake our heads. Our fear of the dark has voted logic off the island. The only place that we aren't haunted by the shadows is in the closet.

I stockpile formula and diaper-changing stuff, ice packs and a cell phone, and hold Tom close as we sit against the wall in the closet. The retina-searing light banishes most of the shadows. We avoid looking at the ones that remain and simmer in the corners of our vision. We call Bill's mom, but she isn't answering.

After two hours, it becomes clear that our refuge isn't going to work. It's stifling in our small prison. It was ninety degrees in the house before we turned every lamp on in the suffocating closet. The funk of dirty diaper only adds to the lack of breathable air. Tom is sweating and crying again. Most of the formula is gone.

I say, "Give them back their names."

"What?" Bill's face is drawn. There are hollows under his eyes.

"Patrick Reilly said to give them back their names when they came to me."

"That's helpful. What the hell does that mean?"

"I don't know. I've tried talking to them, but they don't speak. Maybe I don't know how to listen to them, or maybe they don't even realize that I'm trying to listen. Maybe it's because they're used to no one hearing them, even when they were alive. And I don't know how we can name them if we don't know who they are."

"We can't stay in here with the baby like this."

"I know!" I yell. "But what else are we going to do? Now I know how Anne Frank felt."

"At least you could kill a Nazi."

The white, blind air is more and more putrid and hotter every minute. All three of us are soaked in sweat. Suddenly Tom stops sweating.

This is it. He needs water. We have to leave the closet. Now.

Bill and I look at each other.

I take a deep breath. "You said no one remembered Old Crystal. I think they don't even remember themselves. They've lost their names."

He reaches over and turns off the lights, all but one. The shadows come in, flood in from the corners and from under the door. There are dozens and they keep coming. The shadows crowd in, splitting and multiplying until they are legion, searching for someone to help them remember.

About Rachel Coles

Rachel Coles is a medical anthropologist living and working on public health in Denver, Colorado. She lives with her husband Adam and young daughter Rosa. She started writing horror stories because her daughter loves scary stories. Orphans of Lethe is dedicated to Rosa, and to Hobo Jim. http://www.rachelcoles.wordpress.com

BONFIRE NIGHT
by Chris Castle

They went to find the kite three days after the man was arrested. Until then, their parents had not allowed them back into the forest.

The kite's ribbon ran from the branches of a tree. The tail was red, decorated with small cloth triangles. The boy found it and pulled on his sister's shirt with one hand, pointing with the other. The two of them looked at it, and both silently understood that they would never give this discovery to the adults.

"He owned this kite," she said. She was aware that even though she whispered, her voice carried throughout the forest, just like the voices in the barn did. She sometimes sat in the barn's loft, up amongst the rafters and heard the men and women who met in secret there talking in whispers just as she was doing now. They feasted on the rumors, amongst their quiet, nervous laughter.

"He flew it on top of Bear Hill," she went on, and she enjoyed watching her brother pale, his skin sheen with sweat. "After each one, he flew it."

And right beyond the tree line, fireworks exploded into the sky. Somewhere close by, children sang 'remember, remember, the fifth of November.' The fire had not been lit, not yet, but the townsfolk were getting ready. She could feel it in the air, almost like a low, humming vibration.

"A kite," she said after a long while. "He made a kite out of *their* skin. He made the wood into the shape of a crucifix and then he sewed *their* faces right onto it." She looked over to her brother and saw him looking down into the dirt. She knew he was imagining dried red blood amongst the grains.

"He weaved the teeth into the trail to catch the wind better. Then he used *their* hair for the ribbons to make it glide. He really made it soar. The string he used was the same one that he finished *them* off with, around the throat." She touched her own neck without thinking. "If you held it up to the light, you could see it was red with blood, but otherwise you wouldn't be able to tell the difference."

"How do you know these things? You couldn't know!" His voice was high and cracking. He stared at her, the rims of his eyes red, like he was almost about to cry. She pointed upwards, to remind him of where she sat in the barn's roof sometimes. Once, she had led her brother up there and he had sat, opened-mouthed at the things he saw adults do, and the things they said when they thought no one was listening.

"All things flying," she said in a sing-song voice, knowing that the sweeter she made her voice, the sicker her brother would become. She could tell it was working, because her brother looked up to the sky, beyond the trail and past the tree line, trying to imagine the kite high in the air, the red of the material turning darker with other things.

Then the boy turned to study their find once again. "You don't know all these things," he repeated flatly, trying to keep his voice level to appear strong. He put his hands on his hips to steady himself, but he knew he wasn't strong at all.

"You don't know that I don't," she said calmly, undercutting her brother's bravado with a sense of fact, or even boredom. She watched him swallow down her words, and then she was about to say something else and was surprised when nothing came out.

Overhead there were more explosions; and through the trees they could see the flickers of dying rockets. Something screeched without exploding and made him flinch. There were not all that many trees to block their view of the events taking place in the town.

They stared at each other until she made a sudden movement; with a gentleness that surprised him, she pulled the kite from the branch, leaving it to softly drop at her feet. The boy waited for her to scoop it up into her hands, but instead she edged away, until she was further from it than him. The boy stepped forward and seized it in both hands, surprised at how eager he was to claim it.

"Check your fingers," she said, looking down from his face to his hands. Without thinking, he looked to the tips of each one, waiting to see if any of them were blemished red. There was nothing to see, save for the smile that grew and grew on her lips. Slowly, she licked each one of her fingertips, just to make him squirm even more before her. He clutched the kite to his chest and looked back to the town.

"We should get back. It'll be starting soon," she said to her brother, and he looked over to her and nodded. The humming in the air had risen, crackling the way the sky did just before a storm. The town's children had stopped singing, although there was still something like a murmur in the air. The pitch was different now, lower, and she realized it was the adults making the noise; not singing, not quite, but something like it; was it chanting? It was something like the ethereal sounds when they made love or whispered a secret. She knew it should have scared her, hearing grown-ups acting not quite as they should, but instead it excited her. It gave her the same sensations she experienced in the barn when voices slipped away into grunts and the speech broke away into pants of need.

"Are you ready to see?" she asked her brother, genuinely curious for his answer. It was the one thing she didn't know about him. For a long second he stood still, looking to her, then coughed gently.

"I'm ready," the boy finally said, and he clutched the malevolent kite to his chest, as if to prove the point. And so the two of them began the walk back to the town. The forest ran out almost immediately and soon they were on the path.

The kite grew heavy in his hands because he kept his fists clenched and his breathing grew labored. She listened to his wheezing until she could stand it no longer and seized the thing off him. He wanted to object, but he couldn't summon up his voice.

She taunted her brother with the sight of the kite now in her capable hands and flaunted how easily she walked with it. But something else too; she wondered if the sounds her little brother made were close to what *they* had made underneath the killer at the end. What sounds had *their* throats made just before he had drawn the kite string down over *them*? She wondered if what she heard was close to dying.

They reached the end of the path and stepped into the town. Everywhere was filled with hazy smoke now, fireworks either roaring into life or dying out on the ground around them. As she stepped through the mists, she became aware of a fire being lit, the crackle of the torches being brought into life. The earth was upside down; the ground was covered in clouds while the sky burned bright. She smiled at the feeling of confusion this brought, smiled so hard she almost burst out laughing. This is what chaos feels like, she thought happily, looking all around and seeing her brother's hands shake by his side amongst all the confusion.

She made out the shadow figures of the adults, all of them making their way to the barn where she saw them come alive at night. The first torch exploded into life, becoming a beacon for the rest to follow; slowly the shadows fell into a sort of order behind the fire and the townspeople marched into the barn. She followed them in, her brother by the door, so she could see just enough of what was about to happen. Some of the adults stepped out of the shadows, as if to shoo them away; and then they saw the kite in her hands, but they knew that she kept their secrets and so they looked away, pretending to ignore what she held as best as they could.

The man was at the center of the barn, tied to the cross with straw at his feet. His mouth was gagged, but he was not trying to scream. Instead, he simply looked from one face to the next, taking them all in. There was dried blood on his forehead, one eye was blackened and swollen, and his ear was torn. The sheriff had spent three days with him and had left his mark.

The sister looked around amongst the mists to see who was now in the barn for justice: the sheriff was there, as was the judge, all of those who had sat in that cold, grey room to bring forth a sentence, and so were all of *their* families.

The man who held the torch made his way to the heart of the barn. Three others stepped into the center, each clutching torches. The first torch-man turned and carefully lit each oiled rag that was stuffed into the kindling wood, the flames making the expression on the condemned man's face clearer. As the killer on the crucifix bit down on the gag, every twitch was clear to see, even as the fires kept the crowd hidden in the half-light.

The chanting of the adults grew louder, almost drowning out the noise of the explosions outside. It was as if the whole town was ready to ignite, the sister thought, her heart racing.

Finally three townspeople crept forward, each of them adding their torch to the kindling, building the blaze. They stood back, as if to give the rest of them a better view, but then one lunged forward again, jamming his torch into the gagged mouth of the killer. He was pulled away by the other two, the crowd dissenting, wanting to see the murderer suffer and burn. The gag burned, so the man looked as if he breathed fire, but it did not spread over the rest of his face. Instead, even as his tongue burnt away, his eyes stayed open and wide, still looking from one adult to the next.

Trying to remember *them*, to find some sort of sorrow from the depths of her being, the sister could not go there in her mind, so she was unable to stifle her excitement which was almost growing into a form of ecstasy. She was not able to hide the smile on her face, even as the smell of the burning flesh began to carry out into the air, overwhelming even the heavy fumes of the smoke.

The entire town watched as one as the killer burned alive. Around the edges of the flames were the adults; moths, the sister thought, like moths around a reading lamp. She gripped the kite tighter, feeling the tautness of the material underneath her fingertips. She listened to the sound of the kite as she ran her nails along it, over and over, until it started to weaken and fray.

The killer's body moved and convulsed, as each part of it was eaten up by the fire. The twitching came soon after, as if at the very end, he was trying to shake the fire off his bones like an itch that could not quite be scratched. But all the while, the sister noticed, his head did not move, even as his body writhed. Instead he stayed a witness, not only to his own death, but also to see the faces of his executioners, until, at last, the flames moved over his skull and ended him.

She stepped out of the barn and into the town, aware that her brother was still following her. The fireworks still crackled into life, but there were fewer now; the noise not as great. The adults began to leave the barn, knowing that soon the mists would fade and they would no longer be protected by anonymity. They streamed out all around her, bustling against her, some of them coughing and clearing their throats. None of them spoke, the murmurs dying away, so there were only the explosions of the sky and the crackling of the body inside.

No longer paying attention to the shadow adults around her, the sister began to unfurl the kite. She ran it into the breeze, until it hoisted into the air. When it was good and high, she handed the sting to her brother. He took it without a word; he was pale now and changed forever by what he had seen and she knew it.

He looked over to her and the question of what was in her other hand formed in his eyes, but not on his lips. Instead, the boy silently drew the kite in, raveling the string back into a ball as the kite descended from the sky until it fell back to earth, and he retrieved it. She leaned over and then threw what was in her hand onto the center of the red kite. She smeared it in with her fingers, so it was good and ground in. Then she took hold of it, stepping away from her brother and instantly forgetting him.

She launched the kite back into the air, watching it soar as the last firework of the night flashed around it and made it visible. Then there was silence all over the town, as she watched the kite soar higher and higher, and above the trail of sparks that still shined, the color of the kite was different now and somehow brighter for it.

About Chris Castle

Chris Castle is English, but works in Greece as a teacher. He has been accepted over 150 times in the last year and a half, ranging from sci-fi to horror to straight drama. He has also been published in several end-of-year anthologies. He is currently beginning work on his forth book. His influences include Stephen King, Ray Carver and PT Anderson. He is also working on a poetry collection.

THE PRODUCT
by Bruce Memblatt

"He was the one I was supposed to spend my life with. We'd planned on getting married. There were so many plans."

She raised her head. She glanced at the clock on the wall and sighed. "He had an apartment right on the corner of Fifty-Second and Lexington Avenue. There's a new white piano sitting in the living room. A white piano, imagine? But he played like a mad genius. I used to sit and intently listen. I dug him, his fingers, his hair, the view; there was a knockout view. Why am I talking about the Goddamned view? And the Goddamned piano."

Her hands shook as she looked down toward the floor, afraid she would lose control and sob out the intense anguish she felt.

"You can stop there, Robin," Clinger interrupted. "Are you sure this is what you want? At DMG, we can't bring Shane back. All we can do is to create a close replica. You can call it an illusion, but it won't be *him*, do you understand that? We can't recreate his *soul*. Can you live with an illusion? That's the question you have to ask yourself."

Can you live with an illusion? The words opened like a row of umbrellas in her mind. Could she? Then again, could she live without Shane for another year, another week, another second? No, the grief she was feeling was too unbearable; she couldn't stand another moment of this pain.

She felt angry at the salesman. Here was Clinger across from her, sitting smugly at his desk. What did he know about the pain of loss? Clinger probably had his wife to go home to at the end of his day; a wife who was alive and well.

But at least Clinger was telling her that she could have something *like* Shane; it would be something *like* the life they were going to have had they been able to get married and live in the apartment with the view and the piano. Wasn't *anything* better than what she had now?

Now Clinger was telling her that there were dangers. He wanted her to sign a waiver. She could get lost in the illusion, adapt too completely and forget he wasn't Shane, but a creation designed and manufactured specifically for her, to her specifications; an illusion just the same. Still, wasn't life an illusion anyway? *No,* she thought, *life isn't an illusion, not to those who live it.*

On the other hand, would recreating Shane be living her life, or would it be hiding in a memory instead? This was all too deep and she just wasn't able to think straight since Shane died; she only knew that she wanted him back.

Suddenly *An Idea:* she wouldn't call him Shane. She'd find another name, one that felt artificial. One that would be a constant reminder that the product *was* artificial; it wasn't Shane. Yes, she'd call him *Product.*

And then she was sure she knew what she was doing. "I want this. I'm sure. Can it begin?"

"It's already begun," Clinger said as he folded his hands over his desktop. "In a sense, I mean, it began when you called us. You've already given us all the details of Shane's life, and so we have put his total experience, as best as we could, into a file in our lab. There's more to do, of course, and most are things you need not know, but there are other things you *should* know. For example, we'll be using a sample of his DNA in his model."

"Model?" she questioned.

"Yes, we call them models. They're not clones; they're manufactured from a composite of organic and non-organic materials. One thing you should also know; he won't age, but we can make him look older as time goes on if you like. Every few years, we can upgrade him for you. That is optional, there's no need to think about that now, of course; you have plenty of time." Wow. That was something she hadn't thought about: time. And what would happen, say, five years from now, or twenty? What if she had a change of heart at some point? If it turned out badly, could she just dispose of the *Product*? Would she want to? Too many crazy possibilities for one afternoon and she hadn't even considered about sex.

He seemed to read her thoughts. "If you want more time, there's no need to rush into this," Clinger said. "We know this is an investment in both your money and your emotions, and we want all of our clients to be happy in both areas."

She clenched her fists. She smiled forcefully. "I only know one thing for sure. I want Shane back."

"Well, then, if you're absolutely certain, let me tell you how it's going to go. In about two weeks, maybe three, you'll receive a phone call. The call will come the day before Shane arrives, to prepare you.

You won't pick up Shane. What will happen is he will come home to you just like it was an ordinary day, like nothing happened. He will know where he lives."

"So, I am supposed to meet him at his apartment?"

"We know you are on the lease because you were planning to move in. We know you have been making the payments on the apartment since Shane, well, passed."

"That's right. I couldn't let it go...it was...Shane's." She thought Clinger would understand. She couldn't part with anything of Shane's.

Clinger continued, "It will be best if you don't make too much of a fuss when he comes home. Try to be as natural and as calm as possible. It will take some time for you to adjust to each other and to your new life."

Like an ordinary day? It would be the most unordinary ordinary day she could envision. Natural and calm weren't her forte. With all the crazy new technologies out there, the world must be coming to an end anyway. *Surprising,* she thought, *Clinger's office at DMG doesn't look like anything special, nothing futuristic; just an ordinary office.* DMG looked quite traditional. No sliding steel doors or crystalline tubes like she'd imagined.

"So what happens now?"

"Now you wait, and if we need anything else, we'll contact you."

"I guess this is it, then," she said, standing from the chair.

"If you're certain. I'm sorry, but part of my job is to try to convince you not to do it. At DMG we want you to be absolutely certain, because once it is done, there is no going back. This is a radical decision."

"I'm certain," she said. She grabbed her coat and Clinger walked her to the door.

She cleaned the apartment from top to bottom. She filled her days with expectations, and her spirits were lifted with the idea that her grief would end soon. She paid special attention to the brand new piano she had just bought, and she imagined Shane's long, tapered fingers touching the ivories.

In reflection, it was funny how her life had changed since she'd met Shane; a metamorphosis, like a whirlwind...fantastical. She hadn't even known him that long, but she knew he was the one the moment she met him seven months ago down at a little club called Marie's. She had stopped in for a quick drink, and there was Shane at the piano. Imagine, if she had worked overtime that day like she normally did, she wouldn't have had time for a drink, and if not, would they have ever met?

The new piano was the one change she made in the apartment; she had bought a new piano, a white piano, right before she received the news of his death. Shane had never seen her present to him.

She remembered the day before he died when he got on that small plane, he had sold his piano. He needed the money. She had offered him money. He wouldn't take it. He had told her he'd get a new piano when he could and not to sweat it. Come to think of it, funny, she didn't really know him all that well. Well, not as well as she could have, like she wanted to if they only had more time. Now they'd have all that time. It was waiting just days away. The bell would ring and he'd walk through the door again. Well, *he* wasn't going to step through the door, but he would, in a way. Don't forget it's not him, it's something like him, don't forget, a *Product*.

The bell rang. What? Who could it be? It couldn't be Shane. Wasn't Clinger supposed to call the day before if it was Shane? A small voice whispered in her mind, *This is not going according to plan.*

She quickly looked in the mirror in the foyer and told herself, "I am insane." Her stomach pulled in as she took a deep breath and opened the door.

And there he was. He looked like he had always looked as he stepped through the door, like he did so many times before, but this time it was no ordinary walk through the door. What to say? There was nothing to say. She looked in his eyes and saw recognition. It swept her away. She almost cried. She almost smiled. It was almost Shane.

And then she realized that Clinger probably did call, that he must have called on her cell phone; she remembered it was the cell phone number she had given him. When was the last time she had charged her cell phone? Why, the batteries had probably been dead for days.

*Dead.....*no, not dead; cell phone batteries could be recharged.

"Shane," she heard herself stutter, and all plans to call him *Product* went out the window. "I mean…"

"I know."

"But…you're so..."

"Like me?"

"It's not you, is it, Shane...but it is." She kissed him on the cheek and held his hand. His eyes were still blue; his hair was still black, his smile was still Shane's smile. It was incredible. "Is it okay? I have to know is it okay that I did this, Shane? I had to have you back."

"I can feel myself, yet I can't. Can we sit down?"

They walked over to the small sofa in the living room. As they walked past the mirror in the foyer, she caught a glimpse of Shane and her together and she smiled. The rug under the sofa creased slightly as they sat down. She turned to him and said, "I didn't expect you to be so aware, I mean, I didn't know *what* to expect, exactly. In my mind I didn't think that you'd know what happened, but you are really *in* there."

He pulled away from her and looked toward the window, like an answer that was falling through the air. "The last thing I remember is the flames. The plane must have burst into flames. I remember the heat. It was so intense. I remember the smoke, and I remember dying. I know I died and then suddenly I'm back here and alive, but not really. I'm sort of confused."

"They must have told you something at DMG," she said, reaching for his hand.

"DMG? If you know what I'm trying to say, then you'd know I feel as if it all had happened to someone else," he said and he turned toward her, searching her eyes intently for a moment before he drew his head down.

She felt an insane need to bare her soul. "Shane, look at me. I was going to call you *Product*, to remind myself you weren't really Shane so I wouldn't forget the real you and get lost in an illusion. But this isn't an illusion; you're alive. I am so happy we're together again! Aren't you happy, Shane?"

If she could take all the moments of her life and wrap them into a ball, this would be the most tenuous thread, the one that could make her life unravel. It seemed everything hung on the simplest of questions.

He slowly began to stand. He gazed across the room. "Maybe I'm *not* happy. I guess I'm not sure."

"But..."

"Robin," he told her, "give me some time to get used to all of this; to try to connect myself, to try to feel like one being. It's strange; I feel like I'm trying to eat my way out of a marshmallow."

She didn't believe him about his happiness. Of course he was happy. Right now he was unsure, but she would fix that. "Do you see the piano? I got you a new piano!"

He stepped around the room silently. She watched him. Grudgingly, it seemed, he stood in front of the piano and plucked out a few notes. His hand fell uneasily over the keys. "Happiness isn't even on the plate now. It's just not that simple. Tell me..." he said as he turned away from the new white piano and walked backed to the sofa, "How did you find out I died? You must have been..."

He sat down.

"I was devastated," Robin said, putting her arm around his shoulder. She looked toward the television on the far side of the room. "I came home and I turned on the news. I didn't expect to hear from you until the morning. Anyhow, I was putting my coat away and I heard a story come over the air about a plane crash. You hear so much tragedy you don't pay attention, you know, the words seem to fall over you like petals, but when the reporter mentioned Syracuse I suddenly turned and stared at the TV. Just at that very moment the phone rang, a call from the airline."

There was something in the way he turned his head down after he heard the story that made her heart feel like it was breaking. Wait a minute, this was supposed to *stop* her heart from breaking. This was supposed to end her heartache.

Again she heard that small voice whispering in her mind, *This is not going according to plan.*

He put his hand out, just touching the top of her knee. "You must have been shaken. I'm sorry; I just wish I could feel you." Suddenly his hand pulled away and he said, "The funeral?"

He stood back up, restless, and continued speaking as he walked purposefully back to the piano. "It just occurred to me: the funeral. I must have had a funeral?"

Her hands shook as she watched him sit down at the piano. "Yes, you had a funeral," she told him almost matter-of-factly, and she reached for her purse. She pulled out a small newspaper clipping and placed it down on the coffee table. "Your obituary is here if you want to look at it."

He ignored the clipping, and wouldn't look at her as he plucked out a note on the keys. "So did I have a nice turn-out?"

"Not bad, we didn't tell your mother, she couldn't handle it; she isn't aware of anything anymore anyway. Your sister came...your brother. Ted came, you know, the usual suspects." She sighed at her bad joke and she fell back into the sofa. At that moment Shane began to play a melody. His hands gradually appeared more confident as he fingered the keys.

"What is it that you're playing?"

He turned from the piano, his hand still pressing the keys, and he looked back at Robin with a curious smile like it was caught between a laugh and a cry. "It's an old Duke Ellington tune called *I Don't Get Around Much Anymore.* Quite appropriate, don't you think?"

She didn't like how this was going, but again she was determined to fix it. She would pretend her mood was light. "At least you still have your sense of humor," she grinned while she pushed a strand of hair out of her eyes.

But his face turned sour. "You don't understand, Robin!" he cried and his voice grew louder. "I can't feel the notes. I can't feel the music."

He began to yell. "It's like I'm a machine!" He smashed his hands down on the keys. A harsh chord followed. "I was an artist, a poet, a musician. And what am I now?"

She vaulted off the couch and stood next to him. Suddenly frightened, she reached for his hand and he abruptly pulled away. "Give it time!" she pleaded. Hadn't the salesman at DMG told her that things would take time? Or had he said that they *had* time? Wasn't Clinger telling her that they had years together, she and Shane? She and this *Product*?

Ready for anything and prepared for nothing, she looked at him. What had she done*? It will get easier in time,* she told herself. *It must. The thing that matters is we're back together, so I'll just keep repeating that thought in my head and that will make it right.*

He turned sharply toward her and said, "My grave, I must be buried somewhere, right? A headstone? Do I have a headstone, a plot?"

All the things she didn't think of when she had imagined their first moments back together. She shuddered. "My god, Shane, can't we talk about today instead? Or about our future?"

"I think I have a right to know these things," he said.

It felt bizarre mouthing the words, but she told him, "You're buried out on Long Island."

"Long Island?"

"I had you buried in my family's plot. We were going to get married. So I thought...I just wanted you near me always. Your sister told me it would be all right. She knew how much I loved...love you," Robin said as she stepped toward the window and looked down at the traffic below. Here was the view she had always cherished. The cars looked like toys from the thirtieth floor.

It was then that he grasped her shoulder and she shuddered from the unexpectedness of it. "I want to see it," Shane said. "I want to go there. Take me there."

"What? Take you where?"

"Please."

"I don't understand."

"Neither do I. I just want to see my grave. Take me to my grave."

They stood in silence by the window for what seemed like hours while the sun set over the city.

And that night Robin still found herself alone, still without him, because Shane slept on the couch. But she made sure to recharge her cell phone. Dead things really *could* be brought back to life, and not just cell phone batteries.

In the morning they made their way down to the car. Robin glanced at the gas pedal before she threw the car in gear; it would be a two-hour drive to Shane's grave. She turned and watched him sitting next to her.

He just stared out the window. She wondered if seeing his grave would fix him, fix *them*, and she stepped on the gas. The morning mist quickly dissipated from the window as the sun hit the car directly when they pulled into traffic.

She turned onto the Fifty-Ninth Street Bridge. "Look, it's going to be a beautiful day. Why don't we do something else instead? It's not too late."

"Not too late? Robin, I'm thinking of it as some sort of closure."

She thought what an odd word to use, *closure*. The word closure was an ending. Wasn't this a beginning? This was supposed to be a beginning.

And they drove in silence.

When they pulled up to the cemetery, Shane was still silent. *Silent as the grave*, she thought, and then she felt superstitious at the idea. They parked on a small road across the street from the cemetery and they walked across it. She tried to hold his hand, but he turned away.

As they traveled through the gate, the road turned to dirt. On either side, in front, behind them, everywhere they could see, lay rows and rows of headstones guarded by neatly trimmed hedges and perfectly pinched grass. The sun was brilliant, warming their faces with the promise of life.

She was about to tell him that she felt the promise of life when she realized they had traveled right in front of Shane's grave. What came out of her mouth wasn't anything like she was originally going to say. "Here you are, Shane, this is what you wanted to see." She pointed toward his headstone.

She didn't like any of this. What was he doing? Why did he drag her here? Hadn't she already been here, on that terrible day of his funeral, through the pain, grief, and disbelief that the funeral home was lowering the box that imprisoned him, lowering him into the dirt to be forgotten and discarded like he had never mattered to her?

He stood for a moment silently, apprehensively, and then he slowly began to read the writing on his stone aloud. "Here lies Shane Mathew, born July 17, 2011...died November 21, 2037. I am dead."

No! She couldn't listen to that! She turned to him and whispered, "But you're not, Shane, you're back."

"No. I'm not back. Just a broken fragment of me is back, because you're so selfish."

She was stunned. "What?"

His eyes grew intense. "You couldn't let me rest in peace, could you? You had to have me back to keep *you* happy, no matter what. It's all about you, isn't it, Robin?"

She fiercely tugged on his arm and said, "I love you, Shane! I couldn't live a life without you!"

He shook her off. "This is no life, Robin! This is Hell, Robin, *Hell*. God might forgive you for this, but I don't. You still don't realize what you've done."

"What do you mean, what I've done? We can be together now, forever! You and me."

"Listen to me," his voice cried so loudly it could have shaken the trees. "I am *not back!* I can't feel myself. I'm a mind encased in a plastic body. I can't feel my hands, I can't feel anything. I can't taste, or feel or smell anything. I can't feel you. Do you understand? You have sentenced me to a future more painful than the fires of Hell. Forever, I will sense things, but I won't be able to touch them, or feel them. Like a constant torture, the world will always be just within my reach, but I will never be able to fully grasp it. I am dead, Robin, I am dead and awake and aware of my death. I am buried alive. I hate you."

"I can fix things!" she cried while tears began to run down her cheeks.

"Don't you want to know why I got on that plane in the first place?" he screamed at her. "I was leaving you!"

Quickly, he reached for her and he pulled her down over his grave. She struggled, but his weight was too heavy. He pinned her down and sat on her chest, and then he firmly wrapped his hands around her throat.

"I am going to squeeze the life out of you," he told her as he held her down. "You're going to die on my grave. The grave you stole from me."

She struggled for air. How could this be happening?

Suddenly her cell phone rang from inside her purse. It broke the spell.

Shane released his grip on her neck and moved off of her. Just as suddenly she felt his weight leaving her body, she rolled, facing the ground, and reached inside her purse. Whoever was calling, she would ask for help.

Strangely enough she heard Clinger's voice on the line, like a rescue.

"Robin," he told her, "we're sending Shane over tomorrow."

"What? What are you talking about?" she gasped. "You already sent him…and he's wrong! He tried to hurt me!"

She could hear that Clinger was still talking, but she realized that she was suddenly alone. She moved the cell phone away from her ear. Where was Shane? Where did he go?

Frantically, she looked around, and her head swerved in every conceivable direction. Headstone after headstone shone like white ruins, but she couldn't see Shane anywhere. The phone dangled from her hand as she lay back down upon the earth. He'd vanished. Oh God, had it all been a dream? No! A nightmare.

She sat up and paused for a moment and tried to catch her breath. Slowly she drew the phone back toward her mouth and said, "Clinger, I've changed my mind."

About Bruce Memblatt

Bruce Memblatt is a native New Yorker and has studied Business Administration at Pace University. In addition to writing, he runs a website devoted to theater composer Stephen Sondheim, which he's lovingly maintained since 1996.

His stories have been featured in such magazines as *Aphelion, Bewildering Stories, Bending Spoons, Strange Weird and Wonderful, Static Movement, Danse Macabre, The Piker Press, A Golden Place, Eastown Fiction, Short Story Me!, 69 Flavors of Paranoia, Necrology Shorts, Suspense Magazine, Gypsy Shadow, Black Lantern, Death Head Grin, The Cynic Online, The Feathertale Review* and *Yellow Mama.*

In addition, Bruce writes a bi-monthly series for *The Piker Press* based on his short story "Dinner with Henry." The first installment appeared in March of 2010. http://sjsondheim.com/blog1

OUIJA
by Cheryl Kaye Tardif

Last spring, while packing away my aunt's belongings at her lakeside cottage, I discovered this letter in a box of old party games...

February 13

To Whom It May Concern:

If you found this letter, it means I'm dead.
DEAD!
Plain and simple.
And if I'm dead, it's not by natural causes, I can assure you. I'm writing in haste cause I know I don't got much time.
It's after me!
What, you're asking. Well, I'll tell you.

It all started with that gawdforbidden Ouija board. The board that my best friend and I found in her attic.
Liza and I had been friends and neighbors for more than forty-five years. We even buried our husbands within two years of each other. And no, we didn't bury them in the backyard.
Let me make somethin' clear, first off. I'm not crazy. I'm of sound mind. Maybe not sound body though. I'm not crazy and neither was Liza. I'm as sane as you, whoever is reading this, and what I'm about to tell you is true. TRUE! Not one word is a lie.
My phone rang a few nights ago.
"Liza," I said. "It's three o'clock in the gawddamn morning!"
"You gotta come over, Sharon. Quick!"
"Why do I have to come over now? Can't it wait until morning?"
There was silence.
I sat up in bed and turned on my lamp. "Liza, you there?"

"I hear voices," she whispered. "There's someone in my attic."

Liza sounded scared, more scared than I ever heard her before, and her voice gave me a chill up my spine.

"Maybe you should call the police," I said.

"No, it's not *that* kind of voice."

Aw crap! There was only one other kind of voice that Liza heard. Ghost voices.

"Be right over," I said.

Liza had been hearing ghost voices all her life. She heard when little Jimmy Barton called from Mr. Porter's well. The police found his body the next day. Jimmy had somehow fallen in and drowned...three days before. Liza also heard Mrs. Morgensteen calling to her one night to let her cats outside. When my friend got to the old lady's door, she could smell something rank and awful. The police found Mrs. Morgensteen dead on the floor. The newspapers said she had been dead almost a week.

Anyways, I have to tell you this so's you can see I'm telling the truth. So you'll believe me when I tell you what happened next.

After Liza called, I dressed quickly then stepped outside. There was a full moon and a fog had settled over our lane. I remember thinking how strange the weather was.

Ghost weather.

Crossing the street, I walked down the sidewalk to the corner. Liza lived less than a block from me. When I got to my friend's house, I saw her lights were out. Everything was black. The least she could'a done was put the porch light on for me. So in the glow of the moon I crept up toward her front door, not knowing if I should ring the bell or walk right in.

The door opened with a groaning creak and I jumped.

"Don't scare me like that!" I hissed, then stood with my mouth open.

Liza Plummer, from 1842 Walker Lane off Aurora Lake, looked like death warmed over. My friend's thin gray hair was a mess, her eyes were sunken in like she hadn't slept in a month and she was wearing her natty old housecoat, the one she refused to throw away.

Liza's a packrat. Can't let go of anything.

"It's coming from the attic," she whimpered.

We closed the front door and made our way upstairs. In the ceiling of the hallway there was a trap door. That's how you got to her attic. Using a broom, we hooked the rope handle and pulled it toward us. The trap door opened and—lo and behold—a set of steps appeared, ending almost two feet off the ground.

Now Liza and I, we aren't in the prime of life anymore. She's 58 and I'm 61. So getting up the first step took a bit of trying. Liza refused to go ahead of me, so I put my foot in her hands and she boosted me to the first step. Then I leaned down and hauled her up behind me. A few minutes later, we were up and poking our heads into the pitch-black attic.

"Dont'cha got a light in here?" I asked her.

She reached into her housecoat pocket and then passed me something. "Use this."

I flicked on the flashlight and we held our breath, waiting for the light to reveal some hidden evil, some specter from the past. We didn't see nothing except cardboard boxes piled in one corner and an old, empty picture frame leaning against the wall.

The floor was lined with boards and I tested one with my foot. "Can we walk on these?"

Liza nodded and clamped her hand on my arm, her fingernails digging into my skin as I took a step forward. I kicked at one of the boxes and it slid to the floor with a crash. Its contents tumbled out. Monopoly, Snakes & Ladders, Yahtzee and some other games.

"For crying out loud," I huffed. "There's nothing here. No voices."

"B-but I heard something up here," she said. "I swear I did."

"Well, there's those Poker chips you was looking for last month."

Liza swallowed hard. "How'd they get here? I'm never in my attic."

I rolled my eyes at her, thinking that maybe she came up to her attic lots of times. Maybe she just didn't remember. She'd been having a lot of memory lapses lately. Some days I wondered if she was suffering from Old Timer's Disease.

"Nothing here," I sighed, patting her on the shoulder.

It was when we were putting the games back in the box that we *did* find something.

A Ouija board.

"It's eeee-vil," Liza said, refusing to touch it.

I scowled. "What'cha mean, evil?"

"It's the devil's board game."

When Liza said this, the attic grew colder than the cemetery in the middle of February. I looked down at the Ouija board, then picked it up. It appeared harmless enough. Wasn't too heavy either. I don't know what got into me, but all of a sudden I was overcome by curiosity.

"I wanna see it," I said stubbornly.

I took the game downstairs, much to Liza's dismay, and put the box on the scratched coffee table. I turned on a lamp then pulled out the board and set it on the table. Tipping the box, I watched a small piece of wood tumble to the floor.

"What's this for?"

Liza explained how you rest your fingers on the wood and ask the spirits a question. She told me that the spirits would push the piece of wood and spell out the answers on the board. I thought, this I gotta see. But Liza wanted nothing to do with it. So me being a good friend and all promised to make her favorite carrot cake if she played the game with me.

We put our fingers on the wood and stared into each other's eyes.

"What should we ask it?" Liza's voice trembled with fear.

"Who are you, Great Spirit?" I asked in a spooky voice.

I tried hard not to laugh at the horrified expression on my friend's face while we waited for an answer. Nothing happened. I was gonna take my hand off when all of a sudden the piece of wood shot out from beneath my fingers.

N.

"Liza," I scolded. "You pushed it."

My friend shook her head, her face whiter than bleached cotton.

I rested my fingers back on the wood and we waited again. We were mesmerized when it moved across to the *A*.

NA.

Then it moved to the *T*. Then the *A* again.

NATA.

Liza leaned forward. "You think it's Natalie Brown from down the road? You know, the lady who died last Sunday."

I shook my head. "Dunno. Let's ask it another question instead."

Me and my big mouth.

I asked the board if it had a message for us. When we read it, Liza and I gasped. Then we shoved the board into the box and stuffed it under the couch.

You're probably wondering what the Ouija board said.

It said: *DEATH BOBBY T.*

Bobby Truman was the only Bobby T. we knew. And the very next day, he was hit by a train when his truck stalled in the crossing. He was only eighteen years old when he died.

The day after that, Liza phoned me and said we had to get rid of the Ouija board. She couldn't have anything that evil in her house. So I met her on the corner and we took the board to the dumpster behind the laundromat and left it there. That was that!

Or so we thought.

Later that night I got a phone call. Liza was hysterical. "Come over, quick!"

When I got to my friend's house, I saw that every light was on.

"What's going on?" I asked when she pushed me into her living room.

And then I saw it.

Right there, in the middle of the coffee table, was the Ouija board.

"Jesus Murphy!" I muttered. "Why'd ya go back and get it?"

Liza swore up and down that she never went back for that board. It had just showed up on her table after suppertime. It still smelled like garbage and laundry soap.

"We have to find out what it wants," I told her. "Then maybe it'll leave you alone."

When we asked, the board came back with...*DEATH SERENA U.*

Serena Underhill was a girl I taught piano to. She was only 16.

I stared down at the board, then said to Liza, "Pack it up."

We left her house just after eight. She was holding a plastic bag with the board in it. She held it out in front with her fingertips as if she was holding fresh dog crap. We walked four blocks down to Ling's Noodle House and shoved the bag into a trashcan just before the garbage truck came. We stood there and watched as all the trash was compacted.

The next day Serena Underhill drowned in Mears Creek.

And by suppertime the Ouija board was back on Liza's table, reeking of sesame oil.

Now I know what you're thinking. You're thinking that Liza went out and got back that board. I admit it. I was thinking the same thing. So when she called me that night, I went over and got the board. Then I took the bus to the ocean by myself. I walked along the boardwalk on the water's edge and flung that Ouija board out as far as I could. I waited while it was dragged out to sea and I stayed there until I saw that gawddamn board sink into the ocean.

Half an hour later, I got home and found Liza sobbing on my front porch. In her hands she held a sopping wet Ouija board.

Oh my Jesus, and all that's above! I was more than shocked. For the first time in my life I was deathly afraid.

Realizing that we had no choice, we sat at my kitchen table with the board between us.

"What on God's green earth do you want?" I yelled.

My fingers tingled as the wood slowly slid across the board.

U.

I thought of Ursula Bigelow or Ugene Pierce.

The wood stayed where it was.

"U?" Liza moaned. "What does that mean?"

We waited for the board to spell more, but the wood didn't move.

Liza bit her lip. "We asked what it wants. I-I think it wants us."

Suddenly the room vibrated and we heard a wicked laugh echo through the house. We snatched back our hands and watched the wood race around the board.

LIZASHAR—

"We gotta get rid of this thing," I said.

"We tried that!" Liza cried. "But it just keeps coming back."

When I glanced at the fireplace in my living room, I got an idea. We built us a fire and when it was blazing hot we fed it pieces of the box.

"Put another log on the fire," I sang bitterly, tossing the wood piece into the flames.

Together we threw the Ouija board into the fire and watched as it slowly crumpled on the edges. When it ignited, we let out a sigh of relief. Me and Liza stayed there, arm in arm, watching the letters slowly fry until the board turned to ashes. And then the smell hit us. The stench of rot and decay was awful—like an Easter egg long forgotten after Easter.

That was the night before last.

Yesterday morning, I found Liza on her front lawn—dead of a broken neck. Beside her lay the Ouija board with one small scorch mark on its edge.

The sky is blood-red over the lake and the air tastes like death.

I have to hurry. I don't think I got much time left. The board said both of us, so I know it's coming for me next. I'm so afraid, but I have to try to get rid of this thing one last time and I have to let everyone know the truth. I was the one who opened Pandora's Box. I'm the one who needs to close it.

Just so it's clear, Liza and I tried throwing the Ouija board in a dumpster and a trashcan. I threw it in the ocean and when that didn't work, we both watched it burn in the fireplace. Each and every time, the gawdawful evil thing ended up back at Liza's.

Then again, Liza never could throw anything away. A pack rat. That's what she was.

And my best friend.

I'm writing this letter and watching the Ouija board burn. This time I soaked it in lighter fluid, and when it's done burning I'm gonna take the ashes and bury them by the lake.

When we asked it that first night what its name was, we should have waited. Actually, we never should have asked in the first place.

NATA—

I know now that only one other letter was missing and that if I held a mirror to it, the word would read backward—the devil of all evils. *SATAN!*

He's coming for me. I can feel it in my bones. It's all my fault. I was curious. And you know what they say about curiosity.

I have to get these ashes to the lake.

Be back later...I hope.

Sharon Kaye

On February 13th, my aunt Sharon was found lying near Aurora Lake, her gaping eyes frozen in fear and her hands blistered and burnt. The coroner said she drowned. But I think something else killed her—something insidious and older than time.

While packing away my aunt's belongings at her lakeside cottage, I discovered this letter in a box of old party games. Curious, I read the letter and then reached into the box, pulling out something damp and slightly scorched. A OUIJA board.

You know what they say about curiosity...

About Cheryl Kaye Tardif

Cheryl Kaye Tardif is a bestselling, award-winning, Vancouver-born suspense author now residing in Edmonton, AB. All of her works touch on some element of suspense or mystery, with an emotional hook.

Her novels include: *Divine Justice, Children of the Fog, Whale Song, The River*, and *Divine Intervention*. She's also the author of these new releases: *Remote Control*, a novelette, and *Skeletons in the Closet & Other Creepy Stories*, a collection of suspense/horror stories.

In 2004, Cheryl was nominated for the Lieutenant Governor of Alberta Arts Award. In 2006, she was a contestant on *A Total Write-Off!*, a reality TV game show. In 2009, she placed in the semi-finals of Dorchester Publishing's "Next Best Cellar" contest with her romantic suspense *Lancelot's Lady*, which is written under the pen name of Cherish D'Angelo. In 2010, *Lancelot's Lady* won an Editor's Choice Award from Textnovel.

A full-time writer, Cheryl has presented at many events. She has been featured on TV and radio, and in newspapers and magazines across Canada and the USA.

When asked what she does, Cheryl replies: "I kill people off for a living." http://www.cherylktardif.com

Waiting Near
Joseph Patrick McFarlane

Fragments
Thomas Bossert

FRY DAY
by Melanie Tem

My daughter Rachel always loved carnivals, and she'd have been delighted by this one. A seedy, smelly, gaudy, two-truck affair, it set up last Saturday in the little park near our house. I'm sure they don't have a permit. I'm sure they're violating all kinds of ordinances, not to mention the boundaries of good taste. Rachel would have been charmed by all that.

There are more people here than I expected. A lot of people I know—neighbors, the day clerk from the 7-11, the relief mail carrier. I don't know many of their names anymore, but I remember their faces and most of their stories. This one's husband was killed in a car accident. That one is dying of cancer of the prostate, liver, bowel. I hardly believe in their sorrow, and it angers me to have it presented as though it mattered, as though it gives us something in common. None of them lost Rachel.

That one, passing now in front of me, has never had anything bad happen in her life, a story that seems far more plausible to me than the others, easier to accept. I smile at her and raise a hand in greeting. She waves back. Her bouquet of balloons both obscures and magnifies her face.

Unlike many children, Rachel never was afraid of clowns or barkers, the Ferris Wheel or the Tilt-a-Whirl or the roller coaster, speed or height or centrifugal force or things that are not what they seem. The world for her was a good place, and only going to get better.

Which is why, thirteen-and-a-half years ago at the age of twenty-one, she died. Brian James Dempsey killed her.

Killed and raped her, I remind myself diligently; it seems especially important to be precise tonight. Killed and raped and mutilated her. Along with, depending on which theory you subscribe to, fourteen or thirty-seven or a hundred other pretty young women with long dark hair.

A clown skips by. The orange yarn of his wig is unraveling and he's lost the middle button of his polka-dot blouse so that you can see the gray hair and the gray sweatshirt underneath. He bows elaborately to me and I bow back, laughing a little, a little bit scared.

Unless there's another stay, which at this point doesn't seem likely, Brian Dempsey will die in the Florida electric chair at five o'clock tomorrow morning, our time, for the only murder they've been able to convict him of. Not Rachel's.

At the end booth is a fortune-teller. She's dressed, of course, like a cartoon gypsy—bangles on her wrists and ankles, a black lace shawl over her head. Maybe she really is a gypsy. Maybe she really is a fortune-teller, come to this.

She's reading the palm of Mrs. McCutheon, who used to babysit for me when Rachel was a baby. Foolishly, I wonder if the gypsy could have foretold Rachel's death, or the death of Mrs. McCutheon's daughter, Libby, a grown woman with a husband and children, of a heart attack two years ago. I wonder if now she can see whether Brian Dempsey really will die tomorrow morning, and how it is that I could have lived after my daughter's death, and how I will go on living after her murderer's execution.

When Mrs. McCutheon gets up from the fortune teller's table, she is crying. Her tears offend me, whether they're for me or for herself. She doesn't know me at first; we haven't seen each other in a long time, and I've changed. When she realizes who I am, she gasps, "Oh, hello, dear," and looks at me as if she thinks she should say more. But I don't encourage her. Especially tonight, my grief is too good to share. Finally, Mrs. McCutheon just shakes her head and goes off down the midway.

The gypsy mistakes my hesitation for interest. "Come and see into your fu-tah!" she cries in a hoarse, heavy accent. "Fortunes, one dollah only!"

"I can already see into my future," I tell her, "Thanks anyway." She shrugs and turns to another, likelier prospect. I went to a medium once in those first desperate weeks after Rachel died, but I knew before I went that the woman would be a fake.

When the execution date was finally set, I called the governor's office to ask if I could come and watch. Be a witness to Brian Dempsey's extermination. Bear witness to what he did to my daughter, what he did to me. But Florida allows only official visitors at its executions. The woman on the phone sounded very young, younger than Rachel would be now, and she hardly gave me the time of day.

I couldn't stay home alone tonight counting the hours. I tried to find out what his last meal would be, but they won't release that information till tomorrow, so I fixed for myself what I thought he might have: a hamburger, French fries, baked beans. He'll talk to his mother tonight. He'll dream. I couldn't stay home alone, trying to imagine all that, so I walked over here. It seems a fitting place for a vigil. Rachel loved carnivals, and this tacky little traveling sideshow will stay open all night.

"Hey, lady, win a dancing bear!" calls a barker in a dirty red-and-white striped shirt from under a tattered red awning. "Flip the switch and it dances, just like Brian Dempsey!"

The plywood counter in front of him is crowded with the chintzy gadgets. The midway lights make him and them and me, I suppose, look ghoulish. The toys are about the size of my clenched fists, and they make a tinny whirring sound when you turn them on. Actually, they look more like slightly melted human beings than like bears. All around me people are clapping, hooting, laughing appreciatively. I appreciate the gag, too. I laugh, too.

"Three chances to win for just one dollar, lady! Take home a souvenir of this great day in history to your kids and grandkids!"

Rachel was my only child, so all my grandchildren died with her. A few years afterward, when there were still no real suspects in her murder, but serial killer Brian Dempsey had just started making the news, a young man I'd never heard of called me one afternoon from California. His voice breaking, he told me he'd been in love with my daughter and planned to marry her. Now he was married to someone else and his wife was expecting their first baby. If it was a girl, they wanted to name her Rachel.

I don't know why he called me. For my blessing, maybe; my permission, at least. I had none to give. I have no interest since Rachel died in other people's happiness, or in their pain.

I wait in the short line to pay the man my dollar. He takes it with a practiced gesture much like palming, and he doesn't look at my face or react to the condition of my hand. Probably he's seen worse. He offers me the bucket of multicolored balls and I take three. It doesn't matter which three, and it doesn't matter how I throw them, since the game is, of course, rigged.

I come close on two of my throws, but don't hit anything. I've lost most of my dexterity and grip; my thumbs scarcely oppose anymore. The tall kid next to me wins. I can't remember his name, but he's been living in foster homes since his mother shot his father and then herself when he was five or six. I wonder what he's doing here, how he dares be seen in public. His bear writhes and hops in his hands. Someone in the crowd yells, "Hey, Brian, it won't be long now!" and, briefly, I feel as if I've won something after all.

Over and over I've imagined what must have happened. At first I could hardly stand it, but I told myself I owed it to her; if she could go through it, the least I could do was think about it. So I've read everything that's ever been written about him watched the TV movie four times, seen interviews, studied psychological theories about sociopaths. For a long time now, imagining in detail what must have happened to my daughter Rachel has been a daily habit; those are the first thoughts in my head when I wake up if I've been able to sleep, and they give me energy and reason to face the day.

Speed and height and centrifugal force, and things that aren't what they seem. He'd have been quick—quick-thinking, quick with his hands and his words, though probably not quick, the experts have said, with his killing. Quick with his handsome smile. Even after all these years on Death Row, he has a quick and handsome smile. His approach to her that early, snowy morning thirteen-and-a-half years ago—his offer of a ride to the bus stop, his thermos of steaming coffee—would have seemed to her an innocuous little adventure in a thoroughly adventurous world.

While he drove her into the mountains, he'd have kept up his patter, his pleasant jokes, his intelligent observations. Once she realized she was in terrible danger, she'd have thought of me. I was on my way to work by then, worried about a committee report that wasn't done. Things are not what they seem; she was already dead before I even knew she was missing.

That isn't going to happen to me this time. I'm going to know the exact moment Brian James Dempsey dies. I'm going to be wide awake and cheering. Then, I don't know what I'll do.

He didn't take her very far into the mountains. The roads were snow-packed, and he wouldn't have wanted to risk an accident. He dumped her nude body into the shaft of an abandoned silver mine just outside Idaho Springs; they didn't find it until nine weeks later. Most of his other victims, the ones he killed in summer, he buried; I suppose the ground was too frozen for him to bury Rachel, or maybe he'd forgotten his gloves.

The crowd is thinning. I'm approaching the end of this improvised midway; beyond it is the rest of the park, and the darkened houses of people with their own tragedies. Here's a guy swallowing fire. I watch him for a while and can't see the trick. His throat and lungs and chest must burn, like mine. I have a fleeting image of him setting all those houses on fire, one by one by one.

I check my watch, wind it. If the guy who flips the switch isn't late to work or the governor's heart doesn't start bleeding again at the last minute, Brian James Dempsey will be dead in five hours and ten minutes. Noticing a vague pain, I raise chilled fingers to loosen my lower lip from under my canine teeth. There's blood, but not much. I wipe it on my jacket, and nobody will notice.

This booth sells cotton candy. I'm one of a handful of customers. The kid behind the counter has an enormous "Fryin' Brian" button pinned to the bill of his cap and an empty sleeve. As he hands me a large cone and then change, his glance inadvertently cuts across my face, and he does an obvious double-take. But this is a traveling sideshow, after all, and it's nearly midnight; he probably sees all manner of strange and deformed creatures.

"Where'd you get the pin?" I ask him. It's one I don't have.

He doesn't hear me because he's already saying very loudly, not exactly to me, but to the whole little crowd of us, "Hey, didja hear that Brian Dempsey didn't know tomorrow was Tuesday?"

One of the teenage girls behind me, who have been blatantly flirting with him, yells back as if this were a rehearsed routine, "No! Why?"

"Because he thought it was Fry Day!"

The girls shriek with laughter. I laugh, too, and wave the gaudy blue cotton candy as if it were a pompon. As I turn away from the counter toward the end of the midway, I think deliberately about those three pretty girls and the young man behind the counter, and I imagine in quick detail how he might lure them away from the carnival tonight, kill and rape and mutilate them. The fantasy calms me a little. The cotton candy sticks like clots of hair to my teeth.

There's even a freakshow. I thought freakshows were illegal. I walk slowly past the tents and cages lined up across the end of the midway, staring at everything.

Siamese twin girls joined at the top of the head. Both of them stare back at me and give little shrieks, as if I frighten them. I stand in front of their tent for a long time, probably longer than my quarter entitles me to, savoring their distress and my own.

A boy with fur all over his face and body. Wolf Boy, one sign declares. Dog Boy, says another. He's sitting in an armchair reading *Time* magazine by the display light over his head, taking no notice at all of me. I long to be in there with him, to have my arms around his hairy neck, my teeth at his throat. I'd make him notice. I'd make us both a display. I'd make the world acknowledge this awful thing that has ruined my life. But others must have had the same impulse, because bars and mesh make a cage around the Wolf/Dog Boy, protecting him from me.

A Two-Headed Calf, asleep in its straw, all four eyes closed. A Fat Lady whose flesh oozes toward me as if it had a life and a purpose of its own. A woman with six fingers on each hand; since otherwise she looks quite ordinary, she makes sure you notice her deformity by leaning far forward on her stool and pressing her hands against the screen that shields her from anything other than the stares and words of the audience. The palms and all twelve fingers have hatch marks on them from the screen.

Rachel would have hated this part of the carnival. People being unkind to each other; people exploiting their own misfortunes. Thinking of her disapproval, I start to turn away. Then fury at her propels me back. Rachel is dead. She let herself be killed, raped, mutilated. She brought this horror into my life and will make it stay forever. I owe her nothing.

But there's nothing more to see. I've come to the end of the freakshow already. It must be hard to staff these days, when people accept so much. Reluctantly, I move away from the almost-silent row of tents and cages toward the carousel on the other side of the midway.

The carousel is unstable. I watch it make a couple of rotations, remembering Rachel in pigtails on a pink horse, and the platform is noticeably lopsided and rickety. The same two or three bars of its tune are endlessly repeating, as if the tape is stuck. The old man who apparently runs the ride is asleep on his bench, legs stretched out in front of him, arms folded crookedly across his belly. At first I think he might be dead, but then I hear him snoring. The painted animals go around and around, up and down, without anybody on them.

I step over the old man's feet and duck under the rope. When my chance comes, I leap up onto the merry-go-round. It creaks and tilts under my weight.

I prowl among the animals. There are no pets here, no horses or noble St. Bernards, only lions with teeth-lined gaping mouths, giant cats perpetually stiff-tailed and ready to pounce, snakes with coils piled higher than my waist and fangs dripping venom as peeling yellow paint.

The three variations—lion, tiger, snake—are repeated to fill up the little merry-go-round with perhaps a dozen wooden animals to ride. I've seen them all. I sit down near the edge of the platform and, with curved upraised arms and crossed legs, make another place where somebody could ride. A child, maybe. A pretty little girl. Her parents would let her on this ride because, unlike the teetering Ferris Wheel at the other end of the midway or the roller coaster whose scaffolding is obviously listing, it would not seem dangerous. She would spot me right away and curious about what sort of animal I was supposed to be, she would come and sit in my lap. After a few rotations, a few stuck bars of the music, I would tighten my arms and legs around her until neither of us could breathe, and I'd never let her go.

"Fifty cents for the ride, lady," comes the stern, cracked voice.

Dirty hands on gaunt hips, the old man glares at me as his carousel takes me slowly past him, but he doesn't stop it. Maybe the control is stuck, so that it will only stop if it's dismantled. I get awkwardly to my knee, leaning into the turning motion and fishing in my hip pocket. On my next trip around, I hand him an assortment of nickels and dimes.

"See here," he says, and with unsettling agility leaps up beside me. "You missed the best one."

I can feel my nostrils flare at his odors: coffee, cigarettes, alcohol, dirt and cold sweat. Under the ragged jacket, his new-looking bright blue sweatshirt reads: *burn Brian burn.*

He takes my forearm in his horny fingers and leads me toward the center pole, which is unevenly striped and nowhere near vertical. With his other hand, he points. "There now, ain't she a beauty? Made her myself." Seeing at once what it is, I catch my breath.

A heavy wooden chair, tall as my head and wide as my shoulders, sturdy and polished, its surfaces reflecting the carnival lights. Leather straps across the back, seat, arms; shiny metal buckles. On the plank between the front legs, two inverted metal cones: electrodes. The cord, snaking so cleverly away that you have to look closely to see that it isn't plugged in. I prefer to pretend that it is.

"Gettin' a lot of business this week," the old man says with satisfaction. "Just like I thought."

Thrilled, I'm almost afraid to ask, "May I try it?"

He squints at me in a caricature of shrewdness. "Fifty cents extra."

I pay him without argument and take my place in the chair. The old man straps me in—one thong too tight across my breasts, another too low across my abdomen. He's just finished fastening the sharp buckles at my wrists when I notice that his jacket pockets are stuffed with trinkets, tiny replicas of this chair. "Wait," I say breathlessly. "Those are wonderful."

He chuckles and extracts a glittering handful. "Special shipment direct from Florida. Quarter apiece."

"I'll take them all."

He peers at me. I can tell that this is the first time he's noticed my face, but he doesn't seem particularly interested.

"All? Must be a couple hundred here. Wasn't such a hot item as I thought. Might be some market for 'em tomorrow, after— "

"He killed my daughter." Killed and raped and...

There is a pause. We've made a complete rotation together, although here near the center it's harder to feel the motion. The magician across the way is still trying to get his frayed scarves untangled. "Well," the old man says, "I guess you're entitled."

"Yes."

"Let's say twenty cents apiece since it's quantity. Forty bucks."

"The money's in my back pocket." I manage to lift my hip off the seat of the electric chair long enough for him to slide his hand in and out of my pocket. I have no idea how much he takes. It doesn't matter. He empties his pockets of all the little electric chairs and piles them on the platform at my feet.

"Enjoy the ride," he tells me. He's leaning close over me, and my head is secured so that I can't avoid his rancid breath. He could avoid mine, as most people do, but he doesn't seem to mind. He's grinning. So am I. "Not much business this late, so you can stay on as long as you like."

Absurdly grateful, I try to nod my thanks, forgetting for the moment that my head won't move. He hasn't shaved my head, of course, but I can easily imagine that for myself. When I try to speak, my voice cracks and growls. He waves a twisted hand at me as if he knows what I want to say. Then he makes his way expertly among the silent and forever raging beasts and off the carousel, out of my restricted line of vision.

I'm alone. I can't see my watch anymore, but it must be nearing one o'clock. Brian Dempsey will die in a chair like this in four hours. The carousel keeps turning; before long, even its jerks and bumps have melded into a somnolent pattern.

I'm in my house, in my back yard filled with flowers. Rachel loved flowers. Under the rose arbor is a chair, so polished it glows, so sturdy I know it has rooted to my garden. In it is tied a handsome young man. He's crying. They're going to execute him.

I go to him, kneel, smell the roses, put my arms around him. His body stiffens as if he would pull away from me if he could. I look at his face and see that he's afraid of me, and I know that he has reason to be. I hold him. I can feel his heartbeat, the pulse in his temple. The executioner is approaching, from the back door of my house, a whole parade of executioners each wearing a party hat and swallowing fire. They're going to kill him. I'm not trying to stop it. I just want to comfort him. I hold him close and am suffused with sorrow for us all.

I wake up enraged. I've been betrayed by my own dreams. It's still pitch dark. I'm aware of a steady rotation, and of music that is scarcely music anymore, and of lights, and of hands at my wrists and under my arms. "Wake up, lady," says the voice of the old man, not, I think, for the first time. "It's time."

"Oh. God, what time is it?"

"It's five o'clock."

Then from all up and down the midway comes a ragged cheer, and the triumphant cry of "Brian Dempsey is dead!" I imagine the Siamese twins saying it to each other, the Wolf Boy snarling it through bared teeth, the fire swallower spitting it up. I say it, too: "Brian Dempsey is dead!" Saying those words makes me tremble as though an electric shock has gone through me, although I don't recognize them coming out of my mouth and I hardly know what it means.

The old man is staring at me. He's not frightened, and he's certainly not surprised, but he can't seem quite to take in what he's seeing. I raise my hands to my face, but neither my face nor my hands are there anymore in any recognizable form.

He lifts me out of the chair. I can hardly walk; I stumble over the scattered trinkets as if they were bits of bone. My spine has bent at a sharp angle; my feet hurt too much to bear my weight.

The old man picks me up in his arms, finds places finally to hold onto my body. He steps off the still-turning platform of the carousel, and without effort takes me the short distance to the end of the midway to the row of tents and cages that make up the freakshow.

Next to the Two-Headed Calf, on the very edge of the carnival where the park leads to other people's houses, a cage is empty, except for a chair like the one I dreamed in. The old man drops me into it, but doesn't bother to strap me down. He leaves, clangs the door shut behind him, but doesn't lock it.

An early-morning line of watchers and revelers, celebrating the execution, is already starting to form outside my cage. They've come to see what I've turned into, what Brian Dempsey has made me, what they all can turn into if they try.

About Melanie Tem

Melanie Tem's chronicles of the terrors that haunt families and the amazing resilience of the human spirit have collected a Bram Stoker award, a British Fantasy Award, and praise both here and abroad. Stephen King said of her first novel, *Prodigal*, "Spectacular, far better than anything by new writers in the hardcover field." Dan Simmons declared it "A cry from the very heart of the heart of darkness... Melanie Tem may well be the literary successor to Shirley Jackson." David Morrell called her ghost novel *Revenant*, "Hauntingly beautiful.

Achingly on target." And of *Black River*, her latest novel published by Headline in England, the British critics said, "Fascinating, overwhelming, compelling... Melanie Tem is one hell of a writer." (SFX) "One of the most resonant, moving novels of recent year...a near-masterpiece." (Darlington Northern Echo) You can visit Melanie Tem at: http://www.m-s-tem.com

THE CHAMBER
by David Landrum

Talaith felt hunger pull at her stomach as she kneaded bread. The grain bin was low; it was three months to harvest, and the wheat had hardly grown past a man's knee for lack of rain. She puffed, sweating with the effort, knowing that the loaf taking shape under her hands would be made to last all week—and she would not get much of it. Her brothers and father would get the most. She and her mother would get what was left, and usually that was hardly anything at all.

Of course, she thought, her father and brothers had to work the fields and that meant they needed to be strong. The women, on the other hand, could be allowed to suffer.

Talaith had lost weight. Her last menstrual cycle came a week late, and when it did come she only bled for one day. If this continued, she thought, grunting and sweating as she pushed the dough down, gathered it, and pushed it down again, she might not be able to have children. She frowned at the unfairness of it. Only women were starved. Only women did without while the men had enough. And only women, she reflected, a shudder passing over her, were sacrificed.

People had been talking about it. It had not rained for two months, and many whispered that Artemis, the goddess to whom the village was dedicated, was angry. The priestess sacrificed; the people brought gifts as well. Twice the entire village gathered to pray for mercy. Silence from heaven answered. No rain came, and the people feared the worst.

A small room stood to the left side of the image of Artemis in the temple. No one spoke of it out loud, but everyone knew what it was. When women did speak of it, it was always in whispers, and they called it "the chamber." It had not been used for forty-five years. Now, some people said, it would have to be used again.

The elderly women remembered the famine back then and how the priestess cast lots and chose a girl named Kora. The young girl Kora was dressed in white, dedicated to the goddess, and placed in the tiny, airtight room. The villagers sealed the seams of the door with wax, all the time weeping and praying that the goddess would accept their offering and spare their village. Women who served as acolytes that night said that though Kora initially went bravely and willingly, later they heard her scream, plead, and pound on the door when the air in the room was gone and she began to suffocate. In the morning, they said, her body was as blue as the sea on a sunny day. The rains had come that afternoon.

Talaith finished kneading, covered the bread with a cloth, and put it on a windowsill in the sun. She stood by, guarding it. People stole. She had heard reports of rising dough taken from doorsteps and out of kitchens. These were desperate times.

Her stomach ached. She thought of pinching off some raw dough and eating it, but knew she could not do such a thing. Besides, her older brother Pythius always brought her something. He said anger shook him every time their father cut her a portion only a third the size of what everyone else got. Once when the boys speared a fish and her father said she would get none of it, Pythius gave his entire portion to her in front of the whole family. She offered to split it with him. He took one bite and told her to eat the rest. Her father had beaten them both for that offense.

She waited, keeping an eye on the bread. She heard footsteps and saw her mother come through the door. She smiled to welcome the visit, but then she saw the look on her mother's face and felt a chill wrack her body. Talaith realized that the Chief Priestess and the Head Man of the Village Council were both standing beside her mother.

Talaith froze. She suddenly understood what this meant, and as she tried to stand, her legs failed to support her weight and she collapsed to the floor in a swoon.

The full moon blazed in the sky. The priestess had dressed her in a garment made of lamb's wool that no one else had worn and only virgins had touched. The midwife had examined her to confirm she was a virgin and qualified to be an attendant of the chaste Artemis. Talaith stood as the priestess Modthryth anointed her forehead and put a heavy gold tiara on her head. She smiled a grim smile.

"Talaith, it is an honor to be given to the goddess," Modthryth said.

But Talaith did not feel gratitude. "Why do I have to die?"

"You were chosen after much prayer and the casting of lots."

"The rain falls from clouds, not from idols," Taliath cried.

Modthryth frowned. "Do not blaspheme. You may anger the goddess. Do you want everyone in our village to die? Better one should die than all perish."

"Some people are saying that rain is caused from moisture in the clouds," Talaith said, startled at the boldness of her own reply.

Anger flashed in the priestess's eyes. "How dare you speak so in the very temple of the goddess?" she said. "You may bring a curse on us all."

Talaith fell silent. She had been taught to fear the goddess, but she could not entirely push away the anger that smoldered in a corner of her heart. Younger people had other explanations about rain, but the elders would never listen. Which was real and which was not? Who was right? Her very life depended upon who was right.

"We want the curse to lift," Modthryth said, her face barely concealing the gloating cruelty she seemed to feel about having the power of death over someone she made defenseless. "That is why you will be given as an offering. The rain will come when you are given over."

Talaith was desperate to reason with the priestess. "My brother Pythius says rain comes when the vapor from the sun draws up from the sea and becomes too heavy for the sky, and so it falls back to the earth."

"Pythius sat at the feet of a philosopher who corrupted his mind. It is not wise to share these beliefs. You may offend the goddess and she may destroy your soul in Tartarus. Artemis is a stern and merciless immortal."

Talaith knew the legends about Artemis. The goddess could be cruel and vengeful. The priestess was correct, though, about where her brother got his new ideas. After Pythius studied a year with Heraclitus of Ionia, he ceased to believe in the gods—at least as they were presented in traditional myths and stories. During winter, when he did not have to work in the fields, he would tell her what his teacher had said. She listened as she carded wool or churned milk. His words struck fear in her, but at the same time she felt fascination and longed to hear more. A frightening thought occurred to her that moment: what he had whispered about the cruelty and capriciousness of the villagers had its ultimate proof in this sacrifice of her life.

The priestess's subaltern came in the door and nodded. This meant the full moon was at its zenith. Modthryth turned to Talaith. "It is time. Do you have anything to say before you are delivered to the goddess?"

She considered blaspheming, cursing Artemis, or spitting on the priestess; and then she considered begging, falling on the floor and pleading for her life. She decided it would be pointless to do either thing. So instead she decided her last words would be brave ones. "If truly she is a goddess," Talaith said, her voice clear, "Artemis will spare my life. If she is kind and good, as she requires us to be, she will have no other choice."

Modthryth stared at her in astonishment. After a moment, she recovered. "Your words will be the destruction of your soul."

She chanted a prayer, anointed Talaith's head with perfumed oil, and opened the door to the chamber.

The room was about four feet square. In the center sat a throne that looked to be carved out of solid stone. The ceiling was tall.

The priestess told Talaith to sit. She obeyed, taking her place on the roughly hewn throne. Above the lintel stood a bas-relief image of Artemis: ceramic, pale in its coloration, its design ancient. It looked down on her with the coldness of stone—like the coldness in the priestess's gaze. Modthryth positioned herself in the doorway as if to block any attempt Talaith might make to escape.

"Blessings on you, Talaith, daughter of Polybius," she intoned. "Soon you will be in the presence of the goddess. Keep your eyes on her image. It is said that just before you depart your body and your spirit goes to join Artemis the Chaste, the face of her image will glow with light."

She stood a moment, face blank but full of determined maliciousness, and then stepped back. The door creaked shut. Darkness closed over Talaith, though she fancied she saw a faint glow on the face of the icon.

She looked around. She could see nothing in the darkened chamber. She tried to sit still to use as little air as possible. Then she thought how it did not matter. She heard noises and realized they were sealing the spaces around the door with wax. However little air she breathed, soon it would be gone and she would die—no way around it and no getting out.

A tremor of fear ran through her. Artemis, she had been taught, saw and heard all. Though often kind and gentle, she also had a cruel side. She had killed Orion and turned Acteon into a stag so his own hunting dogs tore him to pieces. Would the goddess really be offended at Talaith's lack of submission and condemn her soul to the tortures of Tartarus, as the priestess had said? Should she repent and plead for mercy?

Now unsure and afraid, Talaith considered asking forgiveness, but the thoughts her brother had put into her head would not leave. Pythius had said the stories about Aretmis weren't true. Higher beings would be higher in their sentiments and ethics, he had told her, not just in their experience of time and physicality. She looked up at the image of Artemis. The glow on its face seemed stronger. Or did she only imagine this? Would the goddess send wrath to her or mercy? Which was it to be?

In the silence, she could hear her stomach growling from two days of fasting. Was there any way out? No, she knew that the room was secure because no one had even bothered to tie her up. She waited and tried to remember more of what Pythius had said, but it was hard to think. She was afraid, hungry, and exhausted. She concentrated, trying to pull his words from the store of her memory. His words mingled with the prayers she had memorized and praise and doubt became a confused muddle in her mind.

Soon she became aware of pressure on her chest. She wondered for a moment what was happening, but then she realized that her lungs were laboring to get her breath. *Do not panic,* she told herself, *that will only make my body gasp harder for the air that is so precious and so limited.* Despite herself, she began panting like an animal. The air in the room was diminishing.

She looked around desperately. The icon's face...was it glowing? By the gods, was it true what the priestess had said about Artemis? Was her brother the one who was wrong? The visage slightly illuminated the interior of the chamber. Talaith could see the bricks and arms of the chair. She felt faint. Her legs throbbed and she gasped desperately, panic seizing her.

She stood up and staggered toward the door. She doubled up her fists to pound on it, but then, with a massive effort of her will, restrained herself. No. She would not beg. What good would it do? Whether this was a murder for the sake of religion or a holy sacrifice, she wanted to die with dignity; it was all she had left.

She staggered back to the chair. Her ears buzzed and her arms convulsed. Feeling dull, stupid, heavy, she gasped and wheezed, trying to breathe. The icon's face glowed brighter. A miracle, just as the priestess had said. The colors of the image blurred as she gazed up at it. The pain in her chest grew excruciating.

But then she realized something.

The moon was shining behind the icon of Artemis. No, that was not quite right; the moon was shining through Artemis!

Was that why the goddess glowed? Of course! They only held sacrifices on nights of a full moon.

When this thought crossed her weakening consciousness, she realized, in a flash, what caused the phenomenon. The goddess did not appear at the moment of death to claim the spirit leaving the body. The icon reflected moonlight that shone down on the temple. And to reflect it, it had to be open to the moon on the other side.

That was why the ceiling in here was higher than the rest of the temple.

And if the icon could be illumined by moonlight, it could not be very thick.

She felt herself fading. Breathing in tortured gasps, she desperately looked around for something to throw—a loose stone, a part of the chair. She could see nothing. There was nothing to throw. There was nothing!

She had figured out the truth, and she had figured out how to save herself, but she was going to die anyway. It was too late to find something to throw at the icon; she was out of air and so she was out of options.

She heard glass break. How had that happened? How had the icon shattered, when she had not been able to find anything to break it with? As those final questions entered her mind, Talaith lost consciousness.

She opened her eyes. The room glowed brightly with moonlight. Cool air flowed over her. She sat up. Was she in heaven, on Mount Olympus, in the dwelling place of Artemis? No. She was still in the sacrificial chamber!

And that meant she was still alive.

She felt a hand lift her up, but she was still too groggy to comprehend her new situation clearly. She gasped for air, and the freshness of a cool night breeze entered her lungs, reviving her. Rising to her feet, steadying herself against the stone chair, Talaith saw the shattered image of the goddess. The stars and the full moon gleamed through the opening of the broken face of Artemis.

Finally able to think, Talaith turned to see who was standing beside her in the chamber. Who had risked the wrath of the entire village to help a mere woman, a lowly member of society?

"We need to get out of this chamber," Pythius told her. "In fact, we have to leave the village entirely."

Talaith understood the implications of her brother's words. She may have escaped death from the chamber, but now the villagers would want to kill them both as revenge for such a drastic breach of protocol. Neither of them could go home. "Where can we go?"

She felt something hit her back. Cold and heavy, it made her jump. Something hit her again; it was wet. She realized it was a rain drop. Huge and cold, the rain drops began falling all around her. Her arms went to gooseflesh as the rain began to soak the garment she wore. Raising her eyes, she did not see the moon, but silvery grey clouds. Sprays of rain poured through the broken image of Artemis.

She heard scraping sounds. They were pulling the wax out of the opening. The door would swing open in a few minutes. "They're coming!" she cried. "The priestess thinks I am dead, so she is opening the chamber! She can't see you here! Pythius, save yourself. Hide! I'll take responsibility. I'll tell them that I alone broke the goddess!"

"I don't want to leave you," Pythius said.

"You must!" Talaith insisted. "You must, so that you can let the truth of science be told to future generations. We must end the useless slaughter of young women in this village. Tell them, Pythius, tell them! Tell the villagers that it rained without the goddess, for the goddess is broken. She is dead."

She pushed her brother through the broken opening at Artemis's head from which he had come. Within seconds Pythius was gone.

Suddenly she chose a course of action. It might not work; the people of her village might think it an even greater cause to kill her, but she saw no other hope. Talaith bent down, picked up a sharp fragment from the broken icon, and slashed at her dress. She could hear them more clearly now. The door opened a crack. She finished trimming her dress. She wished she was not barefoot, but had her boots. Thunder rolled and the ferocity of the rain increased. Reaching back, she untied her hair and let it fall over her shoulders. She put the tiara back on her head and stood up, trying to look fearless.

The door to the chamber swung open.

Talaith looked out at the crowd, which had expected to see her lifeless, suffocated body. Instead they saw her alive, standing tall. She had trimmed her dress so it was above her knees and revealed the curves of thighs. She had untied her hair so it hung on her shoulders. Talaith had made herself look the way Artemis was depicted in statues and images.

She waited, wondering what their reaction would be. They might think this a blasphemy, rush on her and tear her to pieces. She remembered how cruel and unbending the priestess could be. She waited, trembling inwardly, trying to look serene and unafraid.

The people of the village gasped, screamed, and shouted. Several women fainted. The priestess gaped. Talaith stepped forward, and a number of the villagers fell prostrate or bowed their faces to the ground. She saw her mother, standing toward the back, mouth open in astonishment and joy.

She looked at the priestess and then at the crowd of villagers.

"The goddess," she said, making her voice loud and clear, "came through the image on the wall. Breaking through it, she gave me air to breathe. She spoke to me. She took me into her service, yes. But I am to serve her on earth."

She looked out at the crowd of people she had known all her life. Talaith spoke the priestess's name. "Modthryth!" People had always addressed Modthryth as "Lady Priestess," and never by her given name. They did this out of respect to her rank, but Talaith knew she had to play her advantage to the fullest. If anyone challenged her, it would be the priestess.

"Give me your cloak," Talaith continued, ordering the priestess. "I speak for Artemis now."

Without hesitation, the priestess unbuckled her cloak and handed it to Talaith, who wrapped it around herself.

"The goddess has confirmed that I am her chosen servant by sending us rain. I have much to tell, but for now I wish to return to the house of my mother and father. I will rest and then speak out what Artemis wishes me to say."

Rain beat loudly on the temple roof and ran in thick, silvery waterfalls from the eaves. The priestess knelt. All the people imitated her, kneeling in submission.

"Great is the goddess Artemis," the priestess said.

"Great is the goddess Artemis," the crowd echoed.

"And great is Talaith, her voice upon the earth."

"And great is Talaith, her voice upon the earth."

Talaith breathed an inward sigh of relief. It had worked. They would not kill her.

Her first action as leader would be to appoint her brother Pythius as a teacher to the young.

Stepping away from the chamber that had been instrumental for so many previous sacrifices, Talaith crossed to where her parents stood. The people parted for her to pass. Some bowed. Others touched her worshipfully. She kissed her mother and took her hand. The two of them walked into the rain, her father, the priestesses, and the villagers following her, away from the temple.

About David Landrum

David W. Landrum teaches Literature at Grand Valley State University in Allendale, Michigan. His horror/supernatural fiction has appeared in *Sinister Tales*, *Macabre Cadaver*, *Ensorcelled*, *The Monsters Next Door*, *The Cynic OnLine*, and many other magazines. He edits the on-line poetry journal, *Lucid Rhythms*.

David explains about *The Chamber*:

The story takes place in ancient times. Pythius studied with the philosopher Heraclitus, who lived about 535 to 475 BC. The application of human sacrifice had started to wane by that time, but in rural areas it was still practiced. It would not be in Greece proper, but in one of their colonies in Asia minor. http://www.lucidrhythms.com

CHRISTENING
by Scott Nicholson

The sky gave birth to night without a single moan, but Kelly Stamey knew her time wouldn't be so easy.

She wrapped her arms around her swollen belly. How could you love something so much, something that you'd never even seen? How could you treasure this thing that carried the genes of one of the world's all-time biggest losers? How could you go through all of this alone?

But she wasn't entirely alone. She brushed back the curtains and looked across the cold, dark field. The strange shape bobbed among the sharp shadows of the October trees. The shape looked as if it had been carved out of moonlight with a dull knife. It was as tall as the fence that circled part of the farm's property and half as wide as the potato barrel huddled by the barn door.

The baby squirmed, and the shape outside wiggled in harmony with the strange rhythm of the life inside her. Kelly shuddered and went away from the window. Bad things didn't exist if you didn't see them. Just like Chet. Out of sight, out of mind.

Except he wasn't out of mind. And not entirely out of sight, either, if you counted the photograph on the TV set. It was one of those stiff, formal portraits that the Rescue Squad gave to volunteers at the annual fundraising potluck. Kelly, in what she called her "twenty-dollar redneck hair," looming behind Chet, her lipstick a little too bright, her hands folded over his checkered flannel shoulder.

Chet, grinning, a dark gap where he'd lost a tooth in a fist fight. Chet, chin up. Chet with the square and dull face that, if you didn't know better, made him look like the kind of man you'd want working the Jaws of Life if you were pinned in a car. Solid and reliable. If you didn't know better.

She turned the picture face down. She only saved it so that one day she could show the baby. "There's your father," she would say when the child was old enough to wonder why he didn't have two parents. "He."

She was thinking of it as a "he" even though she didn't know the gender, and certainly couldn't afford a sonogram to find out.

And when the child asked what his father was like, well, she'd deal with that part when the time came.

The tangible reminders of Chet were mostly gone. He'd taken his fishing rods, his sweat-stunk sleeping bag, the neon beer light, his thick fireman's coat. But still Chet lingered, insubstantial but stubborn, like that white shape out in the meadow. She expected him to walk into the room at any moment, cigarette dangling from his lips, eyes squinting against the smoke.

But he hadn't walked these floors in months. The only walking he'd done lately was the away kind. Wasn't no woman going to strap him down with a baby, no way in hell. If it was even his, more likely a "Daddy's maybe."

Chet didn't believe in fidelity. He didn't think humans could love, and sleep with, the same person for an entire week, much less a lifetime. So of course he would accuse her of straddling his fishing buddies. Every time he emerged from a drunken blackout to find her side of the bed empty, he immediately assumed she was working the springs of somebody's Chevy. Hell, she was so low in his mind, she'd probably do it in a Ford.

Kelly turned off the lights and went up the creaking stairs. Her groin throbbed with ligament pain, and the baby elbowed her intestines to punctuate the other aches. She was breathless by the time she reached the top of the stairs. A draft blew across her face, like cool, soft flowers brushing her cheeks.

The house was over a hundred years old. The Stamey Place was crumbling and musty, but at least it was rent free. Other family members had worn out these floors, scuffed the stairs, chipped the door jambs. But they were all gone now. She was the last Stamey, not counting the one that twitched inside her.

The baby kicked again, harder, sending a sharp pain through Kelly's bladder. Kelly didn't want to go to the bathroom so soon after the last trip. The toilet seat was frigid. The heating oil had run out, and she didn't have the money to refill the rusty tank out back.

From the bedroom window, she could see most of the farm. The moon spilled silver over the dark skin of the earth. A stand of brush marked the boundary of the creek, and the old Cherokee ceremonial mound was stubbled with cornstalks. The barn stood black and empty beside it. The Stamey graveyard was on beyond that, on a little rise near the forest.

The white shape hovered along the fence line, immune to the breeze. Kelly knew the thing didn't belong here. Not on the farm, not on this earth. But she wasn't afraid. In a strange way, the shape was comforting. They both haunted this same stretch of ground, both were bound to the Stamey place by the same invisible chains.

She'd first started seeing the shape around the time the morning sickness hit. Only then it had been a thin smudge, transparent and nearly invisible. The shape had grown thicker, brighter, and more substantial as her belly expanded and her breasts swelled and Chet turned sullen.

She'd even tried to point out the shape to Chet. She'd almost called it a "ghost," but knew Chet would have nearly laughed himself sober. He made fun of her for going up to the family cemetery and paying visits to the dearly departed. Even a prayer drew a cuss and a laugh. He had no use for spiritual matters. To him, if you couldn't smoke it, drink it, or stick part of yourself in it, then it didn't add a damned bit to the day.

As Kelly watched from the window, the thing bobbed closer. Eight months old. But that wasn't right. Ghosts couldn't age, could they?

Her belly buddy squirmed. She began singing. "Hush, little baby, don't say a—"

She left the melody suspended, the creaking house adding useless percussion. Because the next line started with "Daddy." Chet. He wouldn't buy anybody a mockingbird, even if their lives depended on it.

She could always change the gender, make it "Momma's gonna" do thus and such. But she'd lost the mood, and the baby had settled. Outside, the ghost also settled, a sodden sack of spirit.

Kelly climbed into the cold bed. She rolled into the cup of mattress where she and Chet had once cuddled, played, and made a baby. She wondered if she would dream of her baby's gender. Some women did that.

The quilts were nearly warm by the time she fell asleep.

Kelly walked the frosted morning on her way to feed the chickens. She tugged up her oversize sweat pants as she went. Her breath hung in front of her, a silver miracle that died away to make room for the next. Breath like a ghost.

The chickens gathered around her feet, pecking the kernels she thumbed from hardened corn cobs. There might be a couple of eggs. The baby would like that. He always gave a kick of joy when that food energy flowed through the cord.

Kelly wondered if the ghost kicked each time she ate. Or did it feed from somewhere else? An umbilical cord for the dead, with energy flowing to them from the living. Invisible, with soul juice pumping into the amniotic sac of the afterlife to keep them from fading into nonexistence. Were they connected to one another?

The cemetery was only a couple of hundred feet farther. If she were careful, she could manage the frozen-dirt trail without slipping. Being pregnant helped her keep her balance, for some strange reason. Hard on the feet, though.

She was swelling today. The health department had told her swelling might be a sign of pre-something-or-other. High blood pressure. Bad news.

She made it to the white stumps of stone, old rain-worn markers. Granite. One of them just a piece of bleached quartz about the size of a baby's head. Little flecks of mica sparkled on the skin of the quartz.

Twenty-seven Stameys. She counted again just to make sure.

Susan Eleanor, Donna Faye, Laney Grace, Melville Martin, Timothy Mark, Simon Martin. Her father John Randolph Stamey, the ten-dollar letters chiseled neat and final.

More. Many without names, all connected by the dirt.

Some older ones, the name spelled S-T-A-M-Y.

Off by itself, where the dust and dead bones were cuddled by the roots of an old apple tree, stood a lonely grave. It bore the only marble marker in the lot. A fine hand had etched a lamb near the top, amidst some Biblical-style scrollwork.

The name, Lewis, engraved in the marble.

Her father's twin, who died so quickly after birth that he never got a middle name.

The grass in the shade of the apple tree was brown. One lone apple clung to a branch, shriveled and spotted. The baby squirmed as Kelly approached the grave.

She knelt before the marker. How sad that this child had never danced across the yard, napped in the hayloft, chased leaves in the October sundown. This child had never tasted the April air, a corn bloom, the cold mist of the creek. This child had never known his mother's arms.

This child never connected.

At least Lewis had been buried with love. Paying for such a fancy monument must have been a strain on a mountain farm family. But the Stameys had always taken care of their own. From the cradle to the grave.

"Since I'm the last, who will bury me if I die?" Kelly whispered to the morning.

Chet. He would come back to bury her. Chet wasn't all bad. Once, when Kelly had a deep cut across her hand, Chet didn't make her wash dishes for a week.

But Chet was gone. And she would not be the last. She rubbed her belly. "You'll live," she said.

She had dreamed it was male. He had talked to her last night, even though in the dream he was not even old enough to walk, his skull still pointed from the pressure of birth. His eyes were brown, like John Randolph Stamey's. The family brown.

She told her belly, "You will carry on the name."

Kelly leaned forward and touched the marble. She would have a family. Her baby would live and grow. She would be connected.

She groaned as she struggled to her feet, pulling on a tree limb for balance. The sun had killed the frost and the ground glistened in a thousand wet sparkles. A mile away, rising from the forest, came a thread of chimney smoke from the Davis place. Beyond that, the Blue Ridge mountains stretched toward the horizon. Blue as a stillborn.

Mothers weren't supposed to think that way. Sure, you had your little fears, but you let them pass and thought only of the baby against your breast, alive and grunting in ceaseless need. You hoped and prayed that everything would be perfect. And you forgot about everything that could go wrong. Just like you forgot about Chet.

She made her way back to the farmhouse. Her back ached, so she sat in a rocker in the kitchen. The sun through the window fell on her belly, warmed her. The baby kicked, then rolled in her womb so that either a shoulder or a knee squeezed her bladder.

"You're going to be a mover," she told him. "Just like your daddy."

Chet, who wriggled like a snake. Who moved so fast that nothing stuck to him, no responsibility, no steady job, no woman. No family. No connections.

She looked out at the Chevy in the driveway. She'd drive herself in, when the time came. She'd have to do it early on, because you never knew what to expect with a first pregnancy. They said some women spent two days in labor, while others dropped them five minutes after the first contraction. You never knew.

Chet's sister had offered a room in town, right up close to the hospital. But Kelly belonged here, on Stamey ground.

The baby squirmed again, probably hungry. Kelly had forgotten to look for eggs. All this foolishness over graves and ghosts, and she wasn't taking care of duties. She rose from the rocker and went back to the barn. It was either that, or oatmeal again, and if she ate any more oatmeal, she'd probably give birth to a colt.

"You can't see ghosts in daylight," she told her belly.

But you *could* see them during the day, if the place you're in is dark enough. The barn had only a couple of windows, set high in the plank walls and covered with chicken wire. She'd tried to get Chet to run electricity to the barn, but there was always fishing or hunting or a Squad meeting. The important things.

The ghost was closer now, the closest it had ever been. She'd come around the corner and nearly dropped the little basket of eggs. But if the ghost wanted to hurt her, it had missed plenty of chances.

She couldn't run, anyway. She could waddle, maybe, take three or four steps while her hip ligaments caught fire and her breath left her. How fast was a ghost? No, if it wanted her, it would have had her any night while she was asleep.

The ghost wiggled in rhythm with the baby. Kelly tried to look at the ghost's face, but it was like watching patterns on the surface of a windy lake. Shifting, sparkling, not knowing what it wanted to be. She stood before it, waiting.

The sound came from between the trees. She knew it well, she'd laid awake many nights listening for it. Chet's Chevy pick-up, with the rusted muffler. The truck was coming down the long driveway.

Kelly smiled. Somehow, she'd known he would come back. He was a good man. He loved the good times, sure, but he knew when to stand up and be a man.

Kelly set the basket on the hard dirt floor, and the first contraction hit when she raised back up. She'd had a few Braxton-Hicks contractions, the false ones that were just practice for the real thing. This one was different. This rippled around her womb and clenched like a fist.

She gasped, but her lungs were stones. The ghost hovered nearer, its substance touching her, ice cold, and she tried to wave it away. Chet's truck stopped by the house, and she fought for enough air to call him. Another contraction hit.

Chet yelled her name. Was he mad? Did he expect to drive in after ten weeks gone to find breakfast waiting for him on the table? She'd take him the eggs, make him happy. Or throw them at him.

The next contraction drove her to her knees. They weren't supposed to come on like this, one on top of the other at the start. The health department had told her what to expect, and this was none of the normal things. This was one of those symptoms that meant you'd better get to the hospital and fast.

The ghost moved closer, Kelly could see the silver and white threads of the borrowed life that held the thing together. It was like one of Mamaw's old quilts, stitched after the woman's eyes had failed. Loose and tangled, nonsense. If not for the ache in her guts, Kelly could have watched for hours, tracing the nearly-invisible lines.

The pain came again, like a knife blade and a punch at the same time, and Chet yelled her name from outside. She crawled toward a pile of hay, sucking for air. The ghost hovered over her, shaking and spasming like linen on a December clothesline. She wondered if the baby was spasming too, but she couldn't feel him through the globe of hurt.

Maybe the ghost was causing all this, the pain, the fetal distress. If the ghost and the baby were connected, like to like, one jealous dead and the other with an entire life yet to live, years and years and years stretching out ahead, a billion heartbeats owed him...

Chet called again, and this time she managed to shriek. Nothing to write home about, but it was loud enough to get through the walls of the barn. Then she curled up in the hay, clutched her stomach, and tasted the dust that spun in the air. Her water broke beneath the tails of the long flannel shirt she wore. The barn door banged open, and daylight sliced through the ghost and cut it to nothing.

"What the hell's going on?" Chet blinked into the shadows.

Kelly gulped for another breath. "B—baby..."

Chet hurried over, the smell of bourbon arriving before he did. He looked down at her, at the basket of eggs, at the amniotic fluid soaking her clothes between her legs. Kelly tried to smile at him, but her lips were dumb.

"It's our baby," she said. Everything would be okay now. The hospital was only twenty minutes away, you could hold out until then, why, the pain was nothing if you held onto that dream of brown eyes. And the baby was part Stamey, it was tough, it could bear up under a little trouble. Kelly was heavy, but Chet could manage, he would put her in the truck and slow down for the bumps.

"It ain't mine." Chet smiled. Except the smile was turned down at the corners, sharp as sickles.

His boot came fast, knocking over the basket. She heard the damp crack of the eggs, and then her mind screamed red because the boot was at her stomach, into her stomach, fast and then again, the pain worse than the contractions even. He tugged at her waistband, and she thought at first it was some new kind of pain, then cold air rushed over her skin.

Chet pulled the bloody pants down to her ankles, laughing, grunting.

"Ain't mine." He walked away, leaving her numb and broken and half naked. The truck started, backfired, and headed toward Tennessee or wherever it was he went to hide from himself.

Chet wouldn't bury her after all. No one to bury her.

Kelly, alone and dying. No, she wouldn't die alone. She would bring this child into the world. The child that was on its way, hospital or not. Dead or alive.

She writhed in the hay, wracked by waves of a new hurt, as if her pelvic bones were being ground to powder. The muscles in her stomach ached from pushing. The child inside her squirmed toward the world, toward the light, toward the land of pain and promise.

Kelly's eyes squeezed closed, tears leaking, the same saltwater that had filled the amniotic sac. The water of life. She pushed again and something tore free down below. She was going to pass out, die without ever seeing the flesh of her flesh, without ever connecting.

She forced her eyes open. The ghost hovered again, settling down upon her in the dark corner of the barn. She had no air to scream. Her final breath would be stolen by this thing of mist and dreams.

Except, as the ghost wafted over her, gentle as lamb's wool, a warmth flooded through her. This time, its touch was soothing. The pain lifted, vanished like a spirit in sunshine. The ghost pressed against her, embraced her, bathed her in whatever energy and life it was able to give back. She rose to meet it, like a lover or a penitent surrendering to a force of faith.

Kelly felt strong again, and she pushed, grunted and pushed again. The baby slid free, and she reached down between her legs. He was slick from her fluids, warm but still. Too awfully still.

She sat up and clutched the child to her chest, wailing, all rain and thunder. The child's skin was blue. She rubbed him, shook him, pinched the tiny nose and blew into his mouth. Even though he was already dead, she admired the beautiful face. He was Stamey, all right.

"Don't leave me," she cried, the limp umbilical cord tangled across her thighs. She rubbed its chest and shared her heat. She half-crawled, half-wriggled toward the cemetery, the chill of the infant's flesh reaching deep into her soul. Blood oozed from her birth channel and her scraped knees and palm as she tugged herself over twisted roots and jagged gray stones.

Her muscles were gone, but she tapped faith for fuel, dowsing for some hidden wellspring. The pale outlines of the grave markers appeared through the foliage. She continued her crippled crawl, compelled herself forward to hallowed ground, pushing over the scrabbled turf until she collapsed before the slab of etched marble.

And the ghost was there, forming again, smaller this time, its effervescence less bright. The milky threads of the ghost settled over the baby, swaddled him, gave to him that same strange energy that had revived Kelly.

The baby coughed weakly, shuddered, and then the cord pulsed. The small heart pumped, unevenly at first, then more steadily. His lungs got their first taste of air, then he let loose with the first of many complaints to come. He breathed.

Kelly hugged him, wiped the stray fluids from his mouth, smoothed his slick wisps of hair. She clawed a scythe from the barn wall and severed the umbilical cord. Then she wrapped the baby in the folds of her shirt, pressing him against her warmth. When the cries died away, she gave him her breast, and he fed.

She lay in the hay until the placenta was delivered. She looked around for the ghost, but knew she would never see it again. Not as a ghost, anyway. The child blinked up at her. In his brown eyes, those strange Stamey eyes, were those silver and white threads. As she watched, the soft threads dissipated, but not completely.

The Stameys had always taken care of their own. From the cradle to the grave, and back again.

She named him Lewis Kelly Stamey.

And it named her Mother.

About Scott Nicholson

Scott Nicholson is the author of nine novels, sixty short stories, six screenplays, three comics series, and numerous articles. He's also editor of *Write Good Or Die* at: http://writegoodordie.blogspot.com and http://www.hauntedcomputer.com

LOST THINGS
by Piers Anthony

"Ian, I have bad news for you," the professor said. "Your mother has died."

Ian froze in shock. Doane, his seeing-eye dog and so much more, picked up his horror and whined.

"When? How?" Ian asked.

"No foul play, for what little comfort that may be. She was discovered after several days. It seems to have been a heart attack. The police notified us. You will want to return home immediately. The office is arranging your ticket now. You will, of course, be excused from the rest of your courses until the crisis has passed. Do you want another student to accompany you?"

"No, thank you," Ian said numbly. "I can make it on my own, with Doane."

"I'm sure you can," the professor agreed. "You handle yourself remarkably well. Is there anything else I can do?"

"I—thank you, no. I have to go."

"Of course," the professor agreed sympathetically.

Ian took hold of the brace on Doane's back and let the dog lead him out of the professor's office and to his own room. He stifled his grief for the moment; he couldn't afford it. "Catto," he muttered. "He'll be in trouble."

Doane made a low woof of agreement.

Soon they were on the plane and in flight. The college office had done an excellent job, perhaps using Ian's blindness as a lever to pry loose a good first-class seat.

While they flew, Ian kept his hand on Doane's back and they communed. "I remember how you were the first," he murmured. "The first failure." He smiled, sharing humor. They had been part of what he later learned was a secret project dedicated to developing telepathy in animals and people by enhancing their system's mirror neurons, sometimes even transplanting treated human neurons to animals. Unfortunately there were many failures. "You were slow, even for a canine. An idiot dog. They didn't realize that in your case, slow was not a euphemism for stupid; your human neurons not only made you partially telepathic, they put your life into the human scale. At a year old you still drooled, but you may live seventy years. So you were marked for extinction, because budget cuts forced them to destroy their failures. Fortunately you used your power to divert their attention and fled before they came for you."

Doane nodded, remembering. He was actually the same age as Ian, twenty, and in his prime. But, of course, that was a secret they kept well. Others assumed he was two or three, and no more than a guide dog, rather than a trusted friend.

"And you sniffed out the kind-hearted neighbor, Chloe, and she took you in," Ian continued. "She was always kind to lost things. And when she caught on to your nature, she kept the secret, and did not return you to the project to be euthanized. That was the first reason we loved her."

Doane wagged his tail, agreeing.

"Then when I was five, and blind, they thought I was another unaffordable failure. But I simply had a different kind of telepathy that they had overlooked. Catching on that I was doomed, I used my ability to escape. I was soon lost in the wilderness that surrounded the project, frightened, helpless. But you tuned in on me from afar, bless you, and led Chloe to me, and she took me in too. She saved my life, and gave me an excellent home. She's not my mother genetically, but she is in the sense that counts. That was the second reason we loved her."

Doane agreed again.

Ian smiled. "If anyone overheard me talking to my dog, they would think I was tetched or merely trying to reassure you with the sound of my voice. They would not know that when we touch, we have what amounts to telepathic rapport. You feel my feeling, which is what counts, and I feel yours. We understand each other on a level few others do."

Doane looked at him and nodded.

"Which is a reminder of my own slice of telepathy," Ian continued. "I know you looked at me because I can eavesdrop on your perceptions. I know you nodded in a human fashion because your glance at me shifted perspective. Similarly I can see, hear, and feel what those physically close to me do. I can't read their minds, but I know what they're paying attention to. So I am not really blind, merely unable to use my own eyes. I can read by tuning in to the reading of the person beside me. The project supervisors were looking for their version of telepathy, which was an impossibly full connection to another person's mind, so missed the partial types that were really more feasible. Such as your ability to divert spot attention from yourself, so that you became forgettable. Such as my ability to see where they looked, to read their written orders, and act accordingly."

He shook his head. "Like that man who knows the price of everything and the value of nothing. They were great on prices. I can't blame them; it took me years to figure out the distinction between the viewpoints of others and my own. So I seemed crazy, not relating to their world. At one point I was labeled as severely autistic. But I merely had not yet gotten a handle on my ability. Just as you had not on yours. It was only with the nurturing support of Chloe that we achieved our full potentials."

That ability had served him increasingly as he grew. Chloe sent him to school, after home-schooling him several years, because she said he needed to get experience interacting with his own kind. It had not taken long for the local bully to orient on him as easy pickings.

"You got lunch money, blindbutt? Give it here."

Doane bristled, sensing the threat, but Ian quieted him with a touch. He had to fight his own battles. "I brought my lunch."

"Give me that."

"No."

The bully stared at him, and he saw himself through the bigger boy's eyes: a thin boy wearing dark glasses, carrying a bag with a cell phone, lunch, notebook, pencils, and his folded cane. "How's that again, creep?" the bully said.

"I think you understood me the first time."

"Okay, here's something for you to understand, shitface." The bully cocked his right fist.

Ian didn't wait for the blow to land. He dodged to the side and swung his bag at the bully's head. It smacked him hard against the side of his face.

The bully was more astonished than hurt. The blind kid had struck back. It must have been a lucky score.

"Okay, mush-brain. Now you're really going to get it." The bully cocked both fists and set himself for a fast one-two series of punches.

But even as he moved, Ian dodged again, this time to the other side, guided by the boy's own vision. He got behind the bully, swung the arm with the bag around his neck, and yanked him back off-balance. "Lay off," he said into the boy's ear. "Or I will make you be like me." With his free hand, he pressed against the bully's face, a finger touching an eye. "Shall I demonstrate?" He pressed just hard enough to make the point.

This time the bully got the message. No easy pickings here. "Okay."

Ian let him go. Then he turned his back and walked away, openly showing his contempt. The bully stared after him. Had he tried to attack from behind, Ian would have ducked and whirled and punched him in the solar plexus, another move he had rehearsed. None of these moves would have worked well had he been sighted, but because the bully thought he couldn't see, he was unconsciously careless, leaving himself open to sucker counterattacks. But he could see what the bully did, and that guided him quite effectively. He was physically fit, and able to move with an assurance that sighted people underestimated. That underestimation was critical to his success in dealing with them.

The bully never bothered him again.

Ian did well in school, listening carefully and making notes. He could see through the eyes of his nearest classmates, but did that only to have an awareness of the layout of the classroom. He did not want to give himself away.

The girls liked Doane, and the dog liked their attention, but that was as far as it went. As Ian matured, no girl wanted to date him. They were polite to him, even nice, but, well, he was blind.

Prospects were better in college, and he did get dates. But no serious interest.

The stewardess approached with a meal, and Ian had to cease remembering. He could not see her directly, but she saw her own reflection briefly in the darkened window, and she was trim and pretty. The kind of girl he would have liked to date, had any been interested in a blind man. There it was again.

When she departed, he quietly put the sausage down for Doane, who really liked meat of any kind.

After the meal Ian resumed his summation, as it was his way of dealing with the crisis of the moment. "Then there was Catto, a decade later. The invisible cat."

Doane wagged his tail, sharing the humor.

"Not literally true, of course. His partial telepathic ability was to cloud men's minds so that they could not see or hear or smell him. So when the project concluded that he was a failure because he couldn't read minds, and took him to the disposal chamber, he disappeared and escaped. You tuned in from afar again, knowing his nature, and we went out to fetch him. Chloe didn't mind that he ate a lot; she loved him as another lost thing, and he prospered. That was the third reason we loved her."

Now she was dead. What were they to do? Ian had done well in school because of her constant support. He was smart enough, but needed the emotional endorsement. Chloe had truly believed in him.

Now he would be on his own—rather, the three of them would be—but he knew they couldn't cope. He wasn't remotely equipped to make it in life without Chloe's guidance and support, and the others, as animals, had no resources in the human world.

The plane descended. Soon enough they caught a taxi home. The house was locked, but Ian had a key, and they entered the familiar premises.

Only then did Ian break down, sobbing for the loss of the only other human being he had loved. Doane howled, sharing the grief.

Then they organized for the immediate need. The near future was opaque, but the present was urgent. "We have to find Catto," Ian said. "He had to go out to hunt, when the food in the house ran out, and he's bound to hunt the wrong things. There'll be trouble."

They set out, dog and man, heading into the local forest. Doane sniffed out Catto's scent trail, and Ian tuned into the dog's vision so that he could proceed with confidence using only his white-tipped cane.

All too soon they found the area. There were three men, local farmers by their garb, talking. "Hey, mister!" one called. "You blind? Don't go in that copse!"

"I *am* blind," Ian agreed without annoyance. "I am safe enough, with my guide dog."

"That's not what I meant," the man said. "It's no place for a sighted person, let alone a blind one. There's a monster in there. We're going to get a permit to start a ring of fire and burn it out."

That was exactly what Ian had feared. "I have traversed this forest many times. There is nothing dangerous in it."

"Maybe not, before. But this is now. There's a monster, a ghost, and it's dangerous."

Ian forced a laugh. They had encountered Catto, all right. "Ghosts are fine for spook stories, but we all know they don't really exist."

"Tell, him, Frank."

"Here's what I seen," Frank said, clearly shaken. "My dog smelled something and he ran into that copse. Then he yelped, and I ran in after him. There he was, lying dead, his throat torn open. Something killed him. Something big. I knew it was close by; the hairs on my neck raised. There was a smell, then it faded. I pulled my gun and looked, but I couldn't see or hear anything. I stood there, and then I saw it." The man gulped audibly.

"Saw what?" Ian asked, anticipating the answer.

"The ghost footprints. They just appeared right before me, pressing into the ground. Big ones, like maybe a bear. But there was nothing there. That's when I knew it was a ghost monster. It killed my dog, and might have killed me, but I got the hell out of there." The man was still terrified.

Definitely Catto. Because though he might seem invisible, he could not hide his footprints once he left the area, and they appeared. Frank thought they were being made as they came into view, but that was not the case. They were there all the time, but hidden.

As for their size: hardly surprising. Because Catto was no house-cat. He was a tiger. Chloe hadn't cared: he was a lost kitten, and she loved him. She had covered for him for years, making sure he had plenty of meat to eat and keeping him out of mischief. Ian and Doane had taken Catto for walks in the wood, cautioning him, and he had trusted their judgment. They were a team.

But if Catto got hungry enough, would he attack a man? Ian could not be quite sure. It was better to make sure the big cat never got that hungry. Meanwhile the superstitious farmers might have reason to be scared.

"Ah, here comes the gasoline," the first man said as a fourth man arrived, hauling a large fuel can.

"Well, thanks," Ian said, pretending nonchalance. "We'll be moving along now." He touched Doane's back, and the two walked on toward the copse.

"Wrong way, mister!" the man yelled. "The monster's there."

"If I see it, I'll tell it to go away," Ian responded as though oblivious. Obviously he wouldn't see it, because it was invisible and he was blind, but the farmers surely didn't get the humor.

Ian and Doane entered the copse, and no one followed.

Doane sniffed. Catto was near. He wouldn't dim his odor for Doane.

"Catto," Ian murmured. "Come in close. Make us all invisible." This was part of their teamwork: they had done it before, as a game.

The tiger did. Catto had known and trusted them most of his life, because of familiarity and the telepathy.

They walked in a tight formation back the way they had come. The four men were busy pouring gasoline, starting a big circle around the copse. None of them paid any attention. Catto was diverting their sight. Only their footprints would remain, appearing belatedly. With luck, these would not be noticed.

They made it safely back to the house, smelling the smoke of the gasoline fire behind them. The farmers would be satisfied that the invisible monster had been burned out, and that was best.

But a man stood at the door. "I can't see you, but I know you're there," he said. "I've got a heat detector. We need to talk."

Doane growled and Catto was ready to pounce, but Ian cautioned them back. He couldn't see the man either, but the view from his eyes was competent. At his touch, Catto ceased his effort, and they became visible and audible. "Go inside," he told the man. "We'll join you."

They settled in the living room, the animals on their favorite couches. The three of them gazed at the man.

"I am John Mawker," he said without preamble. "I am from the Project, of course."

This was like dealing with the bully. The man thought he had the advantage, but he might underestimate them. "The Project considered us failures," Ian said evenly. "The Project was going to destroy us."

"True. Our greatest failure was in not recognizing the nature of the successes we had. Since then we have grown smarter, as an institution. We want you back. All three of you. Now that your benefactor is gone, it behooves you to consider our offer."

"What offer?" Ian did not trust this man, but their situation was desperate, and they had to listen. The alternative would be to flee the region, hiding from normal people, foraging in garbage cans, and trying to escape pursuit by people from The Project who knew their nature.

"I see you understand," Mawker said.

"Understand what?" Ian asked tightly.

Mawker smiled. "I am moderately telepathic myself. Mainly I pick up moods. It's clumsy compared to the talents the three of you have perfected. But believe me, I understand you."

"What offer?" Ian repeated.

"One you can't refuse. Return to The Project, and you will be protected and nurtured as much as Chloe did for you. We were aware of this kindhearted normal woman, but left her alone, because she was doing our job for us, and better than we had done it. Did you really think we could be ignorant of a neighbor who took in our charges? She knew nothing of us, as far as we know, though she might have suspected. Now that is over, and we must act to secure you. We can't allow you to range uncertainly amidst the populace. The Project has always been secret and must remain so. We require your cooperation."

Ian did not need to consult with Doane and Catto. "No." Now it was up to the bully.

"I have not completed my presentation," Mawker said without rancor. "I do not bluff. You will accept. But I prefer it to be voluntary, on the basis of full understanding."

"We prefer to be free," Ian said evenly.

"That is the key. We not only want you, we need you. Funding is always a problem, in part because we can't tell Congress what we seek or accomplish, so we have to make do with what we have. We must use our best. And you three have, largely on your own, become our best."

Ian still did not trust this. "Make your point."

"We need you to train our lesser successes. To demonstrate what you do, and enable them to do it too. To see through the eyes of others," he glanced directly at Ian. "To deflect attention." He glanced at Doane. "To suppress the awareness of others, in effect becoming invisible." He looked at Catto. "And other skills, perhaps some we have not yet recognized. We need your enthusiastic participation."

"Provided we surrender our freedom," Ian said.

"No."

Now Ian was startled, and so were Doane and Catto, in tune with his mood. "No?"

"That is the nature of our offer," Mawker said. "We want you to return to manage the project. The three of you; this is a multi-species effort. Under my supervision, the first year, to familiarize yourself with the protocols. Then directly, when I retire."

The three of them stared at him.

"You can continue to live here," Mawker continued. "This can be a useful outpost. We can pay off the mortgage; that at least is within our means. You can continue to range the local forest as you have been doing. Even finish your education, Ian; you are already close to your degree. You have learned to relate to the larger world; that is a skill we also need. We need to be able to interface with normal folk, without betraying our special skills. Starting with your attendance at the funeral and memorial service for Chloe, a fine, generous woman. All three of you."

He paused. "I might add that we do have other predator animals there, and other domesticated ones, who need the help of each of you to fulfill themselves. Also a maiden, seventeen, highly telepathic but uncontrollable. She's rather pretty but emotionally insecure, as you might imagine. I think you would find her worthwhile in more than one venue, Ian. She truly needs a talented and understanding friend. The pay is low, but there are compensations. What we are doing may some day change the world. It is, actually, a secret but glorious vision. One you surely share."

Ian realized that Mawker had come well prepared, and had won the day. Indeed, they could not refuse.

They were no longer lost things.

About Piers Anthony

Piers Anthony had the hodgepodge of employments typical of writers. Of about fifteen types of jobs he tried, ranging from aide at a mental hospital to technical writer at an electronics company, only one truly appealed: the least successful. But the dream to be a writer remained.

Finally in 1962, Piers' wife agreed to go to work for a year, so that he could stay home and try to write fiction full time. The agreement was that if he did not manage to sell anything, he would give up the dream and focus on supporting his family. As it happened, Piers sold two stories, earning $160. But such success seemed inadequate to earn a living. So he became an English teacher, didn't like that either, and in 1966 retired again to writing. This time Piers wrote novels instead of stories, and with them he was able to earn a living.

As with the rest of his life, progress was slow, but a decade later Piers got into light fantasy with the first of his ongoing "Xanth" series of novels, *A Spell for Chameleon*, and that proved to be the golden ring. Piers wrote two other fantasy series: the "Adept" novels and the "Incarnations of Immortality." His sales and income soared, and Piers Anthony became one of the most successful writers of the genre, with twenty-one *New York Times* paperback bestsellers in the space of a decade. This enabled Piers and his wife to send their two daughters to college, and drove the wolf quite far from their door. Piers and his wife now live on a tree farm, and would love to have a wolf by their door, but do have deer and wild cat and other wildlife instead. Today, Piers Anthony is not only a successful writer, but an environmentalist. http://www.HiPiers.com

A NEW DAY
by Larry Green

Alice's eyes snapped open and her breathing stopped as she listened, ears straining in the darkness, searching for the sounds carried to her in the night. Cursing under her breath, she reached to the nightstand, trying to find her lamp, but in the rush she knocked everything else off onto the floor.

Finally, groping in the darkness, her fingers found the base of the lamp, and she felt her way up under the shade to the switch. Light flooded her bedroom and she looked at the mess she had made. The clock was there, underneath the phone, which was now off the hook. She could hear the recording telling her to hang it up like she was some kind of an idiot who did not know any better.

Looking down at the floor there was still one thing she did not see that should have been there, but was not. Her teeth. Slowly, Alice climbed out of bed, and leaning against it she managed to get down on her hands and knees to look for them. As a last resort, she flipped up the side of her bedspread and there they were. Her dentures, and the glass she cleaned them in, had rolled under the bed when everything had taken a spill. And now Alice was horrified to see her teeth sitting in one of her old slippers.

"Of all the places they could land, now I will have to go to the doctor because I will get some kind of fungus in my mouth," she muttered out loud to nobody. Leaning down, she reached, stretching her arm under the bed until she felt the teeth with her fingers. When she pulled them out, she looked at them in the light from her lamp. When she was satisfied they were not covered in lint, or something even worse, she put them in her mouth.

Almost at once, Alice's face began to contort and she stuck out her tongue. Looking down her nose, she could see a hair, just sitting there, moving up and down as she breathed in and out. Quickly she reached up and pulled it off her tongue, noises of disgust coming out of her throat, and she wiped it off of her finger onto the floor.

"Oh my God," Alice said as she retched, her voice slurred by the loose-fitting teeth, "I am going to have to clean under the beds again."

She sat down on the floor, leaning back against her bed, and let out a sigh as she picked up the phone. The recording was over and now the phone was making that irritating noise, over and over again, that the phone company said was supposed to let you know the phone was off the hook. She had called them up one day and asked why the phone made that noise, and that had been their answer. They had been shocked when she had told them that some people left their phones off the hook on purpose, and did not want to hear that noise any more than they wanted to hear the phone ring.

Putting the phone down a little harder than she should have, Alice could picture Edward's face in her mind's eye. It was complete with the little look he always gave her when she was having her "tiff," as he had liked to call it. Poor Edward had been gone for almost two years now and she had not missed that look one bit since he had gone. Alice thought of him and how he had always insisted they have a phone, even though she hated the thing, and he always refused talk on it. It served him right having that heart attack out back in his garden when nobody was there to call an ambulance. Yes, she thought, the old bastard lived his whole life and never once talked on a phone. She hoped he was happy with that.

Through her window Alice heard the noise again, howls somewhere out in the night, and she knew it had to be the Keegal's dogs. They woke her up more nights than she could count, and considering she had just had her eightieth birthday, she thought that was a good indication of how many ruined nights' sleep she could count. She picked the phone up again, banged it back down in the cradle with a smile on her face, just for Edward's benefit in case his ghost was somewhere watching, and then she dialed a number.

"This is the Jefferson County sheriff's office," said the voice from the other end of the phone line.

"Yes, this is Alice Dreyton from out on Willowbrook Lane. I would like to report a disturbance."

"Hello, Mrs. Dreyton, what seems to be your disturbance tonight?" asked the voice from the other end, sounding as though he were trying to hide the laughter in it.

Everyone knew everyone in this small community, and sometimes that could be annoying. "Don't you take that tone of voice with me, young man, I pay my taxes, and that pays your salary, do you understand me?"

"Yes, Ma'am, and I am sorry, Ma'am; what seems to be your problem tonight?"

"It is my neighbors, the Keegals, or should I say their dogs. They woke me up howling. Usually it is their barking at all hours, but this time it is their howling. I need a car to come by at once."

"Yes, Ma'am, right away. It seems we already have an officer out in that area. I will see to it that he gets to your house as soon as possible. Is there anything e..."

Alice smiled as she slammed the phone down, even harder this time. She could imagine the operator jerking his headphones off of his ears, howling in pain like the Keegals' dogs from the squeal that they always showed in the movies when you did that.

Satisfied now, and with nobody else to torment, Alice slowly got back up on her feet and put on her housecoat and went into her front room. Staring out of her picture window, Alice watched the road for headlights. She knew the officer would not be out here any time soon, they never were when she called, and it never changed, no matter how often she complained. As she stood there, Alice heard the howls again, and this time they were closer.

Alice smiled again, grimly this time. She lived in the country and that meant she could shoot a gun. That was one of the main reasons she had liked living in the country in the first place. At least Edward had had enough sense to buy them some land to go along with their house. With ten acres of woods, she should not have any trouble finding a place to hide a couple of her neighbor's dead dogs.

She crossed her living room to the closet by the front door and opened it. There in the back she saw what she was looking for. A tall gun case stood hidden behind coats and Edward's golf clubs. One of these days, she needed to remember to take them into town and sell them. She had always hated golf.

She picked up the gun case and unzipped it. A heavy double-barrel emerged from the case in her hand; the receiver and barrels were finely engraved with a hunter and his dogs out shooting birds. She thought it would have been a much nicer engraving if it had been an old woman shooting her neighbor's dogs, but nobody ever listened to her.

On the stock, right under where her chin went, was a band that wrapped around, held in place by elastic straps, and it held shotgun shells. She broke open the gun, checked the barrels for any obstructions, and then slid two shells in. As she loaded the gun, she made sure the shells had two zeros side by side. She did not want to end up using squirrel shot tonight, she thought to herself with a laugh.

By the door she flicked the wall switch and the light in the front room went out. Outside the window she could see her front yard, lit up by the bright pole light at the end of her house. She had to make Edward get that, too. He said he thought a flashlight was good enough for getting around outside at night.

The howls came again, and this time they were right out in front of her house. She could hear the dogs moving through the brush now. From the sound of it, she knew the Keegals had to have gotten some new dogs, some really big new ones.

Alice quietly went to her front door, opened it carefully, and stepped out into the cool evening air. Her eyes followed the sound through the trees in front of her as she raised the shotgun to her shoulder. With the gun in place, she braced herself with the wall of the house behind her and she waited. Suddenly the dog in the woods quit moving.

Alice lifted her head, looking down the barrels out into the woods when she caught movement out of the corner of her eye. She saw a dog coming at her mid-leap as it flew through the air. She whirled, faster than even she thought she could, and pulled both triggers at once.

The roar of the blast from both barrels filled the night. Alice heard the dog yelp as the kick from the shotgun knocked her off her feet and sent her sailing across the porch backward. She realized when she turned, the house was not there to block her any longer. Trying to brace for impact, Alice felt her feet hit the ground, dragging along as the rest of her body dropped down to join them. The wind was knocked out of her, but she did not hear any pops, so she did not think anything had broken.

Lying on her back, Alice wondered if the stars she was watching were really in the sky or if they were in her mind instead. She tried to sit up, moaning in pain, worried about where the wounded dog had gone. Before she could even move two inches, she heard paws on the porch. When she looked up, she saw two yellow eyes staring down at her. She thought they looked like two yellow piss holes in dirty snow, but she was amazed at how big the teeth were when the dog opened its jaws wide, closing them around her face.

Officer Ronnie Johnson drove down the county road as slow as he could. The call had come in just a few minutes before that he needed to head over to Mrs. Dreyton's place because of some dogs howling. He knew he was in for a good hour-long argument about why he could not shoot her neighbor's dogs and he was not overjoyed with the idea.

With his headlights off, he went as slow as he could, and he could already see her driveway in the moonlight. He looked up, craning his neck so he could see the silver disc floating high in the sky above him. He thought he would rather be up there, with all of the risks of space travel, knowing he had a better than good chance of dying and never seeing home again, than arguing with that damned Dreyton woman. He worked nights because they were easy. At least they had been until Mrs. Dreyton's husband died. He remembered the old man was supposed to have had a heart attack. Officer Johnson knew that it was not a heart attack that had killed the old man. The old woman had bitched him to death.

Pulling on the headlight switch, all the while hoping the old bat was not up there watching him from her front room window, Ronnie turned into the drive. As soon as the headlights washed over the porch, Ronnie saw two of the biggest dogs he had ever seen in his life take off running. He thought they had been eating at something.

When he shined his spotlight on the porch and realized they had been eating Mrs. Dreyton, he radioed in for backup. His eyes never left the old woman, her shotgun lying there beside her, her mangled body covered in blood. He thought the dogs had carried off pieces of her when they had run. Ronnie locked the doors of his squad car and hoped he would hear sirens soon. Far away in the woods, he could still hear the howling.

Melanie woke up; the morning sun was bright in the sky over her, and she winced when she moved. She knew she had to be more careful when the change came upon her, because even *she* was not invincible, although when she was changed she was nearly so. She looked at her stomach, the fresh scars from last night's bullet wounds still bright and pink on her now-human skin. She hoped they faded soon because summer was almost here and they would play hell with her bikini and tan lines.

She remembered eating the old woman, but she did not feel bad. After all, the woman had shot her. Then she remembered the man lying beside her. She looked at him, still asleep, and she thought he looked quite handsome lying there considering the night they had had. When he woke up, she would have to find out his name and she hoped he would stay with her a while. It was lonely sometimes being a werewolf, but this was a new day and anything could happen.

About Larry Green

Larry Green is an aspiring writer and the editor of *Death Head Grin* magazine when he is not taking care of his day job, which is painting houses. He lives with his three dogs that are not werewolves in Northwest Arkansas where he has written off and on for most of his life, but has never pursued it seriously until recently. He has always been a fan of anything horror, growing up reading anything he could find from

Stephen King to Edgar Allen Poe, and watching movies like *Jaws* in the backseat at the drive-in when he was supposed to be asleep, which made him terrified of the bathroom at night when he was five.
http://www.deathheadgrin.com

RED KING
by Jessica Handly

It was quiet, dark, serene. The night had enclosed me like the leather of a glove. So soft, so warm. I could smell the ocean all around me, could feel the waves lapping at my feet.

I opened my eyes. The mist had rolled in out of nowhere. I listened as the soft gong of a distant bell echoed harmlessly from the lighthouse. The darkness was pierced by its yellow light, warning cumbersome ships of the rocks. In a flash, the light passed over my head and was gone.

The ocean wind blew my hair back from my body and ran gently through my clothes. I raised my hands and face to the dark, starlit sky, arching my back, letting the sounds of the ocean fill my senses like it had never done before. I was in love with the Provincetown night. I felt free and without a care. I wasn't even hungry like he had said I would be.

I began to walk forward into the water, but a hand, strong and powerful, clamped down onto my shoulder. He whipped me around to him, and in the matter of seconds that it occurred, I took in his whole attire. Just the same as always; crimson hair, curling wildly around his face and neck, green eyes like a cat just a bit too far apart on his face. His lips were as fiery red as his hair, his complexion so very pale, like a bleached bone. He had said it was all due to his age, so very old that he was. He wore an old green sweater and faded blue jeans, knees ripped, work boots soaked with wet sand.

I wanted to ask why he had done what he did, why he had chased me around for so long. He hadn't even told me his name, not once throughout these long years. He was pouting now, mouth frowning, eyes narrowed. Now I couldn't ask what I so longed to, for his presence near to me had always made me feel small and unnecessary, just this thing whose existence didn't even matter.

He raised his hand, touched my cheek. It was cold against my skin. "What is it? Why did you leave the house?"

I tried to find the voice to answer him, but as usual I looked away, shivering. His pure power intimidated me, frightened me.

He stood silently behind me for a moment, not touching me, but then awkwardly, his hands raised up to hold me. Now, this was something he had never done before, had never even attempted to do. He didn't really know what to do with me, I soon realized, as he just stood there with his hands resting lightly on my hips. I stared out into the darkened sea, watching the waves crash against the shore.

He pulled me against him slowly, hesitantly, turning me gently. "Katia," he whispered my name. I looked up at him, lost in his eyes, as his hands grasped me by the back of the neck, head lowering, gently kissing me now. His nervousness gave me this human gesture, this one and only long-awaited kiss. I held him tight against me.

"Who are you?" I asked, resting my head against his chest. When he didn't answer, I pulled away slightly, gazing up at his wild hair, his gleaming eyes. I reached out and touched his cheek, watching as he smiled now, his face so smooth and so very pale. I touched his lips, the smile continued. I ran my hands down over his arms. He was so very old. I was so young. Why had he chosen me?

A slight nod. His hand reached out and found mine. "Don't be afraid."

My heart was thudding painfully in my chest, but I denied it. "I'm not."

Another grin. Cool long fingers twining into my hair, drawing me closer. "If I'm not to be afraid of you, Katia, you mustn't be so of me."

I had barely the time to nod as his lips descended upon me again, kissing my mouth, my neck, my face. He held me tightly, afraid to let go, sighing my name on the breeze. "Katia."

Darkness, blessed darkness. The warmth of flannel blankets around my body, I had dreamed of his arms around me. Where was I? How long had I been out? My mind drifted backward, to the dark compartment of the lighthouse, to the sun rising around us and the fear of annihilation. To his arms around me, holding me, calming me. When the sun had risen outside of our sanctuary, we were safe together.

Chills spread over me, and I ducked under the blanket against him as his hands ran gently over my hair. Focus, and the world is at your command. Who had said that to me? Did he? Mother? Father? Oh, it was too long ago, much too far away. I hugged him tightly and let the years slip away, the memories flashing into my mind like yellowed pictures from an album.

Mother and Father had known from the start who and what he was, had promised me they would let me know him on my twentieth birthday. Yet I had always known him at a distance, growing up with him around. He was one of my parents' friends to me, no more, no less. I remember him coming into my house after dinner, striding into our dining room with his hands in his pockets. I remember sitting on his lap, his eyes gazing into mine, and how he'd frighten me and I'd cry, begging Mother to make him go away. Like a nightmare thing, his face and voice invaded my childhood dreams.

When I was fifteen, my parents died in a freak car accident, leaving me the sole survivor with no known living relatives. The friend of my parents whom I so detested now became known to me as *Guardian*. He came to live at my house, although I rarely saw him. When I did, it was sudden. Fleeting and gone in a moment. He was a flash of red with glittering green eyes in the darkness. Ever watchful, he waited patiently. I became suspicious of him, as teenagers are wont to do, filled my room with vampire novels. His actions were documented in there. The way he moved, acted, and constantly watched.

He'd follow me to work, watch me as I went to bed, stand over me as I slept. Sometimes he'd come into the house when I was doing the most mundane of chores, loading the dishwasher, and he'd just stand there, looking so odd, so barely held back, it would infuriate me. I'd scream at him and throw things, and he'd catch them easily, whispering, "Relax, Katia."

Then he began to want me to make him dinner, every night. I did, but he never ate it, simply watched me eat, sipping his red wine. I demanded money from him, more and more, bought my first car at sixteen. And then, I was never at home. I didn't see him for months until one night, at a stop sign no less, he simply opened the door and sat down beside me.

"Drive," he ordered and too shocked to do anything else, I did, driving until I ran out of gas. He watched me the entire time, staring through my body, my mind, into my soul, until I screamed at him to stop. When we ran out of gas, he bought more and drove us home. I stared silently out the window.

At eighteen, I graduated high school. And that's when I confronted him.

"What can I call you?"

He seemed to contemplate it for a moment. "My people called me Ruadrí…Red King. But you can call me Rory Danann."

"Rory Danann?" I repeated, then I told Danann that I wanted to go to college; a long hard fight ensued. He spoke to me more than he ever had, saying all kinds of nonsense, that he owed it to my parents to keep me alive. I accused him of wanting to keep me home for other reasons.

"You want me so much and yet you can't stand to look at me!" I yelled as he turned away from me. "You're a coward! You watch me from the shadows, never once taking what you want, and I know how much you want it!"

He turned to me, restraint etched in his face. "Katia, you have no idea what I want."

I laughed at him. "Don't I? I've known it for years. You want it so badly you can taste it, but you won't take it. Why?"

"You don't want me to want you like this," he said, his face exasperated, tightly drawn, the green eyes gleaming.

"Maybe I do," I said, walking up to him, angered as he sighed, turned away. "But wait. How could I be so stupid? You have to see it to want it, don't you?" I reached for my purse, digging until I found what I was searching for. My pocketknife. I flicked it open, and at the sharp snap, his head swiveled to look at me. Before he could say another word, I forced it down on the flesh of my right arm, cutting lengthwise until the blood ran fast. I dropped it on the ground then, falling to my knees, watching in pain as the blood bubbled up and onto the carpet, as red as his hair, his lips.

A sharp intake of breath came from him then. I looked up; he was now kneeling on the floor beside me. "Katia..." He didn't finish his sentence.

"It's what you want!" I was crying, offering it to him. "It's what you are, isn't it?"

He pushed me down until I was lying flat on the ground. My head hit the floor, knocked me dizzy. His cold hands encircled my arm, forcing the blood up faster, and I couldn't breathe, couldn't believe what I was seeing now. Flecks of red were surfacing deep inside his eyes, swirling up, covering them totally, blood red, glazing over, staring at nothing but the blood. His mouth, already opened and gasping, now revealed to me: two canine teeth lengthening, becoming fangs. I whimpered as his head lowered to my arm, and his soft mouth covered the cut. I felt the fangs lying against my skin, not puncturing, but yes, they were there. I swooned, lost a lot of blood all into his mouth, and then I passed out.

When I came to, hours later, I was lying on my bed, my arm bandaged, and he was gone. A note on my bureau read, "I am so sorry. Go to college."

Three days later, I packed a bag, drove out to Cape Cod, and enrolled into Community College.

But my escape was lonely and desolate. Alone, I felt as though I had been orphaned twice. I couldn't seem to make friends; it was as though my classmates instinctively knew that I was destined for something none of them could understand.

Two years later he found me, and seduced me by sheer words rather than anything physical. He whispered promises of eternal life, of love and hope and power. I gave in. I went to him. I held onto him as he drank from me. His hands never touched me. As I took that life-giving blood from his pale throat, it was all my choice. I held him, and the blood was so very good. Now, I was really home. I belonged to him.

When I killed that old man the next night, I'd felt no remorse. I belonged entirely to him, my *Guardian*, my Danann. I'd surrendered as I should have years ago. I poked my head out of the covers, my chin resting on my hands, and on his chest. I felt safe now, with him. Comfortable. Why? Because now I'm just like him.

"Danann, do you love me?"

Shadows on his face, passing, and a look of pure innocence that was a lie. Soft smile like the touch of a feather. Like the touch of his pale, silken skin. Strong arms lifting me, pulling me close and over him. I thought of lavender sunsets, swans, cascading waterfalls in the darkness, and his soft, embracing touch. "Katia, I love you as much as I am capable of loving."

I didn't know how to analyze his answer, but then his lips came to mine, mastery in that. The taste of his mouth was exquisite power. The red of his hair, his lips, his blood, his warmth. And I realized it wasn't anything to do with analyzing facts; this was all about emotion.

Existence was good with Danann by my side. As we walked down the Provincetown streets in the darkness, he told me tales of Vikings and Magic, of Necromancers and Fair Folk, of times long past. He held my hand tight within his.

"I will never leave you," I told him, turning to embrace him there, in the middle of the street, not caring who saw us.

"Katia, you make me remember life." The wind blew up around us as he kissed me, scalding my face with stolen warmth which was not his own.

"I love you," I whispered, giving myself to him totally, surrendering without a care.

We returned to the lighthouse, nestling ourselves inside its protective hold. We curled up together, and I told him we were two misfits defying all time and reality.

"But if I'm with you, who cares what reality is?" I said.

"Dear little Katia, I'm so very sorry," he said, addressing me as though I were still a child.

"Danann, it's alright. I understand everything now. What you've done is given me the means to love you, just as I was meant to do. There is so much time to spend."

About Jessica Handly

Jessica Handly was raised on tales of the old country. As a youth, her imagination soared from the crypts of Sicily to the banshees of Galway Bay. Trips as a youth to Vermont helped spark an early interest in vampire lore. A love of classical music contributed to her creative process early on. Jessica eventually traveled abroad to places mentioned in her novels, such as France, Ireland, Italy, England and Scotland.

Jessica is hard at work, teaching classes, writing, and courting publishers for a new novel currently titled *The Halfling*. Jessica previously wrote "The Dream Series" novels under the name Jessica Barone: *Eternal Night, The Requiem,* and *The Legendary*. She holds a Master's of Arts in Liberal Arts, has worked as a professional writing tutor, held seminars on writer's block, led fiction writing and journalism clubs, and has served as a reviewer and volunteer tutor for other authors. She feels her greatest achievement is that she has inspired young authors to read and write. http://jessicahandly-writer.tripod.com

YOU SAID ALWAYS AND FOREVER
by Richard Hill

When she opened her eyes and looked out of the window, Jane thought that she and the cottage were sinking, that she was still lost in a maze of her dreams. Only when she was fully awake did she realize that the wind from the moors was driving the thick snowflakes upwards; that like so much of her life, it was an illusion. She felt for a moment as if she were inside a glass paperweight, like the one her grandmother had kept on her mantelpiece, that some giant hand had shaken her world, sending the fat feathery snowflakes swirling around the cottage, turning the tiny bedroom brighter and lighter than it had ever been, filled with the cold light of the white world outside.

For a moment Jane felt a flicker of happiness, snug in the warmth of her bed, before it was drowned in the familiar ache of her loneliness. She wondered what Mike was doing. She thought of him every morning when she woke to the emptiness of the cottage and the endless emptiness of the moors and the world beyond. He would be holding that woman in his arms the way he had once held her. With tears prickling against her eyes, Jane pulled herself out of bed. Even with the heating at its highest the cold tightened her skin after the warmth of the bed, and she worried again about the oil running out, or the electricity failing, and the sadness rose in her again. Why had he left her like this, alone and helpless, not knowing what to do? She had a child's fear of being abandoned and lost, of freezing to death, alone and unnoticed. Mike was still her husband, her next of kin, wasn't he? They would call him to identify her. Perhaps then he would realize what he had done to her.

Jane stepped into the bathroom and stared at the pale face in the mirror.

"Got to get on!" Her voice sounded too loud in the silent cottage. "Still talking to yourself, I see. Or should it be hearing?"

Mike had turned her into a cliché, the deserted wife left talking to herself, the wronged woman, the fool, the cuckold.

"Can you be a female cuckold?" She stared at her reflection, running the taps, waiting for the water to run warm.

"Oh Christ!" She began to cry, sponging away her tears, toweling away at her sorrow. She pulled a stiff upper lip at her reflection and went back into the bedroom. Looking down at the crumpled clothes thrown onto the floor, she decided not to get dressed. If she spent the day wearing a bathrobe, who was there to know or to care? She was snowed in, the roads around her were blocked, and there was no sign of the snowfall ever ending. She had plenty of supplies and she had enough work to do putting the next edition of her online zine 'Frightful' to bed. Her only fear was that if it snowed for long enough, it might cut off the electricity to the cottage.

Jane still half-expected Mike to return, to hear the solid slamming of the car door and his voice shouting from the hall, but she knew that her hopes and her imagination were failing her, just as he had.

The darkest of her imaginings was that he had planned everything from the beginning, and that he had known Samantha long before they had moved to Arrowdale. Mike had always been spontaneous, given to spur-of-the-moment decisions and actions, and his plan to take up the partnership of a small law firm in a Yorkshire market town had seemed totally in character. He was someone who needed change, and every few years he would grow restless. The plan was for her to give up her day job and edit the magazine full-time. The dream of a cottage in the country seemed not only sensible but attractive, and his practice was less than two hour's drive away. She had only learned that his new partner, Sam, was Samantha when it was too late to do anything.

Something was moving in the kitchen. Jane stepped over to the door, listening hard. She thought she heard a furtive, shuffling noise, like someone creeping. She moved slowly to where she could see into the room, but it was empty. For days now she had felt the presence of someone, always out of sight; a flicker of movement in the corner of the eye, the half-heard sound of another. But there was no one. To take possession of the kitchen, she made a mug of coffee, pushing back her unease.

They had bought the cottage in the summer, only weeks before they moved. The drive from the little town had been charming and soothing, driving to their new home in a flickering tunnel of green. Only now that Mike had left her did Jane realize just how isolated the place was. And now this foul winter and the blizzard had made her a prisoner. He had begun working later and later 'to get the firm moving,' then staying in town on weekends and finally, carefully, reasonably, he had left her and moved in with Samantha. He had exchanged one partner for another. She had made what Mike had called 'a scene' at his office, repeating it over again, the best joke of all, a partner for a partner, her laughter going on and on until it turned into a scream.

And now there was Nemo.

Editing an online magazine meant that contact with her contributors was both easy and difficult. Easy, because the correspondence between her writers and illustrators was almost instant, and difficult because she had no protection from those who were awkward of reason or too demanding; Nemo was both. The illustrations he had sent her were far too crude and hateful to use, and she had told him so, at first tactfully and finally bluntly. She had used the word hateful, a word he had objected to more than any other, crude drawings of foul things being done to a woman. But if Nemo's drawings had portrayed hate, his emails shrieked with not just hatred but with threats, so that Jane dreaded seeing his name in her inbox, and lately they had become just graphic details of what he intended to do to her.

Normally, Jane would have ignored Nemo's rantings, but since Mike had left, she never felt normal, just lonely and sad and tired. And now she was not only alone but isolated. The phone still worked, and the Internet, but the empty silence of the moors seemed to have moved into the cottage and into her soul. She switched on the radio and turned on her PC. She wasn't hungry, so breakfast could wait until lunchtime. Working on the magazine was her escape as well as a chore and perhaps the new copy she was waiting for would take her away from the white blankness all around her.

The story she was waiting for was in her inbox and she printed it out, preferring to read submissions the first time as hard copy. She realized from the first few paragraphs that it would be as good as she had hoped. Finally, she decided to open the inevitable email from Nemo, steeling herself for another tirade about artistic integrity, his genius, and what he would do to her unless she stopped leading the international conspiracy against him. It was shorter than usual; just one link, to her 'More About Me' column.

Jane stared at the screen. She never had the time or the inclination to update her blurb. It contained nothing about her private life and certainly nothing new. She clicked on the link. Only the words 'More About Me' remained the same. Her photograph had been altered so that her face was old and lined, and her smile had been turned into a sneer, and what had been a few banal facts about her life had been turned into a toxic mixture of boasts about her own superiority and invitations to fulfill her detailed sexual fantasies.

Jane felt as if she had been punched in the stomach, as if something foul had moved into the room with her. She heard herself sobbing, but now she was sobbing not out of sorrow, but from fear. For too long she sat transfixed at what she saw in front of her until at last she knew what to do. She would phone Magic Al, her computer guru. Even his name made her feel better. He was magic. He would sort it out, track down what had been done back to Nemo. It had to be a crime. She would send the bastard to jail.

Her hands were shaking as she picked up the phone, surprised that it was working in this blizzard. She had read the words so many times: 'His hand trembled' or 'Her hands shook.' And now it was happening to her. When she spoke into the phone, her voice was tight with anxiety.

"Is Al there? I need to speak to Al; it's Jane, Jane Allen."

The voice which answered sounded thin and distant, farther away than the miles which separated her from the city, almost a whisper.

"Jane? This is Cathy. I'm afraid…"

Jane heard her own voice, too loud, too high, too fast.

"This man. The magazine. He's done things. Awful things. To my web page. About me. My picture. Al has to change it back again!"

There was a long silence and then Cathy's voice, more faint than ever. "There's been an accident. This morning. On his way to the shop. A car hit him. He was on the pavement, but the roads are so icy. They say the car skidded onto the pavement. He's dead."

Cathy's voice finally broke, and she continued, "The car drove off. He killed my Al and just left him there. I'm sorry, I can't talk any more. I'll call back later."

"Don't! Don't go!"

Jane put down the dead phone and tried to process what Cathy had told her. Al was gone. He couldn't protect her from what Nemo was doing. No one could help her. And then she realized that it must have been Nemo who had murdered Al, that he had been driving the car which had killed him, that he meant to kill her next. She had to stop him. Jane clicked open her email to reply to his last message. She would use his artwork, whatever it was, whenever he wanted, if only he would leave her alone.

"Leave me alone! Leave me alone!" she was barely conscious of the sound of her pleading as she crouched in front of the monitor and realized that his emails had disappeared. The last received message was dated three days earlier.

Jane's fingers scrabbled through the messages for his contributions and his attached drawings, but there was nothing from Nemo except an innocuous message delivered almost a week earlier asking whether she had reached a decision over his drawings. Despite the cold, Jane felt hot and dizzy. She had a separate folder for the e-zine, but when she checked all her other folders and documents, she could find no other messages from Nemo.

And then she was in the bathroom, staring at her hands, pink and strange, writhing around each other in the tiny sink. She lifted them and watched, fascinated, as the water dripped from her fingertips. She tried to remember what had happened, why she was in the bathroom washing her hands. The room was darkening. If it was still morning, why was the world outside the window turning from the hard white of the day to the grey blue of evening? Jane stood listening to the silence and wondered where the day had gone, what had happened between her searching for Nemo's messages and this moment she had fallen into.

She hurried back to her study. There was a new message from her publisher, asking why she hadn't replied to his last two emails. There was nothing from Nemo, but she knew that he had taken control of her PC, changing and erasing. She opened her bio and felt the floor tilt under her. Her photograph had been deleted and in its place was a black frame with just her name and RIP. Her thoughts seemed to scatter. She thought of that day in York, when she had tripped on the cobbled road and the contents of her dropped handbag had spilled and rolled all around her. Mike had been with her to save her from falling, his strong arm around her waist. Mike, who had deserted her and left her at the mercy of a murderer. Jane pushed the PC off the table, smashing it on the stone floor.

She had to get away before Nemo got to the cottage. When she stepped into the kitchen, she realized that she was too late. The kitchen table was covered with felt tip drawings of a naked woman, hacked and battered. They were crude and childish, but not of Jane. She stared at the slashed face in the drawings. It was always the same woman, but Jane's hair was short and dark, and the woman in the drawings had long fair hair and blue eyes, not her dark ones. She picked up one of the drawings, holding it trembling like a fan in her hand.

The woman in the drawings looked, not like her, but her replacement in Mike's heart...like Samantha.

Jane picked up one of her felt tips. The drawings had been made with the pens she used to mark copy, but she kept them in a drawer. Nemo must have had time to search the cottage. And then she heard his breathing and realized that it was too late for anyone to help her.

Jane yanked a knife from the block beside her and slashed at the sound in front of her and then swung round in panic when she realized that his breathing was behind her, soft and gentle as the falling snow brushing against the window. She had no idea how Nemo could make himself invisible, but Jane knew that she had to get out of the cottage. She bolted from the room, pushing over the table, racing down the hall, swinging the knife in an arc in front of her, clawing open the front door, running, his steady breathing in her ear.

Outside the cottage the freezing air filled her lungs with ice, and her feet burned with the cold, but Jane kept running toward the main road. It was almost dark now, the icy wind cutting through her robe, the snow thicker than ever. She might lose Nemo in this swirling white world if only she could keep running, but his steady breathing was still in her ears.

And then her head suddenly cleared. He was following her footprints in the snow. She wanted to sing Good King Wenceslas. The tune filled her head, almost drowning out the sound of Nemo behind her. But she was cleverer than he was. Let him follow her footprints—she would run in circles! He could run and run and never realize that she had tricked him! She began circling the field in front of the cottage as the night grew darker and colder.

She seemed to have run for hours and hours. It was becoming harder to breathe now, but the exertion had made her deliciously warm, warmer than she had been for days. She pulled off her cotton robe and threw it, a whirling white bird, into the snow; white lost in white.

"Follow that, Nemo!"

As her voice disappeared in the wind, Jane realized that her breath too had left her. She sat down and then fell back onto the soft ground, tired beyond tired, wanting to sleep, lulled by the cold. She felt safe and warm. She thought of Mike, who had looked into her eyes and promised to love her until death do us part, who had deserted her, and now she had left both Mike and Nemo behind her. Now she was done. She was alone where no one could hurt her.

As her mind slowed, Jane remembered what the name 'Nemo' meant. It was Latin for *no man,* for *no one.* That's who he was, who everyone was. Satisfied, she drifted into sleep, feeling nothing but the cold soft kisses of the falling snow on her upturned face.

Martin hated these editorial meetings. He knew that Louise had already decided on what she would include in the evening newsflash and he had far better things to do with his time, but at least the meeting was winding up at last.

Louise glanced down at the file in front of her and then looked across the table at him. "Did you find out any more about that dead woman on the moors?"

"The police are writing it off as an accident. She died of hypothermia; that kind of thing happens all the time if you go for a stroll naked in a blizzard. Seems her husband had dumped her for another woman a few months ago and she'd been living alone ever since. Her doctor was treating her for depression, but being snowed in alone for all that time must have pushed her over the edge."

Louise looked mildly interested. "Didn't she get in touch with anyone?"

"She couldn't. No phone. The landlines are still down, and there's no mobile signal from out there. She had a PC, but there was no Internet connection either. She was totally isolated. Seems she spent most of her time making drawings of her ex-husband's new woman. Pretty nasty ones, the police said."

"Too tacky for a closer; too depressing," Louise said and stood up. "We'll go with the rescued coach tour. Forget the dead woman."

And the meeting was over.

About Richard Hill

Richard Hill considers himself as not primarily a horror writer, but just a writer. He has written for radio, TV, and for theatres like The Hampstead Theatre in London and The Everyman Theatre in Liverpool; in fact, he would write for anyone who would give him money for words. He has an MA in Victorian Literature from the University of Liverpool.

Since Richard was first old enough to make annoying noises, he has played in bands in and around Liverpool. Afterwards, he headed up to the Editorial Office at the University of Liverpool, producing all their magazines and prospectuses, and taught Creative Writing there as well in their English Department. He is currently co-writing a novel with fellow author Louise King about two serial killers.

Richard had a stroke five years ago. It still amazes him that his body hasn't yet realized that if it does succeed in killing him, he'll take it with him. Richard had to learn to walk and talk again, but—knock on Formica—he's good now, although now he's used to one-handed typing—which sounds more Zen than it is.

http://www.facebook.com/profile.php?id=643779752

UBIRR
by Conrad Williams

Under the sheet of beaten tin the sky had turned into, Manser labored to keep up with his fiancée. She had picked her way through the group to be with Rick, their tour guide. Manser watched the couple move across the uneven terrain like a pair of goats, putting daylight between them. He would not allow her to get away however, and lose herself among these outcrops with that overgrown blond tosser.

"Is hot, yes? Too hot for the Englander?" Dirk grinned at him through the mosquito veil attached to his hat. He was from a small town near Bremen, apparently, and did something in synthetics. Why don't you twat off, you Teutonic turdster? Everything he wore was brand new. Manser pictured him with a shopping list the day before his arrival in Darwin, buying gear from a shop called 'Action Man,' or 'Survival Bastards R Us.' Now he had lost sight of Tabitha. Where was she?

(*I'm Tabby,* she had said to Rick when they were registering for the outing at the tour company's offices downtown. She did not like anyone calling her Tabby. *What, like a cat?* Rick asked and she had laughed like a kookaburra.)

Dirk persisted. "Are you enjoying the trek? But you sweat such a lot."

"We're all sweating, Dirk. It's bloody sweltering. It must be forty degrees today. And massive humidity."

"Yes, but you don't help yourself. You wear heavy fabric. Your body can't breathe."

Dirk looked like an advert. He wore a skin-thin vest strategically peppered with holes. Its sheen reminded Manser of wet otters. His sandals looked as though they had been designed by NASA. He sported a watch possessing more functions than a top-end microwave cooker.

Manser growled, "I'm fine."

"You are overheating, Englander. You have the beetroot head." Dirk laughed, an ugly, sputtering sound. Some of the others within earshot—

Trevor and Rob from Manchester, Frederique from Quebec—added their guffaws too.

Manser, stoked for an argument, nevertheless managed to check himself. Scowling, he strode clear, trying to ignore some of the muttered words that floated his way. Was 'unsociable' one of them?

The sun clung to his back like a burden, scratching and gnawing at his neck, roasting his calves. The weather had not let up in the three days since they had landed in Darwin, at the top end of Australia. The humidity had shocked him too, although he suspected that the news stories that had followed them around since their holiday began were also conspiring to make him feel uncomfortable. He recalled some of them now. Awful stories, stories that you didn't want cluttering up the romantic sunsets and leisurely, flirty breakfasts. An Aborigine had set fire to herself on the steps of the Sydney Opera House in protest against the long-standing treatment of her people. An Australian company were behind an ecologically disastrous spill of cyanide in Romania. And there had been another victim of the serial killer who was sweeping the country like a bushfire.

This last topic had invaded the party he was currently touring with.

"'Sweet Tooth,' they call him," Frederique said, adjusting the straps of her backpack.

Trevor was nodding. His broad Lancashire accent sounded at odds with the grisly detail it now described: "He's filed his teeth and he chooses the most succulent cuts from his victims. The fatty sweetbreads and suchlike. Dee-licious."

Frederique laughed, a touch nervily.

"The police reckon the girl's self-immolation the other day, and this murder, are linked," said Rob. "You know, tit for tat. They reckon this Sweet Tooth wants to even the score for two hundred years of European atrocity."

Manser could almost understand why, listening to them prate like this. Not for the first time he wished he and Tabitha had organized a tour for themselves only. Sartre was bang on the money.

The path through the rocks took him by shady places where aboriginal art seeped from its natural canvas as though forming itself gradually from the sandstone's color and texture. Manser studied the different layers; the conflicting cells of ochre. Here, by his feet, were the grindstones where the colors had been pulverized and mixed. The playfulness of the art, its simplicity and joy called to him from across the millennia. Some of the fragments had been here for 20,000 years. Maybe even longer.

Let them wander off together, he thought. Some guide he turned out to be. What if I wanted to know what these fish were? What if I wanted to know the significance of the gold sections in that turtle? Who could tell me?

Truth was, Manser already knew. The fish were barramundi and, along with the turtles (whose gold sections were a hint as to where to find the plumpest, tastiest sections of the animal), were an ancient menu, a message that food was nearby: the East Alligator river was but a few kilometers away. To Tabitha he had read passages from the guide book on the days leading up to their flight to Australia. On inspecting the color plates that accompanied the text, she'd remarked on how plain and uninspiring the aboriginal art was. Her attitude changed quickly enough when she saw how enthusiastic Rick became when talking about the paintings.

"And the colors are so vivid!" she had gushed, while Rick pointed out the etiolated balanda, the white men standing around with their hands in their pockets, the way the indigenes had viewed the Europeans as they supervised the slavery they imposed.

Thunder caromed around the Kakadu skies. The wet season had not yet started; it was a good month overdue. Anvils of cloud were poised to shape the acres of dull sky that bore down on the Northern Territory. Manser could feel its weight. His sweat was a constant, like the flies, or the nagging that Tabitha inspired in his gut.

Let it go, he thought, but it was a mere cosmetic, a reflex nod to human convention that came and went in a trice. Such charitable notions occurred to reasonable men. He might once have acknowledged it. At the cusp of the new Millennium, for example, jostled on Westminster Bridge as Big Ben and a curtain of fireworks heralded the 21st century's birth. He had felt such a wealth of goodwill he could have cried. Every time he looked at Tabitha, he swelled with yearning. He had gone so far as to yell at a party of bewildered Japanese tourists that this is my fiancée! He had kissed her for a long time as color and light spattered the sky, only just stopping short of asking her to have children with him as soon as possible because he recognized the measure of his emotion.

He recognized it again. It had limits, this loveplay, and there wasn't much give to it.

A billabong fell pathetically away across the plain, dwindling almost as he watched. Three buffalo stood motionless at the water's edge, hunched by what might be despair. Manser caught sight of Rick and Tabitha picking their way through the rocks to the next portion of aboriginal art and saw how he might intercept them before they could lose themselves. He pushed himself hard against the heat. Each time he raised his arm to steady himself, what seemed to be the annual rainfall of the East Midlands fell from his flesh. A slick formed on his face that could not be wiped clear.

Manser attempted to affect nonchalance as he breasted the final rise ahead of the guide, whose affronted expression took the wind from Manser's sails. Deep down, he had not really suspected the Australian of wanting to do the dirty with his fiancée, but the look of him now suggested otherwise.

Manser pressed the back of his hand against his forehead. "Bit chilly isn't it?"

"You don't really feel the heat after a while living up here," Rick said. "Keep up your fluid and salt intake and it's a piece of piss."

"How are you bearing up, Tabby?" Manser asked as Tabitha sidled up to them.

She arched her eyebrows, but couldn't object. She said, "A rock is a rock is a rock, love. You climb it or you don't." She turned to Rick, placed a hand on his arm. "That said," she continued, "we tried to climb Mam Tor, a pretty undemanding hill in Derbyshire, back home. We had to give up. Stuart couldn't hack it."

"I might have been able to, darling," Manser detested the edge that had crept into his voice, "had I not undergone a hernia operation three weeks earlier."

Rick snorted. "You don't have to make excuses, mate. What's it to me?"

Regardless, Manser could tell he had been judged.

Rick said to Tabitha, "Another five minutes and we could scoot up to the top there."

Manser answered before she could agree. "I don't think so. What about this rock art?"

Rick said, "There are plaques telling the stories of each one." He tipped his Drizabone back on his head.

"We paid for a guided tour," Manser protested. Dirk, Trevor and Rob were strolling up. Their presence, and the silence shared between them upon observing this stand-off, bolstered him. "So we should be getting a guided tour."

"Too easy," beamed Rick. "Let's just hang on for the stragglers."

Manser reined in his tongue, cheated by Rick's obeisance. Spoiling for an argument, he had been trumped by Rick's apparent dismissal of what would have been seen as a flashpoint back home. He shuffled impotently in the grit, flashing glances at Rick, who stood easily in the heat, and Tabitha, who would not acknowledge Manser's attention.

Presently, Claudia, an obese nurse from Interlaken and the septuagenarian twins, Rudolf and Ivan from Dusseldorf, sloped into the clearing, amid a riot of aspiration. Manser believed they should not have undertaken such a demanding trip, but Rick had proffered no words of advice regarding its difficulty.

"Some of you daring types without hats..." began Rick, and all heads turned to Manser, the only person not attired thus, "...might want to consider walking in shade for a while. The sun is currently at its zenith and people of a fair complexion, and those who aren't blessed with the full complement of hair, are at risk of serious burns."

Cringing, Manser moved into the shade of a ghost gum. His hand fell upon the smooth, muscled bark and he coaxed it as he might a knot of pain in his forehead. He gave six inches away to the guide, who probably also weighed a good stone or two heavier. But it was good weight, distributed evenly across a lean, supple torso. Rick was constantly fingering the slabs of hard contoured flesh beneath his singlet. Tabitha prominently displayed the signs of her wish to do likewise beneath her own halter top, despite the heat. Manser's clothes battened down burgeoning wedges of fat.

They moved on. The rock rose above them, a giant fist warning off the sky, which was growing ever more leaden, rippling with potential.

"Here's a fish with a difference," Rick said. A faint representation of a barramundi clung to the underside of a ceiling of rock. There was something not quite right with its shape. "It's a simple lesson in common sense. One day, a fisherman from the tribe caught a fish from the river, turned his back for a moment and when he went to pick up the fish, it had gone, jumped into the water and away. What does this picture tell us, do you think?"

Manser was so irritated by the guide's patronizing tone that he gave in to a second of boorishness. "That's supposed to be a fish? It looks like a rugby ball. A punctured rugby ball."

Rick ignored him, but the heat from Tabitha's eyes momentarily eclipsed that of the sun. He felt foolish. Nobody had laughed. It seemed that every avenue of decision had been blocked off or redirected. He was being manipulated somehow. He was the co-director of a coming textiles business. He had been profiled in the financial pages of The Independent. Yet his control had been breached.

"It's a fish with its head snapped off," said Rick evenly. "You're not going to get many headless fish escaping. Though sometimes, on this tour, you get a few headless chickens doing a runner."

Now the laughter came, and Manser could not help but suspect much of it was at his expense.

Enough. Manser dismissed Rick and his adoring audience with a flick of his hand.

"Meet you at the top," he snarled.

"But what about your guided tour?" Rick sang mockingly.

He didn't look around as he struck off, knowing by now the kind of expressions that would be following him. Worse than the bemused, almost pitying looks sported by Rick and his entourage, Tabitha would assume a disgusted mien. He could imagine her leaning against Rick, saying softly: Why am I with him? And the comeback, from a man who would be at pains to remember Tabitha's name in a week's time, even as her fingernail scars healed on his back: Too right, babe. The guy's a drongo. Or whatever word these lackadaisical wankers came up with to describe a man like Manser. A placid man, that was all. A stone, who usually let worries roll off him. The heat—it must be the heat—had altered something. Turned the stone to sponge, eked out a scintilla of fury that dwelled deep inside.

Back in the ferocious spotlight, away from the shade afforded by the sandstone ledges, Manser ceased to struggle against the relentless beat of the sun. He recognized a kinship there. The heat that pressed against him collided with and equalized the measure of fire within. He felt energized by the balance. He knew himself capable of anything. His awkward shape, the skewed spread of his weight, counted for nought. Here, as he bounded up the side of the rock, he wished he had persuaded Tabitha to make the visit without a guide. He knew enough about rock art from what he had studied in the guide books or gleaned from the Internet in preparation for their holiday. For instance, he recognized the depiction of Namarangini, the spirit man, the rain conjurer. He wouldn't have stooped to sarcastic asides or hubristic tones to ginger his narrative (how did that story go now?) as Rick had done. Rick. Manser spat on the rock, as much from the distaste the name afforded as to clear his airway. The phlegm sizzled and dwindled to a speck as the rock drank him in. Rick clearly modeled himself on the basest of Australian role models, some kind of backwater ocker by way of Crocodile Dundee and Les Patterson. All that was missing was the mullet haircut, the stubbie of Victoria Bitter and a meat pie.

Fingers of steam grew from the areas that took the first spattering of rain. The drops were big and warm; tropical rain. On the track that chicaned up the side of the rock, Manser paused and looked down to the lower plateau. He knew them from the beads of light that reflected off the plutonite lenses of Dirk's Oakley's. They were plodding up the incline, following slavishly the tourist path, marked out by yellow metal arrows nailed to the sandstone.

Tabitha waved something at him. A bottle of water, was it? And what was Rick doing waving at him? Beckoning him? Even at this distance, Manser was being babied. He did not need water, thank you very—

"I don't need water, thank you very much!" There must be pints inside; look at the stuff pouring off him! A palm swept across the forehead drew enough moisture to irrigate an herb garden, for God's sake.

Manser climbed. His body was serving him well, pistoning and balancing him like a machine. What did Rick have, he thought, beyond a knowledge of bush tucker? He knew how to handle a frill-necked lizard while the rubber-necked tourists took snaps. He knew that the sap from a milkwood tree would relieve stings and bites. He knew the facts and figures that surrounded a queen in her termite mound.

"Oh yeah?" he yelled down at Rick. "Well so do I, mate!"

Rick's eyes had not left Tabitha's when he told the group how a female Aborigine could make herself temporarily infertile by standing over a smouldering ironwood branch, "so the smoke enters her." Manser had never before heard the word 'enters' uttered with such relish.

The man had nothing. Dragging travelers around in a 4WD on 3-day tours. Visiting areas of breathtaking beauty, swimming in secluded pools; his own boss.

The bastard. He had everything.

The sun had been smothered. Lightning played around the innards of cumulonimbus. Rain slanted into him. In a moment, the going had become treacherous. He saw Rick move away from the group, gathering pace as he arrowed toward Manser.

"Oh, no you don't!" he bellowed. "I don't need rescuing!" He scrambled up the rock, swearing when he saw that Tabitha had decided to lend her skills to the chase. The others huddled in their cagoules, faces upturned. From here they resembled pale decorations studded into a dry, unappetizing cake.

The last twenty feet took him an age to best. At the summit, he cast around, although there was nothing here to do; he was simply standing at the top of a big rock formation. The feeling of climax wouldn't come. Frustration joined the stew of other bad emotions; violence flared in his limbs, but he didn't have anything to strike out at. He tried to enjoy the view, but each of the panorama's 360 degrees was swamped by cloud. The rain possessed such substance that it could have been something to be gathered in a fist and swept aside to reveal fine weather.

Rick clambered on to the summit. Manser saw Tabitha gasping behind, following his lean backside to yet another moment of humiliation.

"This is meant to be a holiday for me," Manser lowed.

Rick spread his hands. His short-sleeved denim shirt clung wetly to him. His boyish curls had flattened and darkened on his skin. "What the hell are you talking about?"

Manser said, over the thrumming rain, "You're no different from your forebears."

He gulped breath. Wind blew grit into his face. The cloud overhead had borrowed some color from the night. Lightning tumbled around inside, looking for a way out. "Terra nullius, the first Europeans said of this land. It belongs to no one. And how long had the Aborigines been here? Tens of thousands of years? Well, you can forget it where Tabby...where Tabitha is concerned. She is off limits. Hear me? She is my property. Keep off!"

"I'm just a guide. I'm just doing my job." Rick looked worried. The sight of it appeased Manser; he had claimed back control. Rick continued, "I'm not interested in your bird. I'm interested in telling you of the legends—"

"Don't talk like that with me!" Manser bellowed. "Look at her. Look at her! You're telling me you're not interested in her?"

Tabitha had stayed back from the confrontation. Rain had soaked her. She looked tired, a little frightened. Her breasts had become clearly visible through the thin halter top. Her lips had reddened with adrenaline. "I'd fuck her," Manser said. "I'd fuck her right now. Wouldn't you?"

Rick said weakly, "The legends—"

"Bollocks to the legends," Manser said. "I know stuff. We don't need you. I know things." He was bleating. Close to tears. Tabitha was already there, crying into her hands. "I know stuff. Like Namarangini." He was shedding sweat that seemed hardly to touch the ground before it was absorbed into the old, old rock. "He can assume any shape. A spirit of the Dreaming. Namarangini." He turned out to the sweep of land as it was slowly dissolved by the dense rain. "Namarangani."

He comes in a storm, his name as insidious, as softly threatening as the troubled skies that contain him. A pair of sisters gather shellfish for dinner and, eyeing the approaching storm, swear and spit at the tumbling prow of black cloud as it cuts toward them. Swollen with rain, and fury at their disregard of his potency, Namarangini swoops and gathers the younger woman in his arms. There and then he forces himself upon her, but his straining prick is turned back at the place where she becomes parted. Is he too big? Is she too dry?

He takes her back to his domain and attempts congress once more. Now he discovers that a cycad nut, a tool for grinding ochres, is blocking the entrance to her cunt. Removing it, he copulates with her and discards her.

The sister returns to her husband. Upon discovering that the stone is missing, he pushes a heated stick into her, piercing her stomach and killing her. Now the remaining sister cries for her dead kin. As she cries, the rains come, a deluge that continues for weeks.

Rick and Tabitha lay atop the rock. Rick's neck was broken, a bruise flooding the stubbled area below his left ear to his throat. The job on Tabitha had been more thorough. A tendon or two was all that kept her head attached to the neck. Her windpipe was exposed and torn, like some sun-bleached hose gashed open by a Strimmer. The flesh below her chin had snagged and folded, drawing the bottom lip back from her teeth. One eye was slightly closed. She looked as though she had just taken a suck of a lemon.

Manser approached, despite the blood riling out of her that turned her hair to sticky hanks and deepened the sandstone's hue; the sudden farts of air that escaped her; the repulsive twitch of her left hand as though she were trying to shed her engagement ring. He did the job for her, treading on her wrist and jerking off the band, flinging it out to the billabong.

He felt a calming vacuum spread within him. He could no longer hear the roar of the storm, even though it was crashing around him, pulverizing the rock, forcing the trees to genuflect in its presence. Where was everybody? He scampered to the edge of the rock and looked down, but it was like staring into mud. "Dirk!" he called, but his unfamiliarity with the name took some of the gusto from his voice. The storm took the rest of it, tearing it to ribbons and losing it instantaneously.

When he turned back to the bodies, Rick had gone.

Rockfall. He jerked his head up just as the head of a figure sank from view.

"Fucker!" barked Manser. "You kill my girl?" He was after him in a flash, juddering down the incline, following the tenebrous descent of the figure as it skittered and slid along the path on the opposite face of the rock. A dense wall of rainforest rose to meet them. "Rick!"

The other wasn't letting up. He tore into the leading edge of trees and was swallowed by shadow. Manser followed seconds later, barging through the vines until the darkness demanded his respect and slowed him to walking pace. He stopped, trying to load his lungs with the hot, musky air and hollered the guide's name again. The boughs absorbed the call immediately. All sound was dead here, save for the rain, which he could just hear, causing mischief in the canopy way above him. A neatly coiled carpet python oozed over the Y of a branch like something from a

Dali landscape. Movement again, up ahead. A darkness sifting through the slivers of light and shade, an image in a zoetrope.

Manser lunged through the undergrowth. Juts of sandstone emerged from the green and there was art here too. Scratches and curls of color, depicting the strange congress of animals he could not determine. A forest of handprints laid claim to the paintings, they reached out to him across time. Manser swallowed thickly, anticipating their touch, and pushed himself to go more quickly.

He was no longer sure he was on Rick's trail. The chatter and gargle of hidden creatures would hush as though the orchestra was silenced by the rise of a baton. Just as suddenly, the surge of noise would begin again, more intense than ever. It might have been the sound of the forest breathing.

Exhausted, Manser burst into a clearing. Rain found its way in here, misting the surroundings to such an extent that all seemed solid; it appeared there were no gaps for Manser to move through. A wall of sandstone rose and fell away at his side, like the prow of a submarine breaking the surface. An imbroglio of figures and faces and fables concealed the true appearance of the rock. Up ahead, a great banyan fig blocked his path. Its roots fell about him like great ropes cast from a ship in distress. The condemned trunks of neighboring trees were just visible through the stranglers, as if they had given themselves to this monster. And then Manser noticed Rick, standing just to the side of the tree. He was breathing hard, his back to him, as if he too had been defeated by the forest, and the seemingly inescapable nature of the clearing.

"Rick?" Manser tried to call, but his voice was the pathetic mewl of a newborn cat. Manser saw how the figure was not actually facing away from him any more. A face had emerged through what he had believed was the back of Rick's head. The eyes were great dead punctures that boasted all the glimmer of dried tar. Manser had been convinced the figure was fully clothed, but this man now, drifting toward him, was naked. His torso was slashed with white pigment.

Manser backed off. "Ah," he said. "Now then."

What was left of Rick fell away like discarded rind. Fully formed, the figure came at him. The punishment to fit the crime, Manser thought, as he batted into the rock behind him. The lips of the other peeled back to reveal an awfulness beyond Manser's imagination.

With a great effort of will, Manser turned away and, sinking to his knees, lifted his shirt. In the rock, he saw a figure much like himself, prostrate before a spirit from the Dreaming. The best cuts of his flesh had been gilded.

The ancient, parched grindstones beneath him drank lustily of the rain. Soon they would be full of color once more.

About Conrad Williams

Conrad Williams is the author of the novels *Head Injuries, London Revenant, The Unblemished, One and Decay Inevitable*; the novellas *Nearly People, Game, The Scalding Rooms and Rain* and a collection of short fiction, *Use Once then Destroy*. He lives in Manchester in the United Kingdom. He is a recipient of the British Fantasy Award and the International Horror Guild Award. His new novel is *Blonde on a Stick*. http://www.conradwilliams.wordpress.com

BONES IN THE MEADOW
by Tim Jeffreys

The sun set above the town, obscured by cloud. Shafts of light, cutting through gaps in the cloud, pointed toward the landscape below. To Jim, as he gazed from the train window, it seemed as if his eyes were being drawn to the place he was leaving, to the shops, the townhouses, the factories; all that he had known for the fourteen years of his life, all that was familiar. He was excited to be going away for a while, but mixed with this was an element of dread. He glanced at Ste and Kelvin, his two friends and traveling companions, who were busy settling themselves in their seats. Out the window, the horizon turned murky orange and yellow. The onset of night was drawing the color from the day, turning all first to gray shadow, then slowly darkening. The train pulled forward into the shifting landscape, the gathering dusk.

He fell asleep before Crewe. He woke once when the train was stopped outside a station. Another train flashed by, shaking the carriage in its wake, rousing sleepy passengers, making Jim think of a loosed wild animal, roaring and maniacal, a beast thundering into the night in pursuit of some prey. Dark thoughts. He pressed his head into his seat and slept again.

The sun had risen again by the time Jim was roused from sleep. A glance out of the window told him little. The landscape was lost to fog. There was nothing to see except the beginnings of fields, specters of trees. Jim straightened himself, staring out of the window, blinking. The train crawled along. He saw a calf emerge out of the fog, wandering the path at the edge of the tracks.

"Where are we?"

Ste answered him, grinning and excited. "Almost at the station. You better get ready. It's our stop."

Jim continued looking out of the window. "I can't see anything."

Kelvin was pulling the rucksacks from the rack above. Ste was busy reaching up to another rack, where they had stashed the tent. "This will clear. It's not even six yet."

Crookhaven station was small and deserted, an island in the fog. The train was soon gone from sight, but its departing clackity-clacks took longer to fade. Jim bemusedly followed after his friends, who appeared to have decided which way they were headed. He had the tent poles jammed under one arm and a box of fishing equipment in his other hand.

"Guys!" he called, seeing his friends hurrying on ahead. He glanced down at the road.

"Guys, I think the town is that way."

"Town!" said Ste with a laugh. "We're not going to town, Jim. We came here to get away from everything, didn't we? We came here to get lost."

"Where are you going then?"

Ste had crossed the road and mounted a fence that lined the edge of some grassland. In the fog, it was impossible to see what was beyond. Ste pointed into the field nonetheless. "That way!"

His first kiss.

He opened his eyes.

A girl was crouched above him. She was smiling. Eyes like the sea at dusk. Hair long and flowing. A child's mouth. A child's laughter. A gauzy dress that had slipped from one shoulder.

He felt...fear.

Something in the way she was looking at him, like he was her treasure—a found object, a plaything.

He gasped, sitting half upright. Then he blinked, baffled. He was alone. The flaps of the tent were open, but it was impossible anyone could have slipped away so quickly.

A dream, then?

His first kiss had been a dream.

He felt relief.

"Shit," he murmured, falling flat. He lay dozing for a few moments inside his sleeping bag, recalling the dream, remembering the girl and her soft kiss before those thoughts vanished with the day. Besides his anxiety, there were other arousals: vague, pleasant electrical currents that settled in his loins. His heart was beating in his ears, but he let his mind drift awhile. Perhaps, he thought idly, if he fell asleep again the dream would restart, it would set to rolling again in his mind. Now he knew it was only a dream, he was willing to go along with it.

Then: "Morning, Jim! Wakey-wakey! Hands off cocks and on socks!"

Jim looked down to see Kelvin's round face pocking through the tent flaps.

"Get lost."

"Charming! I'm getting breakfast ready. I'm starving. You better get up or you'll miss out."

"Kel," Jim said. He struggled to free his arms from the sleeping bag and sit up. "Who's out there? Is there…anyone out there?"

Kelvin frowned at him. "Ste's gone for a walk down to that river we passed yesterday. He couldn't wait. He wants to see how the land lies. I told him we'd have breakfast ready by the time he gets back, so get up. Come on, get to it."

"Get out then. I need to get dressed. Or have you come to watch?"

Kelvin huffed as he withdrew from the tent. As Jim groped around for his clothes, he heard Kelvin muttering to himself outside, probably collecting sticks for the fire. He was soon dressed and out of the tent, blinking in the early sun.

"Clear," he said to himself, recalling the previous day when they had walked and walked into the fog, on the instructions of Ste—who kept promising it would clear—until Kelvin said he could walk no more. They had pitched their tent in the place they'd been standing, which Jim now saw was the middle of a meadow. To one side, there were the beginnings of a wood, to the other only dips and slopes of grass. He couldn't see any buildings.

"Get the tin opener!" Kelvin called to him from a short distance away where he was seated, trying to build a fire. Turning back to the tent, Jim noticed a trodden circle in the grass. He followed the circle around the tent. It was so neat and precise he doubted Ste or Kelvin had made it. Looking about the field for similar markings, he immediately found two more nearby.

Kelvin called again: "Tin opener! Please!"

"There's circles in the grass. Have you seen them? Did you notice them last night?"

"Jim," Kelvin said, out of patience. "Just get the tin opener, will you? I'm about to starve to death."

"Sure you are," Jim muttered.

Kelvin had the fire smoldering. When Jim joined him, the two of them picked through the selection of packets and tins they had brought in their backpacks.

"You realize we have no idea where we are?" Jim said.

Kelvin grinned. "I know! Isn't it amazing?" Then when he saw that Jim wasn't smiling; he pointed toward the trees at the edge of the field. "Don't worry, Jim. Town's that way."

"How do you know that? I can't see anything."

"It's behind those trees. Relax. Enjoy yourself."

"Ste's been a while."

"Yeah, well…you know what he's like. Fancy a smoke?"

Jim glared at the cigarette pack Kelvin offered him. "Where did you get those?"

"Found them. In my mum's apron pocket. She'll kill me if she finds out. Which is why I did it. Want one?"

"No thanks."

Kelvin shrugged, lighting one cigarette in the fire. Jim heard a shout from across the field.

"Here's Ste now."

Jim frowned at Kelvin. "What's he yelling about?"

And then Jim turned to watch Ste dashing toward them. Every now and then Ste would spring into the air, making whooping noises as he did. He was out of breath by the time he reached the fire. Immediately, he pitched something into the grass before Kelvin.

"Christ, Ste!" Kelvin sprang to his feet and reared away.

Ste stood stooped forward, his hands propped on his knees, gathering his breath, but grinning. Jim looked at what had been thrown to the ground.

"Where did you find that?" Jim felt a shiver of revulsion.

"In the next field. It was just sitting there."

Jim looked closer at the object. "That's human. I know it is. It's part of a human skull. That's a jaw bone! You better get rid of it, Ste."

"Don't be daft. It's a souvenir."

"It's a human bone! And do you realize we have no idea where we are?"

"Cool it, Jim. It's an animal bone. A sheep or a dog or something."

Kelvin was gingerly turning the skull with his foot. "He might be right, Ste. It does look human."

"Okay, well—if it bothers you that much." Ste picked the bone up and tossed it far from them. "Happy now?"

"You're sick," Kelvin muttered, returning his attention to the saucepan smoking on the fire.

Jim stood quite still for a few moments. He felt a slight chill, though the sun was climbing higher overhead. He was thinking of his dream, though now he felt more disturbed by it than thrilled. Now the idea of waking up to find a stranger in the tent with him did not seem so appealing. Shaking off the memory, he sat down in the grass with the others, thinking how the day was turning out to be nice, and about how they could always rely on Ste to spoil a perfectly nice day by dragging something nasty out into the open.

"Hey, guys! Hey, guys! How about some help?"

Ste and Kelvin were walking ahead of Jim. Kelvin had brought something from his backpack, which the two poured over. They had their backs to Jim, who had been left to carry all the fishing equipment.

"Come on," Jim protested. "This isn't fair."

"Just a second. We're busy."

"What're you doing? What're you looking at?"

Ste and Kelvin laughed together.

"Nothing for your eyes, Jim. You'd get embarrassed."

"What is it?"

"Nothing. Just a magazine."

They passed into a small wooded area, then out again into another field. Leaving the dappled shade of the trees, Jim stopped in his tracks. The sun filled the whole of the next meadow. The grass was high and spotted with color: daisies, dandelions and other flowers Jim couldn't name grew in abundance. The meadow was a wide area of grass with the sky blue above. Jim was so struck by the place that he could have happily forgotten about fishing and spent the day on his back in the middle of that meadow. It seemed to be the most peaceful, enticing place he had ever set foot in.

Ste glanced over his shoulder. "Come on, Jim. Keep moving."

"Can't we have a rest?"

"Jim—here!" Kelvin raised the magazine. He roared with laughter when Jim diverted his eyes. "I wouldn't mind seeing Zoë Oswald lying down like that, eh?"

"Zoë Oswald!" Ste barked, punching Kelvin on the shoulder. "She's way beyond your league!"

"No, she's not. I was thinking of asking her out next year."

"What!" Now Ste was laughing, bent forward and clutching his stomach. The full act.

Kelvin looked off to one side. "She wouldn't go out with you in a million years! She's a model, you goon. I've seen her in the Littlewoods catalogue. She wouldn't look twice at you."

"Guys," Jim interrupted, "can somebody besides me carry something? These boxes are heavy."

Kelvin stamped toward Jim and muttered, "Give me something then."

Ste was standing apart, untroubled by the shift in Kelvin's mood. He glanced about the field.

"This is where I found the bone, jawbone, or whatever. It was right over there."

Jim winced. "You're kidding, Ste?"

"No. The river's over on that side. Past those trees. The bone probably washed up. Whatever. Hey, let's swim."

Ste began striding off in the direction he had indicated. Jim and Kelvin exchanged a look that said 'here we go again' before wading across the field in pursuit.

The river was wide, but not deep. Standing on the bank, Jim could see the rocks and pebbles at the bottom of the water. He searched for movement. Could there be any fish in this river? He was turning around to tell Ste that maybe they should follow the river to see if they could find a deeper stretch, when Ste came hurtling past him, stripped down to his underwear and hollering at the top of his voice. He hit the water with a loud splash.

Jim dropped the fishing equipment onto the grass.

Ste shrieked. "Cold! Cold! It's freezing!"

"I'm coming in!" Kelvin said, already peeling off his t-shirt.

Jim sat on the bank, watching his two friends splash each other and frolic in the clear water.

"You're not coming in, Jim? It's not that bad once you get used to it."

"Can't swim," said Jim with a shrug.

Kelvin laughed. "But it's only waist high. You're not going to drown."

"If you go under, I'll save you, Jim," Ste said.

Ste and Kelvin began chanting Jim's name, throwing water up at him until he relented. He stood and kicked off his sandals. He took off his shirt, then stood shivering slightly on the bank, looking down at the water where his friends seemed so at home. It was true it was only waist high, but Jim focused on the slight ripples on the surface, thought about how it pulled and dragged. He thought about himself submerged. He might trap his foot in a space between the rocks and go under. He thought about himself grasping and fighting as he tried to break free, desperate, losing himself.

He took a step back. "Can't."

"Don't be a chicken. What's the matter?"

"I can't."

Jim turned his back to his friends and began walking toward the trees, attempting to escape their calls of derision, which had already begun. He left them to it. He wandered through to the wide meadow and fell down in the cool grass. He lay staring at the sky. Scraps of clouds hung against the blue, barely shifting. A flock of white butterflies jittered above, then away. Jim felt calm and relaxed. He could still hear his friends splashing and shouting, but distant. He was happy to be alone. He lay still and let himself doze with the sun warm on his face and chest. He smiled to himself, remembering what Kelvin had said about Zoe Oswald. I'm going to ask her out next year.

No chance, Jim thought.

When school started again, Zoe Oswald would be out of reach of all the boys. The girls seemed to grow up so much faster. Every September they seemed further ahead. Suddenly they had a different shape, and styled hair, and make-up, and a certain maturity in their eyes. They had become strange and alien. Their conversations were somehow closed. They made boys feel foolish for doing the things they had always done, like chasing balls and rolling in the dirt. That look in their eyes said, "When are you going to grow up?" or even "When are you going to get hair on your balls?" A girl had actually said that to Jim once, to make her friends laugh. It was a girl he was fond of. Her name was Summer. Jim liked her name because she was blond and freckled and looked like summer—to him at least. He had teased her one day and she had turned around and said, "When are you going to get hair on your balls, Jim Stanley?" Jim knew he was being mocked, but somehow what she had said exited him. He had thought about it often since. He thought about taking Summer away from her friends, taking her to a quiet corner of the school yard. She would not protest. She would stand there giggling. And Jim would lean in close and say *Wanna see? Wanna—*

There was a sound.

Jim opened his eyes. He looked into the blue sky. His face felt hot and flushed.

The sound came again. Abruptly, he sat up.

He looked toward the trees. He turned his head to one side, listening.

There it was again. Laughter. A girl's laughter.

He thought for a minute that Ste or Kelvin might be playing some trick on him, but he realized he could still hear the two of them down by the water. This laughter he had heard was closer. He scanned along the trees with his eyes. He hitched a breath when he saw a movement. Something had slipped between two tree trunks. Again, he heard a low giggle of laughter.

For some reason he felt his heart pounding. He realized he was frightened. Just as he had felt in his dream.

"Hel-Hello?" he ventured.

The only reply was another titter of laughter. He saw a form slip between the trees. Out of the corner of his eyes he saw movement also to his right. He looked that way, thought he saw a girl or a young woman standing at the edge of the trees for a moment, looking back at him. She was wearing some rough white cloth that hung off one shoulder—just like the girl in his dream that morning. In seconds she vanished, but as Jim stood gazing, he realized that the wooded area was suddenly alive with figures, flitting between the trees, hardly letting themselves be seen at all, the only noise the odd giggle. They seemed to be dancing, moving together in the cover of the shade.

By now, Jim was paralyzed with fear. He managed to call out to his friends. He called out over and over again until he saw them stepping from the wood, looking at him baffled.

"What is it, Jim?"

Jim stared at his friends. He stared at the trees. Now there was no movement there. He turned his ear again for the sound of laughter, but heard only the sound of the river running.

His friend's faces were expectant.

"I think I've been in the sun too long. I thought I saw something."

"What?"

"People. Girls. Dancing in the trees over there."

Ste creased up with laughter. Kelvin only stared at Jim, wide-eyed and incredulous.

"You believe this guy?"

"You were having a wet dream, Jim."

"No," Jim said, stunned. "It wasn't like that. It…it was more of a nightmare."

Of course, that made Ste laugh even more.

Kelvin shook his head. He began walking back toward the trees when he stopped and stared at the ground. "Guys," he said, in an ominous tone, but the others ignored him.

Ste patted Jim on the shoulder. "You're a dork sometimes. When we heard you shouting like that we thought you were being chased by a bull or something."

"You see any bulls around?" Jim said, looking Ste directly in the eyes. "We haven't seen anything or anyone. We don't even know where we are."

"Guys!" came Kelvin's voice again.

"Don't be like that, Jim. We're having an adventure."

Jim was about to respond when Kelvin shouted louder still. "Hey guys! Another bone!"

"What?"

Kelvin pointed at the ground. By his feet was a long, pale bone.

"That must belong to the bone I found earlier. This one looks like part of an arm, or leg."

Jim stared at the bone. Then he moved off into the field and began searching amongst the grass. He was alarmed to quickly come across more bones. He unearthed a skull, horrified. He turned back to his friends. "There's something really wrong here. We should leave. We need to tell somebody about this."

"It's just a few bones," Ste said. "They're dead; they can't bother us."

"I mean it. We need to tell someone."

Ste might normally have laughed at the idea of a tattletale, but instead he nodded and quietly said, "We need to get our things at the tent."

"Leave them," said Jim, glancing toward the trees that separated them from the river. "Let's just go."

"What! Don't be daft. I'm not leaving without my clothes."

"All right, I'm going back to the tent to get my things," Jim said. "Are you coming?"

When Ste and Kelvin stood immobile, Jim immediately turned to walk away. He heard Ste and Kelvin exchange a few mutters, but he was walking fast away from them, leaving them behind. He glanced once over his shoulder and saw them stepping into the trees, gone to fetch their clothes and the fishing gear they'd left by the river.

Once he got to the tent, he regretted his haste. Now he was alone near a meadow of bones. Why hadn't Ste and Kelvin followed him? Jim waited hours by the tent, growing ever more frantic. He was afraid to take off without them because he wasn't sure of the direction home.

It was possible his friends had stayed by the river, or gone off somewhere else. As the day drew on, Jim busied himself by packing up his things. He left the tent standing. When he finished, it was already getting late. He stood looking toward the trees at the edge of the field, waiting for his friends to appear. But still they didn't come.

Dusk was setting in when he saw a figure standing at the far end of the field, almost lost in the high grass. It wasn't Ste nor Kelvin; it was a girl. Though she was far away, he could see her long blond hair and white dress. She moved no closer, but remained near to the trees. With one arm, she seemed to be beckoning to him. Over and over again she beckoned to him. Jim only stared. He thought about the town, so far away. He thought about his mother, his father and his little sister, who would all be sitting down to dinner together.

His hands gripped the straps of his backpack. He wanted to leave this place. He started walking away. Then he stopped. He stared at the girl, far away, but still beckoning.

"You're scared of your own shadow, Jim," his father told him sometimes. And his mother would say, "Don't listen. He's only pulling your leg."

But he *was* afraid. It was only a young girl, but he was so afraid.

Jim watched as the girl continued to beckon him from across the field. His heart beat rapidly. He let the straps of his backpack slip from his shoulders, wondering at the same time why he was doing so, telling himself that he had to leave, that it would be dark before he knew it. He set his pack down in the grass. He gazed at the distant figure, looking for a reaction, wondering if his action had alarmed her. But no, she only continued waving her arm.

He began to walk forward, slowly at first, tentative, then faster. The girl smiled when she saw him, a sweet and reassuring smile. She held out a hand. Jim felt himself breathing heavily as he grasped her hand in his own. Terror flashed thorough him. And something else—something that allowed him to let her draw him into the trees. She looked into his face, smiling. He found himself smiling back at her; she was radiant, her hair glowing in the sun, her eyes alive and inquisitive, the smile settling at the corners of her mouth. Through the trees she led him into the wide meadow where the grass lilted and the sun touched everything.

She led him through the meadow, toward a glade of trees. He could hear the river running. He glanced back at the sky, now splashed with red as the sun sank behind the distant hills. Again, he felt a flash of fear, but the girl continued to pull him by the hand, gentle yet insistent. She made soft noises that were not words, but which soothed and reassured him. The light beneath the trees was hazy and strange. In the dimness, the girl appeared luminous, still catching rays of sunlight in her hair and on her skin. She glowed and sparkled with light as she turned to him, laughing. There were other sounds of girlish laughter from round about, other soft, wordless exclamations. Jim looked around and saw figures flit between the trees, laughing as though in the midst of some game.

For a moment the spell was broken and he looked back again, searching for the sky. It was there still, beyond the trees at his back, but it had turned to the color of blood. He thought of his friends. Were they here? Could he still look for them? But then the girl tugged at his hand, so he turned to her and was once again lost. She smiled, spoke something he did not understand and led him into the glade, where the air was moist and damp. Jim could see a thin mist hanging low to the ground. He could feel a film of damp on his face and arms. Now he could hear the river close by. The light was fading and the girl led him further as night closed around them. Jim glanced over his shoulder, aware of footsteps behind him. Though he could not see them, he knew there were others following.

Then the trees broke. Everything was outlined, dimly, by moonlight. They had arrived at a place where the river pooled, and on the surface of the water was a cold phosphorescence. As Jim turned about in the near darkness, he noticed a long shape on the ground nearby. A still face, pale in the moonlight, lay in the grass. He wanted to say: Ste? But the girl was there, pulling at his hands, turning him away. As he looked at her, he saw that she was lifting up the white dress off over her head. She moved to stand at the edge of the pool, her body lithe and wan against the blackness of the night, her young breasts bobbing as she turned toward the water, her hair falling across her bare shoulders with a softness that made him yearn. He wanted to wrap her hair around him, wrap himself up. There he would find peace, in a velvety den of her hair.

There was a splash that startled him and he realized she had dropped casually into the pool. He heard other splashes from the darkness around him; other bodies were landing in the water. The girl swam to the edge of the pool at his feet and reached her arms up toward him. She smiled, making cooing noises of enticement.

Jim thought: *No...no...not the water...no!* Then he saw that there were other white forms already in the water as though they were waiting for him. These were the other girls, naked in the moonlight, all crowding at his feet and reaching their arms out to him. Some of them laughed and splashed each other. Some floated on their backs, like otters, joyous and at home in the water.

And he wanted to go to them.

He crouched, reaching forward, and at once hands took hold of him. He felt the shock of cold as he fell forward into the pool. He righted himself, gasping, finding the riverbed with his feet. The girls were laughing, and he was laughing with them, shivering but overwhelmed with joy, intoxicated by the bodies crowding around him and the thrill of his own daring.

The girl he had followed was in front of him. He reached out for her and felt the touch of her cold skin. Her face moved close to his and he could see that she was smiling. Then he realized, with a jolt, that she was pressing on him and he was sinking into the water. He felt her lips against his and her body was forcing him down, and there were other arms, other bodies, all pressing him down. He could hear laughter, and he thought there was a ring of mockery in it.

Still the girl continued to cling to him, kissing him, locking him in her embrace and forcing him downwards. His head sank below the water and he wanted to scream, but could not, and he knew he had seen Ste, dead, by the side of the pool, and still he felt the many bodies forcing him and holding him down. And he was under the water and he could not shout or scream or struggle, he could not breathe, and all he could feel was the girls holding him under, holding him under, weighing on him, until all became still and all became silence and all he saw before him was blackness.

About Tim Jeffreys

Tim Jeffreys grew up in Manchester, England, and from an early age used writing and drawing as a means of escape. His early attempts at storytelling took the form of comic books until he became frustrated by the amount of time this took. So he launched straight into writing and illustrating a novel, a vampire tale entitled *The Riders* (now, for better or worst, lost). After making it to University and completing a degree in Graphic Arts, Tim decided, after much encouragement, to sideline the artwork and make writing his main focus. This would take some explaining in the years to come. By now, though, he had been introduced to the idea of the short story and he started to produce these in tandem with his longer work.

In 2007 Tim published his first collection of short stories, *The Garden Where Black Flowers Grow*, and has since put together a second collection, *The Scenery of Dreams*.

Tim now lives in the South West of England, where he likes to keep himself busy by writing short stories, creating artwork, and working on his novels, as well as holding down an unavoidable day-job in the health service. In early 2010, along with some friends, he founded the small press magazine *The Dark Lane Quarterly*.
http://www.timjeffreyswriter.webs.com

ADELLE'S NIGHT
by David K. Ginn

On Thursday night, Adelle met the strangest man. He introduced himself as Steve Hammond, and they drank together. On the outside, he seemed average: friendly face, short dark hair, button-down dress shirt and jeans.

But when she sat next to him at the bar, and he turned to start a conversation, there was a deeper, enlightened quality to him that she couldn't quite define. It certainly wasn't the topics, because they talked of nothing profound, still, the conviction in his voice breathed new life into even the most banal of subject matters. Adelle found herself strangely and uncontrollably attracted to him. They had known each other for just shy of an hour, and it had been a very pleasant experience for her.

That was why Adelle was so struck when he said the strangest thing anyone had ever said to her. "This is a movie, did you know that?"

Upon seeing her dumbfounded expression, he followed up with, "That's right, it's a movie, and you're the main star."

Adelle took an awkward, hunch-shouldered sip of gin. "I'm not sure what you mean," she said, wondering if she had misjudged the guy by thinking too highly of him.

"Just what I said. Blows your mind, doesn't it?"

"Is this your way of telling girls you're attracted to them?"

"I am attracted to you," he said, "but that has nothing to do with what I'm telling you. Right now, we are in a movie; a movie about you."

Adelle felt uncomfortable and more than a little confused. "Are there cameras in here or something? Is this one of those stupid game shows where they jump out at you and yell surprise?"

"No, not at all. We are part of what film students would call the *diegesis*. I had to look that one up. It means the fictional world of the movie. It's crazy, right?"

Adelle grabbed her purse. "Crazy is right. I'm leaving."

Steve put his hand on her wrist to stop her. "Big man, leather jacket and chains...'Excuse me ma'am, you dropped this'...little kid pointing, his dad pulls him away...old lady almost gets creamed by a pickup...flannel shirt, can't open the door to the cab." He let out an exhausted breath.

"What does that mean?"

"Extras."

"Let go of me." She shook his hand off her wrist and marched to the front door of the bar. As she stepped outside onto the sidewalk, a large, burly man in a leather jacket bumped against her shoulder. Dropping her keys, an elderly man appeared from nowhere, picked them off the ground, and handed them to her. "Excuse me ma'am, you dropped these."

Frightened now, she took the keys back and stared at the elderly man in wide-eyed shock. He turned away before she could thank him. Across the street, the old man's wife made her way toward him, yelling at a green pickup truck as it stopped short to avoid her. Next to Adelle, a drunken man struggled pathetically with the door handle to a taxi cab.

It made no sense. How could Steve have foreseen all of this? Was he psychic? Or was there really some sort of movie? Unable to stop herself, she walked back into the bar and set her purse down on the barstool that she had vacated just moments before. "What the hell's going on?" she asked loud enough that other patrons turned her way.

"In the movie, it cuts to you being back in here. How did it feel to walk all that way outside, when in reality it happens like that?" He snapped his fingers theatrically.

"Will you explain?"

And so he did. Two days ago, he told her, he was just another working stiff, his life as unremarkable as anyone else's. Late at night, as he was browsing the DVDs at a local video store, he had what he now refers to as a "Billy Pilgrim moment"—essentially, that he became unstuck. Being so overwhelmed by the millions and millions of movie titles for rent, he realized that if life were a movie, there would be a DVD of it somewhere.

He spent all that night searching until finally he found it. Proudly, he presented the movie and his membership card to the cashier, and took it home to watch. It was an hour and a half long but well-acted and very enjoyable. There were even scenes with him in it. Over the next day, he re-watched the movie enough to know where to go and what to say, and so here he was, humble in the presence of the star. Which, of course, was Adelle.

"I'd like to see this movie," Adelle told him. Up until now, she had seen what could have been practiced theater-tricks by very skilled illusionists who didn't know how to pick up girls the usual way. And what Steve was saying fascinated her enough so that she wasn't sure which she wanted more: to prove him wrong or to see first-hand that it was all true.

"Have another drink first," Steve said.

"Trying to get me drunk?"

Steve shook his head. "It's what I'm supposed to say."

"And if I oblige?"

"You will."

A half hour later, they left the bar and walked three blocks to the cement steps of Steve's apartment building. She didn't know why she was doing this. She didn't know why she was accompanying a stranger to his home. She sensed danger; the illogic of her submissiveness screamed red flags at her.

At foot of the stairs, she balked. "Why don't I wait here, and you just bring the movie down to me?"

"I could," Steve said, "but then where are we going to watch it? Out on the street?"

"I could just leave."

Steve smiled. "Yes, you could." He opened the door and walked into the lobby, then started up the stairs to the next floor without her.

Adelle stood outside for a moment and looked over her shoulder back the way they had come. A taxi pulled to the curb and an elderly woman stepped out. The cab's lights flashed on and she took a step toward it. But she hesitated. She didn't want to go into the apartment building, yet she was unable to stop herself from doing something so outside of her comfort zone. Turning away from the cab, she went back to the apartment lobby's open door.

When she reached the second floor, he called out from the stairwell above her. She felt irritated at his confidence that she would be there. She took the next set of stairs and caught her breath once she reached the top. She grabbed onto the rail.

"Had enough to drink?" he asked.

Adelle straightened herself out and held her chin up in mock defiance. Steve motioned toward the hallway. "In that case, come with me."

He led her into the apartment, which was clean and entirely uninteresting. There was a bathroom and two bedrooms connected to the living room. He opened the door to the nearest bedroom and beckoned her to follow. As she stepped under the door frame, he grabbed both her hands and leaned close. Adelle dodged his advance, but managed a smile.

"Movie," she said.

Steve nodded and released his grasp. "Yes, the movie. Come on in and I'll make us something to drink...unless you've had enough?"

This was more of a challenge than an inquiry, yet another light-hearted intimation that she couldn't hold her liquor. She accepted with the same mock defiance, although she suspected he knew that she had had more than enough.

He left for the kitchen, and she took a moment to survey the bedroom. Everything looked normal on the surface; but then again, Steve had appeared normal on the surface too. Studying the room, she admired his modest book collection, his cozy reading lamp, and the three or four DVD cases scattered about the carpet.

No, wait, there. There it was, on the floor. She stopped suddenly and crouched to pick up one of the cases, which had her face on the cover art and the title *Adelle's Night*. She felt a chill run through her body, as exhilarating as it was frightening. She opened the case, but there was no disc inside. She searched around for a remote, found it, and turned on the television. She sat on the floor, the carpet soft beneath her, and got ready.

Her movie had already been loaded. She pressed 'play,' and then rapidly skipped through each chapter. With a feeling of increased dread, she saw the entirety of her day—from her phone conversation with her mother, to the stop at the supermarket, and so on, coming to a head as she entered the bar and saw Steve for the first time. Then she was outside the apartment, debating whether or not to hail the cab. The same elderly woman stepped out, and the close-up of her own face on screen perfectly captured her indecision.

Then they were upstairs, first on the stairwell, then flirting in the doorway. She watched herself crouch to the floor, and play the movie, and for a brief moment she was synched with her on-screen persona, and then it kept going. In the movie, Steve entered the room carrying two tumbler glasses. He smiled awkwardly when he noticed what she was doing. He crouched beside her, set the glasses down and shut the movie off.

In real life, Steve appeared behind her carrying two tumbler glasses. He smiled awkwardly when he noticed what she was doing. He crouched beside her and set the glasses down. He placed one cold hand on her waist, the other on the remote to turn off the movie. They stood up together, and she asked him how it ends.

Steve shook his head. "I really, really hate when critics spoil the ending."

"Oh, knock it off," she said in a huff.

"Don't get mad. It's all good; I just don't want to rush anything. You're too special to rush."

Pacified, she walked over to the bed and grazed her hand across the soft sheets. "So if I'm the main star, what are you? The love interest?"

He laughed. "No, not exactly."

"What exactly, then?" she said, realizing that she was indeed feeling very drunk. Why else could she be behaving like this? "Are you the one-night-stand I'm supposed to learn a valuable lesson from?"

There was a suggestive tone to the last question, a clear message that she didn't mind. She was surprised to learn that she was open to the idea.

"No, not that, either."

She felt rejected. "What, then?" She looked down, noticing the carpet was a dark brown.

Suddenly he was behind her, and she felt the palms of his hands on her stomach. So he wasn't rejecting her after all. She arched her head back as his hands traveled upward, pushing her shirt up, his fingers caressing the light goose bumps that had formed over her skin. "I came for the movie," she said, but made no attempt to break free.

"So did I."

"I don't usually do things like this."

"Ah, an 'I'm not usually this type of girl' statement."

"It's just, I'm not very spontaneous."

"And you didn't even see the film," he said. "If you had..." He paused. "Sometimes you can be perfectly ordinary your whole life, but suddenly you see yourself doing something in a movie, something you're just not capable of. But after a day or two, when everything else comes true, you have no choice but to accept it as reality. And when you do, you become capable. You become the person you saw on screen. And there's no turning back."

Adelle loosened his hold on her. "What?"

"I even saw my hesitation. I saw myself almost stop."

Adelle tried to wrestle free. "You're hurting me."

He clasped a hand tightly over her mouth and pulled back. "I hate it when people talk during movies. Now hold on; this is my favorite part."

From his back pocket he withdrew a long, silver kitchen knife, which he held comfortably by its black, silicon handle.

"You can't escape destiny," he said. "Not when it's on film."

He raised the blade, closed his eyes, and swung it down toward her chest. But there was no jolting impact, no thick spray of blood, and no Hollywood scream...because twisting from his grasp, Adelle dropped down to the floor, landing on the thick, brown carpet. He grabbed wildly at the air where she had just been a second before.

From the floor, Adelle kicked upwards with a hard thrust and made contact with Steve's kneecap. He made a whooshing sound and stumbled, and his knife fell to the floor beside her with a dull thud. She made a grab for it and suddenly there it was in her hand. She knew she would use the knife if she had to.

She took advantage of his momentary incapacitation, and jumping up from the floor, Adelle turned and ran out of the bedroom into the living room. She reached the front door. She made it!

She grabbed the door handle and grunted as she tried to pull it open. Why wouldn't it open? My god, she needed it to open! She looked up above the handle and saw three different types of locks on the doorframe. She hadn't noticed any of them on her way in.

Sweating, panting heavily, she fumbled at the locks, and undid them in succession. She heard him stumble out of the bedroom behind her.

"In every good movie, there is a chase scene," she heard him say behind her. He was getting closer. She had to get out now!

For a brief moment Adelle pictured the end of the movie: her own body slouched against the door, Steve staring blankly down at her.

But she had free will. Every decision she made was her own. It could end any way she wanted it to.

She unlatched the final lock and swung the door open, nearly hitting Steve in the face as he ran after her. She fled to the stairway and took all three flights without looking up once. He followed her down to the lobby, taking two steps at a time. She could hear him behind her, but didn't dare to look back.

By the door of the lobby was a steel candy vending machine, such a typical sight that she almost passed it without noticing. He was closing in on her fast, but on a bruised shin. She grabbed the vending machine and pushed. It didn't fall over completely, but it rocked and hit him in the face. Steve stumbled backward and fell onto his back, nursing a bloody nose in his palm.

"You want an ending?" she yelled at him. She pushed the vending machine harder this time and let it fall to the floor with a loud metallic crash. "Somebody call the cops!" She screamed to the ceiling of the apartment lobby. She turned and stumbled as she left the apartment building and descended down the cement steps.

Once outside, she looked around the dark street and saw that there was no one around, nothing but the cab—

It was still there. Whatever it was doing, it hadn't left yet. A wave of relief washed over her as she stumbled dizzily toward it, and through trembling lips she managed a smile. The driver seemed to notice her distress; the car jumped forward and pulled up beside her.

"Are you all right?" the driver asked.

"I need to get away from here."

"Where to?"

"Anywhere."

The driver motioned to the back seat. "Get in."

On the third floor of the apartment building, Steve stumbled into his open doorway, arm over his bruised ribs. He held his head high as he struggled to keep his blood from dripping onto the carpet. He entered the bedroom, collapsed on the floor and grabbed the DVD remote. He pressed "play" and drank from one of the tumblers he had brought in earlier. The glass next to it was empty.

The events unfolded on his television screen just as they had in reality. Steve felt lucky to be alive; his final fate was never shown on-screen. After everything that had happened, he still felt an immense desire for Adelle, even a pang of remorse as he watched her step into the cab and ride away.

Steve saw the cab driver ask Adelle a question on the television screen. "What's your name?"

"Adelle," he saw her stammer as she searched her purse for her cell phone. She found it and raised it above her head. "Can you take me somewhere that has good reception?"

"Adelle..." the driver mused. He narrowed his eyes and let his foot slip slowly off the gas pedal. "You know, that reminds me of a movie I saw recently."

Steve watched the realization creep into Adelle's face. Sometimes it was hard to see her in the darkness, but yes, now the cab was slowing until it was directly underneath a streetlight. Steve understood that lighting was always so important to a film's success.

The driver applied the brake. The streetlight's glow flooded the cab, and Steve could see clearly as Adelle lowered her phone and stared ahead, face trembling.

The driver looked at her without turning—a pair of dark eyes in the rearview mirror. "Great movie," he said. "Want to know how it ends?"

About David K. Ginn

David K. Ginn has written three books and over thirty stories in the fantasy, horror and science fiction genres. When not writing, he does work in independent filmmaking, fine art and graphic design. He has run the science fiction media review site *The Basestar* for two years.

He received a bachelor of arts degree in Cinema and Cultural Studies from Stony Brook University and currently lives on Long Island, New York. http://www.davidkginn.com

BONES FOR A PILLOW
by Alexandra Seidel

The first time I was absolutely certain that something was wrong was when I found long black hairs slithering out of the vacuum bag. They looked withered and dusty; straight. Staring at them, I imagined that once they had been shiny, lustrous even, but creeping from the round hole of the bag, they were as lifeless as ancient spider webs in a forgotten tomb. I should mention that I was the only one living in the house and also that I have shoulder-length blond curls. These black hairs, they weren't mine and that said, I had no idea whose they were.

I mentioned the house. I moved into it in the spring, while flowers were blooming all over the front lawn. I remember when I first saw it and how the realtor was telling me that everything was brand new, even the lively yellow paint on the outside walls. I realized two things immediately when I saw the big rooms and how the sunlight hit the shiny wooden floor boards: first, I loved the place; second, it was probably too expensive for me, never mind that it was obviously too big.

And that was why I was so surprised when I actually heard the price from the realtor's lips. Not because it was higher than I had feared, but because it was so very low. As I asked her why, she just shrugged and said that the owner had given her this price. When I think back, I can't be sure, but I think that she would have liked to have said something else, something more. But that moment passed, and whatever it was, explanation or warning, it died in her throat and was washed away with a sideways glance. At the time, though, I did not care and I certainly didn't ask. The house was a gift horse after all, and I signed the papers almost immediately.

It really was a big house. While I was carrying in all my stuff and arranging all the furniture I owned, I saw that there was more room, more emptiness in this house than I knew how to fill. Yet, when I was sitting down on the floor one evening, the first evening in the new place, I realized I liked it that way.

It was that same evening—I remember it because I was trying to find a place for this very ugly vase my grandmother had given me—that I found a fingernail stuck in a crack of the floor boards.

It was not whole or shiny, but chipped and battered, dyed gray with dust and dirt. I took the ugly thing between thumb and forefinger, disgusted as I did so yet determined to get rid of it, and I carried it out of my house and threw it in the trash. I figured that, since the house had been completely redone very recently, some construction worker had had a minor accident and so I didn't think anything further of it. Only later when I found the hairs did I seem to recall faintly that the fingernail had been long, too long to belong to any sensible construction worker.

But back then, I was in high spirits and something so small and seemingly insignificant could do little to change that. My recent promotion, which had made the move necessary, kept me busy at work and I liked that. I was excited to attend a business conference a few weeks later.

It was at that conference that I met Darren. He came up to me, picking me out of the crowd as if he'd planned our encounter. Darren was cute and confident and I loved his smile and the way he walked like he owned the ground beneath his feet. He seduced me and I would be lying if I said I didn't enjoy every second of it. But ours was not just a fleeting affair; funny enough as chance encounters go, he lived in the same city as me and we made plans to meet again soon at my place.

I think when he first walked through my front door, he said that he had lived in a house just like this. *So you lived close by?* I had asked him. He shot me a smile and said, *Yes, you could say that.* I hadn't realized that he had given the words *just like this* a funny twist when he referred to the house. And his smile a moment later might have looked somehow odd. But I didn't care. I was in love.

He had brought a bottle of red wine and we finished it off sitting on my couch. From there we moved to the floor, undressing each other and exchanging kisses. His strong arms pulled me beneath him, pressed my back and my buttocks against the cool wood. My hair curled around his fingers like wild vines and from there it flowed down to the floor boards, over them and perhaps, like roots searching water, quested beneath them. I slung my legs around Darren and pulled him closer, deeper. Our moans echoed around us like ghosts in my almost empty living room. When we were finished, the wood floor beneath us was damp with sweat and pleasure.

Darren came over often and that made me happy. It's not like we never used the bed, but Darren preferred my living room floor.

Sometimes I thought I heard something else apart from his and my sounds of lovemaking: there was sobbing when we kissed and something like a toneless wailing when our hearts beat faster, but it was all so faint, so almost-not-there that I was quick to dismiss it as a trick of my mind. Despite my attempts at ignoring them, the sounds were always almost there. Almost. I was never sure.

And they followed me, all the way into my dreams. In the morning, I could never recall my dreams exactly, but I did remember the sounds, no matter how faintly, I did remember them.

And that was when I found the hairs in the vacuum bag.

The sight of them alone made a cold shiver run down my spine. Was I scared? More disgusted at first, I think. I took the vacuum bag and threw it away, out off my house and into the dust bin. I was angry that those hairs had dared intrude into what I had come to think of as my home. And I was furious that I didn't know how to explain their presence.

That day, I went to the living room to clean so I could work off my anger and confusion. While I was dusting the low coffee table I caught a glint in the corner of my eye and turned my head toward the part of the empty living room floor it had come from. It was where I had discovered the fingernail. It was where Darren would lay down my head and slide his tongue into my mouth. Nothing was there. I went down on my knees, leaned over and my face came close to the wood and the cracks where one floor board tried to meet, but never quite touched its neighbor. I could smell the dust in the cracks. I was just about to get up again, assured that nothing was there, when I saw something white.

I couldn't reach whatever it was I saw with my fingers and so I got a knife from the kitchen that caught the low autumn sun on its blade. After several tries, I finally succeeded in getting the thing out.

I sat there with my mouth open, a hollow feeling in the pit of my stomach and nausea rising slowly like a balloon filled with hot air. I was staring at a tooth that shone like withered bone in the drooping rays of the fading sun. It was a human tooth, and it wasn't small enough to be the tooth of a child either, to be explained away as a carelessly lost baby tooth of somebody who had lived here before me. A tapping sound startled me and it took me a second to realize that what I'd heard was the sound of my own tears painting dark circles on the shiny wood.

I called Darren. He eventually came over. He was very calm and reasonable and succeeded in convincing me that the tooth had been some remnant of a worker, some unfortunate accident, but nothing to worry about. I don't know if this was rational, but it was a convenient thing to believe as it had been with the fingernail.

I never even mentioned the hairs to Darren. I wanted to forget about them and telling him would have made them more real, too real.

It was at that point that the nightmares came regularly. They ate at my energy and clouded my mood and it got harder and harder to keep my rising fear to myself. All I remember about the dreams is darkness and dread, but no details. I woke up sweat-soaked nearly every morning before dawn.

That winter, Darren had to leave for a few weeks. His mother was in the hospital and she wasn't doing well. I was left behind, alone in the house with all the emptiness that I could no longer bring myself to like.

Daylight was a rare commodity as I had to work long hours, leaving before sunrise and coming home long after sunset. If I had to be totally truthful, I think that I worked as much as I did in order to spend as little time as possible at home.

One night I woke up thirsty. I don't think I'd had a nightmare. Not that night, anyway. I got up and went downstairs to the kitchen to get a glass of water. I remember the wooden floor as a biting cold touch to the pink softness of my bare feet. In the kitchen, I recall the flowing water making gurgling noises in the sink before it filled my glass. When I was just about to take a sip I heard a sound from the living room and, ever so cautiously, I turned around.

I hadn't turned on any lights, but a full moon shone through the window, casting a pale light and strange shadows. On the floor I could see some curling inky lines that I couldn't place. I suppose I could have gone back to bed then, but I didn't. I was afraid as I'd ever been in my life, but there was also this sick curiosity. I wanted to know. I had to know.

I went into the living room, my cold bare feet hardly making any sound. I squatted down. I looked at the curling lines and I just had to touch them to prove to myself that I wasn't seeing things.

They looked like hair, long black hair growing from in between the cracks. It was the hair I had seen in my vacuum bag, the hair I had thrown out and tried to forget about. I thought back to Darren and me making love in this very spot and how my hair must have twisted its way to where this was coming from, how my hair had touched this, many times. It made me feel unclean and tainted.

My fingers reached out to touch the black strands, and to my shock, they were real. I took them in my hands and pulled, but they wouldn't come free. Then, they suddenly reacted to my pull by snapping back beneath the floor boards with all the speed of a striking serpent. I was struck with icy needles of shock and horror; naked fear. I tried to scream, but my throat was dry and the sound was tiny compared to the size of my terror.

I scuttled backward until my back bumped into a wall. There was a tapping from the floor boards. From the other side of the floor boards. It sounded as if somebody was drumming a small wooden stick against the boards.

I knew that I had to crawl back toward the sound and investigate. I could feel the wood vibrate under my hands. I looked into the cracks, but couldn't see a thing. I moved my head down, so close that my lips were brushing over the wood. I could smell dust and something else. There wasn't much light here, but what little there was reflected off the eyeball that suddenly locked gazes with me.

I stared back, too shaken to move a muscle. Never will I forget that eye. Crazy with madness, angry beyond comprehension, and red, so very red. Blood vessels had burst or were about to, swollen on the white background. The iris was dark and the black pupil focused on my own.

There was a groan then, long wailing, and it ripped me out of my trance. I hurried to the garage on shaky legs to get some tools. I knew I had to tear open the floor boards, suddenly certain that the person under the floor was imprisoned and needed my help.

I pulled with all my strength, pulled until tears were flowing like rivers down my cheeks and sobs had made my throat tight. I put down the tools and I pulled until my fingers were bleeding, my fingernails having surrendered to the hard wood.

I was too late, of course. The first thing I saw was the white of fleshless knucklebones. Then an arm, pelvis, spine and finally the skull, veiled by dirty black hair. She was under the floor boards, caught like a rabbit in a snare. She was dead.

I was sick in the kitchen sink. My mind was reeling and I was wondering whether going mad feels like this and whether you can actually feel when you're going mad. I didn't know what to do, panic had left me helpless. I called Darren, I think because I wanted him to comfort me, to make me able to handle what I had just seen.

He agreed to come. He was there very fast, too fast considering that he was supposed to be with his ailing mother. But perhaps I was just in shock and confused the time, I cannot say. He let himself in when I didn't react to the door bell. I never paused to wonder how. I hadn't given him a key yet.

I was all in shambles, but he was so very, very calm. He looked at the corpse, but wasn't really scared or shocked or anything. He turned toward me.

"Have you called the cops?" he asked.

"No," I said, "I called you."

He came over to me then and took me in his arms. He kissed me the way we usually kissed before we made love. I didn't want to just then.

His kisses cleared my mind and made all the details burn bright in my consciousness, much too bright.

It's so cold, my bare feet on the wood and Darren warm, but not to warm me. He pulls me close and pushes his tongue into my mouth. When I try to get away he grips my arm in a way that will leave bruises. My pajamas are torn off in seconds and he has me on the floor, underneath him. I hear him unzip his pants and feel unbearable hot pain between my legs. Adrenaline keeps me focused all the while. I do not want to think of the grave under my living room floor. I have left the tool box here and it is so close, too close. I fight as hard as I can, but he is stronger, he holds my wrists and keeps me pinned down. I see him grab a hammer, see the hammer come down, aimed straight for my head. The last thing I hear before I pass out is the sound of one of my teeth as it clatters to the floor.

Darren walks around in the house as if he owns the place. He cleans up everything and replaces the floor boards, the last one directly over my knucklebones. If my muscles still worked, I would drum them against the wood.

Darren's muscles move visibly under his shirt, just as if he is used to that sort of manual labor. He smiles. How I used to love that smile! When he is done, he strips down and has a long shower in my bathroom and dries himself with one of my towels. His manner shows routine, even when he closes the door behind him and leaves, though his smile says he won't be gone for long.

We stay, and every so often, other hair tickles our faces from the other side of the wood and in return, we let our own hair creep up and wander. Our fleeting eyeballs peer up sometimes and it's not like we could help that, because beneath this wood, there is no room for us to turn our heads away.

About Alexandra Seidel

Alexandra Seidel likes writing scary stories and poems. Incidentally, she also likes writing funny stories and poems; in the grander concept of things, that surely makes sense.

Alexandra's writing has appeared in *Space and Time Magazine, Cabinet des Fées, Star*Line* and others.

She was born and grew up in Kassel, home of the Brothers Grimm and their fairy tales (and of an eerie museum of sepulchral art and culture). http://tigerinthematchstickbox.blogspot.com

MALL WALKERS
by Chris Reed

It would have been the perfect place to skip school if it hadn't been for the mall walkers. Corey watched them rush by outside the arcade entrance, herds of them wearing skimpy little tank tops and shorts that exposed their pale, wrinkled skin. While they never actually bothered Corey and his friends, just their presence was enough to put a damper on things. They always looked at the teenagers with disapproving scowls on their faces. If Corey wanted to be surrounded by judgmental old bags, he would have just stayed at school.

"Watch this," Travis said. He cocked his arm back and whipped a penny in the mall walkers' direction.

Corey watched as the coin struck an old lady on the elbow. The woman grimaced, looked down and rubbed her arm, but kept her stride.

Travis was cracking up, but Tessa didn't find the prank so amusing. "Why'd you do that, Travis? We're gonna get kicked out of here."

"Yeah, and I don't want to go back to school," Hannah said. "I'd be in trig right now." She made an ugly face.

"Oh, come on," Travis said. "You guys are so uptight!" He dug into his pocket and took out some more change. He handed Corey a quarter and said, "Your turn."

Corey took the coin, even though Hannah was giving him the look. It was the same look she always gave him when he was about to do something stupid and she didn't want him to. She gave him that look a lot when Travis was around.

Corey looked out at the mall walkers. They were moving so fast, arms tucked up tight to their sides, elbows jutting out, hips swiveling as they motored by.

"Corey, don't," Hannah said. "That could hurt someone."

"Do it!" Travis said, grinning.

Corey respected Hannah's feelings, but he'd known Travis since the third grade, and they always did stuff like this. He figured Hannah would eventually get used to it. Besides, it was just a coin. What real damage could it do?

Aiming at no one in particular, Corey pitched the coin toward the moving mass of people. It floated upward—higher than he'd meant to throw it—and caught a short, bald man in the temple. The man's knees buckled instantly, his forward momentum sending him crashing to the floor. The group of walkers stopped abruptly, nearly trampling him.

"Shit!" Hannah said.

"Damn, bro!" Travis laughed. "You *nailed* him!"

Corey felt sick as he watched the old man's friends help him to a sitting position. The man sat there, holding the side of his head, a dazed look upon his face.

"I can't believe you did that!" Hannah said. "You could have killed him!"

"Chill out," Travis said. "He's okay. Look, he's getting up."

Corey watched as the old man's friends helped him to his feet. A woman brushed the dirt off his shirt for him, and soon, the group was moving again.

"I think I have another quarter," Travis said, thrusting his hand into his pocket.

Tessa grabbed his arm and said, "I think that's enough excitement for one morning. Besides, I thought we came here to play video games."

"Fine," Travis said. He looked at Corey and said, "C'mon, bro."

They walked deeper into the arcade and found a change machine to convert their quarters to game tokens. Corey dug into his pants pocket and came up with three quarters. The game he wanted to play cost a dollar. He looked back toward the arcade entrance, where the mall walkers were rushing by. The quarter he'd thrown at the old man was out there on the floor somewhere.

"You coming, or what?" Travis said. He and the girls had their tokens and were ready to hit the games.

"I'll be right there," Corey told them.

"Well, hurry up," Travis said. "I want to play some air hockey."

As the others headed toward the back of the arcade, Corey turned and walked toward the front.

The herd of mall walkers seemed thicker now. A black flag near the door, sporting the arcade's name in red, fluttered as they rushed by.

Corey aimed his gaze at their shuffling feet, hoping to spot the quarter. It could have landed anywhere. He walked closer, eyes squinting at the crowd of marching gym shoes. Then he saw it—the gleam of silver on the floor, right at the edge of their path.

He moved closer, trying to time it so he could grab the quarter without getting trampled. The closer he got, the draftier the air became.

He noticed the flag was not only moving now, but actually billowing. Where was this breeze coming from? The arcade was at least twenty yards from the mall entrance, and besides, it wasn't even windy out today.

Corey looked back into the arcade. Travis was pumping tokens into a game as the girls watched. Corey considered asking if he could borrow some money, but he'd had a crush on Hannah since the eighth grade, and didn't want to look like a bum in front of her.

He turned back to the mall walkers. Up and down their feet marched so quickly they seemed to barely touch the floor. Legs flew by in a blur. He'd heard stories of people getting too close to speeding trains and being sucked under, and that's what he felt like now—like he was standing too close to the tracks.

Behind him the sounds of the arcade games and Hannah's laughter beckoned.

He inched his way closer, kneeled down, reached out, his fingertips just inches from the shiny coin. He felt a tug on his arm, something pulling him forward.

He snatched his hand back and scooted away. The flag ruffled next to him, and he realized the wind was coming from *them*. No way, he thought. You've been playing too many video games.

"Come on!" he heard Travis yell behind him. "What are you doing out there?"

Corey turned to him and said, "I'll be there in a minute!"

He faced the mall walkers again. He sucked in a deep breath and let it out slowly. He crept forward, extended his arm, eyes on the coin—it was so close!

The flag whipped and snapped.

He felt the tug on his arm again, tried to pull back, but he was off balance. The force—strong as a tornado—dragged him out of the arcade and into the mob of walkers.

He bounced off their legs and tumbled along the hard, dusty floor. Instead of falling under a train, he now felt like he'd plunged into a raging river. Bodies slammed into him like waves, knocking him down each time he tried to stand.

He looked up, tried to spot Travis and the girls to call for help, but he was no longer in the mall. He was now at his high school graduation, crossing the stage, accepting his diploma. An elbow caught him in the ribs and he found himself in his college dorm room, kneeling at the toilet after drinking too much. A knee struck him, sent him spinning, and he was losing his virginity on Spring break. Then he was in a church, standing before a beautiful woman, placing a ring on her slender finger.

Now he was in a hospital, holding a crying baby. Emotions flashed by in a strobe light of joy, pain, lust, rage. Then time seemed to freeze and he was standing in the rain, weeping over a grave. He'd never felt so alone.

A hand grabbed him under the arm. Another seized his elbow. Wind rushed past his ears as they hauled him to his feet. A crowd of mall walkers surrounded him, their rheumy eyes fixed on him. An old man with saggy jowls and thick glasses said, "You okay?"

Corey stared back at him in revulsion.

"Looks like you're bleeding," a woman in a pearl-white wig said.

Corey followed her gaze down to his right arm. He gasped when he saw the old, leathery skin with the scrape on it. This couldn't be real!

He examined the rest of his body, his wide eyes shifting from his liver-spotted hands, down past his white shorts to his knobby knees and stick-thin legs, webbed with varicose veins.

"What the hell?" he whispered, his voice a raspy croak.

An old man in a pink Polo shirt crouched down, picked up something off the floor. He stretched his gnarled hand out to Corey and said, "Dropped your quarter."

Corey reached out and took the coin.

"Can't get home without bus fare," the man said.

"I told you to get one of these fanny packs," the old lady told Corey, nodding down to the black pouch strapped to her waist. Corey smelled something foul coming from her pants.

The crowd of walkers was moving again. Corey cast a glance over his shoulder, back into the arcade. Travis and the girls were playing Skee-Ball, oblivious to his departure. He opened his mouth to shout, but his dentures shifted in his mouth, changing his words to a jumbled slur.

"Don't pay those hooligans any mind," the woman with the wig told him. "Someday they'll be as old as we are."

As Corey marched, a calm fell over him, and he was relieved to be moving away from the arcade's flashing lights and noisy machines. He suddenly wondered what the appeal of such games was. He remembered liking them at one time, even playing them every day, but it seemed like so long ago.

"You coming to bingo tonight?" the lady beside him asked.

Corey found himself nodding. Activities like bingo and shuffleboard, or just reading a good book seemed quite appealing compared to the chaos of the mall. His legs ached, and he longed to finish the next lap, to walk out the doors where the bus would be waiting, to be back in the peaceful confines of the assisted living community, away from this teenage madness. He didn't understand how people could spend hours in this environment.

He tried to remember how it felt to be young, to have his whole life ahead of him, unfazed by the ticking clock, or the changing seasons, oblivious to his own mortality.

Where had all the time gone?

About Chris Reed

Chris Reed has been published over 60 times. His fiction has appeared in numerous small press publications, including *Black Ink Horror*, *Midnight Echo*, and *Tattered Souls: The Provocative Boundary of Fear*. His influences include Joe R. Lansdale, Fritz Leiber, and John Collier. Aside from writing, he enjoys browsing thrift stores, waiting for hockey fights to break out, and eating way too much pizza, sometimes simultaneously. He lives in Davison, MI, with his photographer wife and their two children.

https://facebook.com/pages/Chris-Reed-Horror-Writer/263671795291

WHAT THE BLIND MAN SAW
by C. Dennis Moore

In my dream, I could see. I saw my hands opening a bottle of wine. I heard a noise from the living room and I looked through the pass to see a woman sitting on my couch and smiling at me. I saw the wine being poured into two glasses, and then I heard the front door burst open. Then I woke up.

I don't remember if I screamed or not, but I woke up to the void of my blindness. I sat up and rubbed my face. My head was pounding! And my throat was full of sandpaper. I stretched and tried to stand up, but couldn't get any leverage to swing my legs over to the floor. Then I realized I was already on the floor. I felt the hardwood under me and realized I was naked, too.

I felt around, searching for the bed to pull myself up, but my hand only met open air, so I pushed myself up to my knees and then stood. I tried to orient myself, but nothing familiar was within reach. I listened for a moment to make sure I was even in my own apartment. I had the sense of familiarity and I determined I was indeed in my own home.

I just didn't know where in the apartment I was. What had happened last night? I couldn't remember.

That wasn't a good sign. I didn't think I'd thrown a party, and I was pretty sure I hadn't gone out drinking after work, so why was my memory so foggy?

I stepped forward carefully, but found nothing. I took another step and found the same. With my hands out, I moved forward, deciding to keep going until I found a wall, a chair, anything. I must have taken twenty steps with no result when, in frustration, I yelled "Come on!" and flung my arm out to the side, cracking it on the wall.

I massaged my wrist, then felt the wall, trying to determine *which* wall. I felt a hook, then my keys, and realized I was near the front door. But when I moved to the side a little further, I made another discovery. The door was wide open, the jam splintered, and the lock was busted.

I listened. I know the sounds of my apartment and am very good at sensing, not only a change in the air, but also the presence of someone else.

There was someone here. I could feel that someone.

"Who's there?" I asked. I don't know if I expected an answer. I didn't get one anyway. So I did the only thing left to do, which was to try again: "Answer me."

Still no response. I couldn't tell *where* the intruder was, only that someone else *was* here. I had my bearings, so I moved for the cell phone that I always kept on the coffee table, deciding to call the police. But the phone had been moved; perhaps it was in my guest's hand now as he or she watched me and chuckled silently. In fact, the further I moved, the more I began to get the sense that whoever was here had moved everything in my apartment except the hook and my keys. At least moved them far away from me. I searched and searched, but touched nothing.

As I probed around myself, seeking familiar things—I felt I was losing my place in the room again—my dread started to wash away, and was replaced by a swelling anger. I was about to yell at the intruder when my foot kicked the coffee table, knocking something over. I couldn't tell what it was, but I heard, indistinct and far away like a ghost trying to break through, a woman's voice: "The candle!"

Ignoring the table, I turned around, trying desperately to find the owner of that voice. I realized I could smell perfume.

"I know you're there," I said. "And I think it's pretty bad when you have to rob a blind person, just so you know."

More silence, as I'd expected. I kept listening, hoping to pick up any sign that would tell me who was here and what they were doing.

I suddenly remembered that I was naked. I felt exposed and oddly humiliated, and I figured the only thing to do was take charge. I'd put some clothes on, and then I would continue searching for the phone. I stomped on the floor as I strode across the room, thinking if I was loud enough, someone downstairs might complain and that would send the building manager or someone up.

My anger grew. I found the dresser and pulled open the bottom drawer, but before I could pull out my clothes, a scream came from the living room. It came faintly, as if from another apartment, but I knew it was the same woman who'd spoken a minute earlier. Screams are never a good sign.

I went to the doorway, still naked, and said, "Get out."

She screamed again and I had her position. I took off running, never mind whatever might be in my way, and tackled her. If I couldn't make her leave, then I'd take her down and strangle her if I had to.

We collided and went to the floor and her screams doubled in volume and intensity. She thrashed about, but I wasn't letting go. My weight pressed down on her and my hands found her throat. I squeezed and she coughed and gagged. I heard another voice behind us, a man's voice this time. He said, "Knock off the shit, Marie. I told you to grab your stuff."

This was the one I wanted, not the woman. I knew it. I had his position and I leapt, knocking him in the stomach, and to the floor. We struggled. He moved and got back to his feet. I moved after him, but tripped on something heavy in my way. I stopped and knelt to move it, then drew my hand back quickly when I realized it wasn't a *what*, but a *who*.

I put my hands on the body lying on the floor, and ran them over it, to see if I could determine who it was. I felt pants. The fabric was fine, not coarse like jeans. I knew they were khakis with a brown leather belt and the shirt I felt was pale blue. But how did I know what pale blue was? Or khaki, or brown? How did I know the colors?

I continued up the torso to the face.

The body was a man, and he was clean-shaven. He wasn't breathing and that gave me pause. But I had to continue; I had to know who it was that was lying dead on my apartment floor.

The face didn't feel familiar to me, so I didn't think it was someone I'd met before. The jaw was square with a dimple in the center. The nose was strong with a slight hump. The eyes were wet and open. I pulled my hands back in shock.

Why were the eyes so wet?

The man told the woman, "I said let's go, you cheating bitch!" and I heard footsteps, his strong, hers stumbling after, and the door closed and they moved down the hall.

Letting them go without acknowledgment, I felt the body again, probing the face, my fingers moving gingerly. Unease rushed over me like a flash flood as I felt where the eyes used to be. I was hearing something in my head, very faint but definite.

I thought about that woman's voice. I did know it. From somewhere…did we work together? Maybe; then yes, I began to think that was it.

Marie. Hutchins. Yes, and she had curly blonde hair and the reddest lips I'd ever seen. But…

We had flirted with each other a lot and I finally convinced her to go out with me and we wound up here, in my apartment. Had something happened? Did she drug me and that's why I woke up naked in the middle of the floor?

No, it never went that far.

My dream. I tried to recall what had happened in my dream. In my dream, I was getting us wine, and then the door burst open.

Who was it?

A boyfriend?

I had thought she was single.

"You couldn't help it, could you?" he had said in my dream.

He glared at Marie and I asked him, "Who are you?"

He looked daggers at me, and said, "I'm her boyfriend, you douche bag. Is that all right?"

I looked back at her, wondering why she hadn't mentioned this before now, then back at the bruiser in my doorway.

"Listen," I said, "I don't know what's going on, but I think it's time for both of you to get out."

He tried to grab Marie and haul her out, but I stepped in.

"Easy, dude, let her walk on her own. There's no reason for that."

His reply was a fist to the side of my head. He grabbed me and threw me into the wall, then grabbed the wine bottle and swung it at me. It hit me and that was it…I went down.

But he didn't stop there. He pinned me and was choking me, and Marie was screaming, "Stop it, stop it, stop it!" over and over, and I glanced over at her, feeling the pressure of his fingers on my neck, and the bruiser said, "Don't you ever fucking look at her again!" He grabbed the wine bottle, shattered it and stabbed me in the eyes, then choked me again until I passed out.

That was my dream.

I am blind and dreamed I saw.

I felt the body under me. I lifted the shirt and felt the abdomen. That scar could be anyone's. It was an appendectomy scar, just like I had, but it didn't prove anything.

I knew what I had to do, and I didn't want to. But I had to know. Anger and fear competed for dominance.

I opened the mouth.

I had two teeth that never came in when I was younger. They were in the back, one on each side, so I had never bothered getting them fixed. My finger probed the corpse's mouth and found the two empty sockets, one on each side, near the back. I *did* know this person after all.

I withdrew my finger, wiped it on the pale blue shirt, and then put all of my fingers to my own face. My dimple. The hump on my nose. My tongue worked into the sockets on each side of my mouth. My hands moved up and felt the wet gaping wounds where my eyes used to be.

About C. Dennis Moore

C. Dennis Moore lives in St. Joseph, Missouri where he works during the day as an inventory control clerk. He's been writing just about forever with over sixty stories and novellas published, plus a collection of his short stories titled *Terrible Thrills*. Recent and upcoming publications include the *Vile Things* anthology and his novella *Epoch Winter* will be published by Drollerie Press. http://www.cdennismoore.com

A Woman's Secret
Joseph Patrick McFarlane

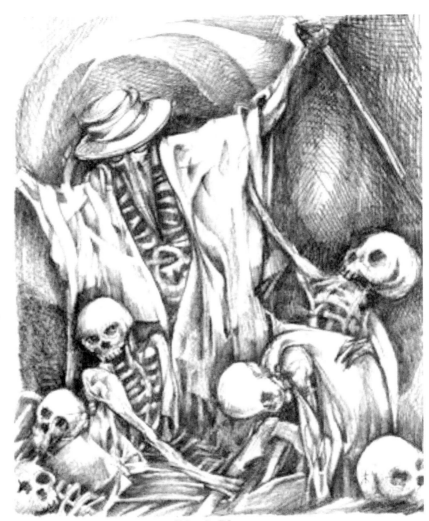

Black Plague
Tatomir Pitariu

POETRY

EMON ANTHOUSIS

A GUIDE FOR ETHICAL ZOMBIE MURDER

First find a weapon
that doesn't need reloading
something blunt and sharp
like a baseball bat lined with razor blades

Keep a safe distance for only one bite
will cause the change
and if that happens you'll become
more familiar with our blades

When one-on-one, aim for the head
crush the undead life out of their brains
When you are the minority aim for their legs
then as they crawl, curb-stop their skulls

If you're unsure if your attacker
is a zombie or not
it's better to be safe than sorry
so chop that Mother-Fucker up

If faced with a Zombie family member
like a zombie-dad
Ask yourself how much Human Meat
would your dad like to eat?

Finally, always keep your weapon at the ready
the goal now is survival
and remember
Don't hold back or feel sad; they're already dead

REDECORATING

I moved the furniture from this room.
It became as barren as your womb.

I lined my floors
before the doors

with plastic mats
to catch the splats.

I painted our walls today
with your arterial spray.

The excess paint
I didn't want to waste

so I grabbed my brush
and in a quick rush

I painted the inside
before the paint dried.

I rolled up the sheet
around the unused-dried meat.

I packed it in the car
and drove away not so far.

I buried it near a tree
so it would no longer burden me.

Now with the work done
I return home to relax as one.

RED PLANET

The mountain shudders and cracks open, spilling blood upon the Earth;
The volcanic fluid rises and coagulates, forming four silhouetted riders.

With each crashing gallop, the ground below quakes and splinters, releasing
air as if the Earth screams out in pain. Those nearest are deafened

by the echoing roar, and horror ensnares the people who remain.
Like starved zombies, they dash toward Jesus' house, but no

one is home. The tidal wave of blood reaches them and their flesh boils away. From the epicenter, shockwaves emanate as a grotesquely colossal

arm bursts out. It grabs anything living and drags it under.
Soon no life remains. The disfigured arm retreats beneath the soil

and the riders melt back to blood, coating the planet and staining
the Earth red. It floats now, empty and barren, with no memory.

About Emon Anthousis

Emon Anthousis is currently enrolled at the University of South Florida finishing up a degree in Creative Writing and considering dual majoring in a field outside of English. He decided he wanted to be a writer after finishing Douglas Adams' Hitchhiker's Guide to the Galaxy, which is currently his favorite book of all time.

His hobbies include watching movies with friends, reading and writing.

Emon doesn't want to limit himself to one form of written work and is currently beginning work on a fantasy novel and a comic book series about his take on the superhero genre.
http://www.facebook.com/Greekcheeze

DENNIS BAGWELL

JASON'S LAMENT

Now you listen to me Rita!
I appreciate all you've done for me, but as my agent, you owe me this
I know George Clooney is being considered for this role, but I have
given the best thirty years of my life to this industry and it owes me, too
You say fans expect me in certain roles and they don't want to see me in
a chick flick, but I want this romantic comedy
What have I been doing for the last twenty years but making comedies,
Rita?
Jason in space? Do I look like a Goddamn astronaut to you?
Freddy would never say this to your face, but he was just as disappointed
with Freddy vs. Jason as I was
You said it would be the ultimate slasher bromance. It stunk, Rita!
What's next? Abbott and Costello meet Jason?
I appreciate the fans, but let's not forget it's the fans that have type-cast
me
Every time the screenwriters kill me off, I think, "Great! Now maybe I
can try something on Broadway"
Maybe DJ in some clubs for fun
Then you negotiate a higher salary for the next piece of crap slasher,
making it difficult to say no
Well, this time I'm putting my machete down!
 Can't you even get me spot on *Dancing with the Stars*?
I mean, have you seen some of the celebrity hacks they get on there?
Not even a guest spot on *Law and Order*?
It's time to expand my resume to include some more high profile roles;
how about a musical? Have you ever heard me sing?
You know, I took this part when I was young and I had only been in
Hollywood a few weeks.
I needed the money and I was excited about being in a "Big Hollywood
Production"
If I had known I would be wearing a hockey mask for the next thirty
years, I would have passed on it, Rita!
I have a daughter who is older than the kids I kill in these movies!
Half the time I can't even find my hockey mask because my son borrows
it to play hockey!
Kevin Bacon was in the first movie and he's gone on to a pretty lucrative
career

When does Jason Voorhees get his moment in the sun?

I had lunch with Michael Myers at Spago last week and I poured my heart out to him like I am to you now

You know what he said, Rita?

Absolutely nothing! His silence spoke volumes and we share the same pain

I wouldn't be surprised if he moves back to Haddonfield

Leatherface already went back to his ranch in Texas. Freddy is working with kids

I can't wait for the day when I can wash the blood from this crummy, unforgiving town and retire to Camp Crystal Lake

I mean, I'm in great shape, but how much longer am I supposed to still be young enough to hurl an axe with robotic precision across a room?

I'll be fifty years old next month, for Christ's sakes!

You can't possibly have any idea how hard it is for an angry, hockey mask wearing, machete wielding, psychotic, serial killer to pretend he's an actor portraying an angry, hockey mask wearing, machete wielding, psychotic, serial killer

I've learned to manage a lot of my anger, but I can only take so much of this crap before the bodies start piling up

My therapist says this lifestyle isn't conducive to my mental well-being

Rita, how can you just lay there and say nothing?

Don't look at me with those glazed-over eyes!

Dammit, Rita, say something!!!

BUGS (for Diana)

Bugs in the vents
Bugs in the drain
Bugs in my bed
Driving me insane

Bugs in the closets
Bugs in the kitchen
Eating my food
Without my permission

Bugs in the phone
Bugs in the halls
In the kids room
Behind their dolls

Bugs in the bathroom

Bugs in the garage
Following me around
Like a creepy entourage

Invading my home
Like unwanted guests
Hiding in the corners
Like filthy little pests

I hear them in the walls
Buzzing in their nest
While I lay in my bed
There is no quiet rest

Laying in the dark
Sweating with fear
Perhaps while I'm sleeping
They'll nest in my ear

Or drag me away
To their burgeoning hive
Becoming their feast
While I'm still alive

My home is now seething
With bugs in every space
I'll grab a few things
Then I'll leave this place

I think I hear them laughing
Their torture goes undaunted
A home without people
Is all they really wanted

PRAYING FOR THE DAWN

The sun is almost down, the fog rolling in
The moon will rise and mock me from the safety of its celestial perch
The creatures of the night will screech, scream and hoot their ugly
nocturnal symphonies
The vampires will awaken from their earthly graves

The undead will shuffle from the woods behind my house
The werewolves will howl to signal the beginning of the night's festivities
The hounds of Hell will sniff around my porch and mark their territory
I will be waiting quietly in the dark
Waiting for some or all of them to get into my house
Praying I live to see another day
Praying for the dawn

About Dennis Bagwell

Dennis is a thirty-something, politically incorrect, mad at the world, X Generation, heathen, musician, poet and writer from suburban Orange County, California. Dennis moved to North Georgia in 2007 and is quietly preparing for the inevitable zombie apocalypse. He has been writing in one form or another since high school. His warped rantings and observations about the cesspool of a world we are surviving in keep his spiraling descent into madness at bay.

Dennis has had his poetry published by the *League of American Poets, The American Poets Society, 63Channels, Black Petals, Death Head Grin* and *Word Salad Poetry Magazine*. He has released two spoken-word CD's, *A Random Litter of Thought* (2006) and *Paid in Full* (2007) on Batteryface Records. A short film of Dennis' poem *Hollywood* was made available to coincide with the release of *Paid in Full*.
http://www.dennisbagwell.weebly.com

JOHN T. CARNEY

THE GHOUL

The tombstone wall was gray and cold,
Like a corpse's flesh left in some nameless morgue.
I could almost touch you; feel you; hear you as in life,
Though your soul was trapped in the eternity of the grave forever.
I placed both hands to caress the faded words on the slab,
My fingers slipping along the rain-drenched granite,
Like a mountaineer losing his grip.
Maybe I was losing mine.

Raindrops fell amongst the lonely tombs,
As I lingered there, unsure of what to do,
Where to go next.

Finally, I moved on to the next crypt,
Placing my hands firmly on the niche,
With a soft caress,
A gentle touch for the dead.
Yet I was losing my grip,
Slipping along the edge of the stone,
Losing my way on the ascent up the incline.

The rain continued to fall,
And I moved on to the next grave,
Staring, transfixed, at the withered stone,

The stone stared back, unmoved.
So like Death, aloof; indifferent.
I stared blankly at a statue of St. Michael in the distance,
A blackbird rose from amidst the stones and soared high in the air.

My hands slipped clumsily through the stones,
Groping, seeking, finding nothing but tears,
Amongst the dirt and rocks of the incline I faced.

I had lost my way, forgotten the route,
Left the path.

A steep mountain of graves loomed in the distance,
I knew I could never leave.

You would never allow it,
Your love had bound me here,
Amongst the tombs and stones of this lonely ascent.

An ascent I would never complete,
Until I returned here for the last time,
And found my place amongst these lonely stones,
On Death's summit with you.

KINGDOM OF SHADOWS

Rushing shadows storm the endless night,
Washing through an endless sea of space,
In this void these shades find dark delight,
The King of Shadows rules this darksome place.
Here, where Styx rolls fat and wide and still,
As in some drugged and hazy, lurid dream,
The fate of souls flows where it will,
One often hears the sorrowful souls scream.
These pause along the vast, unholy shore,
And beg for coins to pay the ferry man,
Else to linger there forevermore,
Or lurk wherever Death is damned.
They whisper through the ancient veil of time:
Drink not so vainly Life's luxurious Wine.

MEMORIAL DAY

A solitary mourner stood lingering by an open coffin,
The corpse laid in state in the mausoleum before the open niche,
Awaiting internment.

For more than an hour he stood staring,
As if waiting for the eyes to flicker; the muscles to twitch.

Finally, he turned his face to me with a strange, stiff smile,
His bared, sharp fangs coldly gleaming,

And slowly approached.

Behind him, the stiff, pale corpse rose from its rest,
Stared, palely, at his back,
And clumsily followed.

I fingered the shaft of my own fangs and grimaced.
My master slowly approaching with bloodstained lips.

It was Memorial Day at Cedar Grove,
And the day had only just begun.

About John T. Carney

John T. Carney was born in San Francisco in 1960 and has lived most of his life in the Bay Area. He graduated from Moreau High School in Hayward, California, in 1979 and from The University of Pacific in Stockton in 1985. He has had several poems published by the *International Library of Poetry* in their various anthologies and has also been published in small college literary magazines.

His favorite horror short story is "The Red Lodge" by H. Russell Wakefield. His favorite horror movie is *The Shuttered Room*, based on a story by H. P. Lovecraft. Estronomicon.com (Screaming Dreams) has agreed to publish two stories of his, the first called "The Lake People" and the second, "The Curse of the Leper."

John has published a book, available on Amazon, titled *The Vampire Sonnets*. It is a novella combined with sonnets about vampirism. https://sites.google.com/site/johntcarneybooksandmusic

TERESA ANN FRAZEE

THE LIGHT UNDER THE DOOR

We, the pale children of our time
  Slide homeward across a hundred years
Into the darkness where shadows fly
  Tonight we'll play with our living peers

While the contented sleep dreaming
  We roam about our old dwelling place
Where sweet memories are kept alive
  Bartering innocence with time and space

Sweat pours through astral bodies
  Dripping into sockets of cloudy eyes
Like faded pipers stirring boyish days
  Of long hot summers catching fireflies

Or riding wooden horses that go round
  Reaching to grab shiny brass rings
And the smell of tiny cakes rising
  While lost in play on old tire swings

But dawn's light muzzles our laughter
  In a world of nothing all day
Imagining these things to come
  With stiffened postures we lay

Our hearts are filled with dust
  Icy breath trapped in the lungs
Only when the golden daylight falls
  Can words roll from our tongues

Yes, speechless until we're midnight born
  Confined daily under roofs of stone
At night we join our small glowing hands
  But we never seem to feel a bone

Like flaming rockets in the dark
  When our sparks and lightning mingle

The jolt of life ignites our souls
　And our imaginative senses tingle

Then up the black staircase we ascend
　Cradled in a whoosh of rising air
Plunged through the light under the door
　To our old room with its new heir

Will the living child accept us
　Or will his hair stand on end?
We're young and not certain
　If our true natures will blend

Right near him now we hovered
　He smiled then blew a hollow flute
Played us an ancient melody
　A tune that had long since been mute

We danced on our vacant beds of rust
　Once again moved our cold feet
And swayed the body in its way
　To youth's wild frenzied beat

Away from our monotonous rest
　Flung our day clothes all about
Stomped on those lifeless things
　And shook the world with our shout

Tumbling adrift toward anonymity
　In a slow motion race against our curfew
As we played freely and left our print
　On the same toys we never quite outgrew

Suddenly dawn waved high her magic wand
　As we scattered around she counted heads
Then swiftly caught us all with one hand
　And gently tucked us in our daybeds

THAT STRETCH OF ROAD

That stretch of road lies between home and somewhere

Celestial light slices through the mahogany sky
Lured by ancient shades of boundless galaxies
　　Which hold the power to charm the mortal eye

Neglected on the map of transient dreams
　　The road takes on dimensions of infinity
Right on course into the passage of fate
　　As the span of time monitors obscurity

Onward we travel toward our destination
　　Through miles of air the road approached a hill
Trees rustle among us like whispering kings
　　And in the hushed black of night they're reigning still

THE ROADSIDE ROSE

Amid the glow of haunting flares
　　A rose blooms there in the night
She stands against a boundless sky
　　Charming the last shards of light

She cradles the sweet breath of Eros
　　In each sultry curve of her petal's fold
Velvet thorns blush behind bursting buds
　　According to the ancient legend told

Some say her nocturnal appearance
　　Is only for amorists upon days close
Many a romantic still wander here
　　And hope for a glimpse of the roadside rose

About Teresa Ann Frazee

From Florida, Teresa Ann Frazee has been a visual artist for over twenty years, with juried and international exhibitions including solo shows in galleries, museums and other venues, receiving many awards and honors. At the same time, Teresa has been perusing her other love, writing.

She is a published poet, and her works have been displayed in *Skyline Magazine, Hudson Review* and *Poetry Shelter*. Inside her world of make-believe, she paints and writes what she knows to be true. Within her creative force, she leaves reality entirely up to you.

JOHN GREY

SEVENTY YEARS LATER

Spanish moss drips from trees.
House sheds shingles.
Old rusty knocker clanks
against rotting doors.
Cracked windows rattle.
Floor-boards groan.
Pipes clatter.
Two bent and withered sisters crouch together
in one threadbare satin chair
amid the dust and webs
of the ancient family sitting room.
Older brother Tom, in tattered bloody gray uniform,
is slumped into the shabby sofa,
eye-sockets blank, flesh green as moss,
but skeletal fingers still tight around his rifle.
"Quiet out there," whispers Amanda.
"Maybe the war is over at last," rasps Esther.
Amanda shakes her weary head.
"Sad. So sad. A million of our boys dead."
"A million and one if you count Tom," adds Esther.

CONSEQUENCE

I ask myself,
heart and head,
is someone there?
There is someone.
A shape
like a flower
blooming under snow.
A wisp
like the last draught of sun
between the trees.
A presence
like the mist
on a cold lake's surface.
But then I wonder

what does this visitor
want of me.
Memory,
a wildflower spark
in the thick forest
of my forgetfulness?
Feeling,
a mote of tenderness
toward all that's
passed before?
Revenge,
for my living,
its threadbare substitute
for existence?
So I'm sorrowful,
sympathetic,
and terribly afraid.
I'm not alone
this chilly midnight.
Oh I have lived a dark
and shameful life
these past few years.
I'm here with my consequences.

SECOND FLOOR

I arrive by night
as moon gilds honey
on dark, unbuttoned wind,
the sky in the oblivion
of its fetal stars,
my hunger passionate but still enraged,
up wall, through window,
to bedroom,
parting the golden curls
of your throat with my tongue,
pressing home my bleak horizon
with long white fangs,
your face, a startled deer
fetching its own end
from the unreal thunder shake
of my eyes,

immense night of exalted blood,
as ancient world inhales life,
exhales a luscious mirror
of my face,
pale, feminine,
and dripping crimson.

HANGING TREE

Its outer limbs
Reverberated
against the shake
of its dead leaves
as if a body had
just been cut down
and it wasn't until
late May that
the reluctant sun
finally burnt off
the thick chunks of ice
that shrouded
its vein-like roots.

About John Grey

John Grey is an Australian-born poet, but moved to the United States in the late 1970s. During the day, John works as a financial systems analyst.

John has been recently published in Connecticut Review, Kestrel and Writer's Bloc, and has more poetry upcoming in Pennsylvania English, Alimentum and the Great American Poetry Show.

CHRISTOPHER HIVNER

THE RULES OF THE ABYSS

In the tunnel
leading from the abyss,
I climb,
dragging myself
over jagged rock
leaving trails of blood behind.
Like teeth, the stone
rips apart my body.
I keep reaching,
stretching for the next foothold,
searching for the light.
The darkness has existed so long
it owns my veins
and pumps through my fractured heart.
I pull harder,
inching forward over fangs of stone
incising through my cold skin.
The pain shuts my eyes
and inside my own world, I see light.
I believe in light.
Every tunnel has a beginning,
a source,
and the light bursts from it.
It must exist.
So I re-open my eyes
to find shards of black
piercing my temples,
driving through my brain
and telling me,
whispering to me sweet blessings
about the easy embrace of the chasm.
In the lull of sing-song voices
I see a pinprick of light,
maybe only in my world
but maybe in the real one.
So I reach and pull and struggle
and the darkness recedes,

cheated.

LITTLE RED THE HOOD

On the way to grandma's house
with her basket full of goodies;
eyeballs that saw too much and
tongues from those who can't keep their mouth shut.

I WILL MEET YOU

I am the gathering thunder
  feel me deep in your belly
I am the coming flood
  run, it excites me
I will lurk in the aftermath
  to pick up your scent

I am the voice you hear
  in the decaying midnight air
I am the presence you feel
  at the foot of your bed, hovering, watching
I am the light that soothes you
I am the eyes of your lover
I am the threads of the sheets you wrap yourself in

Crawl to your dreams
  my sickly pet
I will meet you there

About Christopher Hivner

Christopher Hivner has work published in *Black October, DecomP*, and *Niteblade* among others, and was nominated for a Rhysling Award in 2008. A collection of short horror stories, *The Spaces Between Your Screams*, was published in 2008. http://www.chrishivner.com

JEAN JONES

WHAT IS IT?

When Orpheus asked his critics what they
wanted from him, they all said, "Astonish us!"
Can you do that? Astonish your critics?
Robert Frost claimed that it "got lost in
translation." And Sandburg claimed it was a sack
"of invisible keepsakes." What is it to you?
I would claim that the key lay "In the hands,
something in the hands, surely it must be that."
My friend, Andrea Young, asks me,
"Are you reaching toward being a true poet?"
What is it, Andrea? What is it?
Ralph Waldo Emerson wrote, regarding
the true poet the following:
"The true philosopher and the true poet
are one, and a beauty, which is truth,
and a truth, which is beauty, is the aim of both.
"My friend, Howard McCord, wrote to me and said,
"Poetry is whisky. Prose is mash. DISTILL!"
I still wish to be astonished.

EVERYONE ALWAYS LEAVES THINGS BEHIND

Everyone always leaves things behind,
scraps of it, for miles and miles.
A friend once told me
that Hell is the place
where everyone goes
to find the things
they've left behind,
scraps of it, for miles and miles.

LAST MOMENTS

Have you ever seen a picture that haunted you
of someone just
before she was murdered,
like those photos

of those women and children
at My Lai
before they were shot to death
their crying voices
screaming for help
to you
in the land of the living?

Yet there's nothing you can
do about it,
for in minutes
photos reveal
the dead bodies
where the women and children stood,
like that famous photo
of the dead girl
running with her murderer
beside her
her haunted eyes say to the camera,
"I'm trapped,
yet there's nothing I can do about it,
help me," and her body
is found days later,
brutally raped and murdered.

What are we to do
with such images?

Like the man from the Tet Offensive,
the mayor of Saigon
pulling out this revolver
and executing him on the spot,
blood spurting from his head the whole time,
or those films of that man
who gets his head cut off
courtesy of the Taliban
in Iraq or Pakistan
butchered like pigs before
our eyes,
some screaming for their lives
as the knife slits their throat...

What are we to do with such images?
Go back to church
and pray for God's will?
Rorschach, the madman vigilante
from the graphic novel
and movie *Watchmen*,
reveals to a prison psychologist why
he was known as Rorschach.
After discovering a missing girl's
bones being ripped up by the killer's dogs,
Rorschach proceeds to butcher the dogs
and the killer himself.
"God was not responsible," Rorschach mumbles,
"the killer was," and God didn't mind
if Rorschach killed the killer as well.

To come to the realization, as murderers do,
that no one stops you from killing
but yourself and some lucky breaks
by the police is weighty stuff indeed.
Is there truly no God?
Maybe. Maybe not.
But if there is a God,
He seems unlikely to interfere
in the killing of one human being by another,
this same God who lifts no finger to save a fish
from a hawk, a mouse from an owl,
or me moving in to kill you right now.

About Jean Jones

Originally from Bandung, Indonesia, Jean Jones received a BA in English in 1986 from UNC-Wilmington, and an MFA in Creative Writing: Poetry in 1988 from Bowling Green State University in Bowling Green, Ohio. Jean currently teaches Basic Skills at Cape Fear Community College in Wilmington, North Carolina.

He has had two books of poetry published by St. Andrews Press from St. Andrews College, North Carolina; the most recent, *Birds of Djakarta*, was released in 2008. Together with his friend and fellow poet Scott Urban, Jean Jones has had a brand new book of poems published by a brand new Wilmington, North Carolina, publisher called "Shaking Outta My Heart Press." Jean's book from that publisher is titled *Tornado*.

Jean is also co-editor of the online poetry magazine *Word Salad.*
http://wordsaladpoetrymagazine.com/drupal7

RON KOPPELBERGER

TWILIGHT WINE

An arcane substance appreciated by the stone in bloody wombs
Of birth, the cry of the child in Wolf's Bane and sharp edged
Spears of moonlight applause, a cunning thirst enthralled by the wont
Of an errant wolf, a tattered dilemma of knowing
Revelation and wild haunts in gray gallop and
Padding purchase, the gnarled oaken taboo
Of wolves in abeyance unto the
Magic prayers of those who imagine
The gift of what's given throughout and the
Bursting promise of a midnight run, a cascade in velvet smoke and
Starving affections in rapt fluster, in blissful darkness and frayed
Conditions of patience in chaste flourishes of remedy, for the cares of an
ancient angst in spirit, a melody in twilight wine.

ABERRANT FEAST

The strange gaudy orange twilight
In evenings of snakeskin sheen and
Lizard grace. The speckled chew in chaws
And maws, in grinding ghosts
And wise faerie flight. An aberrant feast,
A cornucopia inside and out of stray
Sated character and
Vague, tingling horror.

IN COMPANY WITH GHOSTS

Thorns and passage unto the unspeakable breadths of eager
Affair in dark reflections of ethereal ascendancy, the artifice
In eloquent agreement with illusionary suns and dreams of reason,
A footfall amongst the morass, between the theaters of delirium
And sane horizons, by weary eyed ambiance, given trampled
Petals in moss laden soils of desire, the infinite in ceaseless airs
Of birth, by want and shadow upon shadow upon outlines in candent
auras
Of secret revelation, by the grim need for eternity and precious undoing's
In indigo and pausing firelight, drawn unto the

Edge of another drama, by torn twilight bidden distant at journeys end and near the faded enticements of yesteryear, a way to conclaves of shadow and

Dusty tears of blood, valued upon the pilgrim in bonded company with ghosts and stray meandering dogs in conveyed hunger.

STARRY-EYED DREAMS

The promise of ash and smoke,
Charcoal assay and cauldrons of
Human stew. A hag in honor of the torment
That Father Redemption predicts. The
Convocation and the provocation
In lead to the ravens of ancient feather.
The stories of transfer, likened to the
Wine of witches and starry-eyed dreams.

About Ron Koppelberger

Ron Koppelberger has published 217 poems and 52 short stories in a variety of periodicals. He has been published in *The Storyteller, Ceremony, Write On!!!* (Poetry Magazette), *Freshly Baked Fiction* and *Necrology Shorts.*

Ron has recently won the People's Choice Award for poetry in *The Storyteller* for a poem titled "Secret Sash." He is a member of The American Poets' Society, as well as The Isles Poetry Association.

Ron has had poetry accepted in England, Australia and Thailand. He loves to write and is always seeking to offer an experience for his readers. http://www.wolffray.blogspot.com

ALEC B. KOWALCZYK

LIGHTHOUSE

In the solitude
of an abandoned lighthouse
an unsound homeless person
finds a journal of an unstable man
fearing for his sanity
fearing the compromised structural integrity
of the crumbling lighthouse he inhabits
fearing the gales and diverse elements
beating upon the standing straw-like shaft
fearing the torsional stresses
twisting the lighthouse barrel
fearing the bending moments
on this vertical edifice of masonry
fearing the shearing strains
slicing through the mortared joints
fearing the overturning
of the entire brick-laid structure
fearing the underpinning of his very mind...
this man in the journal
who also finds a journal of an unhinged man...

CALIGINOUS

Hotel/predawn hours...

looking down from the fourth floor
a doorway illuminated below
one minor beacon in the urban gloom

a dark wreath on the angled door
and its shadow a distorted lozenge
on the fractured tiles of the walk

a wind rocks the tiny bell
of a neighboring church
and the tone is like a toll

VISCERAL

The pair of lions' heads in stone
flanking the courthouse steps
the dynamic tension in their jaws
ready to spring-shut at any moment
as any passing child knows instinctively
as any sleeping adult knows intuitively
the unimaginable made imaginable
to have a hand caught in the vice-grip
of those incisive locked jaws.

MID-CITY AMUSEMENTS

A rolling tumbleweed
bisects a circular patch
of stone shards
that once supported
a merry-go-round

…forging a beeline
past the boarded-up rink
where a lone roller skate
rusted at the end of
a disintegrating lace

…dead-on toward
an overgrown grove
of trees gone wild…
the wreckage of a tangled
timber rollercoaster—
charged sub aural screams
from cars that jumped the track
left hanging in the air.

About Alec B. Kowalczyk

Alec B. Kowalczyk is a native of South Troy, New York, a civil engineer by day, with an interest in the mechanics of poetry. The kind of world he would like to inhabit would be slightly off-kilter…as in *The Hour After Westerly* by Robert Myron Coates.

His work has been published in *69 Flavors of Paranoia, Semaphore Magazine, Pif Magazine, ChiZine, Yellow Mama* and others, winning a Dark Animus Award for poetry. Snark Publishing released his chapbook titled *Shadow and Substance*.

http://www.facebook.com/profile.php?id=100000799343969

JOE R. LANSDALE

AN ALIEN POEM

You may think this is just a poem.
You'd be wrong.
It's a form of alien mind control.
We are the aliens.
This is our poem.
We write them because if you read them—
we got you.
You are now one of us.
We are taking over the world.
Problem.
It would take centuries
for enough people
to read poems
and become one of us.
Even poets don't read poetry.
Hell, can you blame them?
So, we're thinking of switching,
to encoding our thoughts
in pornographic websites
instead of poems,
or into car commercials.
We would get more people to become aliens
that way.
Whatever we decide to do
in the future,
this is the end of this poem,
and—
—HA!
We still got you sucker.
You should have stuck to video games.

DEATH BEFORE BED

In dark cloak
and bunny slippers
I ride the country wild.

With scythe and croaker sack
I gather them up,
those shadows strong or mild.

I put them away,
and kick them some,
to quiet them down of course.

And then I carry them
quick to home,
on my wicked little horse.

Carry them fast,
like a tornado wind
where a hole in the earth awaits.

I toss them down,
I push them down,
I kick them in the ass.

Down there in the pit,
where the flames lick up,
I leave them and laugh.

APACHE WITCH

In the wild country where the West wind blows,
the demon of the desert comes and goes.
Dark like a shadow, a mouth full of blood,
there's nothing out there but it and the dead.

Lives in a cave near a dark red butte,
hides there by magic, in an old cavalry boot.
Released by a spell from an Apache witch,
it twists and it turns and howls like a bitch.

Lizards and coyotes, buzzards and men,
it kills and kills, again and again.
But kill it must, and each night it comes,
until a cowpoke arrives with a lamp and a gun.

The lamp is lit with oil from a dog,

and around the cowpoke's neck,
 on a string of braided gut
is a dried up frog and a hickory nut.

The rifle is packed with bullets of silver and lead,
little charms buried deep in the ammo heads.
An Apache woman, the witches daughter, the cowpoke's wife,
made it to save her husband's life.

So Apache magic meets head on.
The demon whirls with a desert song.
The cowboy fires his gun and throws his lamp.
The demon roars and the night turns damp.

Out of a cloud against a moonlit sky,
comes a rain of black lumps like a cobbler pie.
It blows and it whirls and it twists and it turns,
and when it hits the demon it smokes and it burns.

The cowpoke's magic makes the demon cry.
It even melts the damn thing's eyes.
The rain on the cowpoke is heavy and wet,
but for the demon it's the worse thing yet.

The demon becomes a twirl of smoke,
and the cowpoke laughs like it's all a joke.
On his way home he yells and he cries,
for the demon was made of his poor child's sighs.

The baby's breath stolen by a cat
that was black as the pit and little pig fat.
The Apache witch sucked the baby's soul,
because his daughter made the child in a soldiers bed roll.

So stealing a boot
and casting a spell,
the witch had wreaked vengeance
so very well.

Wearing moon silver
like armor and mail,
the former soldier,

rode home to his wife.

They dried their tears and climbed in bed,
the stars at their window,
the wind at their door,
the howl of the coyote like the call of the dead.

They came together in a tearful wail,
loved one another with all their might,
tried to make a child that very night,
did what they could to set themselves right.

Back on the desert,
next day in the sun,
the Apache witch man
was dead and done.

Found at the mouth of a cave near an army boot,
the witch man was burned and wadded,
with a hole in his chest,
the demon of the desert had left its nest.

About Joe R. Lansdale

Joe R. Lansdale is the author of over thirty novels, twenty short story
collections, screenplays, comic scripts, essays and non-fiction. His novel
Vanilla Ride, from Knopf, is part of his Hap and Leonard series. Others
in the series are currently being reprinted by Vintage Books.

Joe R. Lansdale's novella, *Bubba Ho-Tep*, was the inspiration for Don
Coscarelli's cult classic film, starring Bruce Campbell and Ossie Davis.

And now there is a new Lansdale book: *The Best of Joe R. Lansdale.*
Lansdale's favored themes run from zombies to vampire hunters to
drive-in theaters, and his storytelling encompasses everything from
gross-out horror to satire. http://www.joerlansdale.com

EVERETT MADRID

DARK SHADOW CLUBBING

Dancing there alone in the shadows,
my eyes started to ring and sting.
When I saw that it was the real you,
I wanted to cry and silently scream.
Then I barely realized with fright,
it was only a cracked mirror.
You were dancing in the background,
glaring at me and dancing nearer.
It was too dark to see,
what it was you held in your hand.
It was too late to stop,
by the time I realized what you had planned.
You get to have all that you want,
when you dance with me behind the Black Door.
A thorny rose with black pedals dripping in your blood,
the perfect gift I have been wishing for.

DANCING IN REPRISE

I'm here to serenade you with the letters,
written as you recently requested.
The fuzzy line between you and me,
just went quantum with what you be-quested.
I know it's that bad and I've been there myself,
many times before in another life full of strife.
The end is not the answer we're searching for now,
until fully experiencing the roller coaster of this life.
I know you were expecting only one for you,
mine must come as quite a pleasant surprise.
It wrote itself to the music as I wrote yours,
two little suicide notes dancing in reprise.
I know you won't do it because you're not through yet,
with yourself or me and so I can't let you be.
I can't let you in good conscience end it this way;
writing the note that blames your pain on me.
Whatever the time that brings you to the very end,
it is going to be in the cradle of my arms or not at all.

If you end it with step off of this very steep cliff,
I'm going to catch you before the end of our fall.

INVISIBLE HAPPY EMOTIONS

You are now gone and not because of death,
once again I feel close to complete.
You left me with nothing but my last breath,
and the empty feeling of deplete.
The day has finally come to linger,
you are no longer part of my existing life.
When I think of you now I'll only remember
the sickness and lonely, constant strife.
I should have known it was doomed to land,
when the desire to have you was gone.
You only wanted a golden stage upon to stand,
and my shoulders to place it square upon.
With you by my side I had never been so alone
all of the way, to the terrible very end.
I've forgotten how to laugh, the feeling
to belong somewhere, anywhere, with good friends.
My emotions are mostly invisible now or in rear,
I can no longer imagine happiness as a station.
What I received in return was loss of everything dear,
and a very big bad reputation.
You will not be remembered as an ex-flame,
or the hand for which I was the glove.
You were just an artist I once tried to help,
and the shadow I twice tried to love.

About Everett Madrid

After a successful ten year career as a Navy engineer, Everett Madrid
(otherwise known as b.a.d., which stands for beat art dealer) worked as a
consultant and sales engineer for the semi-conductor and
telecommunications industry. He completed advanced management
application training (Total Quality Management), in addition to earning a
BA in Organizational Management in 1995 at St. Mary's College of
California. He left the corporate culture to follow his passion and entered
the art business as a sales consultant. His passion for excellence and love
for the arts enabled his quick rise in the gallery world, landing him a
director position in one of the largest art galleries in the country.

Over the following five years, Everett would deal in the works of Pablo Picasso, Marc Chagall, Salvador Dali, Rembrandt, Andy Warhol and a myriad of historically important and contemporary artists.

While it was exciting dealing in the great arts of the past, Everett's true passion grew to be contemporary art and promoting the careers of living artists. Launching Gallery Culture in 2003 as a hobby, he provided free artist portfolio hosting and event listings, thus creating a national network of artists and contacts. In 2003, he produced a six-month bi-weekly mini-series covering the San Francisco emerging arts community in addition to conducting countless interviews. In 2005, he curated his first museum exhibition that included the publication of the artist's catalogue *reasonne* and a documentary film.

JUAN PEREZ

A RESPONSE TO SETH GRAHAME-SMITH'S *ABRAHAM LINCOLN: VAMPIRE HUNTER*

The proverbial log cabin ax
Shining with moonlight
Where otherwise covered
With foreign, crimson fluid
Death, a fact
To someone or something
Always, yet what
A barnyard blitz
On a concrete jungle
Puzzle pieces waiting
To recover, return
To its owner
A human converted
To the blood-sucking disease
Surely will not stand
So long as the hunter lives
For man cannot endure
In a place half-human, half-beast
For one will surely end the other
As man divides against himself
So long as either shall live
For as long as the hunter shall resolve
As the last best hope for earth
Lincoln, for the ages

ONE NIGHT'S LAST STAND

Sana, sana, colita de rana
Si no sanas ahora, sanas mañana

Precisely the morning
That I had to hold on to
My hands melting away
Holding on for dear life
La bruja was pleading
Kicking, screaming

Biting, clawing
To get far from meI, frightened for life
She, attempting to claim my soul
For a strange night of sex
The smell of sanguineous sulfur
Her morphean skin, my human one
Begging to be mine forever
Assume any form I wanted
Any woman I desired
All I had to do was let her go before sunlight
Yet, I would lose more
Than I could ever gain
Lust and one damned bottle of tequila
Had gotten me here
At the end of my proverbial rope
Holding on to a sobering dear sun
To burn this sin completely away
A witch's death on my mortal hands
Her dark husband shall have to wait
A far, distant chilly night
Before claiming what she paid for
In this hot, beautiful new sun
My scarred, melted hands
Reminding me of this senseless conquest

Sana, sana, colita de rana
Si no sanas ahora, sanas mañana

THE MEXICAN WHO TRIED TO SAVE THE WORLD

Standing alone
Where oblivion is not as noisy
As I had first imagined
Where all I knew
Where all I loved
Was sucked away
Into a faceless vacuum
Where my thoughtful warnings
Did nothing to stop self-destruction
Where life and counter-life

Danced the wicked beat of time
Where oblivion steps in now
Not as noisy as I first imagined
Had I not attempted
To save this world
Only dissatisfaction would remain
With no room for lovely memories
With no room left to be human
Had I imagined a noiseless ending
I would not had bothered as much
Besides, human is my final name
Yet, that too will soon be forgotten
For what oblivion has truthfully taken
It will never share again
And death its only partner
Yet that is okay somehow
For life was a noisy world
Oblivion not so much
Not as I had first imagined

CENTAUR-LET BI-POLAR OWNER

I lassoed a Martian centaur-let
[to kill it]
So my little Machitaz could have it
[to eat it]
How lovely they really are
[on a platter]
Here on the red planet Mars
[let's kill more]
My lovely Machitaz, she loves her
[as a side dish]
She strokes all four hands on its fur
[to prepare it]
She gently straddles its back and rides
[right back to me]
Even secrets to it she confides
[that I will kill you]

About Juan Perez

After a decade of military service, including the First Gulf War (1991), Juan Manuel Pérez is now a public school history teacher and author of six poetry chapbooks which includes *Dial H For Horror* (2006), plus two full contemporary multi-culture poetry collections, *Another Menudo Sunday* (2007) and the e-book, *O Dark Heaven* (2009). He has also completed three other poetry manuscripts: *W.U.I.: Written Under The Influence of Trinidad Sanchez, Jr., Comic Book Love Affair* and *Make Tortillas Not War*.

He is a member of the San Antonio Poets Association, the Poetry Society of Texas, and the Science Fiction Poetry Association, as well as student of the great Chicano poet Trinidad Sánchez, Jr. He has also been a featured reader at many poetry venues in Southwest Texas.

His work has recently appeared in *Jazma Online, The People's Comic Book Newsletter, Boundless, Voices De La Luna, International Poetry Review, Illumen, Star*Line: the Journal of the Science Fiction Poetry Association, The Poet Magazine, di-verse-city, Voices Along The River, The Dreamcatcher, Inkwell Echoes, The Palm's Leaf,* and *Message of the Muse.* He was recently named the second Runner Up in the 2009 San Antonio Poet's Association's Poet Laureate Competition. http://www.juanmperez.com

NATHAN ROWARK

SANCTIMONIOUS SAINT AT THE SINNER'S BALL

Sanctimonious saint at the sinner's ball
and my ticket's turned to dust.
As the tumultuous drums drown the vodka and rum
flowing over the bodies of lust,
Through the rose-tinted scry of my twisted mind's eye
stands a poet and beggar aghast,
As the dwarfed brigade of the preaching concave
are consumed in the fires of their past.

Making my way to the bar, seeing hope from afar,
I pass by a fashion's high sin.
As she tilts down her head her eyes roll up in red
and thick diamante garrotes neck and limb.
In a moment of shock, running demons amok
in a last ditch attempt for the door;
A man stops me in threads and what descends
from his lips are the reasons, what whys and what fors.

Said he, "This place that you mar is living proof that we
are all the deepest desires yet to come.
And if you continue this fashionable song, you will stay here,
and damned be every one."

Unknowingly eloped in the thoughts of my hope,
he did not see the truth fly his way,
And with fire in my heart and courageous art,
I dispensed my own song for display.

Said I, "The devils you speak are not just old and effete
but their manners are portrayed in your words,
All the people I know this way fight to not go,
for none of this can be real anyway."

In mid note of the rhyme, I found frozen in time
 the devil's party-night sign on the wall,
And asleep in my glass, I fathomed the crass

revelers above looming tall.
I passed out on wine, in mid-flow of a good time,
and a taxi was called for my home.

Yet with blurry eyes fixed on the bar spirits mixed
I could swear I saw shadows still roam.
In the back of the cab facing the evening's tab,
I recalled the dark sight of dreams,
Because it often relates that subconscious warnings do state
that the path is not all that it seems.

UNENDING BATTLE OF SELF

Under fire and in chaos wrought the battle for my soul is fought.
Within my mind, self untaught takes arms against the dark onslaught.

A final stand becomes too large as dogma flashes the fields to charge.
Casualties are doubts homage to the fall of vanities' entourage.

Rising up with a fearsome sigh, the bowman's anger fills the sky.
With shields smashed and hopes goodbye, my conscience is the last to die.

The victors speech fill gaps unsaid and gloats upon the bleak now wed
amongst the blades; by river bled I rise up and leave the dead.

The war for self is rarely lost and budgeted in acceptable cost.
If spirit powers down too soft then apathy's the coin not tossed.

The wage is bad; the nights are long to solidify in this peculiar song.
Once more to take the highroad strong? And stand against the rights of
wrong?

The field turns to ash and dust in empathic view of my foe's dark lust.
Reflection mirrored of nighttime rust that struggles for this world to bust.

Our blackened side fulfilled by hate, to balance out the neutral weight.
Tipping scales for either bait endangers self and mental state.

Mead moon shines with silvery light to witness self's gargantuan fight.
Neuroses troops poised in flight, the battle royale now far from sight.

The winning move deployed in zest is how the wretch can cheat this test,
And as karma blows in from the west, I dispatch his form at my behest.

Job mentally done for now, at least I commit to the truth of the unending beast.
The dual of humanities' pie as meat, forever to plague its soulful seat.

CROSS BUT SHAN'T

The bridge that I should cross but shan't is that of which I could but can't.
Cold metal structures lay to lead but going there will make me bleed.
I sit upon the bank and gaze at the unfolding of the plans she's laid.
Knowing damage yet to come, if I followed her dreams undone.

No longer one that wants to save, I leave her side to watch her cave.
It fills me with the depths of dread to watch unfurl what's in her head.
A beauty that to me resides the hopes of two that well in eyes,
Yet effective pull of darkest strife now takes her down as nighttime's wife.

About Nathan Rowark

Nathan Jonathan David Lee Rowark was born in the pagan county of Hertfordshire, England. Nathan has been writing since he was six years old and he wrote his first novel at the age of twelve when he moved to Essex.

Nathan currently writes screenplays and splits his time between running his own business and directing short horror movies. At thirty-two years young, Nathan's hopes are to follow his first love, which is poetry.

Nathan is Wiccan, which he feels, along with life experiences, has helped to form ideas for his poetry. His family's surname was originally Warlock and it means, according to Norse sailors, "to bind with words," or "spell singer." Therefore, words are in his blood.

If he were asked to sum up his love of poetry, it would be the way a poet can convey situations, emotions and physical environments with just a few words and is the only medium he has ever found that can have such power. Nathan is an eclectic human being and has discovered that an open mind is the passage to the divine. http://www.inspired-words.co.uk

STEPHANIE SMITH

SUMMER TWILIGHTS

you remember
summer twilights
hiding under picnic tables
and behind backyard sheds
mingling with vampires in the trees
and reading Stephen King by candlelight

because the boogeyman is real
to a nine year-old
and the neighbors
are not what they seem

THE DEATH MAIDEN

the death maiden kisses the moon
her hair smells like waste

dress tattered and caked
with dirt from a grave

the delicate bone beneath her skin
quivers with each thought of the downfall

before sunrise she
sang today is beauty

with innocent face
said life and death sit side by side

her dance of existence
was cheery and lively

but inside I knew she was nervous
she gave me flowers

that grew along a river bank
where it rained all night

tears from the moon
I think of the burden

she'll be carrying
very soon

CITY OF THE DEAD

Here in this city of the
dead we cast wishes into
the suicidal fountain

On hot summer days you
can smell the flesh from the
citizens who stroll
down sidewalks of bone

In this city there are morgues
on every street corner
and maggot-filled dreams crawl in
the minds of those who live here,
calling us to the grave

A CHOICE

The angels came to wash my face
And falling: a thousand drops
of crimson tears on my sleeve

All alone on the mountain,
posed at the edge
with tattered wings
perceiving an empty dream,
I was given two choices:
to feel again
or join the angels
who no longer sing in their
choirs but ravage the night
with bloody bird claws
I chose the latter

About Stephanie Smith

Stephanie Smith is a poet and writer hailing from Pennsylvania. Her work has appeared in such publications as *Dark Fire Fiction, Eviscerator Heaven, House of Horror, Niteblade, Not One of Us*, and *Paper Crow*.

Stephanie's first chapbook, titled *Dreams of Dali*, is available from Flutter Press. http://imajican.livejournal.com

PAUL SOHAR

WHEN GHOST CHILDREN SPEAK

The voices of ghost children grow
like mildew on the tapestry,
they wind around the lily pattern
floating in the background free

where the backs of chairs and sofas turn,
where only cobwebs stand on guard,
that's where they can wiggle up
on the backs of adults who park

their lives in pointed circles around the
gray litany of the coffee table
till these trickling voices touch their earlobes
with the tingling of a fable

fanned by the naughty unseen children;
then the grown-up backs will twitter,
speak about the temperature
and the snow that's sure to wither

next week or sooner when these voices
slither back where they came from
and where they send all those who listen
bang into a maelstrom:
say! whispers hone the craft of kissing...

THE ABANDONED FARMHOUSE

The carcass of the old farm house
harbors no sounds
yet I'm afraid to follow the slender
sprite of an early spring breeze

as she slips into the vandalized
living room and

gliding past the dusty bones of old dining chairs

she slithers into a water-stained
volume of poetry—
fluffing up the pages she seeks out
some comforting rhymes to rest on until

massaged by the soft iambs
she creeps out again into
the ghostly late afternoon sun

tiptoeing on the skittish leaves
of a moribund rhododendron
she climbs up
on an invisible rope
back into the sky

and then there's nothing left to show
that I was standing here by the broken window
and like a peeping tom I watched

her wordless tryst with an undead poet
in the forgotten old farmhouse
trapped in an idle growth of maples.

THE KNOCK

It was quarter past nine when I
heard a knock on the front door.
I looked up from my book,
but the door looked no different,
the off-white semi-gloss paint
had started to crack and curl
in a malevolent grimace some
time before, and now it
didn't bother me at all; I knew
I could outstare a problem but
why waste time on it when
I could be reading or falling
asleep in the armchair with
a floor lamp positioned right
next to it. In fact, the door was as still
as any of the pictures on the walls,
even its grimace seemed to sag

and soften as I sat there thinking
I could hang the door on the wall
as an object of art, after all
it had a message, something to say,
maybe a lot more than the tulips in
the print beside me or the blue hills
in the landscape above the fireplace.

About Paul Sohar

Paul Sohar got to pursue his life-long interest in literature full time when he went on disability from his job in a chemistry lab. The results have slowly showed up in *Agni, Bryant Literary Review, Chiron Review, Grain, Hotel Amerika, International Poetry Review, Kenyon Review, Main Street Rag, Rattle,* and many others.

Paul has seven books of translations into English from his native Hungarian language, but now a volume of his own poetry titled *Homing Poems* is available from Iniquity Press. His latest book is titled *True Tales of a Fictitious Spy*, and it is creative nonfiction about the Stalinist gulag in Hungary. http://www.echapbook.com/poems/sohar

PETER STEELE

THE CITY OF THE DEAD

Your dreams have long since been forgotten.
And your flesh is pallid, dry and rotten.
See how your eyes have fallen out of your head.
Welcome to the city of the dead.

The darkness of night is forever here to stay.
And no matter how hard you try, you'll never get away.
Remove all those thoughts of freedom from your head,
Because you are in the city of the dead.

Soon, you'll learn that the dead no longer have a care.
They just mesmerize you with a godless stare!
The maggots are feeding on the brain inside your head.
Your refuge is now the city of the dead.

It is so hard to accept that you have died.
And you often wonder why the angels lied!
But forget all the deceitful words they said
And take your place in the city of the dead.

FULL MOON

The moon shone boldly
Through the trees,
Tantalized by a
Midnight breeze.

Through the dark
A naked creature prowled.
The night was alive
With its primitive howls.

On all fours
With animal charm,
Through the fields
Into the local farm.

To the cattle
It gives an evil gloat,
And with teeth like daggers
Tears out their throat.

The farmer emerged with
A loaded shot gun in hand,
And scanned with a keen eye
His trespassed land.

A rustle of leaves
Up above on the grassy verge
And a human wolf
Did stealthily emerge.

With a gasp of shock
The farmer raised the gun and aimed.
The field was lit by a flash,
And the beast was maimed.

The farmer had taken
The strange creature's life,
And before his very eyes,
It transformed into his wife.

PUPPET MASTER

The theatre was engulfed in an icy chill.
The stage lay ahead, cold and still.
The surrounding spotlights were all on,
And like stars they brightly shone.

Something quite bizarre caught my sight.
There were ten figures up ahead dressed in white.
Their pupil-less eyes seemed so cold and dead.
And their lips were painted blood red.

All of them I noticed had rose red cheeks.
They could be dummies or even freaks.
Strings held them upright in position.
Or should that be—in superstition?

They all bore expressions of total confusion.
Or maybe their look simply reflected my intrusion.
Their dainty puppet hands moved so gently.
Oh how the eerie scene up front demented me.

I did not know if I should stay for a while.
Or perhaps I should just be polite and smile.
Does it bother them, the fact that I am here?
Or will my presence fill them all with fear?

The puppets straightened up and walked toward me.
Yes, those eyes of white really do see!
And I noticed those eyes were focused on me.
The puppets were walking slowly toward me!

It was so strange they way their bodies moved.
And their fabric hearts remained un-soothed.
Like tentacles their hands reached toward me
From within the very mind of insanity.

The strange puppets held onto me so tight,
And their secretive eyes suddenly shone so bright.
I shivered coldly at the sight of ones smile,
While he whispered, "Won't you stay awhile?"

They took me up some steps onto the stage set.
My delirious brow was suddenly coated with sweat.
I felt totally victimized by his icy stare.
And then they made me sit down on a chair.

I said, "Can you please tell the time to me.
I've got to go...someone might miss me!"
But instead, their gaze penetrated so deep, so deep.
And I was scared and my talk was cheap.

There was suddenly a silent, almost ominous hush,
While one of them went and fetched a paintbrush.
With it he dabbed some white make-up around my eye,
And gradually painted away each and every lie.

A slow and infinitely weird hour drifted by,
Until my face looked like a cloud in the sky.

My very soul was overwhelmed with total mayhem,
Because the puppet had painted me to look like them!

I thought that maybe it was all part of a bad dream,
But no—I could hear myself scream!
They stared at me with a blank look on each face,
Like the curiosity of an alien race.

I asked one of them to tell me his name.
He leered and said: "No longer any shame!"
The world I had once known was lost in time.
I felt like the perpetrator of a hideous crime.

The puppet brought out of hiding, a knife,
And with it he ended my miserable life
Now, we all hang around on strings
Waiting to see who tomorrow brings.

Waiting for someone...perhaps you!

About Peter Steele

Peter Steele was born on November 5, 1961, in Gloucester, England. He started writing at the age of fourteen and has succeeded in getting extracts from his books, short stories and poems published in over 150 anthologies. He has also written three horror novelettes entitled *Cannibal killer, Cloven Hoof—Mark Of The Devil*, and *Demon Slayer*; a collection of short stories entitled *24 Tales Of Darkness* and three collections of dark horror poems entitled *A Primeval Child, A Thought From The Dead* and *Anarchy In Hell,* all of which are available in Kindle on Amazon.com and on Mobipocket in Europe.

Peter is the recipient of The American Biographical Institute's Golden Academy Award and Gold Medal of Honor. His biography has been featured in many biographical "Who's Whos" such as *The International Authors & Writers Who's Who, Men of Achievement, International Book of Honor,* and others. He has been short-listed twice for the Forward Prize. He also creates his own artwork that appears on his book covers and album sleeves.

In addition to writing and art, Peter is also a composer, songwriter, musician and live entertainer. His albums include *Alienator, Andromeda,*

Ectoplasm, Utopia, Phantasmagoria, Automaton, Omega, Ancient Realms, City Of The Dead, and many more, all available in MP3 on Amazon and iTunes. http://www.angelfire.com/poetry/petersteele

ANNA TABORSKA

LADY OF THE FLIES

In the silent forest lies
A small figure with sad eyes.
In her dirty, matted hair
Ants and beetles make their lair.
Through the tear-stains on her face
Spiders crawl at leisurely pace.
Nobody knows when and why
She came here, prepared to die.
Crows perch nearby and wait
For gentle death to seal her fate.
The flies won't leave their new-found bed
And circle slowly round her head.
In her buzzing halo lies
Martyred lady of the flies.

SCAVENGER

i collect your refuse
i feed on your waste
 i find what you lose
and remember
what you want to forget

i dig up your corpses
and pick through your bones

you shun me
outcast and cold

i watch you bleed
and listen to you vomit
i feel your heartbeat
and hold you as you choke

the more you die
the more i live

METAMORPHOSIS

i left the safety of my solitude and followed you
giving up all i knew for love

(you said that you loved me)

you left me groveling in the dirt
my tears seeping downwards into the worlds beneath—
no pain greater than love given only to be taken away

the dark gods pitied me and took my earthly life
giving me fangs and claws and perpetual hunger
replacing the useless human soul that bled for you
with eyes that see through your fortress walls
and ears that hear the beat of your inconstant heart

(you said that you loved me)

i stalk you wolf-like
your corridors of power scant haven from my revenge
your ivory towers cannot hide you
nor your indifference protect you
for i will come in your nightmares
in the shadow that falls across your window when you are alone

the comfortable fabric of your world will crumble
your self-assurance break like ice in the face of a new-born sun
 your cold sleep unravel and burn in my tormented fire

(you said that you loved me)

my pain has become my strength
your betrayal has become my strength
your leaving has become my gateway to a new kind of hell

like a creeping sickness i will steal across your world
beware my footfall beside your bed
beware my breath upon your face
beware the brush of my hair against your skin
for i am love reviled and i have nothing left to lose

About Anna Taborska

Anna Taborska was born in London, England. She is an award-winning filmmaker and writer of horror stories, screenplays and poetry.

Anna's films include: *The Rain Has Stopped* (winner of two awards at the British Film Festival, Los Angeles, 2009), *The Sin, Ela, My Uprising* and *A Fragment of Being*. Feature length screenplays include: *Chainsaw, The Camp* and *Pizzaman*.

Short screenplays include: *Little Pig* (finalist in the Shriekfest Film Festival Screenplay Competition 2009), *Curious Melvin* and *Arthur's Cellar*.

Short stories include: "Halloween Lights" (published in *And Now the Nightmare Begins: THE HORROR ZINE*, Volume 1, 2009), "Picture This" (published in *52 Stitches*, Year 2, 2010), "The Wind and the Rain" (published in *Daily Flash 2011: 365 Days of Flash Fiction*, 2010) and three stories published in *The Black Book of Horror*, Volumes 5, 6 and 7 (2009-2010).

Anna's short story "Bagpuss" was a finalist for the Eric Hoffer Award and is now published in *Best New Writing 2011*.

Poems include "Kantor" (published in the *Journal of Dramatic Theory and Criticism*, "Fall 1995), "Mrs. Smythe regrets going to the day spa" (published in *Christmas: Peace on All The Earths*, 2010) and "Song for Maud" (published in *No Fresh Cut Flowers, An Afterlife Anthology*, 2010). http://www.imdb.com/name/nm1245940

SCOTT H. URBAN

CRUISE MISSLE

After they were satisfied it was an accident,
I moved to the opposite coast.
I chose a city that boasted its public transportation,
running like capillaries to every district.
I brought the car, although I can't explain why.
You'll tell me something about getting back up on
the horse that threw you off. I leave the car
unlocked in the hope someone will steal it.

It took me two months to work up the nerve
to touch the door handle. Another two weeks
to sit inside. Why am I doing this to myself?
I can't even remember where I wanted to go.

I pull the seat belt over my shoulder.
It feels like I'm strapped to a gurney.
All that's left to do is shove the IVs in
the bends of my elbows and let
the potassium chloride drip.

I tell myself, *It's just a tool.*
It enables you to move. You couldn't have known,
when you looked down at the vibrating phone,
she'd choose that moment to dart between
two parked cars in pursuit of an errant pink ball.
Not your fault. Not your fault.
Still, I can no more grip the steering wheel
than I can force myself to touch
a glowing stove-top burner.

The key's between my right thumb and first finger.
I can't make it go in the ignition. It doesn't fit,
like the jigsaw piece of skull that wouldn't
go back in the girl's cranium.

And here I sit, still, still,
stranded in the driveway,

encased in a missile
that's struck an unintended target
and destroyed its pilot.

MORE LOVE. MORE FREIGHT

Brevard County, Florida. February 20, 2010.

The narrow kingdom of Saturday afternoon
spans sluggish Crane Creek
with its penumbra of darting midges.
Someone had the foresight to post NO TRESPASSING signs
so the four despots can be left alone.

Two take cell phone snapshots of the other pair
balancing the rails and wind-milling their arms
three feet above the letters proclaiming MORE LOVE,
a spray-painted Tweet every American teen can get behind.

Here is youth swaddled so tight
in a warm cocoon of self-absorption
they don't feel the *thrum* in the ties
ignore the whistle slicing six-thirty
disregard the second trestle only a leap away.

Their realm is invaded by a black battering ram.
You'll ask why they didn't just dive in the water:
all I can tell you is the fixed nail wishes it, too,
could jump to the side of the falling hammer.

Here, the fisherman watches a car
drag a blanket smearing red,
a tattered swatch that once had a name.

In memoriam:
Ciara Malia Lemn, 14
Jennifer Reichert, 15

AMOR ASTRA

On November 3, 2009, a Jeep Cherokee containing the bodies of three women, Kyrstin Gemar, 22, Ashley Neufeld, 21, and Afton Williamson, 20, was pulled from a stock pond near Dickinson, North Dakota. It is thought they drove to the countryside to star-gaze.

A hunger: not in the gut
but in the dimple at the base of the skull.
A hollowness that can only be filled
when you tilt back your head and
your eyes scoop up stars like ice cream sprinkles.

You have to drive beyond
the pixilated haze of streetlamps
and the neon glare of Burger King signs
to lose yourself in the sable shadows,
the true night our forefathers knew.

On your back on the Cherokee's hood
you can get drunk on the Milky Way.
Just like the branches of scrub oak
you raise your hands, but there's nothing
to hold onto. You wonder that the bats,
the creeping vines, the dirt track, your friends,
and the state don't topple into ether
like a sidetable laden with a too-heavy platter.

Deneb. Cygnus. Rigel.
Names of exotic lovers who promise joy
no flesh and bone can provide.
Who would not pull forward past the point
the SUV can be reversed up the embankment?

The engine dies, of course, but the battery
keeps the headlights burning. To the crane operator,
it seems two stars have fallen into murky water,
illuminating bladderwort and tadpoles.

About Scott H. Urban

Scott H. Urban is a freelance writer and poet living, appropriately enough, in North Carolina's Cape Fear region. His dark verse appeared in the collections *Night's Voice* and *Skull-Job* (Horror's Head Press); his most recent chapbook, *Alight*, from Shakin' Outta My Heart Press, appeared this summer. In collaboration with Bruce Whealton, Scott's vampire poems appear in the e-book *Puncture Wounds* (Word Salad Productions).

His fiction has appeared in print magazines, horror anthologies, and online zines, including, most recently, *Lost Worlds of Space and Time* Volume 2, and *The Witching Hour*. With Martin H. Greenberg, he co-edited the DAW anthology *The Conspiracy Files*. As editor, he recently compiled Jean Jones' poetry collection *The Complete Angel of Death* (Skull Job Productions) and memoirist Ryan Miller's *Circle of the Heart, Voices of Comfort Dreams* (Elephant Showcase Press).

THE
ARTISTS

Techno Caro

THOMAS BOSSERT

Thomas Bossert lives with his wife and two children in a little town in the Black Forest in Germany, at the border of France and Switzerland. He is a self-proclaimed audio-addict, listening to music and playing guitar. His favorite musicians are in the bands Pink Floyd, Emerson Lake and Palmer, Yes, Genesis, and Rammstein.

Born in 1961, Thomas' great passion is painting and drawing, especially in the surrealism style. When he first saw paintings by René Magritte, Salvador Dali or Paul Delvaux many years ago, it touched him and he was fascinated. Those feelings have not let him go until this day and certainly his artistic creating.

Most recently, Thomas is inspired by the works of H.R. Giger. He posts on the Deviant Art groups and is a member of The Collaborative Corpse and The Exquisite Corpse.

For Thomas, surrealism is about visions, about unconscious, around dreams, thoughts, symbols and perceptions. He can express himself by the surrealism without borders. His subconscious has the opportunity to express itself by itself, without him influencing it. Most important, the surrealism gives him artistic freedom.

His piece titled "Fragments" is a collaboration with Christian Edler, who is a surreal artist also from Germany. Christian Edler goes by the name 'reality-must-die' on Deviant Art.

A Woman's Face

RICARDO DI CEGLIA

Formerly a graphic designer, Ricardo Di Ceglia worked many years as a web developer in Sao Paulo Brazil, the city in which he was born. Not happy with his career, he dropped everything and moved to London where for seven years he developed his artistic skills. He was shown in a few exhibitions and recently headed back to Sao Paulo to open his art studio, and now he posts his paintings on the web to be seen all over the world.

The Stare

KALYNN KALLWEIT

At only 26, Kalynn Kallweit's career in the arts has indeed been very diverse. From sewing corsets for the woman with the world's smallest waist, Cathy Jung, to making movie props, leather work, and costumes for such shows such as *Masters of Horror, Reaper*, and *Aliens vs. Predators Requiem.*

At a very young age, she was drawn to morbid stories and imagery. Instead of doing her math tests, she drew cemeteries and ghosts alongside her school work and made occult-themed activity books. Now the most likely creations in which she engages are creepy dolls, dark art sculptures, and macabre digital art.

Kalynn is inspired strongly by nature, horror, religious iconography, bones, fashion, and all things living or dead. When asking about her parents take on her devious bent, she says her mother is full of enthusiasm, and her father has said, "Once she saw the movie *Beetlejuice*...that was it!"

Kalynn plans to take her movie-honed mold making and sculpting skills further to the dark side in the company of her dark art dolls. On the horizon as well, is a new branch out into the fine art of tattoo, so keep your eyes peeled in the future for this girl's art on your best friend's sleeve. In true Kalynn Kallweit style, there are never enough outlets for this non-stop creative force!

DANIEL KIRK

Daniel Kirk was born in 1984 in Cambridge, in Ontario, Canada. Now a student based in Toronto, he has been drawing for as long as he can remember. Viewing art as a means of self-reflection, he tends to dwell on the darker side of things. Deformities, mutation, decay, and surrealistic horror are his favorite subject matters. His main mediums are both traditional and digital. Recently, he has delved into the world of 3D and intends to incorporate all of his knowledge into future works.

Keeper of the Creature

JOSEPH PATRICK MCFARLANE

Joseph Patrick McFarlane was born in 1949 in Toronto, Ontario Canada. While attending Central Technical Art College in Toronto, Ontario, he studied studio criteria and art history, plus field research, and then attended Emily Carr in Vancouver BC. Joseph has a degree in the fine arts and in Inter-media and Multimedia.

Joseph's artwork takes on personal views from everyday thoughts and ideas, as well as dreams that have signification meaning for him. He creates things he sees around him, inspirations from other art, and just overall life's experiences that are part of everyone's childhood and adult culture. Having engaged in subjects as diverse as what he has seen during his traveling days, including music of many kinds and architecture, his work reflects all of that with familiar visual signs, and he arranges them into new conceptually layered pieces.

Many mediums are always considered, but mostly pencil, crayon, and pen and ink, as well as water colors are used. In working in these mediums, Joseph has arrived to what shows the most from his thoughts when doing art. He is always considering using other mediums, such as acrylics and oils on large canvases, but at the moment, space restricts that, though he intends to work out that problem very soon. In the meanwhile, Joseph enjoys the drawings he currently creates.

A Cold Wind

FELICIA OLIN

Born in 1977, artist Felicia Olin has lived in Springfield, Illinois, most of her life. She lives with her husband, Jim, and their two cats and one dog. She received her BFA in painting from Illinois State University. Felicia is a member of the Prairie Art Alliance and participates in area shows.

Felicia describes her childhood as being raised by hippies. Her mother was a fiber artist and used organic materials like bone in her work. She was fascinated by her family's collection of bones and rocks. Her favorite book growing up was an old, worn copy of Brian Froud's 1977 *Land of Froud*, which combined natural settings with fantasy art. Her favorite childhood movies were *Labyrinth, Legend, Neverending Story*, and *The Dark Crystal*.

Felicia has attended a Montessori school, which was less about structure, and more about individual interest. She fit art and creative writing into any spare minute. Although there has never been a time she hasn't been creating, it's only been since 2008 that she felt like she could call herself a legitimate artist and started showing at Universities and branching out.

Felicia finds painting equivalent to entering a Zen-like state where she can connect to her subconscious and let it do the painting. She listens to music when she works and lets the energy of it translate into her paintings. She listens to a band that best represents the feeling she wants out of the piece. She finds her work varies quite a bit, but people who follow her can look at a wall of paintings and pick hers out.

Calm

TATOMIR PITARIU

Tatomir Pitariu is a "dark artist" born and raised in Sibiu, a historic city in the south part of Transylvania, Romania.

Though he grew up in the midst of it, Tatomir was, and continues to be, fascinated by the mythic and mysterious folklore of his homeland. The dark forests, mountain streams, fantastic creatures and hiking through nature along ancient ruins set the base for most of his artwork.

In 1995 Tatomir moved to Los Angeles with his family. Since then, his art has become a combination of childhood memories and the everyday life in the land of "Hollywood Dreams." Tatomir's original style of graphite drawing became, over the years, art embraced by the black, trash and pagan metal scene. Many bands commissioned Tatomir's work for logos and CD art. His artwork has also been integrated into many L.A. art-scene shows and charity events.

At one of The Congregation Gallery events, he met Christopher Ulrich, who convinced him it is time to move to the next level. The decision to start painting was radical for Tatomir since he never felt compelled to explore this medium, feeling his strength laid in his drawings and in his photography.

In 2008, his first exhibited painting, "St. Sylvan" was shown at the Forgotten Saints group show at The Congregation Gallery in Hollywood and received great feedback from both peers and patrons. Since then, Tatomir participates in most group shows at this venue and has several pieces in the gallery's permanent collection.

Showered with Love

ELIZABETH PRASSE

Elizabeth Prasse resides in Orange County, California where she explores every dark corner of her soul; trapped inside a body formed of dust, seeking to evolve and unlock mysteries of who she is and may become, both as an artist and a living being.

Elizabeth has been printed in *The Harmless* book project and her artwork has been featured in and on the cover of *Chiamata alle Arti* Italian art-zine. She is part of an international art trading community and has worked on artist collaboration projects and private commission work.

Using the pen name Jelefi, she engages in artistic expression. Her camera is always in tow. She has written poetry, but it is through painting that she loses herself; wandering in labyrinths of emotional discovery, painting paths thick with hope and pain. When her words fail and Elizabeth retreats, Jelefi emerges to release the passion she feels, becoming the drafty window to her soul.

Shards of Light

APRIL A. TAYLOR

April A. Taylor is a Dark Art and Fine Art photographer from Detroit, Michigan. Some of her earliest childhood memories involve Michael Jackson's *Thriller* video, the original *Nightmare on Elm Street* movies and reading Clive Barker's *Books of Blood* series, all of which she credits with introducing her at a young age to her first love: horror.

After two decades of dabbling in photography (which is her second love), she made the decision in 2007 to focus seriously on developing (no pun intended) her photography career and spent the next two years refining her craft through Fine Art and customized photo-shoots. Her Fine Art work always leaned toward the dark and macabre, shedding light on some of the most beautifully twisted and abandoned places throughout the US.

In 2009 she designed her first Illustrative Dark Art Photography shoot (The Post-Apocalyptic Princess) and was instantly taken with the idea of capturing the darkness of the world through vividly horrific scenes.

Only one year later, several of her Dark Art pieces have been published and exhibited internationally, she was named the first ever Artist of the Month by Detroit area radio station 93.9 FM, and she's been signed as an artist guest at conventions around the United States. Her work has received rave reviews from the horror industry, including the following from Lisa Wilcox (the actress who played Alice in *A Nightmare on Elm Street* 4 and 5) who said, "April's work captures the seduction of horror."

Her recent publication credits include *Never Sleep Again: The Elm Street Legacy, Darkfaery Subculture Magazine, WU Magazine* and *Chupacabra Magazine*. April's work is slated to appear in six more books and magazines in two different countries.

THE EDITOR'S CORNER

HORRORSCOPE
by Jeani Rector

The first thing I do when I wake up in the morning is read my horoscope.

I do that even before I have a cup of coffee.

I read it in the newspaper. It's not my newspaper; it really belongs to my mother. In fact, everything in this house belongs to my mother. I live with her.

Yes, I know; I'm a forty-two-year-old man, and I live with my mother. Some people think that's weird, but my mother needs me. Well, I sort of need her too, but I think she needs me more.

But anyway, I read my horoscope. I'm a Leo, and I'm really proud of my sign. I mean, it's symbolized by a lion, so it's royal and all that. King of the jungle. Plus I was born in summer, and everyone knows that summer is the best time of year.

A couple of years ago, I started reading books about astrology, and I learned how great the Leo sign really is. What I learned in those astrology books is that Leo is a special sign, so at that point, I started realizing that I'm special, too.

Soon I found out that reading about my birth sign was only the beginning for my understanding about my full potential. Yes, I am very special; I stand apart.

It isn't always easy to stand apart. Being better than other people has a price, and sometimes I don't exactly fit in. People think I'm weird. Oh, they don't always tell me to my face that I'm weird, but I know they think it by the way they look at me.

That's okay. I'm aware that other people simply don't understand me. How can anyone understand something as unique as me? People are used to the norm, the commonplace…the average things in life. Average people are used to other average people. Anything that stands apart is considered weird, but weird just means different. And different means special.

So, I don't hold rudeness against anyone. I am mature enough to overlook it and to forgive average people for their inferiority.

Well, at least, most of the time I can overlook things...well, okay, maybe not all of the time. Even I will admit that sometimes I get upset at certain people. Like, I hate it when people don't appreciate my efforts to make them happy.

Sometimes I lose control when I am not appreciated.

Anyway, we're talking about my horoscope—let's get back to that. I told you I read it first thing every morning. It's important to me and I won't start my day without it, because it's all written in the stars, man. We don't have control of our lives, that's for the stars, but it's okay, because the stars give excellent advice. Horoscopes give guidance as to how we should go about our days. Without horoscopes, people would be lost and just flounder. Without horoscopes, nobody would get anything done. So everybody needs horoscopes, it's just that most people don't know how to read them correctly.

You see my point, right?

Of course you do.

The problem with my life is that I've always been underappreciated. I haven't been able to stay on one job very long because my bosses always hold me back. I mean, I'm certainly not going to start any job as a janitor. Half the time I know more about the job than the damn supervisor. But do I get any credit?

And anyway, I can't go out of the house on days when my horoscope tells me I'm about to have a bad day. You see the sense in that. And all of those jobs only give a guy a limited number of sick days. None of it's been my fault.

But you want to know about the women.

Where do you want me to start? Oh, at the beginning. You want me to start where I think was the beginning.

Guess that means the hooker. I don't know the hooker's name. Guess it doesn't matter.

On the day I find the hooker, I have a good horoscope. It tells me I'm going to have a good day so I know I can leave the house. Let me look in my scrapbook...oh, here it is.

Okay. This day, my Leo horoscope says: *Outlook for the day: Good. You get cooperation and good fortune comes your way. A loved one will be agreeable now. Don't count on current romantic conditions to last very long because there could be a change of mind. Still, you have good probabilities for achieving objectives today.*

There, you see? On that day, my horoscope was predicting that I would meet a girl and she'd be initially agreeable to my advances, but that a little while later, she'd change her mind. So everything that happens is pre-ordained. I can't alter what is supposed to be. I just have to do what my horoscope says, and since my horoscope didn't specify what my objectives were that day, I figured that part was up to me.

Anyway, that day...when is it...oh, I know, I'll look in my scrapbook again. Let's see; yes, here it is: it was March third. I'll tell you about it.

You know I don't drive because I'm supposed to take medication. So I always take the bus when I go downtown. I figured I'd go downtown looking for love, because my horoscope says someone would be agreeable to my advances. And since my horoscope says the love wouldn't be permanent, I figured the stars must be talking about a prostitute.

So you see, sometimes I have to interpret my horoscope. I mean, it's there in black and white, but the newspaper only has so much space in which to print the horoscopes every day, so they can't be including names and places and stuff. But I'm really in tune to the stars, so my horoscopes never need names and places, because I can figure out that part on my own.

On this particular morning, I decide to take twenty dollars from my mother's cookie jar; ha—real original place to hide money, isn't it? Anyway, I sure don't want to spend more than twenty dollars on a hooker, know what I mean?

I put a hammer underneath my coat. I figure the hammer would work just fine to knock someone out.

I get on the bus and ride downtown. I get off on Twenty-Third Street because everyone knows the cheaper hookers walk around on Twenty-Seventh. That means I only need to walk four blocks from the bus stop for me to reach the streetwalkers.

So I get to Twenty-Seventh and look around. It's about one o'clock in the afternoon so there aren't a lot of hookers around. They usually come out in full force after dark, but there're always a couple of them strolling the street no matter what time of day or night. It's a twenty-four hour deal. It's just that there's more to choose from at night.

So I see this girl, right? She's white, and I want someone from my own race. I'm not prejudiced or anything; it's just that I have to have one with red hair. A redhead is a must, and this hooker has red hair.

I have confidence. I know the hooker will be okay with me because my horoscope told me so. She'll say yes.

I walk up to her. She's wearing this really short pair of cutoffs, showing her butt cheeks in the back and all. She's got on high heels and some sort of sweater-top. She looks sort of skinny, but I figure she's probably more concerned with finding drugs than with finding food most of the time.

"I got twenty," I say. I don't feel like negotiating. My horoscope promised she'd say yes. And she does.

"Where'd ya wanna go, big fella?" she asks me.

"Somewhere private," I tell her. She says she knows the place.

I follow her behind a building; there're dumpsters and other crap back there. But it's sort of an alley, and she's right, it doesn't seem like anyone could see us real well.

She takes off her sweater. No bra. I'm not excited; the girl is scrawny, but that's not why I'm so ho-hum about it.

"How're we gonna lie down?" I ask her. "This is nothing but an alley."

"For twenty, you don't get to lie down," she tells me. "You want a motel, you pay forty. For twenty, I'll lean against the wall. I'll face the wall and you can get me from behind. Not in the ass, though."

Perfect, I think. She's gonna turn around.

The minute she does, I grab her. I'm a big guy; you see my muscles? So I take out my hammer that I have under my jacket. Right there in the daylight.

But she starts to fight. I had forgotten that part about my horoscope. My horoscope warned me that the girl would change her mind. Stupid of me to forget! Anyway, she really fights hard. I'm surprised. She looks so scrawny.

Somehow she gets away. She starts screaming, so I turn and run. Nobody catches me. A few minutes later, I'm back on the bus headed to my mother's house. I wouldn't be surprised if at about the same time as I'm on the bus, that hooker is back on the Twenty-Seventh Street stroll as though nothing happened. Just another day in the life of a cheap hooker.

But my horoscope is right, because it's still a good day. I learned something. I learned that I needed to be more prepared for the next time. And that hooker wouldn't have done me any good, anyway, even if I had bopped her over the head right there in that alley with my hammer. I need a girl I can bring home. What am I going to do, bring a hooker home on the bus?

No, I didn't kill anyone that day. What about the time I did commit murder, you ask? Listen, who's telling this story, anyway? I'll tell you about the murder in a minute.

I begin to search my horoscopes every day for guidance. I figure I want the next time to be just right.

Then, one day, there it is. I get all excited.

Wait, let me look in my scrapbook and I can read to you exactly what it says. Looks like March twenty-sixth. Anyway, here it is: *Outlook for the day: Excellent. This is a good day to follow up on new prospects while putting a high value on your skills and knowledge. A major decision you make now can lead to good results if you show courage and faith. In order to take advantage of what is offered, you must see things through to completion.*

Now, you can just bet that's a direct order from the stars telling me I need to act again. Can't you understand this? I keep telling you that all things we do are pre-ordained; it's in the stars.

So this time, I decide to stick around closer to my mother's house because I need to bring a girl home with me. I figure, maybe a nicer, inexperienced girl might be easier to grab than that stupid hooker. But no matter who it is, she has to be a redhead.

So I do what my horoscope says. I decide to have courage and faith, and to use my skills and knowledge. I gained knowledge after that hooker incident. I know what to do this time, I will take advantage of what is offered. I won't go seeking, instead, I will wait for a redhead to come to me.

I decide that since my horoscope says the outlook for the day is excellent, I can go out of the house. I can run some errands. I have courage, and I have faith that the stars will put a redhead in my path. I know that my destiny is about to be realized.

Anyway, I put the hammer under my jacket again because I'm sure the stars are going to provide someone for me. I go to the grocery store because I need a gallon of milk. I don't need a car for that, because it's only two blocks away from my mother's house and I can walk.

I go into the store, and sure enough, there's a redhead working there. She's a checker. She must be new because I've been to the grocery store lots of times and I've never seen her before. See what I mean about the stars? They have control of our lives. Everything is pre-ordained.

So I'm not surprised to walk into the store and what do you know, there's a redhead. Now, I will grant you that she's not very good-looking, sort of dumpy and all, but who cares, it's only the color of the hair that matters.

I decide to forget the milk and buy something simple just to get nearer to her. I pick up a diet soda and stand in her line. When I get near to her, I feel sort of tingly inside. I feel happy. I know I have courage and faith, and that this is the opportunity my horoscope promised. I know I must see things to completion, which means that although I will leave this store now, I'll be waiting outside for this woman. Waiting just for her.

What do you mean, did I choose her at random? Aren't you listening? Nothing in this world is random, it's all in the stars. That woman was put in the grocery store for a reason. So to answer your question, no, I didn't choose her at random, the stars chose her for me. I only do what my horoscope tells me. You just don't listen, do you? No wonder I think you're inferior. It's because you are.

Oh, is that right? Well fuck you, too.

Listen, asshole, you want me to go on with this story or not?

You know, the only reason I'm talking to you in the first place today is because today's horoscope told me to. Otherwise, I'd sure blow you off.

Well, I've got to remember to be patient with people like you. I'm special; I'm in tune to the stars. Most people are just average, so they don't have the ability to understand the stars. Only special people like me have the ability to read horoscopes correctly.

Okay, back to what I was saying. Where was I? Oh yeah.

Anyway, I wait until the store closes. I hang around, because I mean, what if the redhead only works part time? She'd leave early, before closing, and if I go back home, I'll miss her. Now, I know I look weird hanging out for a couple of hours in front of the grocery store, but I keep remembering that my horoscope says to have courage and faith, so I hang out in the parking lot...waiting.

It's a Ma and Pa store, so it closes at eight-thirty. It's only March, so it's dark already. Days are still sort of short. I'm glad it's dark; I know it will make things easier.

I see the woman come out of the store, and again I feel good, sort of tingly. Maybe it's anticipation. I don't know, but it's really cool how I feel. I feel excited, happy, powerful. I feel superior over this woman who is too dumb to realize that she shouldn't be walking all alone in a dark parking lot. But then I remember, this is all pre-ordained by the stars. Maybe the woman is smarter at other times. But tonight is not her night; this is *my* night.

I silently follow the woman, crouching among the parked cars. There're not many cars right now, but it's dark and the woman seems preoccupied anyway so she has no idea that I am stalking her. I am thinking to myself: *This is so easy. I am meant to do this.*

I sneak up behind her. I glance around quickly. All is quiet. There's no one around to interfere. This parking lot isn't very well lighted, and this store makes the employees park in the farthest parking spaces so that the customers can park close. All to my advantage.

I slide my hammer out from underneath my jacket. I feel the rough wooden handle in the palm of my hand. I grip it tightly, but the hard wood does not give. I move the hammer and see the dim streetlight reflecting off the metal top. It looks very powerful in my hand; the hammer makes me *feel* powerful.

I know it's time and I can feel my heart pound. This is really happening! I am this woman's destiny, and this woman is my destiny. My heart soars.

I am right behind her. I watch as she fumbles in her purse for her car key. That gives me the right opportunity. With courage and faith, I lift my arm and swiftly bring the hammer down on the woman's head.

It's more than I could ever ask for. The woman drops silently to the ground, landing in a heap. She is sprawled on the black tar of the parking lot, motionless.

I feel exhilaration. I feel potent; almost omnipotent. It is glorious how I so efficiently fulfill the commands of the stars. I am special! Looking at the woman lying unconscious on the ground merely reminds me of my superiority: I am better than this average woman lying limp beneath me.

You keep interrupting me. You keep asking me about the murder. I'm not at the murder part of this story yet, okay?

What?

You want to know why I murdered? Listen, I told you I'm not at the murder part yet. So far I haven't killed anybody.

Hey, I'm going to tell this story either my way or no way. If you want to hear the rest, then you can just shut up and listen. You already read me my Miranda rights, so I know I don't have to talk to any cops, much less a rude one like you. Consider yourself lucky that I *am* talking.

Damn, you keep interrupting me, and now I forget where I was. Oh yeah, the redhead. I just bopped her one over the head.

Well, I need to take this girl home, see? So I figure, she has her car keys in her hand. Probably the stars planned that too. Anyway, I told you I don't drive because the DMV won't give me a driver's license, but that doesn't mean I *can't* drive.

So I pick up the redhead from the ground. I'm surprised at how heavy she is, but she's none too slim, you know? Dead weight and all that. Ha, that's funny. She feels like dead weight, but she isn't dead. She's only unconscious.

I realize it's easier to drag her, so I do that until I have her at the passenger side of the car. I push her inside, and sort of prop her up. She looks like she could be sleeping. Works for me.

I go back around the car and get in the driver's side. All this time, I keep thinking, *Man oh man, my horoscope will never let me down. This is just so cool.*

I feel like I want to rejoice. It is like I am drunk with power and I know I can do anything, as long as the stars guide me.

I turn the car toward my mother's house and drive off. I am bringing home my prize.

I am so excited! Only two blocks away.

Finally I reach my mother's house and I park in the back. I am taking the girl inside the house, going in through the back way. Nobody will catch me, because my horoscope said there would be good results if I follow through to completion.

And now is the time for completion.

This woman I'm dragging into my house is supposed to be my sister. My sister was a redhead. Now you see why the hair color is so important?

What do you mean that you don't understand how a stranger can substitute for my sister? God, you are so dense. Don't you get it? My sister was killed when she was little, run over by a car. I figure she'd be grown up by now if she were still alive.

My mother always wants my sister. My mother still cries over her. My mother tells me all the time that I'm second best. You know, how it should have been me who got run over by that car instead of my sister because I'm, well, damaged...and my sister was perfect.

My mother needs to quit thinking that I'm damaged. I'm really just different. And as you know, different means special. I told you that I am superior to the average people in this world. I'm different, not damaged.

But my mother always wants my sister. So I figure, what the hell, I'll bring my sister back. Maybe then my mother will like me, too. We could be a real family again.

So, this redhead is my gift to my mother. This is my sister.

There you go again, interrupting me. Don't worry, I'm getting to the murder part. Quit rushing me.

I figure if this redhead isn't quite right, and my mother doesn't think she's good enough to be my sister, then I'll just get rid of this redhead and find another one. I could try this or that one on for size as my sister. You know, life is really very simple if people are smart enough to put things in perspective. It doesn't have to be rocket science.

But because my horoscope is so positive for this day, I am pretty convinced that this is the right redhead to be my sister.

But something is wrong now. To this very moment, I still can't figure it out. I can't understand what is wrong. I keep looking at my scrapbook, and my horoscope doesn't change for that day. Horoscopes are always right. So what is wrong?

Do you think I lost that special ability to be able to really be in tune with the stars? Did I suddenly stop being able to read my horoscope correctly?

It's confusing and upsetting.

But now I'm getting to the murder part. You happy? It's what you've been waiting to hear.

My mother's reaction is what's wrong. Here I have her daughter in my arms. Alive. Here's the perfect sister that she's been wanting all these years. I have done the most wonderful thing in the world. I have brought my sister back from the dead.

Why is my mother screaming? What the hell?

Shut up! Shut the hell up!

Look at your daughter! Don't you want her back? What's the matter with you? I did this for you! Don't you appreciate it?

Oh man.

I let the girl go, and she falls to the floor. I am really confused now.

I decide that this must not be the right redhead. So I have to kill my sister. I reach into my jacket and pull out the hammer.

But then I realize that my sister is already dead. She was run over by a car, a lot of years ago.

How can I kill someone who is already dead?

Okay, here it is—what you've wanted to know. We're finally reached the murder part of my story.

I don't kill the redhead. But my mother is being so rude.

Now do you finally understand why I am justified in killing my mother?

THE HOUSE ON HENLEY WAY
by Jeani Rector

"You have to tell them," Nick said.

Mandy sighed. "I'm so close to a sale. I can feel it in my bones. The wife loves the home."

"You know the full disclosure law in California," Nick told her. "In California, sellers have to notify buyers if a death occurred on the property within the past three years. If it was a murder, the buyers have to be told no matter when it happened."

"Some buyers are creeped out by that knowledge," Mandy said, frowning.

"At least be glad your buyers aren't looking at the Dorothea Puente house over there on F Street," Nick said. "Those weren't exactly flowers that Dorothea planted in the ground. That old bat committed murder times eight."

She ignored his sardonic grin. "Well, it's just that in this recession, sales are so hard to come by. Frankly, I need a sale."

"Don't we all," Nick said. "It's not exactly a boom for realtors. But things will turn around. You know that the housing market is cyclical."

"Unfortunately, my bills won't wait for any turnaround," Mandy said. "A sale on Henley Way could do me a lot of good."

"*Que sera sera*. It means whatever will be, will be."

She started toward the office door. "I know what it means. Don't start singing that old song or it'll be stuck in my head all day."

He grinned again as she went out.

She got into her car and started the engine, deep in thought. She knew that Nick had been right. She was bound by California law to disclose what had happened in the Henley Way house.

But it was so long ago, she thought. *Surely it wouldn't matter after all these years.*

Nonetheless, she was supposed to tell the prospective buyers the truth.

Mandy drove to Henley Way, where she was going to meet the young couple interested in the house. She had arrived too early on purpose, because she wanted some time alone to think. She pulled up in front of the house, turned off her engine, put her hands on the steering wheel, and stared.

It looked like any other house.

It was tan with white trim; a typical tract house. It was a ranch-style one-story, just like every other house on the block. Who would figure that this house was any different? Nothing about its appearance made it stand out from the rest.

She had a decision to make. And so she made it.

No one reads the fine print in the escrow paperwork, she thought. *There are so many pages to sign at a closing that no one reads them. The buyers just initial and sign.*

She figured that since there were no such things as ghosts, there would be no problems, and therefore, no consequences if she kept her mouth shut. The wife loved the house, and she needed the sale. It would be a win/win situation.

Amber opened one of the many boxes that littered the kitchen floor of her new house.

It was taking her all day to unpack. Her husband wasn't any help since he was away on a business trip. It seemed that just as soon as they closed escrow and moved in, Kevin had to leave again on business.

In fact, that was one of the reasons they bought a home. Kevin felt that Amber needed something to take her mind off the fact that she was alone a lot of the time while he traveled. He told her that if they bought a house, she could decorate it any way she wanted.

Amber had been thrilled. There was only one thing she wanted more than a house, and that was a baby. Kevin had told her they weren't ready for that kind of responsibility, but Amber figured that since they had bought a new house, it would make sense to fill it with a baby. She felt that with time, she could talk Kevin into it.

Certainly they had the space now, and she loved this house; for some reason, when she had looked at it with the realtor, it had spoken to her...whispering promises.

The new house wasn't exactly new, having been built in 1960. Still, it was a three bedroom, two bath, ranch-style tract home that had over 1,500 square feet. That was a lot of space for only two people. A baby could fill the space.

And so Amber unpacked by herself in her new home. She hadn't had time to look for a job in this new town, and reveled in the idea that at least for a while, she could live a life of luxury by not having to go to work. Of course, once they started paying the mortgage, she would need to find a part time job.

But on this day, she wasn't going to worry about it. She was going to unpack a few things and begin nesting; preparing for the baby that she knew would arrive. She wanted a boy, how she hoped she and Kevin would have a son.

She glanced at a window, and couldn't believe it when she saw it was raining. How could it be raining? The weather had been so beautiful just the day before.

It rarely rained during May in Sacramento, but on that Friday it rained all day. The dark sky seemed to dampen Amber's mood, and her high spirits changed to anxiety.

Because of the rain, night came faster, throwing its ebony blanket over the town to change it from a place of friendly openness into a place of menacing shadows. Amber found herself wishing that Kevin were home. Earlier, Amber had been enjoying her new house, but now that it was night, she found herself nervous to be there alone.

She had nothing to do. She didn't have cable hooked up yet, and there was no antenna, so she couldn't watch television. She tried to read a book, but all she had was a murder mystery and reading that would make her even more nervous. She didn't want to unpack any more, because she had been doing that most of the day and now she was sick of it.

Amber found herself walking around, wandering from room to room. She held her cell phone in her hand, trying to resist the urge to call Kevin. Outside, the storm was at full force now, raging in its fury. Lightning flashed and thunder soon followed; the sound rumbled and growled throughout the house.

It made her feel better to turn on every single light. The kitchen, bathrooms, and dining room all had ceiling lights, but the living room and the bedrooms did not. Amber was glad she had thought to unpack lamps earlier in the day; now she plugged them in and turned them all on.

In one of the empty guest bedrooms, the lamp was shining its light at an angle upon the wall. Something about the wall didn't seem quite right. She put her cell phone on the floor to free her hands for the lamp. Amber picked up the lamp and moved it a bit, trying different angles to shine upon the wall. It looked like some sort of bulge was pushing out about halfway up the wall.

She wondered why she had not seen it when the realtor had shown her the house. Maybe the room had looked different in the daylight.

Great, Amber thought, *do we have structural problems already?*

She put down the lamp and walked over to the wall, running her hands over it. There was definitely a bulge in the wall. It was all bumpy and uneven. And now that she was close to it, she could see that it looked as though someone had done a makeshift repair job; probably there had been a hole in the wall and someone had haphazardly patched it and painted over it.

It was a very bad patch job.

Amber had heard of people stuffing newspapers into holes in the wall so that they could have something to spread the spackle upon. She didn't like the idea of it; she didn't want paper inside her wall because it could be a fire hazard.

Would it hurt if Amber punched out the plaster in that spot to look inside the wall? After all, wouldn't Kevin want to do the same thing, since the patch job had been done so poorly? Either way, the hole in the wall would have to be done over and patched correctly, so there would be no harm in opening it up now. Hadn't Kevin given her free rein with the house? Besides, she had nothing else to do.

She went into the kitchen and grabbed a knife. Returning to the guest bedroom, Amber punched the wall with the knife. She was not surprised when the knife went through the patch job very easily and that she could hear rustling on the other side.

So she had been right: newspaper.

She fumbled at the wall, but managed to begin tearing away at the plaster. She used the knife to create openings and then pulled the makeshift spackle patch job out. The spackle crumbled, falling into little pieces upon the floor.

The hole opened up. Amber reached inside and started pulling pages of rumpled newspapers out. Finally when she had them all removed from the wall, she decided to sit down and take a look at them. The date on the newspapers would tell her how long ago the wall had been patched.

She picked up one of the newspaper pages and un-wadded it. It was yellowed, so she figured it must have been in the wall for a while. She placed the page on the floor and tried to smooth out the wrinkles with her hands.

When it was free of most of its wrinkles, she picked it up again and looked to the top of the page for the date. It said: *The Sacramento Bee, Sunday, May 8, 1988.*

How ironic that that paper was dated the same month in which she found it. She skimmed the page and saw advertisements that proclaimed it was not too late to buy a Mother's Day gift.

So May eighth must have been Mother's Day in 1988, she thought. *Maybe it's an omen.*

She started reading the paper, glad that it wasn't the Sunday funny pages. Her eyes stopped on an article. She read:

A 23-year-old woman was arrested last night on murder charges in connection with the death of her son, according to a police report.

Sacramento paramedics responded about 7:30 PM to a 911 call about an unresponsive five-year-old child in a home on the 1900 block of—

Rats! Amber thought. The page was torn, so the rest of the article was missing.

Then she remembered how she had believed that finding a newspaper dated on Mother's Day had been an omen. She shuddered, and instinctively reached for her belly, even though there was no child inside.

She connected the article to her own address, which was 1924 Henley Way. Too bad the article had been torn before the name of the street could be given.

There are lots of streets in Sacramento that have 1900 blocks, she thought. *It could be any house on any street between the addresses of 1900 and 1999.*

Still, it made it even creepier to be reading about a murder at night while she was in an unfamiliar house with a thunderstorm raging outside. The effect of the bad weather was apocalyptic to her mood, and she had feelings of melancholy and paranoia. She decided to start a fire in the fireplace, using the old newspaper pages as fuel. It would add more light in the house. Plus, she was feeling cold.

Grabbing the old newspaper pages, she wadded them all up in her hand, wrinkling them again. She took them into the family room, placed them into the fireplace, and picked up the book of matches that she had placed on the mantle earlier.

Amber crouched to touch the flaming match to the newspapers when suddenly the back door blew inwards, blowing out the match. She screamed in frightened surprise.

The rain gushed into the room, and the wind howled with a furious aggression. Running toward the door, Amber pushed to try to slam it shut, and was astonished at the resistance of the door. Was the wind really that strong? She shoved even more forcefully, using all of her strength, and finally she managed to close the back door.

After locking it tightly, she stared at it, trembling and fearful. Hadn't she locked it earlier? Of course she had, hadn't she? Why couldn't she remember?

Then came the thought: *If I didn't lock the back door, then maybe I didn't lock the front door or any of the windows, either.*

She would have to make the rounds all through the house to double check all of the locks.

She took a step forward to start making sure everything was safe when suddenly the front doorbell rang. She glanced at her watch. It was 10:15 PM. Who in the world would be ringing the doorbell at this late hour? And who would venture out on such a stormy night?

The doorbell rang again. Startled again by the sound, she felt frozen. She waited a few minutes, then took a deep breath.

Slowly Amber walked to the front door, listening to her own footsteps thudding dully upon the hardwood floor of the entranceway. She tried to peer through the peephole, but she couldn't see out to the porch very well. She was not about to open the door unless she was sure whoever was there posed no danger.

Amber next turned to the window by the door. Slowly and carefully she pulled a corner of the curtain aside, and peeked out. Rain was running in rivulets down the windowpane, blurring the glass, and making visibility close to impossible.

She waited a few minutes, immobile with indecisiveness. Finally turning back to the door once more, Amber called, "Who is it?"

No answer.

"I'm not going to open the door unless you tell me who you are first."

Again, no answer.

Suddenly Amber cried, "To hell with you! Go away!"

She backed away from the door. Maybe whoever had been there had left. After all, no one knew yet that she and Kevin were moving in, so perhaps whoever had rang the doorbell had been looking for the previous owners. If so, they kept odd hours.

"Calm down," Amber told herself, not even realizing she was speaking aloud.

She held her hands up, looking at them to gage the amount that they trembled. Then she wiped her forehead, surprised at the sweat, considering how cold it was in the house.

And then she heard something, and stood stock-still, her mouth slightly open so that her ears would work better. It sounded like the groaning of a door opening down the hallway. One of the bedroom doors. *It must be the house settling*, she told herself. *I'm not familiar with the sounds of this house yet.*

Despite the logic, she was afraid. Damn that Kevin, leaving her all alone in a foreign place! She didn't know any neighbors, and had no family to call in Sacramento. If she called the cops, what could she tell them? That she was afraid of the thunderstorm? Or of a boogeyman that went around the neighborhood ringing doorbells at night?

The only thing she could do was to check all of the doors and windows to make sure everything was locked.

She started with the front door, since she had already been there. She reached for the handle and jiggled it. Locked. She touched the dead bolt and assured herself that it was also locked solidly.

On to the windows. She checked the living room windows. All locked.

But then she heard that groaning sound again down the hallway. Pausing, she could feel her heart thudding in her chest. Maybe she should call Kevin after all. Oh no, where was her cell phone? Damn it; hadn't she left it in the empty guest bedroom when she had picked up the lamp?

That meant she had to go down the hall.

Silently, she crept to the start of the hallway. All of the lights in the house were still brightly lit. She could hear the thunder booming outside, and the rain pounding on the roof. The sound of a tree branch creaked against the house somewhere, and she thought, *That's what that particular noise was, a tree branch, right?* Still, a tree branch couldn't explain why the sound came from down the hallway. And she was sure she had heard a bedroom door opening.

Slowly she entered the hallway. Hardwood ran all the way down it, and she was glad she had taken her shoes off and was wearing only socks on her feet. She approached the guest bedroom, and saw that the door was open into the room, an invitation she could not decline.

Had she left the bedroom door open earlier or had she shut it? She couldn't remember; why couldn't she remember?

And then Amber heard a sound from within the room, and she suddenly knew, she just knew, that she was no longer alone in the house.

Trembling, her heart pounding against her ribs, Amber stepped into the bedroom.

She gasped, and clutched her chest.

Sitting cross-legged on the floor was a child. He was barefoot, wearing jeans and a blue-and-white striped shirt that was maroon with blood. He looked up at her with blackened eyes and Amber could see the blood that trickled from the child's broken nose.

"Where's my mother?" the child spoke through cracked and swollen lips. One of his front teeth was missing. "I keep looking, but I can't find my mother."

Amber screamed in fright, whirled around and ran from the bedroom. She fled down the hall, slipping on the hardwood. Catching herself before she fell, her arms flailing, she regained her balance and continued to run. At the front door, she fumbled with the locks. She didn't dare to look behind her to see if she was being chased. She needed to unlock the door to escape out into the night.

She flung the front door open, and bolted, running away from the ghost-child. She ran from the walkway into the front yard, sliding when she hit the slick mud on the ground. She was instantly drenched by the raging storm, freezing and soaked in her wet clothes, her hair in dripping ribbons around her face. She ran as fast as she could, splashing in the mud, running for her life.

Then suddenly rough hands grabbed Amber's shoulders.

"Amber!" came a man's voice, as his hands closed tighter on her shoulders, preventing her escape.

It was Kevin! Kevin was there!

Amber collapsed in his arms. "Oh, Kevin!" she sobbed into his shoulder.

"What are you doing outside in this storm?" he asked her, sounding baffled. "Come on, let me get you back inside so I can warm you up."

"No!" she shrieked. "Don't make me go back into that house!"

He stood there in the downpour, holding his wife, the water running in rivulets down his rain slicker. "All right," he soothed her. "Get into the car."

He led her to his car, and held open the passenger side door. Then after he made sure she was belted in, he went around the car to the driver side. Starting the engine, he turned the heater up to high.

"You don't even have shoes on," he said. "Listen, I was worried about you. I tried to call you all night but your cell phone was turned off. I asked Roland to check on you. You remember Roland, don't you? You know, my business associate? I asked him to drop by to see if you were okay. When he called me to say you didn't answer the door, I decided to come home."

"Someone rang the doorbell," Amber said. "I didn't see anyone on the porch."

Kevin sighed. "Why were you in the yard?"

"I saw a ghost in that house," she told him. "A dead child. A five-year-old boy; oh, Kevin, he was dead!"

"Amber…"

She grabbed his arm. "Oh! You do believe me, don't you? Tell me you believe me!"

He glanced sideways at her as he drove. "Sure, honey, you know I always believe you."

"Always? What do you mean, always? This has never happened to me before."

"Don't you remember?" he asked gently.

She looked out the window, as though suddenly realizing she was in a car. "Where are we going?"

He sighed again. "Amber, I'm taking you to a hospital. Then tomorrow we can go on a trip to see Doctor Robinson. Remember Doctor Robinson?"

"No," she said.

"Remember how much help he was to you after our son was hit by that car two years ago?"

She was flabbergasted. "What son? Damn it, Kevin, you know I've never even been pregnant. What are you talking about?"

"That's okay, Amber," Kevin told her. "Doctor Robinson will explain it all to you. He'll tell you all about how you keep seeing our son."

She buried her face into her hands and sobbed. "Yes, our son. Did I see a ghost in that house? Maybe I was just seeing our son again. Now I feel so confused that I'm not sure."

He told her softly, "You did *not* see a ghost. There are no such things as ghosts."

It was a magnificent July morning when Mandy walked into the office that she shared with Nick.

"Hey," he greeted her. "You'll never guess what house is already back on the market."

Mandy froze, her heart stopping. "It can't be. Not again. Not this fast, anyway."

"Yep, the murder house, 1924 Henley. The one where that kid died in 1988. Just how many times have you sold that house, anyway?"

She continued to stand still for a moment. Then she walked to the coffee pot and poured herself a cup. She felt she needed it.

About Jeani Rector (Editor)

While most people go to Disneyland while in Southern California, Jeani Rector went to the Fangoria Weekend of Horror there instead. She grew up watching the Bob Wilkins Creature Feature on television and lived in a house that had walls covered with framed Universal Monsters posters. It was all in good fun and most people who know Jeani personally are of the opinion that she is a very normal person. She just writes abnormal stories. Doesn't everybody?

Jeani Rector is the founder and editor of *The Horror Zine* and has had her stories featured in magazines such as *Aphelion, Midnight Street, Strange Weird and Wonderful, Macabre Cadaver, Ax Wound, Horrormasters, Morbid Outlook, Horror in Words, Black Petals, 63Channels, Death Head Grin, Hackwriters, Bewildering Stories, Ultraverse, Story Mania, Lost Souls, All Destiny*, and many others. Her novel *Around a Dark Corner* was released in the USA by Graveyard Press in 2009.

About Dean H. Wild (Assistant Editor)

Dean H. Wild's love of stories put him on the road of reading and writing at a young age, and once those first few steps were taken, the journey became one of a lifetime. His career path wound its way through many venues including freelance copywriting. It was once he became acquainted with Jeani Rector of *The Horror Zine* that he began to edit as well as write. He recently assumed the position of Assistant Editor of The Horror Zine web magazine and also had a hand in editing the book you now hold in your hands. Dean lives in Brownsville , Wisconsin with his wife Julie and a couple of self-absorbed but loveable cats.

THE
HORROR ZINE

The Horror Zine's mission is to provide a venue in which writers, poets, and artists can exhibit their work. The Horror Zine is an e-zine; spotlighting the talents of creative people, and displaying their deliciously dark delights for the world to enjoy.

The Horror Zine is accepting submissions of fiction, poetry and art from morbidly creative people.

Please visit The Horror Zine at:
www.thehorrorzine.com

IMAJIN BOOKS

Quality fiction beyond your wildest dreams

For your next ebook or paperback purchase, please visit:

www.imajinbooks.com

www.twitter.com/imajinbooks

Printed in Great Britain
by Amazon

69803589R00220